"COME ON, HAVE A DRINK."

Scylla took it, but not to drink. As Marchey started to withdraw his hand she clamped her other hand around his wrist. Her ceramyl talons hissed from their sheaths in the backs of her fingers and locked with a menacing *snick*, razor-sharp points dimpling the soft gray fabric of the glove he wore. Not hard enough to crush, but more than enough to crack his infuriating indifference.

Much to her surprise his wrist was unyielding. The look of apathetic patience on his face never faltered.

She hissed in a fulminating mixture of rising anger and baffled frustration. She dug her talons into his upper wrist and pulled. The cloth shredded like tissue under the ceramyl blades.

But instead of being rewarded with an agonized screech as his wrist was flayed to the bone, there was a shrill *skreeeeeee* that vibrated up her arm and set her teeth on edge. Still Marchey stared back at her, looking . . . amused.

Although it felt like a minor defeat, she dropped her gaze. Scraps of gray cloth dangled from her talons. His hand and wrist were silver—a silver exactly like her own angel skin. . . .

FLESH AND
SILVER

Stephen L. Burns

A ROC BOOK

ROC
Published by New American Library, a division of
Penguin Putnam Inc., 375 Hudson Street,
New York, New York 10014, U.S.A.
Penguin Books Ltd, 27 Wrights Lane,
London W8 5TZ, England
Penguin Books Australia Ltd, Ringwood,
Victoria, Australia
Penguin Books Canada Ltd, 10 Alcorn Avenue,
Toronto, Ontario, Canada M4V 3B2
Penguin Books (N.Z.) Ltd, 182–190 Wairau Road,
Auckland 10, New Zealand

Penguin Books Ltd, Registered Offices:
Harmondsworth, Middlesex, England

First published by Roc, an imprint of New American Library, a division of
Penguin Putnam Inc.

First Printing, August 1999
10 9 8 7 6 5 4 3 2 1

Cover art: Bruce Jensen

 REGISTERED TRADEMARK—MARCA REGISTRADA

Printed in the United States of America

For Sue-Ryn

ACKNOWLEDGMENTS

This book never would have been written if Dr. Stanley Schidt at *Analog* had not rescued a story titled "A Touch Beyond" from the slush pile. A few years later he published "Angel," the second part of the Marchey/Angel saga. When I tried to sell him a third part, he said what this really wanted to be is a novel. But don't blame him.

A million thanks are due to my wife, Sue-Ryn, for protecting me from the rest of the planet during writing season and gently and patiently dealing with the zombie I become. Thanks are also due to friends and family who encouraged me; to my agent, Joshua Bilmes, for helping sell this story to a good home; and to Laura Anne Gilman and her crew at Penguin Putnam for getting it into print.

"You think the technique we're perfecting here is inexplicable? That it smacks more of magic or psychic mumbo jumbo than science? Listen, when it comes to the human brain we still have more questions than answers. All higher-order mental activity remains essentially an enigma. Hear the music in the background? That symphony was created by the blob of meat in Mozart's head! Can you explain *that*?"

—Dr. Saul Bergmann during an interview by Dr. Susan Stanach on the Sysnet medical magazine *Cutting Edge* thirteen months before his death in 2049.

1

Medical History

Dr. Georgory Marchey cracked open his second quatriliter of Mauna Loa of the evening and refilled his glass. His movements were smooth and precise, his hands steady as the proverbial rock.

Mauna Loa was a pale, golden whiskey made on Kilauea, one of the Hartman habs orbiting the volcano-riddled, seething sulphurous surface of Io. Named for an active volcano back on Earth in Hawaii, the liquor was famed systemwide for its flavor and potency. Marchey raised the glass to his lips with a gray-gloved hand and took a sip, again savoring the faint hint of rumlike sweetness it left on his tongue.

He put the glass back down by the half-eaten remains of another local delicacy served by the Litman Memorial Hospital commissary, force-grown prawns the size of his thumb fresh from Callisto. Poached in wine with slivers of garlic and tomato chunks, then served in the resulting sauce over angel hair pasta and dusted with grated Romano cheese, they were good. No doubt about that.

But the whiskey was better. Even if it only came in little runty quatriliter bottles.

The truth of the matter was that he would have given the whiskey more attention than the food even if it had only been the flavored algaecol that passed for liquor most places off Earth and the Moon.

After all, you couldn't get drunk on shrimp. Even when they've been poached in wine.

Drinking more heavily than normal after a procedure was as much a part of his routine as another surgeon's scrubbing up beforehand. Usually this sacred rite was observed in the austere privacy of his own ship. He'd retreat there as soon as possible after his work was done and start knocking them back the moment the hatch closed behind him.

Here at Litman Memorial, the larger of the two central hospital wheels augmenting the many smaller clinics scattered throughout Jovian space, he'd been derailed. Upon arrival he had been informed that a crew from a local shipyard was standing by to give his packet its triannual hull-integrity check, and given not quite two minutes to vacate. At that very moment the interior spaces of the ship he called home were charged with inert gas at a pressure of over four times normal—hardly a homey atmosphere. The test was slated to last at least another couple–three hours.

With luck and dedication he'd be passed out cold long before then. Which meant he would have to stay the night in the room he'd been assigned here. Not a pleasant prospect, but drinking would make it bearable. Drinking made *everything* bearable.

Layovers happened, and you made the best of them. As he would then. Denied the safety and solitude of his ship, he would have opted for a private restaurant and the anonymity it could provide. The nearest one was on a hab a measly five thousand kilometers away, but the next shuttle there didn't leave for over two hours. The need for a drink was far too immediate to make such a wait a workable solution.

Which was how he'd ended up in the staff section of the hospital wheel's commissary. *In the midst of the enemy.*

The food was quite good, the service tolerable. The decor was deplorable, the ambience execrable, the company overtly hostile. The important thing was that they served alcohol. Not every hospital provided that amenity.

Almost as if purposefully devised to make his situation as uncomfortable as possible, the only free table had been dead square in the middle of the room.

He'd taken it anyway. There was some liquor back in his room, but not quite enough to get where he wanted to go. Besides, getting his hands on some Mauna Loa was the only enjoyable part of this stop. There was no place to buy a flagon or three outright, but the commissary bar stocked it, table service only.

So there he sat, well aware that he was very much the center of attention, enjoying the sort of guest-of-honor status accorded the cadaver in a dissection. All around him his erstwhile colleagues eyed him coldly, probed and prodded with harsh whispers pitched just loud enough to reach his ears. Even without the silver biometal pin on his chest they would have known who and what he was. Hospitals were like small towns. Word travelled fast. Pariahs can expect no privacy. Union rules.

Whatever else Bergmann Surgeons lacked or had lost—and the list was considerable—their unhappy notoriety remained.

What these fools didn't know was how little their hatred and contempt meant to him anymore.

His bland, indifferent gaze settled on one particular couple scowling at him from a table in the corner. He thought he recognized the woman from that afternoon. Maybe a cardiovascular surgeon? His only real lasting impression had been of a dark, hawkish face and bile-bitter comments, some in Arabic.

He raised his glass toward her in salute, grinned and winked like they shared some sort of joke, then inhaled the three fingers of whiskey. Her face closed like a fist.

Marchey barely noticed. His attention had drifted back to the alcohol warming his insides. Over the

years that had become his sole criterion for judging
the places he was sent: *How was the booze?*

The commissary was a wonderful place. Top shelf.

Other than that, the hospital was indistinguishable
from the last and would be no different from the next.
The same sterile steel/stone/ceramic corridors swallowed him up and spat him out. The same faceless
insensible strangers were his patients. The same
blurry, disapproving faces watched him do what they
could not, outraged by his presence—his very existence—and impatient to see him gone. The same half-
heard ugly comments greeted him, dogged his heels,
bid him bitter farewell. This afternoon, now, next
time; all were only moments from a past, present, and
future that twisted back on itself like a Mobius treadmill that kept him plodding blindly along in the same
place in spite of the millions of kilometers he
travelled.

He knew he was at Litman Memorial only because
of the crest inscribed on the dinner plate before him.
Beyond that it was just a name. He hadn't the faintest
idea or slightest curiosity as to where he was being
sent next. And as for where he'd been, well, most of
it was indistinguishable from where he was then.

Most, but not all.

His smile twisted into a grimace as he refilled his
glass. Half of it disappeared in one swallow.

Since he was one of the barely thirty surviving Bergmann Surgeons, and as such followed the itinerary set
for him by MedArm, the branch of the UN Space
Regulatory Agency in charge of all facets of off-Earth
Health Care, Marchey led a life sharply divided into
two unequal parts.

Ninety-nine percent of it was solitary. Safe. It was
spent home aboard his automated ship, crossing and
recrossing the vast desert of vacuum between human
enclaves as he was shuttled from place to place and
patient to patient. His adaptation to this part was
nearly perfect. He could spend days, even weeks at a
stretch adrift in a tranquil sea of alcohol, breathing

in the endless lotus scent of nothingness, becoming a rootless, pastless, futureless part of it.

Here he sat in the middle of the other, smallest part. The ruins of his professional life. The part he lived for. The part that was slowly killing him.

The part which evoked unwelcome reminders that there had once been more to life than this bottle and the dogged pursuit of oblivion. Love. Respect. Idealism. Hope. Friendship. A sense of place. Satisfaction. Optimism. Even imagination. One by one they had withered away, or been amputated by circumstance.

But what the hell, he thought, a small, rueful half smile appearing as he slumped back in his chair. Getting his nose rubbed in the pile of shit his life had become was just one more thing he had to endure if he wanted to continue being a Bergmann Surgeon. One more drawback. Not that it was so much a matter of *want* as being completely unable to imagine giving it up. The very thing that had blighted his life redeemed it, an irony of which he was well aware. At times it was even funny, a joke of the rubber crutch or exploding suppository variety.

Still, places like the commissary were dangerous. The pervasive, unmistakable hospital atmosphere, the being around other people; any number of things could summon up the unquiet ghosts of his past. There was no way to tell what might set it off. It might be a voice, a face, a gesture, a scent, or just the continual pointed reminders that he no longer belonged among his former associates. He no longer belonged anywhere, and sometimes situations like this cast him helplessly adrift on the anywhen between past and present.

Well, that was just one more reason to drink.

I think we definitely need some more anesthesia here, Doctor, he told himself, topping off his glass.

A snatch of conversation from somewhere behind him caught his ear, a sour comment about the way he was drinking, and a forgiving soul suggesting that maybe it was because of a woman.

Not anymore, he answered silently, *Or at least hardly ever.*

But this reminder sent his thoughts skidding back nearly ten years, conjuring up a tall, thin, green-eyed woman with skin and hair so pale she could almost pass for an albino in the empty chair across from him.

He closed his eyes and drained his glass. The whiskey went down like water.

But it didn't wash away the memories. . . .

There they were, sharing a restaurant table after more than eight years apart.

Ella Prime drank it all in. The soft music, the candlelight and wine. Erratic flickerings of the old electricity leaping the gap between them. And *memories.*

So many memories. Crowding around the table at their shoulders and whispering in their ears; the best friends and most implacable enemies of two people who have come back together to see what remains of a lost love.

Ella watched Marchey refill his wineglass, wondering if he always drank this heavily, or if it was seeing her again that was driving him to it. She didn't ask, and whatever the reason, at least it did seem to be helping him unbend a bit.

The four months of waiting for him to work his way to Ixion Station had given her plenty of time to dream of this moment. She had imagined their reunion as joyous and passionate, quite often fantasizing them going straight from the shuttle back to the privacy of her microhab, where they could peel the years off with each other's clothes and start making up for lost time. Such thoughts made her ache with longing for his touch.

The first crack in the fantasy had come when one of her bug's main thrusters had flamed out on the way in from her hab. She had gotten in all right, but that stranded them on Ixion Station until it was fixed.

Still, the where of it didn't really matter that much, and the revealing blouse of sheer ivory silk and the skintight black skirt that showed off a mile of leg she'd worn for the occasion had been calculated to make the critical parts of her plan come to fruition in her fallback venue. As had her suggestion that they go to the room she'd hastily rented so they could "freshen up"—a code phrase from the old days.

He'd caught the signal, but pleading bad food on the shuttle, asked if they could first go someplace to eat.

The way she'd thrown herself at him it was no wonder the poor man had ducked! Cursing herself for moving too fast, coming on too strong, she'd brought him to this restaurant. She had to remember that a lot of water had passed under the bridge since she'd seen him last—a bridge she herself had burned. Building a new one this many years downstream was going to take time and patience.

But being near him again made that so very hard.

"What's with the gloves, Gory?" she asked, to break the silence which had crept up between them. "Getting kind of obsessive about protecting those surgeon's hands of yours, aren't you?"

He laughed. "Something like that." She couldn't help noticing that his smile looked a little pained, and his laugh sounded forced and unconvincing. Avoiding her gaze, he inhaled half the wine he'd just poured.

"Hey," she said, wondering what she'd said wrong and wanting to repair the damage. "That's *nothing*. I've got mine insured for one hundred and fifty million."

That made him look directly at her. "Really?"

She nodded, holding them up and wriggling her long thin fingers. "Bet your ass. These babies can turn fifty credits worth of clay into several hundred thousands' worth of sculpture."

"You're getting that much now?" He chuckled and shook his head. "I remember the first time you cracked the thousand mark."

Ella smiled. Now *there* was a memory . . .

"So do I." But not as clearly as she remembered

celebrating that event with him. He'd made the night unforgettable with dinner and champagne, a suite in a five-star-hotel and ten-star sex. Yet it was his absolute and utterly unselfish delight in her accomplishment she remembered best of all.

Less than four months later she'd broken it off, tired of coming off as second choice to his Bitch Mistress Medicine, and incidentally freeing herself to devote all her time to her art and the search for even greater fortune and fame.

Even now she couldn't say for sure which had been the reason and which the excuse.

"It sounds like you're doing pretty well, Ella."

Career-wise, anyway. She shrugged. "That's what my agent and my accountant tell me."

The truth of the matter was that she'd grown almost absurdly rich and famous since then. Her rise in the art world had been meteoric. Now they called her a living legend. Each new piece she offered set off a bidding war. Almost pathologically reclusive, solitude had always been extremely important to her. Now she had it in spades, living in splendid isolation in a richly appointed microhab all her own just off a research station in one of the most isolated places imaginable. She had everything she'd ever wanted.

Except a life.

She gazed at Marchey, wondering if it was the sharp scent of her desperation that was putting him on guard. It was probably pouring off her in *waves*.

He had turned out to be the one big love of her life. Oh, there had been the random lover in the years since then, but nothing like what they had shared. Not even close.

Over the past couple years she'd begun to feel as hollow and brittle as a porcelain bust of herself. Her thoughts kept returning to the time Gory had been there for her, and seeing it as the high point of her life. Looking ahead, she'd felt like she was on a greased slide to the lowest. God, even the frigging critics had begun to talk about the "melancholy sense of existential loneliness that has come to permeate her work."

Terrified by the future she saw hardening around her, she'd sought to re-create the past. She hadn't quite begged Gory to come see her, but that was an option she'd been prepared to take. Just knowing he was coming had filled her with a hopeful new energy. The most recent works she would be shipping sunward on the returning transport would fetch the highest prices yet, she was sure of it.

Her imaginings of seeing him again and reality differed in yet another way. Of course she had expected him to have changed, but there had to be more than just time between the image in her mind and the man sitting less than a meter away.

His hairline had retreated to the back of his head, only a few discouraged strands of his lank black hair remaining on top. That happened to a lot of men, but most cared enough to have it replaced. Where once his face had been round and glowingly robust, now it was pared down to the austere bones underneath, fatigue chiseled into every hollow and line. His gray eyes had retreated into their sockets, bruised-looking bags under them. He had also lost a lot of weight, which left his broad, blocky body looking rawboned and starved.

The change was so radical that when she'd seen him appear in the shuttle's airlock her first thought was that he'd been sick. He had the look of someone with something relentless and unforgiving gnawing at his insides.

But holding him close again, feeling the warmth of his arms around her and his face snuggled against her breasts had brought back such a rush of sensation and memory her knees nearly buckled under her. It was like coming home after far too long out in a place cold and comfortless.

In some ways he was still the sweet man she remembered. Yet in others he had become a complete stranger. Although he seemed genuinely glad to see her, there was a subdued air about him, a guarded remoteness that gave her the uneasy feeling that he was hiding something.

Or maybe he was just afraid she'd break his heart again.

That wasn't going to happen. If there was a problem, she'd deal with it. Now that they were together again, nothing could come between them.

Ella seemed to come back from some far-off place and gave Marchey a smile. "I know I'm repeating myself," she said shyly, "but I've really missed you, Gory."

"Me too," Marchey agreed. He had never really stopped loving Ella. The worst of the symptoms might have subsided over the years, but the condition itself seemed to be incurable.

He'd known that seeing her again might put him at risk of a major reinfection, and tried to convince himself that he'd developed emotional antibodies that would keep him from finding her as attractive as he had in the old days.

One look at her had blown that theory all to hell.

He knew Ella wasn't all that beautiful by most men's standards. She was almost freakishly tall, and thin to the point of emaciation; less than forty-five kilos of lean flesh and pale, almost translucent skin spread over more than two meters of angular jutting bone. Her long, narrow face wasn't the sort to launch a thousand ships; it was rescued from being plain only by big white-lashed eyes of an unusual bottle green.

Still, something about those impossibly long crane-like legs, those tiny cupcake breasts, that body with every muscle and bone as starkly evident as that of an anatomy illustration, those big green eyes, even the pale austerity of her face turned in his heart like a key in a lock. It always had, and it seemed it always would.

He'd lost her once. Watching her eat and listening to her talk and catching tantalizing tastes of her scent,

he wondered how he could have let himself gamble
with losing her again.

This was not a new line of reasoning. The long,
labyrinthine trip out to Ixion Station had given him
plenty of time for doubts and second thoughts.

The place Ella had chosen to live was not exactly
an easy one to reach. The big wheelhab named Ixion
Station hung halfway across the barren gulf between
the orbits of Jupiter and Saturn, pacing the latter.
Only twice a year would a passenger-and-supply transport make the long journey into the vast emptiness
beyond the orbit of Jupiter's settled moons to visit.
The UNSRA labs, observatories, research and training
facilities—along with the small but thriving society
that had grown up around those installations—rated
no more than that as yet.

While it was a jumping-off point for the first tentative explorations of Saturn's mysteries, as yet only a
few were allowed to make the leap. Settlement on the
moons of that ringed world was so sparse and austere
there was nowhere for them to go. Yet.

Someday that would change, and the trickle would
become a steady flow. Until then Ixion remained hu-
mankind's farthest flung permanent outpost.

If getting to Ixion was difficult, arriving was disconcerting. Cut off as they were, the Station's inhabitants
treated the transport's arcing flyby and the shut-
tleloads of goods and personnel it brought them as a
cause for celebration. Nearly everyone dropped what
they were doing, turning out to greet the new arrivals
and hurling themselves into an almost desperate round
of partying they called ShipTime.

This meant that Marchey's first glimpse of the place
had been the sea of upturned faces filling the receiving
bay. The people below laughed and clapped and
stamped their feet. They whistled and hooted and
waved, treating him and his fellow passengers like vis-
iting celebrities.

The shuttle stewards had warned them beforehand,
so he knew they weren't there to greet him, specifi-

cally. That had helped a little, but already apprehensive about the prospect of seeing Ella again, the welcome had made him feel like he'd been suddenly thrust onto a stage under a blazing spotlight. At any moment the rowdy throng below him might demand that he sing or dance. That he amaze them.

And he could have, if he'd wanted to. How did it go?

Observe carefully, ladies and gentlemen. You'll see that I've got nothing up my sleeves . . .

Then he'd seen her, sudden panic nearly sending him fleeing back into the shuttle.

"I'm just so glad you really came," Ella continued, her low husky voice sliding liquidly into his thoughts. Her face was so serious. He knew she had more riding on this than she was saying. Well, so did he.

He made himself smile. "So am I," he agreed, neatly managing to lie and tell the truth with the same three words.

Her invitation had taken him by surprise, as had his spur-of-the-moment decision to take a break from his frustrating, fruitless search for a permanent place to practice.

It had been the act of a man grasping at straws. She was his last tenuous link with the sort of life he'd led before his idealism and dedication had led him to join the Bergmann Program.

Her green eyes sought his, a glint of desperation in them. "Sitting here like this, you and me together again . . ."

She bit her lip. "It's so much like before. That's—that's what I've dreamed of. It's what I want for us, Gory. For things to be the way they were before."

"We had some problems," he said carefully.

She dismissed them with a careless flick of one thin hand. He saw that her nails were bitten to the quick. "Then things will be *better*."

"Maybe . . . but you know our work can still get in the way," he said, reminding her of their earlier relationship's greatest obstacle, and taking a half-hearted swipe at being honest about the one it faced now.

Total dedication to your vocation took the best of what you had to offer, leaving only sloppy seconds for the one you loved. Theirs had torn them apart and driven them in opposite directions. Ella had begun her journey outsystem and up the ladder, at last holing up out here at the edge of nowhere.

He had certainly found his own extremes. She hadn't been able to accept how much of himself he gave to medicine then. And now?

Nobody else did. Why should she be any different?

First emptying his wineglass, he crept up a little closer to the matter.

"I've changed, Ella." That was a bit of an understatement, but he had to start somewhere.

She nodded. "So have I. That's why I think we can work it out now."

Her face, her voice, all echoed with her need to have it be so. He recognized his own loneliness in her, his own need to fill the emptiness, to find something to cling to.

"You *have* changed," he said, smiling as he backed away from treacherous ground. "You're more beautiful than ever." That was true, but it avoided the candor she deserved.

His deceit had been calculated, and had begun before he left the shuttle. In the time between leaving his seat and reaching the lock he had nervously checked himself over one last time. The gray-velvet gloves he wore were clean and secure. The darker gray sleeves of his jacket were snug at the wrist. The fly of his baggy black pants was shut.

Lastly, unconsciously and by habit, he had touched the gleaming silver biometal pin clipped to his red-silk shirt over his heart, half-hidden by the lapels of his jacket.

It was the Bergmann Surgeons' emblem: two arms crossed at the wrists, arms ending just below the elbows, fingers spread wide.

When he had realized what he was doing he took his hand away, clasping it with his other hand to keep it from straying there again. But his awareness of the pin—and what it meant—remained at the fore of his mind.

He had considered leaving the pin behind when he came here, or at least leaving it off, but found that he could not. Not so much out of honesty, but because it was a part of him, branding him as one part of an experiment that was both an incredible success and a dismal failure: medal and stigmata all in one.

There he sat, the silver pin barely peeking, feeling like a cheat and a liar. Sleeves and gloves might hide the path he had taken from her for a while, but she would find out in the end.

Until then all he could do was try to make the best of their time together. The wine helped.

Ella had ordered a large bottle of genuine French wine, never batting an eyelash at the price, but had taken no more than a couple polite sips from her glass.

Marchey felt no similar reticence. In the years since joining the Program, alcohol consumption had increased to the point that someday it might just become a real problem. But that was a concern for some other time. He already had the bottle down to the halfway mark, and planned to see the bottom by dessert.

Fortifying himself for the moment when he finally revealed his pride and his shame.

Each glass made it a little easier to belive she would understand, and that their love could rise up like a phoenix rather than crash and burn yet another time.

Even with things still a little strained and uncertain, Ella felt more at ease with Gory than anyone else she had ever known. She remembered pushing him away there at the end, and how it had seemed like the right thing to do at the time. Now she had to wonder how she could have been so selfish. So stupid. Had it really been that hard to make allowances for his work?

They were halfway through the main course when their waiter, a thin, smoothly courteous man with a hooked nose and a walrus mustache approached their table.

"I regret the intrusion on your meal," he said quietly, "but there is an urgent call for you, Miz Prime." He held the flat book shape of a communit against his chest like a stack of menus.

Ella scowled at him. "Who the hell is it?"

"The caller is Dr. Carol Chang, Director of Ixion Medical Services. She was most insistent about speaking to you, and instructed me to tell you it was a matter of life and death." He stepped back and waited impassively for her answer.

Marchey's eyes had narrowed at the mention of Chang's title and office. Already suspecting what sort of a call it might be, Ella was staring at him intently. She seemed to be holding her breath. The call might be for her, but obviously the decision was up to him.

Like it or not, he really had no choice. He tried to smile. "Maybe you better take it."

Her mouth turned down. That hadn't been the answer she wanted. She gestured curtly. "Put her through."

"As you wish." The waiter placed the unit on the table facing her, keyed it on, then faded back out of sight.

The image of a diminutive, middle-aged oriental woman appeared on the screen. When she saw that she had been put through, the grim, impatient look she wore shifted to a tight smile. "Ms. Prime?"

Ella inclined her head fractionally. "Yes."

"I am Dr. Carol Chang. I deeply regret the intrusion on your privacy, and would not have called if I'd had any other choices. I understand that Dr. Georgory Marchey is your, ah, guest here. An emergency has arisen, and it is imperative that I speak to him."

"Well," Ella began unhappily, an old old resentment still there inside her, as good as new. It was *always* an emergency, she remembered. Every damn time. How many times?

"Please," Marchey whispered.

"He's right beside me," Ella said tonelessly. She turned the unit toward him, then snatched up her wineglass and drained it.

Chang's features lit in a genuine smile when she saw him. "Dr. Marchey, this is indeed an honor. Again, I apologize for the interruption."

Marchey glanced away, watching Ella refill her glass, her jaw set with anger. He closed his eyes a moment, then faced the screen again. "You said there's an emergency?"

Chang nodded. "Yes. One of our young people, a girl named Shei Sinclair, somehow managed to build a toy cannon and make powder for it as a way of celebrating ShipTime. It exploded in her face the first time it was fired."

Marchey grimaced. Ella stiffened, wineglass halfway to her lips.

"We have removed most of the fragments and stopped the worst of the bleeding, but her condition remains extremely grave. Two fragments entered her skull through her left eye socket, their flattened profiles making them follow curving paths. The damage they did is considerable. Both are lodged deep within her brain, one impinging on the medulla. There is steady intracranial hemorrhaging, and her autonomic functions are failing fast. We are already using machine assist to keep her breathing. I am afraid that cardiac function will soon fail as well. The fragments must be removed, but going in for them would be extremely risky. I am prepared to try if I must, but—"

The oriental woman paused to take a deep breath. "I was reviewing the medical records of our new arrivals when this happened," she continued in a rush. "Yours was a surprise. I have read about Bergmann Surgeons, but never thought I would see one way out here. Now I have to look on your arrival as a gift from God. If you—"

There was suddenly a high-pitched buzzing sound in the background of Chang's pickup. The grating buzz was quickly replaced by a metronomic beeping. She glanced off-screen, brow furrowing. When she faced Marchey again her grim expression had returned and redoubled.

"She just went ECS. Can you help?"

Had Marchey been by himself, he would have already been on his way. But for once he wasn't alone. He turned toward Ella, a strong flash of déjà vu swallowing him up and making him feel unreal. This was so like the times before that the intervening years might as well have been the dream of a single bad night.

Ella's face was blank. She stared past him at nothing, green eyes glazed and sightless.

"Ella?"

She scarcely heard him, remembering the too many times their lives had been interrupted by a call like this. The resentful hours spent waiting for his return. . . .

But only if she let them be resentful. Her eyes snapped back into focus. "Go," she said, digging her fingers into his shoulder.

Marchey's relief was obvious. His sunken gray eyes flicked back toward Chang's image. "You heard?"

The hope on her face said she had. "Yes. Thank you—both of you!"

"Now how do I get—"

Ella's fingers gripped him even tighter. "I know the way. I'm going with you." The look on her face defied him to argue.

He didn't plan to. "Good."

He knew then how she was going to learn what he'd been hiding from her. The end of the suspense gave him no real comfort. This might just be the best way, but would it make any difference in the long run?

He pushed all those thoughts to one side. There was no turning back, not for any of it. All he could do

was keep going and try to cope with where events
carried him.

He shoved his chair back and stood up, Ella rising
to her feet beside him as he took a last look at the
screen.

"We're on our way."

"I have seen your Dr. Marchey's name in the medical journals several times," Dr. Chang said as she
poured two cups of tea. She smiled back over her
shoulder at Ella. "And please call me Carol."

"All right, um, Carol." Ella had expected to hate
on sight this woman who had spoiled their reunion.
Much to her surprise the opposite had been true.

Chang had greeted them at the door to her office
and ushered them inside.

All Ella could do was wait for whatever happened
next and wish she had a sketchpad with her. Lacking
that, she tried to memorize Chang's every move and
gesture.

The head of Ixion Medical Services stood just over a
meter and a half tall. She was flawlessly proportioned,
uncannily graceful, and had an almost perfect geno-
type with straight jet-black hair, almond eyes, and skin
the color of aged amber.

Though she had to be an unrejuved fifty, Chang
had one of those faces whose beauty time could not
diminish. Ella's artist's eye subtracted her crisp white
coverall and the small silver crucifix worn outside the
coverall's blouse. Dressed in a kimono, she could have
been one of Hiroshito's exquisite porcelain figurines
come to life. But warmer, not so aloof and opaque.
Old, young, and ageless all at once. She planned to
ask the woman if she would sit for her when this was
over. Nude, if possible.

As for Marchey, he might as well have been in another room. He'd asked to see the young accident
victim's medical records and stats the moment they
reached Chang's office, and had been hunched over
her Medicomp and oblivious to all else since.

Ella's nostrils flared at the spicy aroma of the tea when Chang handed her an eggshell-delicate cup. "Thanks."

"You are most welcome." Chang remained standing. That put her and the seated Ella nearly eye to eye.

"It is I who should thank you," she continued. "There are only a handful of Bergmann Surgeons as yet. Your, ah, friend is one of the first and most accomplished of them. Now I know that they are somewhat, well, controversial, but I don't doubt that in the end the prejudice will disappear." She turned her head to gaze at Marchey, hope filling her face. "For myself, I can only say that his being here at this time is the answer to a prayer. His special skills give Shei a better chance than anything I can do for her."

Ella frowned at Chang over the rim of her cup. "I'm not sure I know what you're talking about. You called him that before, a *Bergmann Surgeon.* What's it mean?"

Marchey heard Ella's question. He risked a glance at his old lover. Her whole attention was focused on Dr. Chang as she waited for an answer.

Chang's poise faltered. She took a sip of her tea, her movement uncharacteristically jerky and uncertain. After an uncomfortable pause, she said, "You don't know." It came out as both a question and an unhappy statement all at once.

Ella frowned, puzzled by her reaction. "Gory has always been a surgeon. Is this different somehow?"

Marchey spoke up at last. "Yes, it is." Both women turned toward him, Chang looking relieved and Ella clearly baffled by the sudden tension.

"I must see the child now." He met Ella's gaze. "I want you to come and watch. There's something you don't know about. Something I haven't been able to tell you. The only way to understand is to see it for yourself."

He spoke firmly. His apprehension showed only in the way his gloved hand strayed for a moment to the silver pin over his heart.

Chang put her cup aside and started toward the door. "This way, please." She strode ahead without looking back.

They both followed, Marchey moving with a businesslike briskness, Ella trailing uncertainly behind.

Chang led them to a small combination Surgery/ ICU just two doors down from her office.

The brightly lit, antiseptic-smelling room made Ella even more uneasy. She didn't want to think about the type of things done in such a place. Invasions of the body and dignity. Proof that the flesh could fail in all sorts of horrible and humiliating ways.

Her unanswered questions weighed heavily on her, leaving her off-balance. From the very first she'd felt Gory's reserve, suspected that he was holding something back. Hiding something. It seemed that the veil was about to be lifted. She had a sinking feeling that she wasn't going to like what was behind it one bit.

When she finally made herself look at the small, white-swaddled form on the padded table in the center of the room, took in the tubes and sensors and other medical arcana hooked up to it, the urge to turn and escape screwed tighter around her. There was nothing here she wanted to know about. This was all a part of him she had kept at arm's length the first time around.

Yet she stayed, hovering fretfully near the door. Her hands worried and plucked at each other nervously. Her question remained: *What was a Bergmann Surgeon?*

Marchey went straight to the table, his face intent, and began his initial examination in silence. Chang dismissed the medico in attendance and started toward the table. He waved her back without turning around.

"Will the secondaries take over if I unplug her for a moment?" he asked over his shoulder while checking the pupil response of Shei's undamaged right eye. The other one was hidden under a thick sterile covering. The whole left side of her head was heavily bandaged; her face had been partly averted when the toy cannon had turned into a pipe bomb.

He shook his head at what he saw. Her pupil was dilated and showed only minimal response. *Hang on, my brown-eyed girl. Help is here now.*

"Yes, it's a full table."

Marchey nodded absently at Chang's answer. He sighed, squared his shoulders, then turned to look across the room at Ella.

The expression on his face made her take an involuntary step back. He wore the face of a condemned man, despairing and apologetic, the face of a man saying a final farewell. Part of her was drawn to comfort him, to tell him that nothing could be that bad. But she could only stand there, the anxiety buzzing through her bones defeating that impulse.

Marchey's gaze dropped, and he turned away. First he shucked off his jacket and laid it aside. Next he rolled up the sleeves of his red-silk shirt. The gray-velvet gloves covered his arms up to his elbows.

He began stripping off the right glove. The fabric slid down his forearm, revealing not white skin but burnished silver. His wrist was silver. His hand, palm, thumb, and fingers were silver; gleaming metal shaped into smooth, perfectly sculpted folds and curves, supple seamless biometal shaped to mimic the flesh and bone it had replaced down to each knuckle and crease.

He removed his other glove, his already-bared silver hand gleaming and flashing as it moved like a thing alive. His left hand and arm were the same, a mirror twin of the right. Face burning self-consciously, he put the gloves aside. Through all this he kept his head down, studiously avoiding Ella's shocked and uncomprehending stare.

She stumbled forward a step, protest filling her chest to the bursting point. Dr. Chang caught her arm and held her back, speaking quietly but firmly.

"Not now. *Please.* Wait until he is done."

"But his hands, w-what happened to his—" She swallowed hard, silenced as he held up one shining hand. An implug extruded from his palm like an electronic stigma, hung there on a braided silver cable.

He turned to his patient and gently probed the base of her skull. When he found the impline linking her to the table's life support and monitors he pulled it and substituted the implug dangling from his palm.

Ella shivered and hunched her shoulders. Taps were common, but she had always been revolted by the idea of letting a tap's quasi-alive nanostrands slither into her brain like electronic worms. Just the thought of it made her stomach churn.

Marchey stood there, swaying slightly, the abstracted look he wore making it appear he was daydreaming.

Dr. Chang spoke up before Ella could find voice for her question. "He's linked to Shei's tap and reading her condition. Most imped doctors can do that, but only through a special interface. His interface is built right into his prosthetic."

Ella mouthed the word *prosthetic*. It tasted like tinfoil against her tongue and teeth.

There was a soft snick as he disconnected. He hooked the girl back up to the table once more, gently lowering her head back down onto the padding.

Next he placed a hand on either side of the girl's skull. Keeping them parallel with each other, he moved them in slow wide circles. They emitted the faintest of hums, nearly lost in the background noise made by the other medical equipment.

"Now he's scanning the location of the fragments. He doesn't have to do this, we've taken full scans. He's just being careful. In fact, he could go in cold and do better than I could with every scan and test possible at my fingertips."

Ella watched intently, hearing every word the woman said and even understanding some of it. Her whole attention remained welded to the alien argent metal that replaced the gentle hands she remembered. Marchey seemed lost to all but what he was doing.

At last he straightened up, muttering something

under his breath. One silver hand brushed the dying child's bandaged forehead tenderly.

Something clicked inside Ella. She was suddenly inundated by a flood of jumpcut, staggeringly vivid sense memories of Marchey's hands touching her: a velvety knuckle kissing her cheek as it wiped away a tear; his warm palms and fingers cupping her breasts; fingers trailing sweet fire along her flanks, heating her nerves to the flash point; thumbs and fingers that knew her secret places and what to do there, possessed of a special wisdom of their own; his warm hand in hers in the dark, comforting and reassuring . . .

But those hands were gone. *Gone.* Her skin crawled at the thought of those cold metal *things* touching her, creeping across her flesh like sinister steel spiders.

"*—gone—*" It was a breathless whisper, a crack in the speechless silence, forced out by all the things building up behind it. She started toward him to demand that he tell her what had happened to him. How this horrible thing had come about.

Dr. Chang barred her way, grasping her arms. "Ella," she said sternly, "I know this has to be difficult for you. But you must not break his concentration." Her voice throbbed with urgency. "Shei's life depends on it."

The pleading note in Chang's voice reached Ella. She swallowed the sour wave in her throat, looking down and meeting the other woman's eyes. After a moment she nodded.

Her eyes sought Marchey again. Chang turned to watch as well, but kept a restraining hand on her arm.

Marchey stepped back from the table. He crossed his arms before his broad chest and began to breathe deeply, eyes closed, doing some sort of *pranayama* or breathing exercise. Crossed at the wrist, his silver arms were posed like the ones depicted by the pin on his shirt.

Ella watched in growing bewilderment as his silver hands began fluttering and flashing like mechanical birds in rhythm with his breathing. His face became increasingly strange as his breathing slowed, all expression flattening away to leave a rigid, blankly inhuman mien in its place. The seconds limped by, and his face became colder and stranger still; a sinister Mr. Hyde emerging from the sweet Dr. Jekyll she thought she knew.

She sought the comfort of Chang's hand against the sense of dread climbing up her spine and wrapping clammy, spatulate fingers around her heart. Chang's hand was cold, her grip tight. Was she afraid as well?

Marchey's sunken gray eyes slowly opened, the lids sliding back like shutters over a void.

There was nothing of the Georgory Marchey Ella had known and loved to be seen in them. They were deep dark caves: cold, empty, and forbidding. Not even the faintest spark of who he had been remained in them, every gleam of humanity expunged by whatever radically altered state he had just invoked.

Ella fought the urge to run away from the awful stranger he had become. Had turned himself into, right before her eyes.

Staring straight ahead, his gaze sweeping indifferently across the two women like a scanning beam, Marchey moved to the foot of the table with slow, ratcheting steps. He bent at the waist like a badly made puppet and rested his forearms on it, elbow to wrist flat on the padded surface.

The chrome clockwork birds of his hands were still. His eyes drooped shut. He drew his breath through his clenched teeth sharply, as if trying to lift some impossible burden.

After a moment his breath came out in a long hiss. He slowly straightened up and stepped back. His silver arms remained on the table, abandoned, and somehow obscene. Just below the elbows his arms ended in flat, featureless silver plates. After that, nothing.

Chang clutched Ella's hand tightly. "It's all right," she whispered, her tone reedy and uncertain.

Ella could only stare at her former lover, her face white and immobile as carved bone, her lips pressed

tightly together to keep in the contents of her squirming gut. Had what she was seeing *always* been inside
him? Looking out? *Watching?*

Marchey moved to the head of the table, his movements stiff and jerky. Once there he brought the truncated stumps of his arms down toward the child's
bandaged head, pausing when they were an arm's
length away. His posture, his face, everything about
him made it look like he was about to do her terrible
harm. Ella's insides jangled with the impulse to snatch
the child out of his grasp, but the thought of going
nearer to him filled her with terror.

Then he *reached*.

Had he still possessed hands, they would have been
driven through the skull and buried deep within the
delicate tissues of the girl's brain. He changed position. The silver plates at the end of his arms winked
knowingly. His eyes drooped shut to become glittering
slits. His face showed no more animation or humanity
than that of a granite gargoyle.

Ella forced a question past the knot in her throat.
"W-what is h-he—?" What is he *doing?* What *is* he?

"He is locating the fragments by touch," Dr. Chang
replied softly. She licked her lips. "Since they are
metal, he will trace each path of entry and bring each
fragment back along its path to minimize the damage
inflicted by removal. If he hadn't been here, I might
have tried to do it myself, but even with nanotic for-
ceps I would have done more harm than good."

Ella's bewilderment was total. "But he doesn't h-
have any h-hands," she stammered, tearing her gaze
away to stare at the smaller woman almost accusingly.
"They're *gone!*"

"He has something *better!*" Chang said so forcefully
it sounded almost like a shout. She gripped Ella's
hand tighter and spoke softly, reassuringly. Almost
reverently.

"Let me try to explain. There is a phenomenon
sometimes experienced by amputees called the 'phantom limb syndrome.' What that means is that they

think they can still 'feel' the missing limb. The flesh and bone is gone, but some strange ghost of sensation remains. The intensity of that feeling varies from person to person. Some do not experience it at all. Once the replacement of missing limbs with banked tissue became commonplace it very nearly became a forgotten occurrence.

"Almost, but fortunately not quite. A very great man, a prostheticist named Dr. Saul Bergmann became intrigued by this phenomenon. He began to study it, eventually learning that a small percentage of those who felt it were capable of actually manipulating matter with that *limb image*. The ability was so weak and wildly erratic that it took him years conclusively to prove it existed. But he did prove it, and then went on to develop techniques to help the ability grow stronger and under better control."

Ella stared down at Dr. Chang, trying to absorb and understand what she was being told. It sounded impossible. Insane. As insane as what she had just seen, as what was happening at this very moment. And anyone who could believe in such a crazy thing had to be—

"These very few special people had to work in a deep trance to maintain the concentration it took to use this limb image, but they could do many unexpected—you might even say *miraculous* things with it. The strangest and most wonderful things of all were the things it could do inside a human body. Anyway, once the techniques became better perfected, Bergmann Surgery—"

Ella's gaze had been drawn back to Marchey as she tried to reconcile what she was hearing with him. Her free hand went to her mouth, and the small shocked sound that escaped past her fingers made Dr. Chang turn and stare.

A jagged metal fragment the size of a fingernail slowly emerged from the gauze pad covering Shei's damaged eye. It poked out apparently on its own power, twisted free of the threads, hung there in the

air for a moment, then settled to the white bandaging.
A small bloodstain began spreading away from it,
darkening the snowy gauze.

Marchey was oblivious to their wide-eyed scrutiny.
Sweat sheened his wide forehead. A silver-capped
stump turned toward his head momentarily, and the
sweat vanished. He shifted position slightly and continued his work, the silver plates hovering over the
child's head. Discs of reflected light crawled across her
bandaged face.

Ella shuddered and looked away. This was worse
than knives and bone saws and a rubber-gloved hand
coming up dripping with gore. Those were at least
things you could understand. Horrible, but compre-
hensible. Not like invisible hands on phantom limbs
wielded by the horrific stranger inhabiting Gory's
body.

Chang picked up the thread of what she had been
telling Ella again, but she no longer addressed the
younger woman directly. She seemed to be speaking
for her own benefit as much as Ella's, trying to reduce
what she was witnessing to something explicable. She
clutched Ella's hand tightly. Her other hand was
clasped tightly around the crucifix at her breast.

"Bermann Surgeons perform procedures light years
ahead of conventional surgery. He can wipe away a
tumor or a clot or sterilize an infection. He can coax
an aneurism out, smoothing it away like a bubble in
clay. He can thrust his hands into a living, beating
heart without breaking the skin or altering its rhythm.
Bone, muscle, blood, and tissue—even the very cells
themselves—he can work on any of it directly. Look
at what he's doing here. The strongbox of the skull
presents no more barrier than the surface of water to
him. He can reach through it to work on the delicate
tissues inside as easily as you or I could turn over
stones at the bottom of a fishbowl. No scars, no complications, no blood, no pain . . ."

Chang's voice trailed away. After a few moments

she spoke again, her voice barely above a whisper. "I *envy* him, Ella. Can you understand that?"

Ella stared down at Chang's wan, sweat-glazed face, too numb to answer even if she had known what to say.

"Soon all my skills will be as obsolete as cupping and lobotomy. Surgeons will be like *him*." She grimaced. "Compared to what he has become I am just a crude mechanic with a few blunt tools at my command. He is a *healer*."

She squeezed Ella's hand. "I know this has been a lot to absorb all at once, and it's very frightening to see him like this. But he is not a monster. He is not a cripple." She managed an unconvincing smile. "I saw the way you looked at him. You love him, don't you? This doesn't change that."

Ella's face was that of a shock victim, her skin pale and bloodless as wax. It took all her strength and concentration to speak.

"H-how did he get like this?" Her voice was thin with bewilderment. She pulled her hands free from Chang's grasp and shoved them under her arms as if to protect them from the same fate his had suffered. "H-how was he *m-maimed*? He never said anything about any a-accident . . ."

Dr. Carol Chang was a kind woman. A caring and considerate woman. But she was badly unnerved herself, and she answered Ella's question without stopping to think about what a terrible thing some truths can be sometimes.

She shook her head. "There was no accident. His professional rating was high enough to be considered for the Bergmann Program. He scored well enough in the preliminary tests to become a candidate. Once it became clear that he had something of the innate ability needed, he gambled on success and had his hands amputated. God, I'd trade—"

Ella stared at Chang in absolute horror, her mouth working soundlessly at the word *amputated* but unable to force it past her lips. In her mind a gleaming, razor-edged silver cleaver chopped down, severing his hands, her hands, her heartstrings.

She stumbled back clumsily, her horrified gaze seeking out Marchey. *He'd done this to himself. Willingly. Mutilated himself so he could become this—this—*

Her back came up against the door.

"Gory?" His name came out a heartsick plea for proof that some fragment of the man she loved remained inside what he had become. What he had turned himself into.

No response. *"Gory!"* Louder, shrill with desperation.

Not even a flicker of recognition showed on the cruel cold landscape of his face. His hooded eyes remained dead and indifferent, focused on some crazy mental image, buried in the child's brain. The image burned itself into her retinas, through them into the tender folds of her own brain, into places so deep it could never be erased.

A sob escaped her as she spun around, pushed through the door, and fled, knowing knowing *knowing* she would never again be able to see him any other way.

Dr. Carol Chang watched the door swing shut, her shoulders slumping defeatedly. After a moment she slowly turned back toward the table where Marchey worked. She felt clumsy and stupid. Guilty. Out of place, there in her own clinic.

She shivered as before her eyes another twisted fragment of metal emerged from a place no one else could reach, brought out by a spectral hand she could not see.

Science, she told herself, *that's all this is. Science. Like light and a ruby make a laser, like Schmidt crystals and electricity produce anesthetic fields. He is only a man who has gained a special skill.*

But at what cost?

No triumph showed on the face of the hand's owner at what he had just accomplished, no regret for what he had just lost. He might as well have been a machine—a soulless, inhuman construct empty of everything but fixed, unswerving purpose.

"Dear God," she whispered. She took an uncertain step nearer, but could force herself to go no closer than that. Nor did she voice the name of who it was she wanted God to help: herself, Shei, Ella, or Marchey.

Oblivious and unmoved, he worked on.

Marchey reattached his prosthetics. A mental twist of the wrist and he had solid fingers once more. The arms felt heavy, and even though they were every bit as sensitive as the flesh they had replaced, they still felt like numb dead meat compared to the exquisitely sensitive un-hands he'd just used.

He didn't ask where Ella had gone. Some detached, then-volitionless part of his mind had registered every detail of what had happened.

Now everything from his old life was gone. The circle was complete.

He sighed. "I was able to repair most of the damage. I think the worst she'll suffer is some small memory loss, and perhaps a minor temporary degradation of coordination. You know the tests to run." His tone was as mechanical as his silver hands.

Chang nodded soberly. "You saved her life. You— you healed her face, too." Her voice was husky with awe.

It had been like nothing she had ever seen before, and not something she really ever wanted to see again; at once wondrous and indefinably *wrong*.

First the bandages had parted, threads cut cleanly as if by the sharpest microtome, and peeled themselves away from Shei's face, revealing the mangled, hastily gelsealed flesh beneath.

The gelseal had been swept away and the wounds reopened, chipped bone showing in the deepest lacerations. Then the truly miraculous had manifested itself before her very eyes.

With just one slow pass of an invisible hand Shei's

wounds had been debrided of even microscopic fragments, a haze of foreign materials rising up, coalesc-
ing, and settling down on a tray. Damaged bone had
been smoothed like soft clay. Torn muscle and severed
blood vessels had snaked together and reknit, melding
into one as they were repaired at the cellular level.
She had watched an eye that would have had to be
replaced under normal circumstances become whole
again, and an eyelid that had been blown to bloody
lace mended to smooth-domed perfection. She had
watched subcutaneous tissues move like hot wax,
flowing, flattening, filling in, and sealing. She had seen
burned skin slough off, and lacerated—no, *shredded*—
flesh ripple as it migrated to reshape itself to its earlier
state like water stills after a disturbing hand is withdrawn. Layer by layer, tissue by tissue, the trauma had
been erased without benefit of stitches or staples or
gels, and with a surety and speed a whole team of
surgeons could not have begun to match.

When he was done Shei's face had been almost perfectly restored, the slightly pinker redistributed skin
the only evidence it had ever been damaged.

What she had witnessed was something that went
so far beyond the boundaries of what she considered
traditional medicine that for her it could only belong
in the realm of magic and miracles. Her training and
what she knew about his specialty said otherwise, but
only in a small uncertain voice. It had been unbelievable. Impossible.

Yet she had seen it happen.

Try as she might, she could not keep herself from
maintaining a careful, cautious distance from him.
There was no way she could look at him in the same
way as when she'd first met him, even though she
knew it was a grievous sin against him, and her own
rationality. Just a couple hours ago he had been an
interesting concept in the literature. Then he had be
come her best hope, and in realizing that hope he
had been transformed into something that raised her
hackles and brought a prayer to her lips.

Marchey had been prepared for her reaction. He'd been in a similar situation all too many times before. He shrugged uncomfortably, gazing at the peaceful, now unblemished face of Shei Sinclair.

A life for a love. May she live long, and her second chance turn out better than his had.

"She's very beautiful," he murmured. "It would have taken major plastic surgery to have repaired all the damage. There was no reason to make her live with even temporary disfigurement."

He glanced at the clock. "I gave her a keep-under, so she'll probably be out for another couple hours. When she wakens she'll be almost good as new— though I would test her hearing. I'm, um, glad I was here to help." He made a point of not looking directly at Chang. Had he done so, she would have flinched away.

Fear, revulsion, violent denial, blind hatred, or, as in Chang's case, a kind of appalled theistic awe; these were what he always saw on the faces of the medical people who witnessed him at his work. Always.

This was one wall of the box he and the other Bergmanns had put themselves in. Even those who knew every detail of the Program reacted the same way. What he was and did flew in the face of all their former colleagues knew and did, and that he could so easily accomplish feats they could only dream about made matters worse. The way he looked when in trance unnerved and frightened them, and his having given up his hands to aquire such abilities burned the bridge between his kind and theirs, marking him in their eyes as a dangerous lunatic who had mutilated himself to become some sort of witch doctor.

Somehow *that* was never mentioned in the medical journals. At least not yet. Neither was the relief those same people felt when he or any of the thirty-some other Bergmann Surgeons moved on—driven off more often than not. That nobody wanted them on staff, not even the burn units. He hadn't quite become completely numbed to being a pariah, but he was working on it.

Now Ella was gone. He'd been braced for it, but that didn't make it any easier to take.

He shrugged again, having given up trying to argue his case a couple years before. He began pulling on his gloves so he could get the hell out of there and find that first of many drinks. The gloves were a necessity. There was no way he'd be able to bear being stared at right now.

"I guess that's about it." He cast a last yearning glance at the child whose life he'd saved, wishing he could stay to see her waken. To see those brown eyes open and that sweet face smile.

But that could never happen. Bitter experience had taught him and the other Bergmann Surgeons what would happen if he did, and taught them well. Some memory of his invasions remained inside her, creating a sort of peculiar psychic scarring. If she woke and saw him, she would begin to scream and shriek, gripped by a terror so harsh and primeval it could well kill her.

The *Nightmare Effect*, they called it. At the beginning of the Program several patients had nearly been lost before the lesson was learned.

Dr. Chang took a hesitant half step toward him. "Thank you . . . Doctor." Her eyes met his for an instant, then slid uneasily away. "I—I'm sorry." She hung her head, face burning with shame. "About Ella. About everything."

"The child lives," he answered. "That's all that matters." In one way that was even the truth. It was the sole redeeming value of Bergmann Surgery. Because of it the child and hundreds of others in similar dire extremity lived.

He picked up his jacket and left quietly, without looking back

"Are you done with your dinner, sir?"
Marchey stared sightlessly up at the waitress several seconds before he came back to the here and now of

the Litman commissary. He blinked the past away and focused on her face. Broad and Slavic. Blue eyes. Red cheeks and a strand of sweat-dampened hair curling across her high square forehead. A harried, hopeful smile.

She was on duty all by herself. He'd watched the other people in the commissary ordering her around like a slave, and so tried to keep his own requests gentle and to a minimum.

"Ah, I suppose I am." He checked the level in the bottle near his glass. Running toward empty from drinking on autopilot. That would never do. "I could use another flagon of this fine whiskey, though. When you get the time."

The waitress nodded as she took his plate away. "All right. What about dessert?"

"Why not? Something chocolate. You pick."

"I guess I can do that," she said, not sounding very sure about it. "I'll be back in a couple minutes."

"No rush." She hurried away, veering off to answer an imperious summons from another table.

He poured the dregs from the bottle into his glass, took a meditative sip. Not so many years ago remembering the last time he'd seen Ella would have torn him apart. Now he felt scarcely a quiver. Amazing what enough time—and nearly half a liter of 110 proof whiskey—could do.

Every year he felt less and less. Soon he would feel nothing at all. This was a state he alternately looked forward to and dreaded during those odd times he was sober enough to think about it.

Shei Sinclair had been a child of thirteen then. Now she probably had a husband and children, and retained only vague memories of her brush with death. Perhaps the odd nightmare. He hoped her life was a happy one.

Two days after his interrupted reunion dinner he'd joined the boarding queue and trudged up the ramp, his bag in his hand. As he stepped into the lock he turned and looked back. No one was there to see him off.

He hadn't heard a single word from Ella. Nor had he tried to contact her. Some things were beyond the reach of his healing skills, and would always remain so.

Dr. Chang had sent two messages detailing Shei's condition. Memory loss had been minimal. A slight hearing impairment was already fading. Her most severe aftereffect proved to be vivid recurrent nightmares of an armless monster pawing through her insides, nightmares terrible enough to make her wake up screaming in spite of sedation. The messages were very formal and quietly apologetic.

Just before leaving he had composed and sent a reply:

DEAR DR. CHANG. I AM GLAD THE CHILD IS DOING SO WELL. I WANT YOU TO KNOW THAT YOU ARE BLAMELESS FOR WHAT HAPPENED; YOU WOULD HAVE BEEN REMISS IF YOU HAD NOT ASKED FOR WHATEVER HELP WAS AVAILABLE, AND WHAT HAPPENED BETWEEN ELLA AND ME WAS PROBABLY INEVITABLE. AT LEAST A GOOD CAUSE WAS SERVED.

BUT PLEASE BE CAREFUL OF WHAT YOU WOULD ENVY. MY KIND ARE A FAILED EXPERIMENT. A PHYSICIAN MUST MINISTER TO PEOPLE, NOT JUST BE THE REPAIRER OF THEIR AFFLICTIONS. THAT IS MY LOT. FOR ALL I HAVE SEEMINGLY GAINED, I HAVE LOST EVEN MORE. NO LONGER DO I HAVE THE PRECIOUS CONNECTION WITH MY PATIENTS THAT MADE ME WHAT I ONCE WAS, NAMELY A GOOD DOCTOR. A HEALER.

I HEARD WHAT YOU SAID, AND YOU HAD IT WRONG. YOU REMAIN A HEALER, AND YOUR SKILLS WILL NEVER BE OBSOLETE.

IT IS I WHO HAVE BECOME THE MERE MECHANIC. BELIEVE ME, IT IS NOT THE SAME THING AT ALL.

Once on the shuttle he'd slumped back in his seat, the red edges of a headache beginning to throb at his temples. While sorting through his beltpouch for one of the soporifics he had become increasingly dependent on, the shuttle's steward approached him, a large foil-wrapped package in his arms.

"Dr. Marchey?"

"Yes?" Ah, there was one. He popped the pill out of its blister and put it in his mouth. It tasted bitter, but then again so did everything lately. He swallowed it dry.

"I was told to see that this package got to you." The steward handed it over. "Careful sir, it's heavy."

So it was. Surprisingly heavy.

"Thanks." He lowered it to his lap, dug into his pouch again and located a five-credit chip. "Here you go. When do you start serving drinks?"

"Soon as we debark, sir." He touched his cap. "Thanks."

The steward sidled down the aisle, slipping the chip into his pocket. Marchey put the package on the empty seat beside him, then picked it right up again, unable to contain his curiosity.

Under the foil was a carbon-fiber box, and inside the box—

Marchey sat in the commissary, glass of Mauna Loa in his hand, remembering the moment with an aching clarity. Like it had happened only yesterday, not nearly a decade ago.

Inside the box had been a bisque-fired clay sculpture, the ceramic the color of old ivory. The piece was exquisitely wrought and yet fairly throbbed with raw power and emotion, eloquent proof that her talent remained undiminished under all the hype.

The piece portrayed two sculptors who had begun work on a statue of two lovers embracing. But one sculptor stood helplessly by, gazing hopefully up at the unfinished lovers. His arms lay at his feet, arms crossed at the wrists and tools still clutched in his hands. He cradled a wounded child in the stumps of arms held up toward the sculpture as if in supplication.

The other sculptor, the tall thin woman, huddled on

the ground near him, her averted face a mask of frustrated shame. Her posture was that of someone who
could not muster the courage to pick up her scattered
tools and stand, taking the first step in trying to help
complete the work they had begun. Her face was
turned away from fellow sculptor and work alike.

The lovers were rough-hewn and unfinished, yet
there was no mistaking who they were.

Marchey recalled staring at it for a very long time,
tears streaming down his face.

When the acceleration warning sounded he'd returned it to its box, then belted it into the seat beside him.

She understood. Not that it changed anything, but
at least she understood.

Marchey stared into his empty glass, adrift between
past and present, and finding comfort in neither.

The waitress returned. She placed a plate and fresh
fork in front of him. "Here's some chocolate cake, sir.
I hope it's all right."

He gave her a fractured smile. "It looks delicious."

She replaced the empty bottle of Mauna Loa with
a fresh one. "And your drink. Can I get you anything else?"

"Nothing, thanks. I've got everything I need."

She went away. He opened the bottle and filled his
glass, then forked off a bite of cake, tasted it.

It was delicious.

But the whiskey was better.

"I want to talk to you, *Doctor* Marchey." A pe-
remptory tone and sarcastic emphasis on *Doctor.*

The swarthy, hawk-faced woman whom he'd saluted
with his glass earlier had come to his table for a show-
down. He'd remained vaguely aware of her presense
all through his second bottle of Mauna Loa and memories of Ella. She and her companion had argued in
harsh whispers for several minutes. Finally he left their
table, looking angry.

She'd sat there for a while, drinking coffee and no

doubt working herself up to a fine rage. At last she'd
flung down her napkin and stood up, strode over, and
planted herself at the other side of his table. Her arms
were crossed before her formidable bosom, and she
was radiating enough righteous wrath to make the
whiskey in his glass begin to bubble and steam.

He peered at the name tag pinned to her dark blue
jacket. *Dr. Ismela Khan.* That explained her splendid
command of Arabic invective.

He met her tight-lipped glare squarely. "I doubt
that."

Her dark brows drew down. "Just what do you
mean by that?"

"Just what I said," he answered mildly. "You don't
want to talk to me. You don't want to have anything
to do with me. Nor do you want to *talk.* Harangue,
maybe. Perhaps villify. Insult and condemn, almost
certainly. You can save your breath, Dr. Khan. I've
heard it all before." He picked up his glass, took an
unhurried sip. "If I'm not mistaken, I already heard a
lot of it from you this very afternoon. Why repeat
yourself?"

She gave a grudging half nod. "All right, maybe I
did say some things I shouldn't have—"

"No need to apologize. I was ignoring you anyway."
He waved his glass toward the empty chair across the
table from him. "Have a seat, Dr. Khan."

His invitation took her off guard. She looked
around the commissary, as if trying to decide how the
other staffers might react to her getting cozy with the
outcast, then faced him again. "Thank you, no," she
said stiffly.

"Suit yourself. How about a drink?" Instead of
waiting for an answer, he flagged the waitress down
as she trotted by.

"I'd like one more bottle of this fine whiskey and
a glass for the lady, please," he told her.

The waitress looked uncomfortable, biting her lip
and staring at her feet. "You've already had three
whole quatriliters, sir," she pointed out diplomatically.

A hopeful look. "Wouldn't you prefer some coffee or something?"

Marchey smiled at her, touched by her concern. "Do I look drunk?" he asked gently. "Act drunk?"

"No," she admitted.

He chuckled and gave her a wink. "Well, actually I am. The thing is, being drunk is something I happen to be exceptionally good at. In my expert medical opinion I'm not nearly drunk enough. So please help me continue this great work. All right?"

She ducked her head in acceptance. "All right."

"Thank you." When she hurried off he turned his attention back to Dr. Khan. "Please pardon the interruption. Now what's on your mind?"

"You're an alcoholic," she said accusingly.

He emptied the bottle into his glass. "I suppose I am." He took a drink. "What of it? Want lessons?"

Her upper lip curled in distaste. "You're disgusting."

His eyebrows lifted in mock shock. "I do believe that was an insult!" Then he shook his head sadly. "Not much of one, though. Surely a surgeon of your caliber can do a better job of drawing blood than that."

She opened her mouth to say something, but bit it back because the waitress had returned. Khan stood there, the muscles in her jaw twitching with repressed anger as a glass was placed on the table before her and the empty bottle traded for a fresh one.

She watched the waitress beat a hasty retreat, then scowled at Marchey. "I suppose I shouldn't be surprised that you're a drunk," she informed him in a low hard voice. "It's probably the only way you can live with yourself."

"Maybe so." He shrugged. "What would you suggest as an alternative? Suicide?" A faint pang of sorrow surfaced, sank back into quiescence. "Some of my friends have been driven to just that, you know. Me, I prefer to drown myself one glass at a time. It's really quite pleasant. You should try it."

"You really don't care what you are, do you?"

Another shrug. "I'm reconciled to it." He put down his empty glass and cracked open the new bottle. "I'm reconciled to a lot of things, like the rude, rotten treatment I get from people like you in places like this. But I do my duty and go where I'm needed. Whether you or I or anybody else likes it doesn't enter into the matter. I run your gauntlet. I do what needs to be done. I leave." He poured an amber splash into his glass. "That and happy hour are usually the best part."

Dr. Khan watched sourly as he drained his glass and filled it yet again. On days when he operated it always took a lot more to reach the place he liked to live. Some of that came from the D-Tox he'd taken that morning. Instead of starting with half a tank he had to work his way up from dead empty.

But he could really feel the whiskey now. By the time he finished this bottle he'd be ready to find his way back to his room, have a final nightcap, and pass out. Tomorrow morning he'd reclaim his ship and once again be gone, on his way to somewhere else he could do this all over again. And again. And again.

Even this conversation was nothing new. Once or twice a year someone took his presence personally enough to want to take a whack at him. He knew if he ignored her she'd go away eventually. *The Dead Horse Defense.* Her whip arm would get tired sooner or later.

But maybe if he took a swipe back at her, then the next time a Bergmann Surgeon was sent here she'd leave the poor bastard alone. It wasn't like he had anything else to do while he killed this last jug.

He turned his flat, sunken gray eyes on her. "I'll tell you one thing I'm not reconciled to," he said in a soft, passionless voice. "That's the waste of my skills. In a good month I might get the chance to help three patients. *Three* patients. By all rights I should be on staff in a place like this and treating that many a day. But thanks to narrow-minded prigs like you, my dear Dr. Khan, I'm not."

He picked up the bottle and offered it to her.

"Maybe you ought to take this, sweetheart. Drink to forget that today I gave a patient help you couldn't begin to provide. Drink to forget that I could do the same thing tomorrow for another patient if you hadn't helped make it impossible for me to stay. Drink to forget that you're putting your own petty prejudices ahead of the well-being of your patients, and forcing me to waste skills that make your best surgical technique look like something done with fucking hatchets and meat cleavers."

Khan ignored the bottle in his hand. "Are you through?" she asked, grinding the words out between her clenched teeth.

"Almost." Marchey slouched back in his chair and took a long drink straight out of the jug. "You can choose between accepting what I can do, or only using me when MedArm forces you to. My only choice is between doing what little I'm allowed to do or quitting. I took the Healer's Oath, and quitting isn't a part of it. So I get by. *How* I get by is none of your god-damned business, and since it's you forcing me to live like this, I suggest that you stuff your sanctimonious attitude up your tight judgemental ass and leave me the fuck alone."

He grinned at her. "Now I'm done."

Dr. Khan uncrossed her arms and leaned toward him, resting the knuckles of her clenched hands on the table. "You dare talk about the Healer's Oath," she spat. "At least I'm willing to treat anyone who needs help, as it demands. Not like *you.*"

Marchey stared back at her. "I treat whoever Med-Arm has the Institute send me to treat."

She nodded, her face taking on the look of a prose-cutor who has extracted the damning confession she sought. "Yes, your kind do, don't you?"

She straightened up, pointing an accusing finger at him. "If I was letting myself be used the way you are, I'd probably drink, too." Her mouth twitched into a harsh smile. "If anybody ought to stuff their sanctimonious attitude up their ass it's you. We're not stupid. We know what's going on."

She turned on her heel and stalked away. Marchey watched her, scowling and wondering what he'd missed. *We're not stupid. We know what's going on.* What the hell was that supposed to mean? He could always call her back and ask . . .

He took another swig from the bottle in his hand, the sweet whiskey dissolving the question like a clot dosed with hemaflux. For all he knew she was convinced that the Bergmanns got their abilities from human sacrifice or a pact with Satan. Some of the more fanatic Christian and Islamic sects did.

He sighed and closed his eyes. *Damn* being out around people like her. The talk of choice, and his treating only those people MedArm assigned . . .

He opened his eyes. Another ghost from the past began to materialize across the table from him. He probably could have banished the shade, but let her be. She was one of his few good memories.

When he thought of her now, it was her smile that came to mind through the thickening boozy haze.

A certain special smile he had never seen . . .

Merry put down her glass, the wine hardly touched. She gazed coolly at the man across the table from her, intrigued in spite of herself. "Something better than money, you say."

The night hadn't begun all that well. In fact, it'd been shaping up as a real 4D: Dead, Dull, Disappointing, and ending in Deficit.

She'd been sitting at her usual table in Randy's Rest, gloomily nursing a cheap algae-based white wine and wondering if there was really any point in sticking around when this juan had pushed through the bead-curtained doorway.

He wasn't a regular, she knew that at first glance. So she looked the fresh meat over.

He was middle-aged, nearly bald. Well dressed in loose gray pants, crisp white open-neck shirt that was either real silk or a damn good fake, gray gloves, black-cotton and leatherite jacket, black-suede boots. No jewelry except a silver pin on his broad chest. Tasteful and understated. Not some rowdy dusty rock-jock or smirking tourist out for a thrill.

He'd done what most of the new sticks did, standing there just inside the door and checking out the available talent—getting checked out himself at the very same time, the credit scanner in each girl's head humming over him and reading his paying potential down to the decicredit. This went on during the momentary pause while they waited to see if he got this dumbjohn look of surprise on his face and stumbled back out, having drunkenly mistaken Randy's for Billy's Club next door, where the doe-eyed boys posed and preened in their satin loincloths and tight leather jeans.

These tests passed, there was a lacy rustle as the other girls went into display mode, making sure their charms were shown off to their best advantage.

Merry hadn't even bothered to sit up straight to show off the merchandise, or put her *try me* look on her face. Habit told her she should, but the disgruntled voice of cynicism said *Why bother?*

It was a slow Tuesday night in the Rest, with a dozen idle girls besides herself vying for the attention of this one customer. Much as she hated to admit it, she knew she was well past the first-choice category, and maybe even the second or third. Randy let her keep working there more for old times' sake than for the money she brought in. But he was a practical man. Now her table was way in the back, where the light wasn't too good, and the sour smell that at times wafted from the head just a couple meters away sometimes seemed like a foretaste of her next step down the ladder.

Oh, the men who came into Randy's would take her if all the other girls were busy, and not a one of them wasn't shown at least as good a time as the other talent could give them. Maybe even better, because she didn't try to coast by on looks alone. Besides, if you could get them to become one of your regulars, that meant that you didn't have to hustle so hard. A stable of regulars was credit in the bank, and maybe even a ticket out of the Life. She had a couple, but the poor bastards were almost always as stony broke as she was.

It had been hard enough before, on the downhill side of thirty and competing with girls almost half her age. And now?

There was no way she could hope to compete with those perfect young faces.

Yet this coddy hadn't given any of the other girls a second look. The moment he had seen her his face had gone all funny for a moment.

But not with that *What the fuck happened to you?* look she'd seen so many times in the past months. It was more like he'd seen a ghost, or stumbled across the last thing he had ever expected to find here. Like maybe his wife, his mother, his sister, or a long-lost lover.

After a moment he got a handle on himself, smiled at her uncertainly, and headed straight for her table.

She did sit up straight then, her translucent red skin-suit tightening around her. A smile went onto her face, part habit, part *screw you* to the pouts appearing on the other girls' flawless faces as they saw the trade choosing her over them.

Watching him come closer, she thought about how every so often Fate gave you something besides the finger. This might just be one of those nights. She sure as hell was due for one.

Too many of the juans just waltzed right over to your table and plunked themselves down like they owned it and you, figuring that what they had in their pockets plus what they had in their pants made them irresistible.

They were half-right, anyway.

But this one had politely asked if he could join her, and thanked her when she said yes. He'd ordered a triple whiskey neat from the waitbot, another wine for her, then come right to the point. He wanted to purchase her services for the night.

All-nighters were rarer for her than they used to be, and though she was tempted to shave her price to guarantee he took her, some ornery remnant of her pride made her quote the standard fee set by her union.

Besides, she could haggle if he said that was too much.

The juan's face was broad and craggy, with big dark pouches under eyes of a clear cool gray. It was the face of someone who'd lost a lot of weight sometime in the past, and maybe a lot of other things, too. A widower's face, drawn and dispossessed. But there was humor there, too. He'd given her this puckish smile, and then hit her with this "something better than money" stroke.

"What's better than money?" Merry figured that maybe he wanted to barter. No problem there, Randy could help her convert almost anything into cash. For a cut, of course, but at least he was honest. More or less.

His smile turned wry. "Lots of things. Trust, for instance. Choice is another." He peered slantwise at her, probably seeing the look that had crept onto her face at this line of patter.

"I know you don't know me well enough to trust me," he continued. Most juans said something like that, she'd have laughed in their faces. But there was something about him and the way he said it that made her take his words seriously.

"You seem nice enough," she admitted, "but so does my landlord until I come up short when the rent comes due."

After six years of turning tricks Merry's internal radar was tuned to within a couple microns of dead center, and she wasn't getting any rip-artist readings. That was the only thing keeping her from telling him to go try his line on one of the other girls.

He chuckled. "Point well taken. I'll tell you what. I'll get us the best room this establishment has to offer, something to eat and drink from room service—"

"The price of a suite gets you a snack tray, and there's a free bar in the room," Merry put in. "Drugs and benders are extra." She could have told him the number of tiles in the ceilings of the bedrooms as well, having had plenty of chance to count them. A hundred in the suites and 144 in the singles.

Another chuckle, and a nod of his balding head. "I love the room already. I'll also preauthorize a one-KISC charge to be paid to you tomorrow morning. If you still want it."

He said the number as if it didn't mean anything to him, like it was the number of tiles in a protel ceiling, and it caught her so off guard she had to make sure she'd heard right.

"You said one *KISC*?" Hoping she'd heard right.

He grinned at her in obvious amusement. "That's what I said."

Merry found it hard to imagine *not* wanting the thousand International Standard Credits. It was twenty times the price she had quoted him, the union rate for five full days of an A-list girl's services. Even after Randy skimmed his 10 percent off the top she'd still have over four months' rent on her cubby.

She held out her slim, red-nailed hand. "You've got yourself a deal, handsome."

Her voice dropped to a sultry purr. "Shall we get the vulgar financial details out of the way, darling, then go somewhere more private?"

"I would be honored," he replied, closing his gloved hand around hers to seal the deal. His hand felt strangely hard, but his grip was gentle. "My name is Marchey, by the way. Georgory Marchey. My friends call me Gory."

Merry had noticed that he wore gloves right off the bat, and once again she had to wonder why. But she gave it only a moment's thought. She'd dealt with odder kinks than that. *Much* odder.

Of course that still didn't mean he wasn't hiding a nun's habit, a pink-lace merry widow, or even a chicken suit under his clothes. If so, she could play along. One kay bought one hell of a lot of leeway.

"Pleased to meet you, Gory. My name is Merry."

Marchey made himself comfortable on the suite's shapeless black couch, watching the woman who called herself Merry fix them each a drink.

He knew that Merry was just her working name. Her real name wasn't supposed to matter. While she was Merry it was her job to be whoever and whatever he wanted her to be.

From the back she looked so much like Ella it made him ache. Although not quite as tall, she had that same impossibly thin frame, the narrow waist and small firm behind, the same long lean limbs that would be gawky but for an innate inner grace. She had the same close-cropped, nearly white hair, straggling tendrils curling down her knobby spine.

But when she turned around the illusion unraveled.

Her face was pretty where Ella's had been plain, softer and less severe, underlaid by an elegant bone structure. Her eyes were brown instead of green, with long dark lashes.

He watched her come toward him, one side of her wide, ruby-lipped mouth curved up in a warm smile that showed no sign of artifice. The other side of her mouth—the other side of her face—remained lax and nearly expressionless. That eyelid drooped in what looked like sleepy suspicion.

There was also a scarcely perceptible drag to her foot on that side. It was so slight that only someone trained to look for such things would have noticed the minor paralytic trace.

His observations were by no means all diagnostic. He was also paying close attention to the undulating roll of her slim hips, the rhythmic flexings of the long lean muscles in her thighs, the sweet and subtle sway and swing of her breasts. He feasted on the sight of her, feeding a gnawing hunger, and sharpening that hunger at the very same time. Just knowing he was still capable of feeling it was a pleasure in itself.

It had been almost two years since he had last been with a woman. There were times—usually those increasingly rare moments when he was stone-cold-look-at-yourself-in-the-mirror sober—that he became dismayed and depressed at just how accustomed he was getting to his solitary life and his celibacy. It was almost as if he could feel his libido shrivelling up like some vestigial organ that no longer had a purpose. Before long he was going to have to start counting his balls each morning to make sure he still had them.

Not that he had much choice in the matter. In fact it was better that way. A sex drive firing on all thrusters would have driven him mad, making intolerable a life spent all alone on a ship of his own, ricocheting from place to place like some spacefaring surgical Flying Dutchman.

MedArm called it the circuit, and it had been instituted less than a year after he last saw Ella. That meant he had been on it for over four years. Hard to believe.

Working with the Bergmann Institute, MedArm had created the circuit, giving each Bergmann Surgeon a ship of their own and sending them where they were needed worst. He had no idea how the higher-ups decided where they should go and whom they should treat. It didn't really matter. At least they were allowed to be of some use.

He and his fellow Bergmanns remained constantly on the move, skulking in and out of health facilities like thieves. The circuit's chief advantage was that once he was freed from the schedules set by the regular carriers less time was wasted waiting around to get from point A to point B.

Unfortunately that also meant no more long layovers during which he might at least try to find some companionship, be it a brief flirtation, a one-night stand, or even the boozy camaraderie created by adjoining barstools. He would arrive at his destination, perform the procedure he had been brought in for, and more often than not go straight from surgery to the local equivalent of a liquor store and be in his ship and on his way again before the patient regained consciousness.

Only rarely did he remain anywhere long enough for even an unsatisfying taste of paid sex such as with that prostitute on Ceres two years ago. This stop at Vesta was the longest break from the monotonous treadmill he'd had in months. Not only was he here long enough for two procedures, his ship was undergoing some minor refitting, which gave him a bonus night of his own.

He'd ventured into Gusto Mews, Vesta's infamous pleasure district, looking for something—anything—to fill up some small corner of the emptiness inside himself. Some proof he was still alive, still a man. He'd been resigned to settling for paid sex and simulated affection if that was all he could find.

But when he had caught sight of Merry he'd suddenly glimpsed a chance to find something worth having.

She handed him his drink as she sat down on the couch beside him, folding her long legs under her. "Here you go, love."

"Thanks." He helped himself to a sip, grimaced. It was cheap fake scotch whiskey, algaecol and artificial flavorings, probably made on-site. Not that such distinctions made all that much difference. He would drink the good stuff when he could get it, and whatever was available when he couldn't. Humanity had risen from the tribes in the treetops to cities in space because of its ability to adapt. It was only fair he did his part.

The "suite" was as low-rent as the whiskey. It consisted of a three-meter-by-three-meter sitting room furnished with the lumpy couch under his butt, a chunky foamstone table cemented to the floor in front of it, its top covered with a pink-plastic tablecloth and bearing a platter of unidentifiable soy- and algae-based delectables. Then there was the bar. That was no more than a shallow alcove in one wall equipped with four shatterproof glasses, three smudged decanters, a beer tap, and a metered ice dispenser.

A wide arched doorway led to the bedroom, which was barely larger than the fake-fur-covered king-sized bed. There was a deep narrow bathroom off to one side of the bedroom, complete with pay shower. The suite's black-glazed stone walls were stenciled with patchy red flocking in an Early Bordello design. Bad erotic art hung askew on the walls. Wallscreens faced both the bed and the couch so the happy couple could watch themselves, or some quite likely more photogenic other couple at sport.

Well, he hadn't really been expecting the Mars Grande. At least it was fairly clean and private.

He peered down into his glass. "Not exactly sippin' whiskey, is it?"

Merry's face fell. "Sorry. Maybe I can get Randy to—"

"Don't worry about it. That just means there's no point in sipping it." He drained his glass, knowing the sooner he got his palate numbed the better it would taste.

When she started to jump up to get him another, he restrained her by resting one gloved hand on her thigh. "That's all right. No hurry."

She settled back. "Okay, but if you want more just say so." Her face was turned so that the damaged side was hidden from him, and her smile promised all wonders for the asking. "If you want *anything*," she added, "I'm here to please you." That last was said in such a way there was no mistaking her meaning.

Her eagerness to cater to whatever urges or impulses he might have was a little disconcerting. No doubt it had been sharpened by the size of the payoff he'd promised her. He felt a little guilty about sandbagging her with such a large sum, but he needed even more forbearance than was usual in her profession. One way or another she would feel satisfied with their transaction.

The money meant nothing to him, but if she took it, he was going to feel cheated. Only time would tell.

"Don't worry, I will." He took a deep breath, suddenly feeling as nervous as a boy about to steal his first kiss, and told her one of the things he did want.

"What I would like is for you to tell me what happened to your face."

Merry was a pro. The expression on the working side of her face barely changed. But the warmth in her brown eyes was snuffed out in an instant. "Airlock accident," she answered tonelessly. "Blowout."

Just as he'd thought. "Ah. Savatinian embolism?"

She stared at him in unconcealed disgust. "Look, if you're a cripfreak, that's your business. But it's not *mine*. I may not like it, but I'll put up with you getting your rocks off on the way I look if that's what it takes to earn my money." Her good eye narrowed and her mouth hardened. "But I'll be damned if I'll talk it up just so you can get it up."

This flash of fierce pride made Marchey like her even more than before. He gave her his most disarming smile. "The reason I asked is because I'm a doctor."

She snorted. "Right. And you're here to make me all better with your magic syringe."

Marchey couldn't help guffawing at the image she'd conjured. "No, nothing like that," he assured her, chuckling and shaking his head. "Your condition was caused by hundreds of microscopic gas bubbles bursting numerous small blood vessels in your brain; like a stroke, only widely diffused. Savatinian embolism is a condition that occurs in about one-tenth of one percent of people subjected to explosive decompression."

"You sure talk like a doctor," she said grudgingly.

"That's because I really am one. Here, give me your

glass." He took it from her long slim fingers, carried it and his own to the bar to fix them both refills.

"Sorry I was so touchy," she said behind him. "It's just that I don't like being treated like a freak."

"Believe me, nobody does." Just this morning some of the staff at the hospital had treated him like a radioactive pedophile. And those had been the polite ones.

But that was then and this was now. One hurdle had been cleared. He finished assembling their drinks and prepared to go on to the next.

"As for your being a cripple," he said as he returned to sit beside her, "that's not a word I particularly care for."

"Thanks," she said, accepting the glass he handed her with a nod. "Why's that?"

"Aside from its cruelty, some would say it fits me, too."

She looked him up and down. "I don't see anything wrong with you." Then her gaze went to his lap and a pink tinge of embarrassment crept onto her face. "Oh . . . you mean you don't—I mean you can't . . . ?" She shrugged. "You know."

"No, nothing like that," he assured her. "There might be dust or cobwebs on it, but I'm fairly sure it still works. The thing is, I don't have any forearms or hands."

She gave his gloved hands a look, scowling slightly. "What're those, then? Extra feet?"

"Prosthetics."

Her scowl deepened. "Pro*whats*?"

"Prosthetics. Fakes. Artificial substitutes." He put his glass aside, then peeled off one glove to show her.

Merry gazed in wide-eyed wonder at the silver-metal hand that emerged. "It's beautiful!" Her voice was hushed, awestruck. Even her drooping eye widened slightly.

Marchey was surprised by her reaction. "Well, it's shiny anyway," he allowed. Even though it wasn't some crude hook or whirring, humming antique Cy-

berhand, most people were put off by the sight of it
and its twin. In a world where missing limbs could
be easily replaced or regenerated, and even normal
prosthetic devices were covered by vat-grown skin and
could not be identified except by scan, it was proof
that there was something strange about him.

They were self-contained, powered only by the
whisper of electricity carried by the nerves, self-
maintaining, and all but indestructible, the gleaming
biometal several times harder than hullmetal, yet supple as skin and providing the same degree of tactile
feedback. Most importantly, they were easy to take
off and put on. No synskin covered them, and they
needed none of the structural or cyberneural connections other kinds used. When brought up against the
silver stump-caps the biometal arms melded seamlessly back into them to become one. They were glar-
ingly obvious, but in the beginning there had been no
thought of hiding what they had done. They were all
proud to have given up their hands and taken these
silver replacements.

Now he wore gloves in public.

She started to reach out to touch his hand, hesitated, turning her wide brown eyes toward his face.
"Do you mind?"

He held it out palm up. "Be my guest."

There was nothing cautious or squeamish about the
way Merry handled his hand. She stroked the smooth
curve where thumb sloped into wrist and leaned close
to examine where the fingers met the palm. She felt
the shape of the knuckles and tried to wriggle the
fingers from side to side as if expecting to find them
loose.

"A perfect replica," she said half under her breath.
"Body temperature. Jointed just like a regular hand,
but except for a couple access seams, like here on the
palm, it's seamless. It even gives to conform to the
surface of whatever object you're holding, just like a
real hand."

She looked up at him again, still holding his hand

like it was a gift he'd given her. "This is stunning workmanship. Absolutely perfect. Class I Biometal, right?"

"The best money can buy," he agreed. "I was told that each hand and arm have almost twenty-five KISC worth of biometal in them." He hesitated, marshalling his nerve for the next step, then with his other hand cautiously reached up toward the frozen and drooping side of her face. "May I . . . ?"

"I guess so," she answered uneasily. He doubted that most men wanted to touch her there. But he did. Needed to.

"Don't worry, I won't hurt you," he said softly. "I can juggle eggs with these things." His silver fingers lightly traced the slack muscles around her eye, along her cheek, around her mouth. Not even a reflexive twitch. She sat stiffly, her eyes warily tracking his hand, her full lower lip caught between her even white teeth. "Of course I always end up with two mitts full of scrambled eggs and the yolk's on me."

A laugh burst out of her, sudden and hearty. Marchey felt it filling a place inside him that had been silent and empty for a very long time. Making someone laugh is such a little thing. Such a wonderful, rewarding thing. Only by living without it could you learn just how priceless it was. It felt so good to know he still could dispense the best medicine.

Even if she did take the money—and he hoped she didn't—that laughter, and her easy acceptance of the way he was, were worth far more than the thousand credits.

Things had been going quite nicely until he asked *The Question.* Merry had been afraid he might, and hoping he wouldn't. Now he had, spoiling everything.

"Hard luck." She shrugged, trying to pass the matter off. "It's like gas. Everybody gets their share."

"And it eventually passes. What was yours?"

She stared at this strange man who had purchased her services for the night, feeling torn. How she'd become a pro was her own business and nobody else's. It wasn't exactly a secret, but it was part of her life, not part of her job.

Yet she found herself trusting him enough to tell him. Even wanting to tell him. She wasn't sure why. Maybe it was because he treated her like a lady, like a person. That felt good, and it only made her resent his ruining things all the more.

"You won't tell me how you lost your hands," she pointed out, hoping to derail him that way.

He grinned at her over the top of his glass. "Yes I will. I had a run-in with the Manicurist from Hell."

She snorted derisively. "*Right.* Well, I became a whore because instead of being curly, all my pubic hair's shaped like dollar signs."

His grin got even wider. "Really? That's most unusual. You must show me later."

She gave him a smoldering look. "I'll show you everything I got right this minute." Not that the translucent skinsuit she wore hid all that much. Still, nothing distracted a man like sex. She reached for the sealtab nestled between her breasts.

He reached out and gently closed a silver hand around hers. His metal fingers rested so lightly on hers they might have been foil butterflies.

"Please tell me," he said, looking her straight in the eyes. "You can trust me." He released her hand. "At least I hope you can."

Merry looked away, stood up abruptly. "I need another drink."

She retreated toward the bar, her gait somewhat unsteady. Part of that came from three glasses of wine on an empty stomach. But not all of it. Not even most of it.

To survive as a whore you had to keep your head on straight. Always be the one in control, even when playing the submissive. Keep your emotions out of the transaction. Remember that no matter how nice the juan seemed, he had paid for the use of your body and nothing more. When you lost your handle on all that, you were just asking for trouble.

She knew she was skating on the thin brittle edge of trouble now. Slipping closer and closer, almost as if she wanted to go over it.

Why?

Because this man she had sold herself to for the night was trying to seduce her, and she was liking the way it felt.

Not seduced in the sexual sense, that was already bought and paid for. This was being seduced in the sense of being enticed into dropping her defenses and letting him inside. Of being subtly drawn into the vulnerable nakedness of letting him see the private places she kept hidden by the Merry face she showed the world.

Keeping her back to him, she picked up the scotch bottle and topped off her glass with that instead of wine. Her hand shook, splashing liquor over the rim of the glass, reminding her how rock steady that hand had been once upon a time.

Yes, once upon a time. Didn't stories which started that way always end with *They all lived happily ever after*?

She leaned heavily on the bar, keeping her back to this strange juan who refused to follow the rules.

Tell him this, and the next thing she knew she'd be telling him her real name!

"I was a microtech," she said softly, eyes on her traitorous hands. "Most tech work is troubleshooting and mod-swapping. But sometimes, most often with special purpose equipment, the mod itself has to be rebuilt or reconfigured. That calls for a microtech. The parts are so small and delicate, the circuiting so intricate, it calls for someone with a really fine touch, like a—" she hesitated, searching for the proper comparison.

"Like a surgeon," he supplied quietly from behind her.

She nodded. "Yeah, like that. I had that touch. I

was good. *Damn* good." She had been, too. The best on Vespa and within thirty thousand kilometers of it. She'd made serious money and her rep was solid gold.

She took a swallow of whiskey and grimaced, steeling herself to tell the next part. The hard part.

"One day I was working on setting up the controller-mods of an industrial circuiting machine for Iolus Fabrique here on Vespa. Some clown on the crew accidentally left the bolts off a substrate roller collar. Or they had been left out at the factory where it was built. Whatever the reason, that two-hundred-and-fifty-kilo roller broke loose and came crashing down inside it, flattening the modbox directly under it. A modbox I just happened to have my hands inside."

Retelling it, she shuddered at the remembrance of that sudden blinding burst of pain/surprise/confusion/horror, of stumbling backward, a bubbling scream plugging her throat when she saw the terrible ruined things at the ends of her arms, flopping bonelessly and spurting red in every direction. . . .

The juan, Marchey, was silent. But she could feel his attention wrapped around her as he waited for her to continue. And she would. Now that she had started this there was no turning back. It had to be replayed to the end, just like when you began falling there was no stopping until you hit bottom.

"Both my hands were crushed. Almost every bone in them was broken, and the muscles turned to mincemeat."

The foreman had taken one horrified look at her, turned white as a sheet, and puked all over his shoes. They'd had to put plastic bags over her hands to keep from losing pieces of them, holding the bags in place with tourniquets to keep her from bleeding to death.

She wheeled around to face him. "You know, I really shouldn't trust you," she said in a dead voice.

"Why is that?" Softly, not in challenge. His face solemn, but not forbidding. Willing to accept whatever she said. A bitter wave of spite rose up inside her.

"Because you're a doctor. *Don't worry, you'll be*

fine, they told me." Her upper lip curled in disgust. "Sure, they fixed up my hands so that they look all right if you don't check too close, and I can do most normal things with them. But my career as a microtech ended that day." She shivered. "In fact, I can barely stand to be around machinery anymore. I look at it and feel an itch I just can't scratch."

He nodded soberly. "Believe me, I know how you feel."

No you don't! screamed the shrill voice of frustration, but the words never made it past her lips. A glance down at his silver hands silenced it, telling her that he just might understand after all.

"So you blame the doctors for not fixing you up the way you were before. First with your hands, and then with your face after the embolism."

Merry's thin shoulders slumped. "No, not really," she admitted. Oh, she had for a while, but had gotten over it.

"Why not?"

"I know that not everything can be fixed. Some things just seem fated to end up on the scrap heap." She shrugged. "I guess I'm one of them." The worst part was how long the trip took.

"Why do you say that?"

Merry had to wonder what he was after. Why he cared, if he really did. Yet she couldn't keep herself from answering. It had been so long since anyone had just listened to her, had been interested in her as anything other than something to get their rocks off with when nothing better or free was available.

It was true that some men wanted to talk as much as they wanted to get laid. More of them than an outsider might think. But what they really wanted to talk about was *themselves.* Any questions about her were either nervous chatter, a form of voyeurism, or in some cases a desire to get their money's worth by sticking themselves into her life as well as her body.

She spread her hands. "Isn't it obvious? I knew I'd never again be the tech I had been. My lawyer warned me that it would be years before I got any sort of settlement. I needed a new career because I needed the income. When my landlord offered to eat my month's rent if I screwed him, I heard opportunity's bastard cousin knocking. Even though I was getting a little old for the trade, I was still doing okay until I got caught in a blowout a few months ago."

She fingered the lax side of her face and let out a sardonic chuckle.

"I became Frankenwhore. Now I've got two maybe-someday settlements coming. Now my landlord keeps his fly closed and demands cash. Not only am I getting old, this isn't exactly helping further my career as a prostitute. My body's still okay—"

"Your body looks great." He grinned. "Believe me, I've noticed. As for your face, couldn't you change your name and maybe wear a mask to hide it, and make you more exotic?"

She ducked her head. "I could, I guess. But I was an honest tech. I never palmed parts or faked burnouts. I never padded my hours or strung a job on. I try to be as honest a pro." Her tone sharpened. "This is how I am, take it or leave it. I never fobbed off damaged goods as new when I was a tech, and I'll be damned if I'll do it as a whore."

"It must be hard."

God, you don't know how hard! She wanted to scream it, cry it, let it out of the damaged fist she kept clamped around it.

And this was hard, laying herself open to a stranger. Exposing parts of herself no one saw no matter how many times she removed her clothes. It was unbearable.

She polished off her drink, the raw liquor searing her throat. She rarely drank this much while working unless it was demanded of her, but at that moment it was just what she needed. Anesthetic and fuel all in one.

This madness had gone on too long. It was time to

take control and stop it while she still could. She put her glass aside and forced a smile onto her face.

You're nothing but a juan, she told him in her head. *A coddy. Time I started treating you like one.*

"It's you that should be hard," she purred, keeping her head turned so only the best side of her face showed. Her fingers toyed with the skinsuit's sealtab, and once his eyes were on it she drew it slowly down, opening it from breastbone to crotch. Cool air rushed across her skin, making her nipples stiffen.

She sauntered toward him, putting a lot of hip into it. Planting herself right in front of him she bent over, feeling the front of her suit gape open even wider. "Hard instead of difficult. Difficult won't feed the kitty." She ran her tongue around her lips. "But I can fix that." She trailed her red nails up the inside of his thighs, feeling his muscles quiver.

She looked up into his face. Their eyes met. He was smiling, but it was one of the saddest smiles she'd ever seen.

"I'm sure you can," he said in a thick voice, "If that's what you want to do to me."

Merry had the business of punching a man's buttons down cold. It would be so easy to reduce this one to the level of just another juan. She knew he wouldn't even fight it.

Yet she could not make herself ignore the disappointment shadowing his face and voice, implied by his answer. He wanted her, and badly. But not yet. There was something else he wanted first, wanted more, and she found herself wanting to give it to him if she could.

—Only to earn the big payoff he'd promised, of course.

But what was it he was looking for?

Merry had not become a whore because she was too stupid to do anything else. Tech work demanded superior problem-solving skills, and prostitution had taught her a hundred seminars' worth of applied psychology. Part of her job was figuring out what it was her customers wanted and providing at least some acceptable semblance of it.

She studied the schematic lines of this strange man's face, trying to read what was behind it. He wanted her to trust him, he'd said that at the very start. He wanted her to tell him about herself. The first thing he'd done when they were alone had been to ask about what had happened to her face.

He'd been acting in a very specific manner: getting her trust; asking about the things that had happened to her; how they affected her; how she was dealing with them. There was something very familiar about all that . . .

Something someone who'd spent as much time being put back together by doctors as she had would recognize.

Bedside manner, it was called. Whores had their own version of it. He was a doctor, and had been treating her like a patient. His moves had been subtle, but now she saw them clearly.

Things he'd said took on new meanings. That remark about having an itch he couldn't scratch, for instance. Were those silver hands keeping him from practicing medicine?

Driving him to hire a prostitute to play patient?

All that made her wonder what he meant by that bit about paying her with something better than money. Was he hinting that he could fix her up right when no one else could?

That was a logical conclusion, but it didn't jibe with having to pay someone to be his patient. Besides, how could he fix something every other doctor had said was irreparable? A fried mod was a fried mod, and that's all there was to it.

Still, if her guess was right, then what could she do to cater to him? She doubted he wanted to play doctor like the usual juan might. *Show me where it hurts, little girl.*

"Trying to figure out what I'm up to, Merry?" he asked quietly.

She blinked in surprise, startled from her thoughts. For just a moment there it had been like the old days, getting so wrapped up in trying to solve a problem that everything else faded away. She considered his question. No sense in denying it. None of the usual rules worked here. With him.

"Yes, I am," she admitted.

He patted the couch beside him. "Sit with me, please."

Merry did as he asked, but arranged herself so that he'd get a good eyeful of the merchandise. His smile said that he was, and not minding it one bit.

"If I'm acting more doctor than, um, patron, I'm sorry. I can't help what I am. If I seem to be getting too personal, it's because I like you."

Hearing him say that made her feel absurdly pleased. She fought the feeling by saying, "It's just my body you're not crazy about."

He shook his head. "That's not true, and you know it. It's just one of the many things I like about you, and I plan to get around to it in a while. The thing is, if I'd wanted nothing but mindless sex, one of the other girls downstairs would have been good enough."

His voice dropped lower, as if confiding a secret. "But I want more, Merry. I don't want to settle for an empty package wrapped with a pretty face and a certified disease-free vagina. I want to share my night with a woman who's lived a little, and maybe even died a little. I want to spend my time with someone keeping on, no matter how hard it is or how much it hurts. Someone I have something in common with."

He sighed. Merry saw resignation in his face, and the need and desperation and even despair that lurked behind it. Those things were easy to recognize. She'd seen them all too often in her mirror when she put on her working face, painting them over with that night's good-time-girl smile.

"I'm just like you, Merry. I'm not what I once was." A wry smile twisted his lips. "When you get right down to it, I've become a bit of a whore myself. Good for only one thing as far as most are concerned, and once I've turned my trick for them they want me gone. How I feel about the way I'm used doesn't enter into the matter at all. I don't like it, but I live with things the way they are because I have no choice. . . ."

It was Merry's turn to sigh. "Choice is an illusion, love."

"Is it?" He shook his head. "I sure hope you're wrong. I keep telling myself that it's just something you have to wait for. That if you can just hold on, it will come along sooner or later and give you a chance to escape from the box where circumstance has put you. That it will save you."

"You mean like some knight in shining armor coming along to rescue you?" Merry clasped one silver hand in hers. "Sorry, love, but there ain't any such animal. At least not outside the storybooks."

Marchey still had his drink in his free hand. He took a long pull on it, regarding her over the rim of his glass and pondering what she'd said.

"Maybe you're right," he said at last. "But what if there were? What if that knight suddenly came along, riding out of nowhere on his white charger, and all at once both your face and hands were whole again? What would you do?"

She snorted. "Drop dead surprised."

"No, really," he insisted. "If suddenly, unexpectedly, you had choice again, would you recognize it? And if you did, what would you choose? Would you stay a prostitute, become a tech again, or choose to become someone else entirely?"

Merry shook her head. "I don't know." She didn't even like thinking about it. Thinking like that could make you crazy.

An uneasy laugh escaped her. "It doesn't matter because it would never happen anyway."

Marchey put his glass aside. "I'll tell you what, Merry. Think about it for a while. Let me know what you decide."

"When?"

He gave her a smile she hadn't seen yet. A mischievous gleam lit in his gray eyes and a bawdy twist curled onto his lips. It made him look younger. It made her smile back.

"Later," he said.

She watched those shining silver hands drift toward her. Felt them circle around her waist. He leaned toward her, planting a tender kiss on her numb cheek, then pulled back to look deep into her eyes. Not like a juan looks at a whore, but as a man looks at a woman. Eye to eye. Asking if she felt what he felt. Inviting her to share rather than demanding his money's worth.

Merry gazed back at him, knowing that for all her talk of honesty she *had* lied to him. She'd worn a mask for years, worn it this very night. It was a cold and brittle thing, the name and persona called Merry. It had been melting and slipping all evening long. Looking into his eyes something inside her finally *gave,* like ice melted to the point where it crumbles and slides off what it has sheathed, letting the warm come in. Merry vanished, leaving the woman who had hidden behind the mask naked before him.

"In the morning," he said.

"All right," she whispered, then covered his mouth with hers, kissing him with an abandon Merry had never given a juan. His mouth tasted of whiskey and dreams.

He embraced her, and she closed her eyes and held on tight, transported back to a time when love and happy endings had not seemed out of reach, and hope had not yet become a four-letter word.

It was five in the morning local time when Marchey sat up in bed, wakened by a signal from one of his arms. He yawned and stretched, then took a moment to gaze down at the woman sprawled across the bed beside him. In the low amber light of the bedside lamp her long lean body looked like it was shaped from ivory, coral, and gold wire.

But nothing made of such things could be so soft and warm. So beautiful. So giving.

A fond smile slipped out onto his face as he drank in the sight and smell of her, the very feel of just being beside her. He wanted to fix this moment, these sensations, this feeling in his memory, frame it like stained glass so it could lend its glowing colors to the gray days ahead.

"Thank you," he whispered under his breath, knowing she couldn't hear him but needing to say it. She had given him so much. More than she knew.

There remained one more thing she had it in her power to give, in its own way the most precious of all. But he would have to wait to see if it came to him.

There were things which needed to be done to prepare the way for that moment. Debts to be paid in the most valuable coinage he had. It was time to get up and get started.

He slid out of bed and dressed quietly, even though there was little chance that she would waken. The tab he'd slipped into the drink he'd brought her just before their last bout of lovemaking would see to that.

First he retrieved a pocketcomm from his pouch, carried it into the other room, and made a couple calls. Once those arrangements had been made, he returned to the bedroom.

Leaning over, he planted a kiss on her forehead, then padded to the foot of the bed and began the breathing exercises that would take him into his deep working trance.

Before long he was ready to begin. He laid his silver arms aside and ratcheted back around to the side of the bed.

Had she wakened then and seen him, her trust would have turned to horror at the frightening, forbidding look the trance put on his face.

But the woman who called herself Merry slept on, untroubled and serene.

Merry awakened some four hours later with a dreamy smile on her face. She stretched lazily, yawning hard enough to make her jaw crack, then rolled toward her bedmate to see if he was awake yet. If not, she knew how to bring him around.

She found that she was alone among the tumbled covers. She peered hopefully out into the sitting room, but it was deserted. Just like she had been.

The bed's warmth turned to cold as it was transformed from a cozy lover's nest to a whore's padded workbench in an instant.

She slumped back, squeezing her eyes shut to blot out the sight of her own stupidity. Not even one juan in a thousand wanted a morning after with an old hooker with a messed-up face. How could she have been dumb enough to let herself think this one would be any different?

But she had, damn her. She'd thought he understood just how awful it felt to be used and abandoned. She'd let him raise up her expectations only to chop them off at the knees.

So much for the knight in shining armor.

So much for answering his stupid frigging question in the morning.

Choice. What a laugh! But somehow she didn't feel much like laughing . . .

She couldn't even choose just to lie there and feel sorry for herself. Now that she was awake the messages from her bladder were too urgent to be ignored any longer.

No rest for the wicked, she thought sourly, heaving herself out of bed and padding naked into the small dark bathroom. There was no need to turn the light on. She knew where everything was.

Draining off some of the far too much she had drunk made her feel a little better. Remembering the thousand credits waiting for her made her feel a little better yet, at least partially blunting the sting from the slap in the face.

When she turned up the lights and tried to check herself in the bathroom mirror to see if she looked any better—or worse—than she felt, she found that it had been covered over with the pink plastic tablecloth from the sitting-room table. Something had been written on it in tall black letters so meticulously formed that they might have been machine printed.

Merry frowned and rubbed her bleary eyes, then started reading.

CHOICE it began, **IS BETTER THAN MONEY**.

By the time Merry had finished reading the message Marchey had left her, he was already over two thousand kilometers away from Vespa, the ship around him still gathering velocity as it carried him toward the next place his skills would be used. Where he would be used.

He sat in the small galley nook, nursing a coffee and brandy, and musing on the past day and night.

The two surgical procedures he had performed were routine in that only a Bergmann Surgeon could have done them, that he had not met the patients before or after, and the hospital staff had given him the bum's rush the moment he was done. No one had called him a pariah to his face. They hadn't needed to. Actions spoke louder than words.

The departure from business as usual was Merry.

A fond smile crept onto his face. Her scent still lingered on him, sweet and beguiling. He said her name aloud. Softly, like a prayer or a benediction. *Merry, full of grace.*

She'd treated him like a real person, not a monster or a freak, something you used when you had to and sent packing the moment its purpose had been fulfilled. That alone was such a pleasurable feeling that he was scarcely drinking for fear of blunting it.

Since the circuit began his life had been swallowed up by a friendless, rootless, choiceless monotony. It was as if a night of a thousand days had fallen, casting a tarnish across his spirit. He felt himself corroding, drawing inside and growing a thick rusty skin of apathy to survive.

But when someone took the time and trouble to rub a small clear spot in the tarnish . . .

Marchey gazed down at his gleaming silver arms.

Did a knight in shining armor emerge?

Or had it been a cruel trick on both of them to try to give her what he most wanted for himself? To try to prove to himself that such a thing was still possible?

He pictured it in his mind. The covered mirror and the disassembled comm on the counter below, along with a tool kit he'd had delivered to the room. Taking the unit apart while in working trance had been child's play. In that state he could play tiddlywinks with platelets and strum single strands of DNA like harp strings. After reattaching his arms he had written:

> **CHOICE IS BETTER THAN MONEY. THAT'S WHAT I WANT YOU TO HAVE.**
>
> **PUT THIS COMM BACK TOGETHER. YOUR HANDS ARE AT LEAST 85% OF WHAT THEY ONCE WERE, AND WILL RETURN TO 95% WITH USE.**
>
> **WHEN YOU HAVE DONE THAT, PULL THIS DOWN AND LOOK IN THE MIRROR.**

You did what was necessary to survive, keeping your head down and stumbling blindly along.

But if you were very lucky, every once in a while you got a chance to try to shove the night back a little. If your nerve held, and if you could still believe that turning the grim eclipsing tide was possible.

> **YOU WILL PROBABLY HAVE NIGHTMARES ABOUT ME. I CAN'T HELP THAT, AND HOPE YOU CAN REMEMBER ME FONDLY IN SPITE OF THEM.**

The commboard chimed.

His heart began to race, and his hands tightened on his cup. He had to swallow hard before he could speak.

"Yes?"

"Incoming message," the comm's smooth, sexless synthesized voice informed him crisply.

"Go ahead." He closed his eyes. Some obscure impulse made him cross his silver fingers.

"A one-thousand-credit posting you made on Vespa has been returned to your account," the comm announced. "There is a printed message attached. Shall I read it?"

Marchey settled back, eyes still closed, the better to savor the moment. "Yes. Proceed."

" *'You can wake up from bad dreams, and choose to dream better ones. I know that now. Thank you. If the knight in shining armor is ever on Vespa again and needs some repairs done on his tinwork, look me up.'* The message is signed *Delores Esterbrook.*"

Marchey's face eased into a satisfied smile. In his mind he saw her smiling back at him, her face lit like a lamp raised against the dark.

Both sides of it.

The third—no, *fourth* quatriliter of Mauna Loa was empty.

The memory of that smile barely touched him anymore. And as for choice—

Marchey chose to stand, get his bearings, and head for his room so he could finish drinking himself to sleep.

2

Administration of Tests

The temporary cubby he'd been assigned was in the half-g section of the hospital wheel. The combination of reduced gravity and enough whiskey under his belt to stop most men's clocks had him moving with the slow, exaggerated caution of someone attempting to walk on the ceiling.

His mind precessing like a gyroscope, he considered the day's events. As layovers went this had been about average. Forgettable. In the morning he'd be back on the circuit. In a month the only thing he'd be able to remember about today was the excellent Mauna Loa whiskey.

Next stop . . . where? Ganymede? It didn't matter. Thanks to the splendid efficiency of MedArm he didn't have to know. He would be picked up and deposited there like a chess piece.

Queen to King's bishop 3. The Red Queen, of course. Running like hell but getting absolutely nowhere.

The image made him laugh. But it was a joyless, unpleasant bark that caused a young couple waiting for the elevator farther along the corridor to turn and stare.

He gave them a less than reassuring grin. "Actually," he called cheerfully, "I'm more a pawn than a queen." He blew them a kiss. "Really."

They retreated toward the stairwell, glancing nervously back over their shoulders and whispering. The expressions on their faces suggested that they thought he might be an escapee from the wing with the padded walls.

Marchey's attention had already strayed from them and back to the task of keeping his feet under him. Whispers were nothing new; they were the sound of the blur, signifying nothing. A behind his back shout of *Freak!* or *Quack!* could still penetrate his awareness, but that was about all.

The door to his cubby suddenly materialized before him. He peered at the number closely, even though it had been easy enough to find because it was the last door in a dead-end corridor. That was a nice touch. Whoever said hospital administrators didn't have a sense of humor?

B/164/G. Home sweet home.

He rummaged through his pouch, pulling out the door key with a gray-gloved hand, watching that hand 'face it with the lock as if it were some unconnected piece of arcane machinery operating on its own.

The lock chirped acceptance and the door slid open. He shuffled in, slapping the plate to close it behind him. One nightcap—well, maybe two—and a check to see how his patient was doing. By pad, of course. There was no sense in taking a chance on killing the poor bastard by looking in on him after saving his life in the first place. That would kind of defeat the whole point of having come here, wouldn't it?

Now if he could just remember the man's name . . .

Had they even told it to him? Probably not.

It wasn't until he turned toward the bed that he finally realized he was not alone in the room.

Scylla sat rigidly on the bed, waiting for her quarry to react to her presence.

No matter what he did, she was ready. If he tried

to run, she would bring him down before he could get even halfway to the door. If he came at her, he would quickly learn what a deadly mistake it was to dare attack an angel.

But he only stood there, swaying slightly, staring at her so blankly that for a moment she wondered if he saw her at all.

His face was broad and rough-hewn, a craggy landscape of shadowed crevasses and eroded cliffs. Only a thinning gray-black fringe of hair clung to the back of his head. His lips were twisted into an odd half grimace that was habitual, judging by the deep grooves bracketing his mouth. He was of medium height, barrel-chested and blocky. She decided he was probably quite strong, even though his broad shoulders were slumped as if from years of grinding toil.

It was his gray eyes that bothered Scylla. They were flat and incurious. She saw nothing of herself reflected in them.

He appeared to be willing to stand there, unspeaking, unmoving, and unmoved, forever. Scylla was not used to people failing to react to her. She did not like it one bit.

"You are Dr. Georgory Marchey," she said sharply. "You will do exactly as I say. I want you to sit down. Will you obey me, or must I demonstrate what will happen if you defy me?"

Marchey shrugged indifferently, but complied. He dropped heavily into the cubicle's sole chair. "That's an UNSRA-issue Armark Full Combat Exo you're wearing," he said blandly. "Aside from its armaments, it makes you at least fifteen times faster and thirty times stronger than me."

"You have correctly judged my superiority over you," Scylla said tightly, "But do not spout nonsense. I am an *angel*."

Her prey gave her a mordant smile. "My mistake. I always expected my drinking to make me see pink elephants." He leaned over to retrieve a bottle from the table beside him. "Speaking of drinking, would you care to join me in a nightcap?"

His refusing to take her seriously could not be tolerated. Scylla *moved,* a living lightning bolt as she came up off the bed, streaked across the room and snatched the bottle from his hand faster than the eye could follow.

Then slowly, deliberately, she crushed it to splinters in one silver-coated hand. The small cubby filled with the sharp tang of spilled alcohol. The shards tinkled to the floor.

"No?" Marchey said mildly, staring up into her face. It had been tattooed into a nightmarish red-and-black demon's mask, a face designed to instill fear in the beholder. "Or are you just not particularly fond of gin?"

"What is the matter with you?" Scylla demanded, frustration turning her voice into a caustic hiss. "Are you stupid? Suicidal? What are you?"

Marchey stared unblinkingly back at her, his face empty of fear, empty of anything she could name.

"Thirsty," he said.

This was not going at all the way Scylla expected.

Her world was a simple one, the rules unvarying and unbreakable, and her place in it clearly understood by one and all. People feared her because she was an angel. Angels are made to be feared; they are instruments forged in Heaven to make man comply with the Laws of God, and mete out punishment when those Laws are broken. Only one person in her life and world did not cringe in her presence, and that was Brother Fist. As she was His angel, it was only fitting that it was she who feared Him.

But this man she had been sent to fetch was no Chosen of God. He was an infidel, and she an angel. How could he look upon her and not be daunted?

Scylla knew exactly how she looked, and was proud of it. Her body was no unclean mass of soft, sagging, sweating flesh; she was polished, strutted, indestructible silver nearly head to toe. For her, nakedness was no shame. She was not cursed with a woman's offensive parts to hide. Her groin was smooth, featureless, and unimpregnable. Her breasts were modest silver mounds without nipples to mark her as a suckling beast.

Her face was human-shaped and made of flesh, but it bore red-and-black God-marks etched into her very pores. Instead of hair, her skull was covered with gleaming silver. Her one green eye was human enough, for angels stand halfway between God and man. Her other, angel eye was an unblinking, ever-vigilant steel-framed glass lens. Brother Fist could look out through that eye, seeing His world through her when he wished, and it gave her sight in the darkness so that none could use it to escape the bringer of God's Justice.

She shone like a sword of holy light, and yet this man Marchey was not blinded. He did not even blink.

She watched him pick up another bottle from the table. He drank from it, then offered it to her. "Come on, have a drink," he said. "It'll help you relax."

She took it, but not to drink. As he started to withdraw his hand she clamped her other hand around his wrist. Her ceramyl talons hissed from their sheaths in the backs of her fingers and locked with a menacing snick, razor-sharp points dimpling the soft gray fabric of the glove he wore. Staring him straight in the eye, she squeezed. Not hard enough to crush, but more than enough to crack his infuriating indifference.

Much to her surprise his wrist was unyielding. The look of apathetic patience on his face never faltered.

Scylla frowned, red-scaled nostrils flaring. She squeezed harder. Hard enough to make him scream as bones of his wrist ground together. She was under strict orders to deliver him in one piece, but one way or another she was going to put him on his knees where he belonged, to look into his eyes and see the fear that belonged there.

Scylla knew her own strength. Her hands could

crush granite to sand, twist and tear steel like putty. Yet his wrist was unyielding. His face showed nothing. Less than nothing.

She squeezed harder yet, her black-tattooed lips drawing back from teeth which had been filed to points and capped with a thin layer of bonded ceramyl. Their knife-sharp tips were bright bloodred.

Marchey cocked his head for a better look at her mouth. Against all reason, he smiled. "Nice touch," he said. "Bet it hurts like a bastard if you bite your tongue."

Scylla hissed in rising anger and baffled frustration. She dug her talons into his upper wrist and pulled. The cloth shredded like tissue under the ceramyl blades.

But instead of being rewarded with an agonized screech as his wrist was flayed to the bone, there was a shrill *skreeeeeeee* that vibrated up her arm and set her teeth on edge. Still he stared back at her, looking . . . *amused*.

Although it felt like a minor defeat, she dropped her gaze. Scraps of gray cloth dangled from her talons. His hand and wrist were silver—a silver exactly like her own angel skin. Her ceramyl blades were sharp and hard enough to slash through plate steel like cardboard, but they had not put so much as a scratch on the gleaming surface of his wrist and arm.

Her forehead furrowed, baffled by this impossibility.

When she looked up at his face again he was grinning at her.

"Surprise," he said, daring to laugh at her. At *her*!

"Surprise yourself," she snarled.

Then she shot him point-blank in the chest.

Marchey came to, shook his head groggily.

That proved to be a serious mistake. His brain felt like it had been sucked out his eye sockets, macerated, and squeezed back into his skull through the hole bored in the middle of his forehead. He moaned as it sloshed turgidly with every move he made.

Behind him someone laughed, a harsh sound that drove a blunt harpoon in one ear and out the other. A female someone? His memory coughed up a hazy picture of a one-eyed silver chimera.

Incapable of making any sense of *that,* he squinted at his surroundings. He recognized the high-backed chair under him, feeling a little better when he realized that he was in the familiar confines of the courier ship that had been his only real home for the past few years.

The main board was about three meters away. He managed to focus one bleary eye on the flight-status stack.

He was in transit.

That was strange. He didn't remember—

"We are on our way to Ananke."

That woman's voice again. Maybe he wasn't imagining it. He flirted with vertigo getting his chair swivelled around to find its source.

The silver-armored amazon with the hideously tattooed face hadn't been a hallucination after all. She was sitting at his galley table. Drinking coffee, from the smell.

"Good for us," he mumbled, fishing in his pouch for an analgesic. His fingers found only the bottom. It had been emptied.

She held up the purple foilpak he'd been searching for. "Are you looking for these?"

"Desperately." He heaved himself to his feet, grimacing as the contents of his head ebbed and surged, and stood there a moment to regain the hang of standing before trying to walk. He felt his chest with his gloveless hand. It felt bruised and tender, like he had been hit in the sternum with a sledgehammer.

"I . . . remember you shooting me. Disruptor?" That plus all the booze he'd drank would explain the monster hangover.

"God's Wrath." Marchey watched the woman's face harden. It was not a pretty sight. "You will feel it again if you give me the slightest trouble." She held up one silver arm. A bracer—a detachable weapons package interfaced with the exo's systems and her own nervous system—was wrapped around it. There was another one around her other arm. This meant she was almost as heavily armed as a small platoon. He got the message.

"Perish the thought." He tottered toward her. "Can I have one of those, please," he asked, reaching for the pak. "Or is torture part of this package tour?"

She stared at him a long moment. "I am no torturer." She flipped it at him. "To rely on such things is weakness."

Somehow he managed to catch it. He popped out a derm and pasted it over his carotid artery. He closed his eyes, waiting for the high-powered analgesics to work their sweet magic.

Hangovers were business as usual, but the aftereffects of being shot with a disruptor made him feel as though every neuron were nearing nuclear fission. After a few moments he slumped and sighed as a soothing tide washed through him. He opened his eyes, moved his head experimentally. The brain-slop was gone. Once more he was nearly capable of what passed for rational thought.

Well, that could be remedied easily enough.

He managed a wan smile. "Thanks. I hope you didn't have to break any Kidnappers' Union rules to do that. I just can't rise and shine the way you do."

Although the tattoos made dragonesque fury its natural expression, Marchey found that he could still tell real anger when it appeared on her face. It showed in the curl of her black-webbed lips, the flare of her scaled nostrils, in the cold flash of that one green eye.

"Do not take me lightly, little man," she warned, her voice brimming with unmistakable menace. "I will make you regret it."

It was no mental feat to deduce that being feared was of cardinal importance to her. It explained the face, the teeth, the combat exo, the attitude. He supposed he should be more careful about what he said to her. But when he got right down to it, he just didn't give a damn. Screw her if she couldn't take a joke.

Still, he could be polite. After all, how often did he have company?

He held up his hands in a placating gesture. "I don't doubt that you could tear off my head, squeeze it flat, and eat it like a brain sandwich. I don't plan on trying to overpower you. I'm a surgeon, not a fighter. Besides, I interned in a UNSRA military hospital for a while, and helped install a couple shock troopers in exos like yours. I know how they work and what they can do."

His kidnapper glared at him. "You spout nonsense again. I told you before, I am an *angel*. Do not forget it."

Marchey shrugged. "Whatever you say." He slid into the seat across from her, ordered a cup of coffee. There was a bottle of brandy in the condiment well next to the dispenser. A liberal dollop went into his cup, then he offered it to her. "Want some breakfast?"

She shook her head, looking displeased by his offer. Probably a teetotaler

"Suit yourself." He put the bottle down within easy reach.

"Do you spend all of your time drunk?" she demanded.

"Define *all*." He took a cautious sip of his laced coffee. "Define *time*. Define *drunk*." Another sip, peering at her over the rim of his cup. "It's a semantic minefield. You could lose a foot just thinking about it."

Not even a hint of a smile. If she had a sense of humor, it was better armored than her body.

"Are you really a doctor?" She made the word *doctor* sound like it described something strange and hideous, perhaps even evil and perverse. *Are you really a lycanthropic necrophile?*

He hunched his shoulders in a stillborn shrug. "Depends on whom you listen to, I guess."

That wasn't a subject he particularly wanted to get into this early or this sober.

"What kind of kidnapper are you, my angel?" he asked to change the subject. "What do you expect to get for me? And are you going to tell me your name, or should I just call you Madame Shanghai?"

"Only one question has any meaning. My name is Scylla."

Marchey's ears pricked up at her name. "Ah, were you once a fair maiden, now changed into a monster?"

Scylla's frown deepened. "What do you mean by that?"

"Greek mythology." No reaction. Apparently not a devotee of classical literature. Not many were.

"Homer's *Odyssey*," he explained. "Scylla was a fair young maiden who was changed into a monster. Twelve legs like tentacles. Six heads, each with a triple row of fangs, and a taste for sailors. Let's see . . . *'God or man, no one could look upon her in joy.'* That was poor Scylla after the sorceress Circe was done with her. Circe saw her as a rival for the love of a merman named, um, Glaucus. Turning her into a monster made her a lot less lovable."

Scylla said nothing. There was no way for Marchey to tell what—if anything—she was thinking. His spiked coffee had cooled. He took a long swallow, then asked, "Did someone give you that name?"

"Brother Fist," she said, an instant later looking confused. All expression drained from her face, and she sat there staring sightlessly past him like a robot which had encountered circumstances outside the scope of its programming.

His curiosity mildly piqued, and the brandy beginning to bring back the familiar comfortable buzz, Marchey settled back to see what happened next.

"Brother Fist."
His name was the center of all Scylla was and did. She had uttered it a million times or more. But the moment she spoke it in answer to the infidel's ques-

tion—a question no one had ever asked her before—
a sudden wrenching duality swept over her, her solid
sense of self inexplicably straining in two directions
and leaving her lost in the middle.

She had always been Scylla.

Brother Fist named me.

She was an angel.

*{—a blurred glimpse of a face. Small. White. In
a . . . mirror?}*

She served Brother Fist.

{—another face. Bigger. Beautiful.} (I love you,
Angel. Love you.)

Brother Fist spoke God's Will. .

(Remember, Angel. I love you. Love you.)

His voice was God's voice, His words God's words.
**(ANGEL IS DEAD. DEAD. YOUR NAME IS
SCYLLA. SCYLLA. YOU ARE AN ANGEL.
ANGEL. YOU WILL LOVE ME. LOVE ME. YOU
WILL OBEY ME. OBEY ME. WHAT ARE YOU?)**

An angel! she screamed silently, trying to drown the
bewildering cacophony of voices inside her head. She
was and had always been the angel Scylla! All else
was deception!

*Life is an endless battle against the lies and decep-
tions cast by the forces of darkness to lure the weak in
faith and spirit from the One True Path.*

Brother Fist had warned her of that a thousand
times. Unholy evil was everywhere, made in the very
flesh and marrow of every man and woman. Even an
angel was human enough to be prey to it.

Doubt assailed her. Was she too weak for the task
Brother Fist had given her?

He had ordered her away from her place at His
side. Commanded her to leave the safe Eden of Ananke and venture into the Profane World to bring this
infidel Marchey back to Him. The impious temptation
to argue with His edict had been terrible. It went
against her every instinct to leave Him vulnerable
and unprotected.

Still, He was Brother Fist, and she was His angel.

His will was always to be done. Disobedience was blackest blasphemy.

So she had meekly obeyed, command deciding the conflict.

Deciding, but not resolving. She had left her home and risked her life and soul to capture Marchey, but that conflict was a smoldering ember of doubt buried deep in one chamber of her heart.

An ember that made her wonder what possible use this drunken infidel could be to him. Which led her to wonder—

—could Brother Fist have been . . . *wrong*?

That thought triggered a convulsive burst of pain and nausea, cramping her insides like some fatal poison. Her body stiffened, every muscle twisting into a quivering knot. The cup she held in her silver hands shattered as they clenched into fists.

The spasm subsided, and in its wake a voice howled a litany at the back of her head. A man's voice. The irrefutable voice of her conscience. She heaved herself to her feet in dumb obedience.

She had shown weakness of faith. She had *doubted*. Not just herself, but God's perfect servant Himself. She had sinned most greviously.

And so she must atone.

Marchey watched Scylla go rigid as a steel beam, her one green eye rolling back in her head until only the white showed, crushing the heavy ceramic cup she held like so much eggshell. At first he thought she might be suffering a *grand mal* seizure.

After a moment she seemed to shake it off, taking a deep breath and lurching to her feet. The blank lens that replaced one eye slid blindly past him. Her other eye, the one of the unusual bottle green that reminded him of another woman, another time, another life, was fixed and dilated.

She plodded to the center of the deck space like an automaton, folded to her knees. There was a metallic double click. The bulky silver bracers on the back of her forearms released themselves to dangle loose. She removed them, laying them aside within easy reach.

Out of the utility pouch she wore at one silver-sheathed hip came a palm-sized matte black box. She pressed a catch. Two coiled wires sprang from a concealed compartment. At the end of each wire glinted a long steel needle.

She turned her hands over. Marchey saw that removing her bracers had bared a small patch of exposed flesh at the back of each hand, the pale skin framed in silver. Her ink-etched face a stiff, frozen wasteland, she drove a needle deep into the back of first one hand and then the other. Only the knotting of her jaw muscles betrayed her pain.

Now wired to the box, she placed it before her knees. The heel of each hand went atop it. After a long moment she leaned forward, putting her weight on her arms and hands. The box began to emit a low, sinister hum.

Scylla's arms stiffened. Her back, her whole body clenched cable-taut as electricity surged from one electrode to the other, using her body as the conductor. She threw her head back, her jaw clamped tight on what had to be a scream.

She inflicted that agony on herself for a slow ten count, then let up. After muttering a low, monotonous prayer, she leaned on the box again.

Marchey shuddered and looked away.

Obviously she was punishing herself. A term for what she was doing floated up out of some obscure corner of his memory: *self-flagellation*. Usually it was a matter of the penitent scourging him or herself until he or she bled. Her exo made whipping pointless, even if she were to use a length of chain on herself.

Why was she doing it? He stared into his cup as if expecting to find the answer there, then shrugged and drained it. He refilled his cup, this time with straight brandy.

A strangled moan from Scylla drew his attention. She was panting for breath. Sweat beaded her tattooed forehead. Her whole body trembled as if palsied, nerves misfiring and muscles twitching from the overload. The set of her jaw said she was preparing to scourge herself again.

If he hadn't know it before, this was irrefutable proof that he was in the hands of a madwoman. One who believed herself to be an angel of the sort favored by Revelations. No guests for years, and then this is what he got.

I should stop her, whispered a voice in his head.

He didn't move. There was no point even to trying. As long as she was in that exo, she could be anyone and do anything she damn well pleased. This he knew from firsthand experience.

Back when he'd interned in that UNSRA Military Hospital he'd watched a shock trooper installed in an exo like hers take on a fully armed Ogre tank, his bracers deactivated to even the odds. It had taken the trooper all of twenty-one seconds to single-handedly reduce the battle machine to smoking scrap.

Marchey knew he ought to be scared shitless.

But he really didn't feel much of anything.

He took a meditative swig of brandy, wondering if he'd reached the point where he was past caring if he lived or died.

Interesting question. He didn't think so. When he got right down to it, his present situation wasn't all that different from his normal routine. His destination might have been changed from the one originally set for him, but he wasn't being wrenched off in some radical new direction. Someone else had been in control of his movements for several years now. Someone else chose where he would exercise his special skills, and on whom.

This was undoubtedly more of the same. Sure, this time an armored female maniac was in charge, but for all he knew his itinerary up until this time had been decided with darts, dice, or pigeon entrails.

When his work was done he would be shown the door, shoved back into the old game, still the ceaselessly moving pawn in an endless chess match where the Black Queen ruled the vast and far-flung board. Her name was *Death,* and the stalemates he forced on her had become meaningless events, forgotten by day's end. Fleeting and inconsequential as fireflies in the void or fingerprints on glass.

He played on, but by Survivors' Rules: apathy was sanity; caring would be the kiss of death.

Marchey's right hand strayed up to the silver metal pin he wore over his heart. The metal still shone, even if its gleaming promise had become obscured. He found himself remembering when he had agreed to give up what little autonomy he still possessed.

He was back where it had all begun. Square one.

A meter-long reproduction of Marchey's pin hung on the wood-texed wall behind Dr. Salvaz Bophanza's desk, the initials of the Bergmann Medical Institute under it in gold-edged black. A close look would have revealed a patina of dust on the upper curves and strokes.

The chunky, middle-aged black man behind the desk gave Marchey a rueful smile. "I'd offer you a drink, old buddy, but I had to give it up." He patted his stomach. "Kept eating holes in the tank."

Marchey made a face as he sat down. "That's a bitch, Sal."

Bophanza shrugged. "It's not so bad. I only miss it when I'm thirsty." His smile faded. "You probably wonder why I recalled you."

"I was hoping it was so we could catch Happy Hour on your expense account," Marchey answered in an attempt to lighten the mood.

Sal rolled his eyes. "I wish. No, you're back here because things aren't working out very well the way they stand."

Marchey sketched an ironic bow. "Still a master of understatement, Mister Director Sir."

He'd arrived at the Institute to find it all but deserted, a bare handful of the staff still remaining. The corridors were silent and empty, the air of abandonment palpable. A mood of bleak pessimism had descended, but he'd hoped seeing his old friend would make him feel better. One look at Sal had been enough to kick the slats out of that.

Sal Bophanza appeared to have aged a decade in the four years since Marchey had last seen him in person. His glowing ebony skin had lost its sheen, and he seemed to have shrunk and slumped inside it. What had once been a wild black dreadlocked mane was now a thinning salt-and-pepper fuzz. His body had broadened and thickened, but his face had thinned, and it wore the resolute, resigned countenance of the captain of a sinking ship. As director of the Bergmann Medical Institute, that was uncomfortably close to his job description.

Sal's smile was fleeting. "I try. The fact is we're dead in the water here. When we first started having problems and the word came down our first crop was to be our last, at least for a while, I was angry. Now I'm glad. Jesus could heal, and got crucified for his trouble. Nobody's nailed any of you guys up yet, but it wouldn't surprise me if they got around to it eventually."

Sal came out from behind his desk and began to pace. Marchey remained sprawled in his chair, waiting patiently. He knew Sal was working his way up to something. Probably more bad news.

"It really pisses me off," Sal went on, his voice dripping disgust. "The system will use you when they don't have any other options, but treat you like fucking pariahs before and after. The word has gotten around. Becoming a Bergmann Surgeon is the kiss of death. Even if the program weren't on hold, it wouldn't matter. We haven't had an inquiry or application in over two years."

"That's probably for the best." See, he could do understatement, too. Now to something he'd been dreading. "I heard that Sara-Lyn Neff, Josiah Two-trees, and Grace Nakamura all killed themselves. Is it true?" *Three out of thirty-five. Not a positive trend.*

Sal's face fell, the anger leaking out of him. "It is. So did Ivan Kolinski."

Four. Marchey shook his head sadly. "They were all damned good doctors." Ivan had been an incorrigible practical joker. Once he had "borrowed" one of Josiah's prosthetics while he was operating and replaced it with one made of foil-wrapped chocolate. The look on Josiah's face . . .

It was easier to imagine him playing dead than being dead. Those four—all thirty-five of them—had been so full of life. Bursting with energy and idealism. So committed to the Healer's Oath and to medicine that they had risked all in hopes of breaking ground to a new frontier. Well, they had, and become outsiders in the process.

"The best," Sal agreed in a somber tone. "Ivan's death was the worst of all. It was—" He closed his eyes a moment. "It was partially our fault. We brought him back here after he gave himself a near-fatal drug overdose on Cassandra Station. We had to make him stop practicing. He'd just gotten too erratic to be trusted."

Bophanza stared down at his hands as if Ivan's blood was on them. "He put himself in trance, put his prosthetics aside, and stopped his own heart. He left a note. It said that the way he had to practice now was killing him by inches, but without it he was nothing, and had nothing left to live for."

He looked up at Marchey, his eyes moist and haunted. "He said he knew why we made him stop, and didn't blame us. He . . . *thanked* us . . ."

"You didn't have any choice," Marchey offered, knowing nothing he said would ease Sal's pain.

His old friend nodded mutely, then said, "It's killing you all. I know that."

Marchey made himself sit up straight. "Yeah, and knowing that is eating you alive. But I doubt that you called me back here so we could compare our beds of nails. I'm here. What happens now?"

Sal looked relieved to drop the subject of Ivan's death. He parked his buttocks on one corner of his desk, taking on a brisk, businesslike air. "You go back out. But MedArm came up with an idea that might just make the best of a bad situation. You are each being assigned a high-speed UNSRA courier ship of your very own. No more depending on the schedules of the regular carriers to get from place to place. The ships are fully automated. We will handle logistics and itinerary from this end. See, MedArm agrees that your skills are far too valuable to be wasted. What you can do is still in demand—"

"Even if we're not." Marchey turned the idea over in his mind. "We can cover a larger area this way. Having our own ships will give us at least the illusion of having a place we belong, right?" He watched his old friend nod, and kept on doing his best to look at the idea in a positive light.

"Maybe it will even help our reputation. We're constantly on the move to serve the greater good, not because we're about as popular as tapeworms. High-speed house calls in a back-assward ambulance." He shrugged. "Why not? It can't make things any worse."

Sal leaned closer, his face intent. "It's still not going to be easy. But the couriers are big enough for two . . ." He raised one eyebrow and let the implication dangle like a baited hook.

Marchey snorted. "Then I'll have lots of elbow room." His voice dropped lower, and he looked Sal straight in the eye. "So we're admitting that we've turned ourselves into nothing more than pieces of specialized medical equipment to be passed around on a rotating basis."

"No, dammit, that's not true!" Bophanza snapped. "You're a healer, Gory! A goddamned good one! You and the other Bergmann Surgeons were some of the brightest, most dedicated doctors—"

"*Were* is the operative word, Sal." Marchey spoke

softly, but with steel-clad certainty. "I used to be a doctor. I remember what it was like. Doctors don't give their patients nightmares. The mere sight of them doesn't risk scaring the patient to death. Doctors treat *people*. I haven't met one of my patients in years. They're not people, they're conditions. Diseases. Traumas. Unconscious and broken meat machinery." He thumped his chest. "I know what I've become. Just a meat mechanic. That's all."

"No," Sal insisted stubbornly, "That's not true."

"Bullshit!" Marchey roared, slapping his hands onto the arms of his chair hard enough to crack the veneered plastic. He realized that he was getting angry. But not at Sal, who had trouble enough of his own without being put in the position of an emotional punching bag.

"Sorry," he said, getting up and going to lay a silver hand on Sal's shoulder. "I'm not mad at you. Just at the way things turned out."

"You have a right to be," Sal answered wearily.

"We all do." In one way Sal had taken the hardest road of them all. Marchey smiled and squeezed his old friend's shoulder.

"I remember when you flunked the final tests," he went on. "They wouldn't let you give up your hands. I remember how disappointed you were. How hurt."

He shook his head. "There was already a lot of heat on the program, a lot of controversy about what we were trying to do. People thought we were crazy, and maybe we were. I know how easy it would've been for you to have repudiated us and what we were doing to make yourself feel better about missing the final cut."

He wondered if he could have showed half the guts and class Sal had displayed. "But you didn't. You kept on believing in what we were trying to do. You took an even harder choice than we did, staying on to help us realize a dream that was denied you."

"You don't know how close I came to quitting," Sal admitted softly.

"But you didn't, and now you run the place. Your dream soured, but you kept on serving it anyway. It hasn't gotten any sweeter or easier since then, but you're still here. Still trying to make it work."

He gazed up at the dusty emblem on the wall, recalling the hope it had symbolized, the pride he had felt every time he saw it. "Come to find out, we weren't the lucky ones either. We gained an incredible skill, but lost everything else in the bargain. But we're still keeping on the best we can because it's all we have left. We can still be useful, and who knows, maybe someday . . ."

Marchey let his hand fall from Sal's shoulder, watching him mull over his own maybe-somedays. "I'll accept things the way they are. The way it seems they have to be. It's that or give up completely. Maybe this bit with ships will work, though I have my doubts. I'll try it because I have nothing to lose. But there's one thing I want you to do for me, old friend. For all us poor bastards who will be bouncing around out there all by ourselves."

Bophanza met Marchey's gaze squarely. "Name it."

"Remember the dream for us, Sal. I doubt we'll be able to much longer. Keep looking for a way to make it come true after all."

Bophanza nodded solemnly, then came off his desk and wrapped his arms around Marchey, pulling him close and holding him tightly. That was his answer.

Marchey stiffened and almost pulled away. But after a moment he relaxed and returned his old friend's embrace, feeling his strength and conviction, and allowing himself to remember how it felt to have someone care.

Marchey's hand fell.

That had been the beginning of his endless shuttle from task to task. No home other than this ship, and no end to his journey in sight.

He had been a prisoner in this ship long before

Scylla took it and him over. She was just someone else who wanted to use the tool he had become.

She was still praying, but it looked like she had at least quit hurting herself. Absorbed as she appeared to be, he didn't doubt that she would abandon her devotions were he to approach her or the ship's controls.

Not that he planned to bother. There was no point to it.

He was being moved to another square. But every part of the board was the same; all the long years gone by had shown him that. The game never changed. It couldn't be won. All he was doing now was playing it out to its foregone end. So why should he care about the who and where and why?

What was the difference between indifference and defeat?

Indifference was an empty cup. Defeat was no cup at all.

He looked down. His cup was empty, the spirits all gone.

So he refilled it.

And smiled to himself.

See how easy it is to take control of your life?

"What is that?"

Marchey looked up, startled. "What?"

Scylla slid onto the galley seat across from him, eyeing his plate distastefully. "That stuff you are eating."

He laid aside the real bound book—M. A. Zeke's excellent novelization of Homer's works—he'd been reading while eating supper. The whole day had been pretty much spent reading and drinking. His captor had skulked around so quietly that after a while he forgot she was even there.

Chiding himself for being a bad host, he decided he should pay at least minimal attention to his guest.

"That's steak," he answered, pointing with his fork. "Not real steak, but a tolerable substitute. That's a baked potato. The yellow stuff atop it is cheese sauce, the green flakes are chives. I think the chives and the potato are real, but I doubt the cheese has ever seen any more of the inside of a cow than the steak. The green beans are real, as are the mushrooms."

Scylla absorbed all this with a furrowed brow. "None of that can be real food," she announced. "I do not see how you can eat such things."

"Substitutes aren't that bad if they're real good." He chuckled at his turn of phrase. "Want to try some?"

Her nose wrinkled in disgust. "No. I am an angel. I would not eat human food, even if that were what was on your plate."

Marchey took a sip of wine. "How would you describe human food, then?" *This ought to be interesting.*

"It is a thick green liquid that comes in big blue drums. Each person is allowed two bowlsful each day."

What was that line Sal had always used when he came up against someone utterly convinced of something that made no sense? Oh yeah: *Where you from, son? Nairobi, ma'am. Isn't everyone?*

"Two bowls of green glop a day. Everybody eats like this, you say?" What she'd described sounded like survival-grade Basicalgae; spoilage stabilized, nutritionally and dietary-fiber complete, and tasting just about like what you'd expect from enriched pasteurized pond scum.

"Of course."

"I mean everybody everywhere?"

"What else would they eat?"

"Well, stuff like I'm eating, for instance."

Scylla's tattooed lips pinched tight. "That is not food."

He chuckled again. "QED. Ten points for the lady in the silver skivvies." He speared a forkful of steak, began to chew. "What do you eat, then?" he asked around his mouthful. "Angel food cake?"

That green eye narrowed dangerously. "Do you make sport of me?"

Marchey realized that poking fun at her was about as safe as prodding a pile of gunpowder with a lit match. "Never," he said with what he hoped was a straight face.

"Very well," she said stiffly. "I eat manna."

What else? "Well, I guess you're in the right place."

She stared at him. "Explain."

"Manna falls from heaven, right? Which from Earth is space. Should be regular hailstorms of the stuff out here."

A terse shake of her head. "The things you say make no sense."

"So it seems. My tongue must need a tune-up." He drank some more wine, just in case the problem was excessive dryness.

"Manna comes in a crate." She reached into her pouch and pulled out a foil-wrapped wafer. "This is a loaf."

"Ah, *ratbars.*"

Scylla cocked her head, light gleaming off the polished silver covering everything but her face. "Rat . . . bars?"

"Short for ration bars, no rodents involved. Your exo is able to handle all your wastes as long as they are kept to a minimum. Fluids—sweat, urine, and the rest aren't really a problem. They're recycled, any excess vented off as water vapor. Solids are harder to manage. The ratbars are nutritionally complete, but extremely low residue. If they're all you eat, then you probably don't need to excrete more than what, once a month?"

Scylla scowled at him. "I am an angel," she said at last. "I do not make filth as humans do," she added prissily.

"Of course not. You've got a nanotic colony in your bowels to scavenge what your digestive system misses. But every thirty days or so this cloche"—he pointed at a bulge on her right hip with his fork—"opens. Inside is a lozenge-shaped chunk of grayish matter that you throw away."

Scylla only stared at him intently, her webbed lips pressed tightly together, her green eye almost as cold as the lens that replaced the other.

"Well, am I right?" he prompted.

She shoved herself to her feet, snatching up the ratbar. "I cannot talk to you," she said tightly, then stalked off in a huff.

"Apparently not," he said mildly, watching her go to the farthest side of the compartment and sit with her back to him.

He topped off his wine, picked up his book, and went back to reading and eating. He ignored her, and she him, for the rest of the evening and most of the next day.

The closer they came to Ananke the more keyed-up and fretful Scylla became, the more impatient that this awful task be over and behind her. At long last the end was nearly in sight. Only twenty more hours to be endured.

Scylla sat alone in the galley, feeling like she had been condemned to Purgatory. Her charge was in an unresponsive stupor. He had been so for the past two days, silent and stinking of alcohol.

Yet she dared not relax her vigilance. Steadfastness was one of the defining qualities of an angel. Two days cooped up with the sodden, unresponsive lump in her charge, staying ready for action that never came, left her frustrated and edgy.

The trip out from Ananke in a battered old hopper had taken ten days, but this far swifter return seemed much longer. An eternity. All because of *him*.

At first she had come to the conclusion that this man Marchey was dead inside. People whose spirits had broken were common on Ananke; not everyone had the faith or inner strength to tread the hard steep road to perfection. His cryptic, sometimes sarcastic comments were nothing more than echoes of what he might have once been, like ghost data from a wiped program. She had dismissed him as nothing but an empty shell. Any response to being struck was merely an echo.

But in the evening of the second day her opinion had been forcibly revised.

He had been stretched out on a lounger, reading, listening to music, and as usual, drinking steadily. Where anyone else would have been watching her fearfully, not for even a fleeting moment forgetting that they were in the presense of an angel, he seemed utterly indifferent to her. That was wrong, contrary to all she knew. It rankled, but if he did not challenge her control over him, there was little she could do about it.

Boredom had set her to pacing the confines of the ship's single deck. Back on Ananke there was always something to be done. Serving Brother Fist. Guarding the flock. Overseeing the workers. Hunting out blasphemy. Here she was cut off from all use and diversion.

Her restless gaze had crossed an overhead storage compartment she didn't remember having searched when she swept the ship for weapons. So she unlatched the door to check it out.

Inside, carefully held in place by uniholds, was a bisque-fired clay sculpture. She released it from the clamps and took it down for a better look.

Brother Fist had objects like this. Pretty things, some of them imbued with a strange indefinable something that she could sense, but not quite understand.

This object was beautifully made, and it radiated a raw emotional power that caught her unawares. The harsh lines of her face softened as she stared at the thing in her hands in growing wonder.

It depicted two people who had begun making a single thing together. But the man stood off to one side, staring sadly up at what they had begun and never would finish. He cradled a child in arms that ended just below the elbow. His missing arms lay at his feet. He held the child and stumps of his arms up toward the work in an attitude she knew well, one of supplication.

The woman was tall and thin. She huddled on the ground near him among her abandoned tools. Her face was filled with such shame and loss and frustration that Scylla felt uneasy looking at it. That face was turned away from both the man and the thing they had begun making together.

What they had been making were two people embracing. Although it was rough-hewn and incomplete, Scylla could see that the man's face was Marchey's. It was the woman on the ground he held.

She frowned, disquiet rising with the unfamiliar emotions aroused by the thing in her hands. Something about it drew her, and yet that same thing repelled. It set off an uneasy subterranean yearning she could not begin to define. She had to wonder what her prisoner was doing in it, and why it was hidden. She called his name, turning to ask him.

When he saw her and what she held, his face had gone a terrible bloodless white. He made a strangled, tormented sound that was somewhere between a sob and a snarl, and launched himself at her with his silver fingers hooked into claws.

His drunkenness betrayed him. He stumbled as his feet hit the decking, and he went crashing to his knees.

Scylla had already braced herself to fend him off, angel reactions slowing time to a crawl as she waited for him to get up and come at her. Anticipation perked through her, hot and invigorating. At last a chance to assume her rightful place as she put him in his!

For *nothing*. He remained where he had fallen, hunching in on himself in heaped misery. He began to weep, begging her not to hurt the thing in her hands. He kept repeating a name: *Ella*.

Brother Fist's angel knew that she had finally found a weapon to use against him, a crack in his seamless apathy. That was good.

Yet for some reason whose rhyme still escaped her,

she had carefully returned the thing to its niche, putting its unnerving presence safely out of sight.

Then she had told him that it was safely back where it belonged, and promised that she wouldn't hurt it.

Promised.

How could she have done such a thing? What was happening to her?

There was no escaping those questions. They plagued her waking hours and haunted her dreams when she curled up in a corner and set her proximity alarms to waken her if he came within three meters. He never did—at least not in body. Her sleep was fitful and restless, filled with dreams in which he intruded at will.

Never had she known such inner turmoil. Her sense of self and purpose no longer filled her the way it once had, her certainty complete and unscathable as her silver skin. The more she fought it the worse it became. Like an air leak, it had begun as a mere pinhole when Brother Fist sent her away to fetch this man, and had become a widening rent upon finding him. Only it was her insides escaping, not air.

Him, she thought grimly, watching him take yet another drink and mumble something to himself. He wasn't afraid of her, even though all she had to do was look at the people of Ananke to put them on their knees. He didn't care that she had taken his life in her hands. Where she was taking him and for what purpose meant nothing to him. Outwardly he acted as if he was totally beaten and in her control.

Yet she knew he was not. But for that one incident, she had not reached him. He no longer disputed her angelic state, but she had the unsettling feeling that he was only humoring her.

Every time she talked to him she came away feeling even more frustrated and confused. When she spoke of things she knew as truth, he would give her a tolerant, forbearing smile such as an adult would give a misinformed child. Somehow that smile made her feel small and weak and stupid—she who was made by

God to stand above lowly creatures such as he. When she said other things he gave her a different smile, one that left her feeling absurdly pleased.

Worse yet, he seemed to know things about her no mortal should. Like their talk of food that first night. Only her master knew—He had been the one who instructed her—that once a month she had to unburden herself of the physical manifestation of her own spiritual imperfection. It came in the form he had described, from the place he had indicated. How could he have known such a thing?

There were times she thought that maybe he was a devil who had been specifically shaped and sent to taunt and tempt her. His every aspect baffled her. He was an infidel, yet had the hands of an angel. He wallowed in weakness, but there was strength in him that made him nearly impossible to bend to her will.

Only a devil could have such knowledge or insidious power. Somehow his very presence made her think forbidden thoughts, made her doubt herself and all she knew as true. It was as if his blank indifference turned him into some sort of mirror that reflected back hidden faces of her self while distorting the familiar all out of recognition.

Where had the silver armor of her certainty gone?

For all the times she had asked herself that, she still had no answer. Her only certainty was that her only salvation lay in returning to her rightful place at Brother Fist's side. He would make things right again, just like he had when—

Scylla frowned as the echo of another almost-memory whispered through her mind, a taunting, impossible remembrance of a time before she was an angel, when—

Her silver-clad fingers dug into the galley's tabletop, the hard plastic furrowing and tearing like putty. Her black-webbed mouth tightened into a thin, hard line.

Deceptions. On every side, even on the inside.

As much as the man Marchey troubled her, it was being away from the Eden of Ananke, away from

Brother Fist's love that had exposed her to all this
doubt and deception and confusion in the first place.
He should never have—

Scylla's one human eye squeezed shut and she shivered, aghast at how easily and often such blasphemy
came into her mind. How had she fallen into such a
morass of forbidden thoughts and wickedness? How
had her soul become so tainted?

She must atone. That knowledge—that *commandment*—tolled in her mind in a voice as great as God's.
It was deafening. Irrefutable as the need to breathe.

Yet something inside her clenched as tight as her
silver fists in denial.

No. There would be no atoning this time. If she was
failing a test of faith, so be it. The blame was not
hers alone.

Refusing the commandment to atone brought intense physical pain, an agony to match that delivered
by her prayer-box. Enduring it was a kind of penitence
of its own. That realization allowed her to endure the
torment of refusing the commandment crackling
through her nerves.

The doubting angel rode out the searing pain, until
it passed, and the subtler torment that filled the hours
after, counting each moment until she returned to Ananke as an eternity.

Five days after Marchey had found an angel in his
room, he arrived at Ananke. It was one of the smaller
outer Jovian moons, an irregular stony lump just over
20km in diameter. The screen over the main board
showed its unattractive face as they approached. He
hardly gave it a second disinterested look. Most of his
attention was on the unpleasant descent into the grim
barrens of sobriety.

Apparently Ananke was not a very friendly place.
As they approached it a recorded message came in
over the comm, warning them that under no circumstances would they be allowed to land. All incoming

and outgoing cargo was to be left on their orbital doorstep.

Scylla had given an override command that let them land after all. She told him that his was the first outsider ship to do so in over seven years. Somehow he didn't feel particularly honored.

They passed through an open-shuttered blister on Ananke's pockmarked surface and into its interior. The shutters had closed after them like the jaws of a huge trap, leaving them in a narrow stone gullet. Since the moon had been given some spin, in was up. His stomach insisted on another opinion.

When they came to rest a battered, often-patched locktube blindly sought the ship's lock like an eyeless lamprey. It finally found its mark and locked on. His own airlock began cycling, flashed orange, and aborted. He had to acknowledge a warning about poor air quality before it would finish the cycle. The pressure read as barely acceptable; any lower and he and Scylla would have needed to take antiaeroembolants to avoid the bends.

The airlock door hissed open at last. He wrinkled his nose and shrank back as a staggering wave of foul-smelling, overused air rolled over him. Scylla prodded him impatiently from behind.

Marchey had become increasingly phobic about leaving his ship over the last two years. To make matters worse, the D-Tox tab he'd taken earlier to purge the alcohol from his system had left him feeling wrung out and wincingly sober, his senses shriekingly acute and his nerves like bare, overheated wires.

He stood there at the threshold, all but gagging on the fetid air and on the verge of hyperventilating. Every instinct told him to close the lock back up and get the hell out of there.

Scylla had other ideas. This time she gave him a shove. "Start walking, or I will drag you."

He hunched his shoulders. Taking a deep breath, he forced himself to step through the lock and begin pulling himself through the creaking tube, silver hands clamped tight on the guideline. Ananke's innate gravity was negligible. Most small moons and asteroids were spun up to create a semblance of gravity. Here it appeared that the process had been begun and then abandoned. It felt like there was not much more than a tenth g, which was far too close to free fall for his comfort.

His ship used a combination of acceleration and spin to maintain at least a half g at all times. Most hospitals had low- or null-g sections, but surgical procedures were always performed in at least a half g. Null-g sex might be delightful, but surgery was a nightmare in it. Blood, rather than pooling, tended to cover everything like a thick coat of paint.

The tube ended at an airlock large enough to handle cargo. Both inner and outer doors were open. Scylla herded him through them, out onto a wide, shallow ramp leading down into a man-made cavern used as a receiving bay.

There were eight or nine people in the cold, dimly lit bay, shadowy figures laboring to unload an orbital container. Slowly at first, then in a stumbling rush, they abandoned their work and started toward him. Something about the way they moved reminded him of the street beggars he'd seen on Earth in a city named Calcutta back when he was twenty.

He watched them draw nearer. His eyes still hadn't adjusted to the gloom enough to let him see them clearly when Scylla came out behind him.

The people below cried out as one and flung themselves to their knees on the rocky floor. He turned to see her gazing out over them, nodding in satisfaction. There was something like a smile on her webbed lips.

"Yes, Brother Fist's angel has returned," she called out, her voice echoing hollowly off the stone walls. "Stand and welcome her back into your love."

Scylla took his arm. One by one the people below struggled to their feet and formed a double row at the foot of the ramp. Most had their heads bowed and their hands clasped loosely before them.

Those that could.

They started down. Marchey's eyes had adjusted to the dim lighting by then, and what he saw chilled him to the bone. Each and every member of the unhappy honor guard had the gaunt, haunted look of a concentration-camp victim. The best dressed among them wore little more than rags, even though the temperature in the bay had to be in the single digits.

Every one of them was in one way or another maimed and crippled.

They came abreast of the first in line, a gaunt black man with downcast eyes. He was missing one leg and leaned on a homemade plastic crutch. The hand on the crutch-brace was a blunt misshappen knot. His other arm ended at the wrist. The face of the woman next to him was a mass of purplish scar tissue wrapped around one brown, fearful eye. Similar scarring covered her neck and disappeared down the front of her torn and greasy coverall. Marchey did not need to see the few strands of hair left on her pale, blistered skull or the tremors that racked her thin frame to recognize the signs of severe radiation exposure.

Marchey ached to reach out and wipe the pain away, to see if her face could still be found under the horror that had been done to it. But Scylla towed him relentlessly down the line past a man whose arms had been broken and not properly straightened before they set, which had left him looking like he had an extra set of elbows. Across from him was a coughing woman with black blood on her lips and and a body warped by arthritis.

It seemed he had been brought here for good reason. It appeared he had his work cut out for him.

Still, to make her and these others stand here like this! "All right, Scylla," he said curtly, "I've seen enough. Unless you have a very good medical facility—which looks pretty damned unlikely—I can treat these patients better in the small clinic on my ship."

The angel stared at him as if he had begun speaking in tongues. "You are here at Brother Fist's command."

"Then I'm supposed to treat him first?" Marchey told himself that this Brother Fist character had better be in goddamned rough shape if he was putting himself in line before these poor bastards.

She scowled. "Brother Fist is God's Chosen One. Through Him we know that secular medicine is a cheat and a deception, a blasphemous affront to God's Will. He needs nothing you can offer." She glanced indifferently around at the cringing wretches on either side of them. "These ones will be healed if their faith is strong and their obedience perfect enough."

She had led him along this rue of misery to draw even with a black-haired boy of perhaps twelve. Both his hands were crudely bandaged with dirty rags. One of his eyes was gone, the socket black-crusted and badly infected. The boy's face was flushed with fever and beaded with sweat in spite of the cold. The whole area around his eye was an angry red, and so swollen that the tight and shiny skin looked ready to burst. Under it was a glistening tear track of pus. The sickly-sweet smell of gangrene filled the air. His other eye, dulled by pain and filled with mute appeal, sought Marchey's face.

The boy tried to smile.

Marchey tried to smile back, but could not. For a moment it was as if every cell in his body had stopped motion and function. Then he shivered, feeling fury ignite in a place where there had only been cold ash for a very long time.

He shucked free of Scylla's arm and glared at her. "Listen," he spat through clenched teeth, his voice dripping anger and contempt. "This boy's eye is badly infected. Necrotic. He is going to fucking *die* unless he gets proper care. This Brother Fist character is full of *shit* if he says—"

He never saw it coming. Silver lightning struck him, blasting him off his feet. He pinweeled sideways, narrowly missing the boy and slamming back first into one of the orbital containers. He hung there as if glued to its cold steel side with the wind knocked out of him, dazed and desperately gasping for breath.

Ananke's feeble gravity never had a chance to claim him.

Scylla swept down on him like a chrome harpy. She grabbed him by the front of his tunic, her ceramyl claws raking across his chest like a fistful of knives. She peeled him off and jerked him close. Wrath turned her tattooed face into that of a Chinese dragon. Her breath steamed like smoke in the frigid air.

"*Never* dare speak of Brother Fist like that again," she hissed, black-webbed lips peeling back from her serried teeth. "My punishment will not kill you." Her one human eye narrowed to a glittering slit. The blank lens that replaced the other gleamed with machine-cold menace. "Because death would be a mercy, and there will be none for you."

She slammed him onto his feet. Marchey staggered, but somehow managed to keep from falling. Blood from his slashed chest already stained the pristine white of his mangled tunic. He was at last able to breathe again and sucked the foul air in greedily. It tasted almost sweet.

He was hurt and scared, but his outrage still outweighed his fear. He stood up straight, gathering the shreds of his dignity about him, and stared Scylla straight in her eye.

"Your objection is noted," he panted, "but mine still remains."

Scylla's mouth twisted, her lips drawing back from her mouthful of knives. She raised her hand, talons all the way out now, her next blow a killing blow. Somehow Marchey managed to stand his ground on legs that had turned to jelly under him.

But before she could strike again, a voice rang through the cavernous bay.

"Scylla! Bring the infidel to me now." The voice was a clotted, rasping whisper amplified to the volume of thunder. It raised the hackles on the back of Marchey's neck and sent cold crawling down his spine.

The crippled people fell to their knees. Scylla went rigid as a statue, her armored, blade-tipped hand and arm cocked over Marchey like a scythe. Anger and something Marchey could not name warred across the nightmare landscape of her face. For five endless, awful seconds he was certain that she was going to disobey and he to die.

But in the end she shuddered, let out a strangled, inarticulate sound, and let her arm fall. She bowed her head.

"I hear and obey, Brother Fist." Her voice was low and meek. Fearful.

"Of course you do. Come to me now. I wait."

Her head came up. She eyed Marchey coldly, pointing to the door at the far end of the bay. "Move."

Marchey decided not to press his luck, silently obeying her order. He stumbled into clumsy motion on rubbery legs.

He kept his head high, doing his best to hide the sense of dread that made him feel as if his insides had been filled with chilled formalin.

That awful voice still rang in his head. That its owner could cow Scylla so easily did not bode well.

Nor did this place. If what he'd seen of Ananke so far was any indication of what was to come, then he'd just been brought into the first circle of hell.

There was no way for him to guess what horrors might wait in the inner circles. Humanity—and wasn't that an ironic descriptive?—had long ago proved that when it came to the practices of cruelty and oppression, especially in the name of religion, its inventiveness was nearly infinite.

Caught between Scylla and Charybdis. That was the original rock and a hard place. There was no mistaking the danger Scylla represented. And as for the Charybdis of this Fist person and Ananke—

The door at the back of the bay opened, revealing a gloomy tunnel ahead.

—He'd know more than he wanted to sooner than he wanted.

The door closed behind him. Scylla gave him a push. Once thing was for certain. He was no longer trapped on the old, endless treadmill where he had plodded for so long.

Once he would have said that any change would have been an improvement. Now he was getting an inkling of just how wrong he would have been.

Scylla's metal-shod feet made a sound like the relentless ticking of a bomb against the mesh-covered stone floor of the tunnel. Her face was as set and grim, a bulwark against the furious hellbroth of conflicts and pressures boiling inside her.

Thinking about how close she had come to killing the infidel Marchey made her head pound and her insides roil uneasily. It was not that killing bothered her. After all, God's terrible swift sword was edged so that it might draw blood. All life was His to give or cut short.

But Brother Fist had laid on her the task of delivering her prisoner unharmed. She had come within one furious heartbeat of failing Him.

Of *disobeying* Him. The sin of disobedience was cardinal and unforgivable. That he had provoked her with blackest blasphemy would mean less than nothing in this case. She was an angel, and her obedience was expected to be more perfect than that of intrinsically corrupt human flesh.

She stared at her captive's broad back, watching him shuffle cautiously along the uneven floor in the oversized magnetic slippers she had made him put on. For all the time she had spent with him, she had to admit that she could come nowhere near being able to predict his actions or reactions.

She was sure he had known full well how close he was to death back in the bay, yet he had only reacted with a quiet defiance that seemed to have been half courage and half his usual unbreakable indifference. Still his anger over the state of sinners who meant less than nothing to him had been real enough, if completely inexplicable.

There was anger in him after all, perhaps even in

measure to equal her own. This was good to know. Yet as with so many things about him, the how and why of it remained a baffling mystery.

Brother Fist had not revealed why He wanted this man brought to Him. She had not dared ask; it was not her place to question His purposes and plans. Now that he was here, she had to ackowledge the possibility that her master might wish to speak to him alone.

That prospect troubled her deeply. Marchey was not cowed. He could not be trusted. He might even be a devil sent to hurt her master.

Brother Fist had not seemed quite Himself of late. He said that the Hand of God was heavy on His shoulders. Was it possible that He might overestimate His ability to control this strange, unpredictable man?

She certainly had.

Just thinking that her master might be wrong about anything made the pain and nausea she already felt spike so high that her head swam, and she very nearly lost her balance. Such thoughts were unworthy. Forbidden. Blasphemous.

But she had become used to suffering such pain on the trip back here. She accepted it, endured it.

The silver chain she clung to was the knowledge that she was Brother Fist's angel, His servant, and—most of all—His guardian. His holy person was to be protected at any cost. Pain was a small price to pay when her life and soul were already pledged to that sacred duty.

Scylla knew where the hidden pickups covering this section of tunnel were mounted. As they moved into a blind spot she reached into the pouch at her hip and pulled out one of her Ears. It was a thin, transparent chip the size of a fingernail, perfect for being hidden in the homes and workplaces of those suspected of laziness, ill faith, or blasphemy.

She scraped her finger across its back to activate the adhesive, carefully keeping her Angel eye averted in case Brother Fist was watching through it. By the time they came in range of the next pickup the Ear was stuck tight to her prisoner's belt.

Scylla permitted herself a small, secret smile. There was some risk that Brother Fist would frown upon what she had done, were He to find out about it, but it was worthwhile.

Now she could do her duty, guarding her charge no matter what happened.

Marchey hurt. More every minute.

The slashes across his chest were lines of fire. His back felt like one massive bruise. He could feel his lips ballooning, and his jaw felt half-unhinged. He moved it experimentally. At least it wasn't broken.

He'd been lucky back in the landing bay and knew it. Scylla had only backhanded him—and pulled her blow at that. That exo gave her enough strength to have literally knocked his block off.

Some angel! It would have been funny if it wasn't so tragic.

He was beginning to see her in a new light shed by the abject obedience that had saved his life. Could it be that she was just another pawn in whatever reprehensible game was being played here? He was beginning to think so. Someone—this Brother Fist character, most likely—had turned her into a killing machine with that exo, and somehow brainwashed her into believing she was an angel. That would explain her truncated personality, her flat, knee-jerk responses.

He wished he'd spent the time coming here trying to learn something about the woman hidden—or trapped—inside that demon-faced, silver-metal monster. But he hadn't bothered, had he? Such matters had exactly nothing to do with him, right?

Sure. Besides, why think when you could drink? He shook his head sadly. He might as well admit that she wasn't the only one operating under flatworm-simple programming.

All right, he told himself sternly, *stop using your head for a proctoscope for a change. Pay close atten-*

tion to everything in this cut-rate Eden. Your life might—and probably does—depend on being on your toes for a change.

Not that what he'd seen so far was easy to ignore. The only way to describe the place was unrelentingly grim. The cramped tunnels were cold and poorly lit, the floor grid patched and curling, the unsealed walls and ceiling rough-hewn and in some places crumbling. The flat floor meant that the tunnel's builders had planned to give the moon more spin, making up and down more than a hazy theoretical concept.

The air was only minimally breathable. Not only did it stink of sweat and poorly recycled waste, it seemed saturated to the weeping point with a suffocating miasma of fear, misery, and despair, like the air in a dungeon. Unscavenged water vapor had condensed on the walls, making them and everything else damp and clammy. Every other surface was covered with mildew.

Other than those poor bastards in the bay, Marchey had seen only a few of the inhabitants of this horrible place. Those he and his escort had encountered reacted by either cringing back against the walls as they passed with their heads bowed and eyes averted, or scuttling back out of sight like frightened mice.

If this was an Eden, then it was of the sort created by such infamous utopians as Jim Jones, Pol Pot, and Gerald Van Hyaams. He didn't need to see the mines to know what sort of conditions these people worked in; he'd already observed evidence of enough injuries to close down any normal operation.

It was obvious that human life was as cheap as dirt here. The people he had seen so far were clearly bereft of such basic human rights as comfort, freedom, or dignity. This was not a place where people laughed, or even smiled.

Nor did it appear to be some nest of religious zealots. It was not fanaticism he saw on people's faces, it was fear and exhaustion. Service to God might have been the name of the game here, but the rules were from an old, old practice that went by the name of *slavery*.

It had been a long time since Marchey had felt anything like real anger or fear. Since he had really felt much of anything at all.

Much to his surprise, he found that the machinery for such emotions was still intact, the rusty gears grinding faster and faster. He felt like some piece of equipment that was coming back on-line after years of being on standby.

They turned into a wider tunnel. Scylla stalked beside him now, tight-lipped and impatient. It was all he could do to keep up with her.

He watched her out of the corner of one eye, finally giving the reason she had brought him here some serious thought. Did she know the reason, or was she just unquestioningly following orders? The latter seemed the most likely.

He plotted it out in his mind. She had been sent for him, specifically. She'd known his name and where to find him. How? He had no idea. Why?

Only one answer made any sense. He was a Bergmann Surgeon. Not only competent at all conventional medical procedures, but also able to treat conditions no regular physician could. The inescapable conclusion was that Fist had ordered him kidnapped and brought here because of who he was and what he could do.

According to Scylla, this Fist preached that medicine was a cheat and a deception. She acted as if she believed him, even though she was the one bringing a doctor to him.

Marchey knew he shouldn't be surprised. Fanaticism and blindness to reality always went hand in hand; they were ultimately different faces of the same spurious coin. He was tempted to point out the contradiction to her, but felt fairly safe in predicting that her reaction would be vehement denial at best. More likely it would be violent.

That made him wonder if this Brother Fist had taken into account the chance that she might find out he was lying to her. He seemed to have her on a short leash, but still . . .

Watching her surreptitiously, so superhumanly fast and strong in that indestructible silver exo, he knew that he wouldn't want to be in her master's shoes if her illusions were shattered.

Scylla punched in the code that unlocked the massive steel door that barred the way to her Master's chambers, a code known to her and Brother Fist alone. Hope and fear and doubt and confusion fought for supremacy inside her, making it hard to concentrate.

It would be good to be back at her Master's side. Back where she belonged. It felt like she had been gone for an eternity.

She knew that she had somehow been changed by being away from Ananke for the first time in her life. Just how, she could not quite say, and deep in her heart she had prayed that simply coming home again would make everthing right again.

But it only made things worse. The Eden of Ananke seemed a different place than the one she had left. Smaller. Dirtier. Oppressive and almost . . . *ugly*.

She shook her head to clear it. *Deceptions.* The fault lay in her eyes, not what they beheld.

Even an angel's heaven-made flesh was weak. The doubts that continued to assail her were proof of that. What should have been a joyous homecoming had come under a pall of apprehension as she realized that she would have to go before her Master with an unclean heart.

She could not help but be afraid He would see the black stains on her soul the moment He laid eyes on her, for did He not always say that He could read her every thought? His disappointment would be deep and justified. Ever quick to anger, the way she had failed His trust might provoke Him to rage.

Even if somehow He did not see her failings at first glance, she knew she would have to confess them. To withhold would only compound her transgressions.

No matter which way her sins were revealed, she
would have to be punished to atone for them. She had
meted out many such punishments, and knew just how
high the price of redemption might be set. Many put
the sinner back in God's hands so that He might fling
them down to Hell, where they belonged.

Scylla was an angel. Still, she was close enough to
human to want to run and hide from what she faced.

But her silver fingertips danced swiftly across the
keypad, entering the code sequence that would open
the door as if they knew that the only answer was, as
always, perfect obedience.

*God punishes us because He loves us. To hide from
His punishment is to hide from His love.* She repeated
that truth over and over, but for the first time in her
life she found no solace in it.

The final number was pressed. A low tone signalled
acceptance. Motors hummed. The door yawned open
to admit the fallen angel and her charge into the ante-
room of God's chosen one.

Soon His justice and His love would shine on
them both.

"Sweet Jesus in a bank vault," Marchey muttered
as he watched the two-meter-wide, half-meter-thick
armored door swing ponderously outward. It looked
like a tacnuke would make about as big a dent in it
as an exploding cigar.

This Brother Fist had a really deep and unshakable
faith in the love of his flock, didn't he?

Scylla gave him a look. He stepped cautiously inside, unable to guess what he might find waiting for
him. The door rumbled shut behind them, closing with
a massive and absolute finality. Lockbolts the size of
his arm pistoned into place, sealing them in.

He sniffed the air. It was sweet and clean, the oxygen content at or slightly above normal, heady as wine
after the overused fung of the tunnels.

Separate life support. Brother Fist was a cautious
man. A man of the people, too.

His angelic escort took his arm and led him through an arched vestibule and into a wide rotunda under a high-vaulted ceiling. This hemispherical chamber was as beautifully wrought as the tunnels were crude. Graceful carved pillars outset from the facet-cut walls bracketed the broad mosaic floor. At the far end, a white-stone altar table and real wood pulpit on a raised dais confirmed that it was a chapel.

His gaze was drawn upward toward the source of the golden light flooding the chamber. It came from a glowing one-meter sphere at the center of the ceiling dome. The globe was a representation of the Sun. Around it smaller spheres, the planets and moons, each exquisitely rendered in translucent tinted glass, wheeled in their endless dance and painted their colors on the walls.

Scylla gave him no more than a few seconds to appreciate the loving artistry that had gone into it or the chapel. Or to try to understand the melancholy air that permeated the place, a feeling of disuse. Of misuse.

She pulled at his arm in obvious impatience. "This way." She towed him toward a wide door between two pillars at the far right. A last glance over his shoulder gave him a closer, better look at the altar.

Cold crawled into the marrow of his bones when he saw the thick webbed straps which had been bolted to the sides of the altar table. Its top was scratched and chipped. Dark brown stains were caught in the cuts and gouges. . . .

Scylla hauled him around to face her. "You are going to see Brother Fist now," she warned in a low, hard voice. Her face was an unreadable mask. "If you are disrespectful, I will punish you." Her silver fingers dug into the meat of his upper arm. "If you make the slightest hostile move toward him, I will strangle you with your own guts."

Marchey shivered, knowing that she meant every word. But he was damned if he was going to give her the satisfaction of showing his fear. He forced a smile, even though it made his mashed lips sting and begin bleeding again. "So you're in charge of protocol, too?"

She snatched him off the floor by his arm and shook him until his teeth rattled. "Understand me, little man!" she hissed. "Even if you are alone with him, I will know what you say and do. I am an *angel*! Do not forget that for a single moment. If I come after you, there will be no escaping my wrath, and no mercy once I have you in my hands."

She shook him again, nearly wrenching his arm out of its socket, then pulled him close. So close that he could see every red-and-black line tattooed on her face, could count her red-tipped, razor-sharp teeth. Her voice dropped to a knife-edged whisper.

"If you misbehave I will send you to Hell. Slowly, infidel. Skinless and screaming to die. *Do you understand me?*"

"I . . . do," Marchey mumbled, desperately trying to contain the cyclone of dread whirling through him. The image of that bloodstained altar burned in his mind, lending a terrible credence to her threats.

Maybe she saw through the tissue-thin remains of his self-control and knew that she had him cowed. She nodded. "Very well."

He staggered drunkenly when she slammed him onto his feet, and would have fallen but for the iron grip she had on his arm.

A commbox had been cemented to the wall next to the door. Scylla pushed the callbar. A low, absurdly cheerful tone sounded, then from the box issued the soft, rasping voice he'd heard in the landing bay. Once again the sound of it made him shiver.

"Scylla."

She meekly bowed her head. "Here, Master."

"You may enter." There was the muted clunk of lockbolts withdrawing. The door swung toward them. Marchey saw that it had been backplated with a layer of steel-wrapped, reinforced stonecrete.

Just as when he'd opened his ship's airlock, the first thing to hit him was the smell. It came gushing out in a turgid, gut-twisting wave, so thick it seemed almost liquid. It was a smell he knew, one that could slice through the strongest hospital disinfectant like a scalpel through a rose petal.

It was the sickly-sweet, septic stench of something long diseased and dying.

Scylla froze on the threshold, nerves shrieking a warning and fight response jittering through her.

Her eye narrowed. Nostrils tattooed with scales and barbs flared as she sniffed the air. *What was that smell?*

But she already knew the answer to the question: Brother Fist. It was a smell she knew as well as her own face in the mirror, a sweet perfume He had begun to exude just a year before: His own attar of holiness. Her first days away from His side she had missed it.

Then why did it seem like such a loathsome stench now? Was this yet another effect of her eroding angelic state?

She forced herself to stifle her unworthy revulsion and put one foot in front of the other. This twisting of her senses was a final deception, cast against her to keep her from her rightful place at Brother Fist's side. One word, one touch, and all would be right again.

She stepped through the doorway, and at last she was returned to His holy presence.

Yet seeing her Master did not bring the comfort she so desperately craved. It only made things worse. The time apart, some inner failure, something was making her see Him differently from the way she should.

He was dressed in His black cassock and seated in His usual place, the big thronelike chair near the wall of screens that let Him look into every corner of the Eden He had created. That was as it should be. Yet instead of stern and strong and righteous, He looked old and weak and—

—*sick.*

She tried to smother this blasphemy even as it was being born. It was just that the Hand of God was heavy on His shoulders. It was a failure in her perceptions, a betrayal by her untrustworthy senses. The other was impossible. Unthinkable.

Ashamed that she had been prey to such a profane thought in His presence, she bowed her head, praying that when she looked up again the scales would be gone from her eyes.

"Brother Fist," she intoned with abject humility, speaking His name like a talisman that would give her strength and lend truth to her senses. "I have returned."

"My angel," he replied in a thick, phlegmy rasp. "You have done well."

Scylla hunched her shoulders. That praise heaped on the burden of her manifest unworthiness was a weight greater than even the shining metal armor that proved she was an angel could bear. Heart stuttering with fear, she steeled herself to confess.

She was never given the chance. Brother Fist spoke first. What he said and how he said it instantly banished all thoughts of confession from her troubled mind.

"Leave us now, Scylla." His tone was brusque, impatient, as if she were an annoyance, not His angel and right hand.

Her head snapped up in surprise. She stared at Him in wounded incomprehension, unable to believe that He would dismiss her so offhandedly. She had been away for over fifteen days, braving the Profane World and putting her very soul in peril for him, yet He did not seem to care. His eyes were fixed on the infidel Marchey, and had she been forced to describe the look on His face, she would have said it was one of greedy expectation.

"But—but this man is *dangerous,* Master!" she protested lamely. Suddenly a sickening apprehension crawled through her. *I have fallen so low that I am no longer worthy of His love. He sees. He knows. I have become less than dust in His gaze.*

Brother Fist's eyes had begun turning a yellowish

color some three years before. Another sign that the
Hand of God was on Him, he said; it was the reflection of the golden streets of Heaven. Those sallow
eyes blazed with petulant fury now. A fury directed
at her. It rooted her to the spot, unable to speak or
move.

"I said leave us!" His skull-like face hardened, and
he beat on the arm of his chair with a bony, blue-
veined fist. "Get out, you stupid bitch! *Out!*"

Scylla turned and fled, cringing under the lash of
His displeasure, and knowing He would strike her
dead with a thought if she did not remove herself from
His sight. She stiff-armed the door out of her way,
choking back the bewildered cry of pain and appeal
lodged in her throat.

Her cubby was on the opposite side of the chapel
so that she would be close at hand to her Master, and
it was there she sought refuge.

Her metal-shod feet clattered across the mosaic
floor as she crossed it in a stumbling run. Once inside
her room she flung herself down on the raised foam
pallet that served as her bed, burying her face in the
forgiving softness. Her breath came in hitching gasps,
but she did not cry.

Angels do not cry.

Ever.

To do so would be an abomination. To do so would
be the final damning iniquity.

Biting back some hot wet force boiling inside her
and threatening to burst free, she made herself sit up.
She held out one trembling hand. Her right hand.

At a mental command her right buckler released
itself. She shucked the weapon off and laid it aside.
Gleaming silver metal still covered her palm and fingers like a second skin, but with the buckler gone
the needle-scarred area on the back of her hand was
exposed. Like her weakness. Like her manifest
unworthiness.

She partially extruded the talons on her left hand,
the gleaming white ceramyl blades as sharp as the line

between sin and obedience, between damnation and grace.

Sharp enough to slice into the tattooed flesh at the back of her hand like corruption had insinuated itself into her soul. Blood welled up around each blade, the price Brother Fist said God demanded when He was failed.

Her one green eye slid shut to hold in the strange wetness gathering there. The blood was born in pain, and that was good. Pain was the ladder one climbed to return to grace, and she bore it gladly. Each throb was a rung that lifted her higher.

The pain was cleansing. It washed away the hurt and confusion, leaving only her essential suffering self, naked to God's judgmental scrutiny.

I am an angel.

She gritted her teeth, digging her talons deeper to root out every corrupt tendril of doubt and resentment.

I was brought down to serve Brother Fist. To carry out His will and protect Him.

Blood pooled around her talons, a shimmering ruby set in a silver brooch.

I am His to be used as He will. I am my duty. Without it I am nothing. I must serve with no expectation of reward in this life, and any punishment I earn should be received gladly, for it is just that I suffer for my failings.

Her whole body trembled as she balanced on the knife point of pain. Sweat glazed her forehead. She held her breath, afraid that it might carry a scream if she released it.

There is nothing of me or mine more important than my duty to my Master. If He asks me to lay down my life, I should rejoice that I can pay the price He asks of me.

She closed her eye, the better to see Truth as she recited her catechism.

If I allow Him to be hurt either by action or inaction, God Himself will condemn me to eternal damnation for failing my duty to protect His Servant.

Scylla's green eye opened. She saw her path clearly.

She was Brother Fist's angel. His protector. The man she had brought to him was unpredictable, maybe even dangerous. Her Master was alone with him, unaware of the threat the infidel posed and undefended from him.

He had ordered her away from His side, away from where she could watch over Him. That (*hurt!*) was His right. He had not ordered her to listen in and act as hidden guardian, but then again He had not ordered her *not* to, and how else could God's Will be done?

Her talons retracted, the china white ceramyl smeared with the red of her own blood. She stood up, flexing her wounded hand. It felt aflame, but functioned perfectly. Her angel body could block the pain, but she kept it from doing so. Pain kept the doubt and deception at bay. Pain was truth. Pain was clarity of thought and action. Pain was grace.

It felt good to be back on the True Path once more, the angel once again in her rightful place at Brother Fist's side.

The door closed behind Scylla. Brother Fist touched a stud on the control pad on his chair arm, locking it after her. Bolts thudded back into place, sealing it tight. Marchey flinched at the sound.

"Come, sit down, my dear Dr. Marchey," Fist called, beckoning him closer. He smiled. "I've been looking forward to meeting you." Fist spoke softly, a clotted, wheezing, tubercular rattle to his voice. His tone was arch, ironic.

Marchey looked around, choosing the seat farthest from the wasted figure in the oversized chair. He lowered himself into it reluctantly, gaze averted from his host.

Once he was sitting down he surreptitiously took in his surroundings. The cubby was quite large, the space broken up by foamstone dividers. Fist sat at its center, on one side of him an elaborate, slightly archaic comp, on the other screens displaying views from all over

Ananke. The cubby's walls were lined with book-shelves packed full of antique bound books and per-mem cubes. A few choice art objects were scattered about the room, some grotesque, some quite beautiful.

But for the surveillance screens, it could have passed for a professor's study, modest and comfort-able. Two other things spoiled the effect. One was the nauseating reek that permeated the air, making it smell like a carrion eater's lair.

Then there was the room's owner and occupant.

Marchey had to psych himself up to taking a long hard look at the man who'd had him kidnapped. He raised his eyes hesitantly, pulse pounding with trepidation.

Brother Fist looked like his nearest relative was Sis-ter Death. He was a skeleton draped with loose saf-fron skin, raised from the grave and infused with some sort of awful unlife. His black cassock hung on him like a shroud. His cheeks were gaunt and sunken, his mouth a thin-lipped, liverish slash, his teeth white and sharp. His eyes were jaundiced, feverishly bright, and were fixed on Marchey with a greedy, crazed intensity.

But it was not his physical appearance alone that sent flight-response adrenaline pumping through Mar-chey's system, turning his heart into a clenched fist and making his skin prickle with cold sweat.

The primitive human animal in him scented a rabid sickness that the civilized physician in him would try to identify with meaningless labels like *psychopath, egopath,* or *sociopath.* Words created to describe mon-sters but falling far short of capturing their dark es-sence, just as a word like *bomb* cannot convey a millionth of the horror of one going off on a crowded sidewalk.

Such creatures can be nearly impossible to identify because of their ability to hide themselves, like fatally venomous chameleons. Clever lurking things, discov-ered only when someone accidentally stumbles across a cellar floored with human bones or a storage locker stacked full of severed heads. *He seemed like an okay guy,* the neighbors say afterward. *Pretty much kept to himself.*

But when guile and pretense are discarded, there is no mistaking that it is a thing only nominally human, born of woman but reared in hell and suckled on poison. It is revealed as a cold-blooded and savage thing of unspeakable drives and an absolute disdain for any life other than its own.

Brother Fist laughed, a hacking, mirthless sound that sent a shudder of revulsion up Marchey's spine. "Do I frighten you, Doctor?" he asked, carious yellow eyes bright and cunning.

Marchey bit down on his first reply. *Shitless.*

"Aren't you, um, trying to?" he asked in as close to a normal voice as he could muster.

Brother Fist's smile made Marchey think of the gleeful, grinning *rictus sardonicus* worn by skeletal, scythe-wielding Plague in medieval art.

"Perhaps a little. I so wanted us to get off on the right foot. I may be unwell, but I am undiminished. I have power. Over this place, and now over you." He gestured as if to take in all of Ananke. "This place is mine, created in my image. I have made it into a crucible, my dear doctor. I am at its center. I *am* its center. I am its maker and master, flame and furnace. Tell me, do you know what a crucible is?"

"Yes," Marchey said, the words seeming to come out of his mouth on their own. "It's a vessel for smelting ore."

A nod. "Excellent. The crucible is a means of reducing excess and impurity, creating something useful. I am the smelter. I am the furnace. In my crucible all that does not serve my purposes is burned away. Individuality is cauterized. Autonomy is immolated. Love is cremated. Trust is boiled away. Hope chars to the blackest ash . . ."

Marchey watched those awful yellow eyes glaze as the old man intoned his lunatic litany in a rustling hypnotic monotone. Everything but the old man's eyes and voice seemed to fade away.

"The smelter's art lies in heating the crucible to the proper degree. Razing the human psyche until only fear and faith remain. Until they are fused into one. Fear and faith guarantee perfect, unquestioning service. From the crucible emerges a material fit to be beaten into a tool."

Brother Fist's gaze turned outward again, fixed on Marchey. He felt it bite into him, sharp and paralyzing as a viper's fang. That black knife-slash mouth twisted into a sinister smile. "You've had a chance to sightsee, Doctor. What do you think of my crucible?"

Marchey licked his swollen lips, tasting blood. The man's virulent madness seemed to infect the very air he breathed like some deadly biowar virotoxin, suffocating him, shriveling his wits and will. He squirmed in his chair uneasily, but could not find the strength to look away.

Unaware of what he was doing, he slowly reached up to touch the silver metal pin on his chest as if to find some reminder of his own identity. The emblem was still there, dangling on a bloodstained scrap of his slashed tunic. Metal touched metal with a faint click.

It was almost as if a circuit closed inside him. The sense of who and what he was flowed through him again. With it came the memory of a one-eyed child this man had condemned to die out of a cynical contempt for human life. Out of cold, raw cruelty.

"I think it sucks," he heard himself say. He blinked and sat up straighter, returning anger making him clamp his hands on the arms of his chair. "I think someone should jam some of what you've been dishing out right back down your fucking throat."

Brother Fist lolled back, eyes hooded and smirking. "Perhaps you are correct," he agreed softly.

"Damn right I am."

"You sound so certain. Are you volunteering to be the hand of justice, Doctor?"

Marchey stared at him, imagining his silver hands on Fist's scrawny wattled neck. They tightened on the arms of his chair, strong enough to snap Fist's spine like a twig.

"Think of all the pain and suffering that would be averted."

He already was. Killing Fist would be like curing a disease.

"Come on, Doctor," he wheedled, lifting his chin and stroking his neck in invitation. "Do what is right. Take the matter in hand. Expunge the suffering. Balance the scales."

Marchey stared at his tormentor, but remained where he was. Cold sweat crawled down his sides.

Fist smiled with hateful pleasure. "I thought not. You won't raise a hand against me. Your righteous indignation is a joke. I find it quite hilarious, but do you?"

Marchey looked away, feeling ill. Fist continued to taunt him, making him feel sicker with every word.

"You can't forget yourself. You are sworn to preserve life, not take it. To heal rather than hurt. You've pledged your life to an oath. One that has mocked you for years. That mocks you now, even as I do."

—I pledge my life to the practice of healing—

Marchey said nothing. Fist had summoned up the words he held as the one holy thing in his life. The Healer's Oath. Based on the Hippocratic Oath, but further reaching; an ethical ideal he had upheld through thick and thin, and which had held him up as well. His vocation had become an empty shell. That Oath was the glue that held the fragile, cracked pieces together.

"I'm sick, my dear doctor," Brother Fist continued, smirking as he tightened the screws. "Probably dying. That is why I had you brought to me. Now that I have you here, you will do everything in your power to cure me."

"I won't." Marchey forced the words out, but they were no more than a hollow whisper.

Brother Fist's mocking laughter made him feel like there were maggots slithering through his insides.

"Oh but you will!" he wheezed. "You have no choice. Keeping your ridiculous Healer's Oath is the single fingertip that keeps you from falling into the abyss. It is the one tattered shred of self-respect you have left."

He paused to catch his breath. "I have studied your kind. I know more about you than you do yourselves. Fail your Oath, and your entire existence becomes meaningless. You will have given up everything you hold sacred for *nothing*."

Marchey could only shake his head from side to side like a punch-drunk fighter, trying to get away from the blows hammering into him and backing him into a corner.

—holding every life sacred—

But there was no escape. This terrible old man knew his situation too well, knew precisely which buttons to push.

"You cannot refuse to help me."

—refusing none who seek my help—

"Welcome to my crucible, Dr. Marchey." Brother Fist spread his thin hands. "You think I have turned up the heat beyond bearing, but I have really only just begun. After all, how hot can it be if your scruples are not yet burned away?" He gazed at Marchey with baleful pleasure, closing his hands as if he gripped Marchey's life and fate in them. *"Yet."*

His hands fell to his lap. "Do your duty. Begin examining me."

—because my duty is to save lives, not judge them—

Marchey stood up, feeling sick and doomed, bile on his tongue and lungs clogged with choking despair.

"Scylla said you don't believe in medicine," he protested in a pathetic attempt to escape the nightmare swallowing him up.

His tormentor's laughter hacked through his hopes for a way out like an antique bone saw, leaving them in raw, bleeding pieces.

"Please don't demean yourself by pretending to such naïveté," Fist said, his voice filled with the cloy-

ing sweetness of rotten meat. "I simply don't believe
in letting the sheep have it. It pleases me to hear
their futile prayers. I so love watching them abasing
themselves because their faith isn't perfect enough to
make them whole again. That is one of the brightest,
sweetest-smelling blossoms in my little garden of
pain."

Garden of pain, Marchey thought with numb horror.
*And I'm supposed to give the gardener the renewed
health he needs to continue tending his bitter crops. . . .*

Scylla hunched like a cast-silver gargoyle at the end
of her pallet. Head down. Shoulders sharpened with
tension. Teeth bared. Her one green eye glazed and
sightless.

Brother Fist had—

Her talons were out, and she shredded the foam
pad without even knowing it, hands rhythmically
clenching and unclenching.

He had—

His own voice, the damning words coming from his
own tongue, his contemptuous laughter as he turned
her service to himself and to God into acts of willful
cruelty. Turned Revealed Truth into proof that he
had—

—lied to her.

This was no weakness. No deception sent to test
her faith.

Brother Fist was sick.

He had sent her for Marchey because he needed
a doctor.

Because . . .

God would not heal him.

The orderly walls of her world were shuddering and
cracking, their concrete foundations turned to a quicksand of lies. In the chaos strange things that felt almost
like memories surfaced like raw earth thrust up
through split and buckling pavement. Faces. Feelings.
Sensations. People and things she had no names for,
but which seemed to know her as a sister.

Her mind reeled blindly, buffeted in a hundred directions, seeking solid ground, seeking escape, and all she knew for sure was that if she heard any more she would—

She lifted her arm, reaching out to turn the Ear off. To stop this before she went mad. Her silver hand hung there in front of the stud that would bring silence and safety and sanity.

Hung there. As if reaching for a lifeline.

Hung there. Between truth and silence.

Hung there, wavering—

—trembling—

—then fell.

Almost as if that were some sort of signal to thaw time and start the world moving again, Marchey's voice came to her, breaking the silence.

Marchey had reviewed his options. It hadn't taken long. They had been few, and equally grim.

His only choice was in mode of self-destruction.

Brother Fist had drawn him into a maze where the walls were built from his own moral strictures, and every turning led to darkness and defeat.

He couldn't break his Oath without breaking himself. Brother Fist had seen that with the cynical clarity of a worldview uncolored by honor, ethics, or scruples. He could not bring himself to kill this pestilence masquerading as a person. He could not even let him die if it was in his power to heal him. Those might in one sense be the "right" things to do, but not for him.

He had long ago sworn to accept the precept that every life was sacred, had value. His entire life had been dedicated to that principle; it was the ability to save lives that might have been otherwise lost that had kept him from renouncing Bergmann Surgery and trading his silver arms for flesh. Even now he could not bring himself to abandon that vow.

Besides, even if he could bring himself to refuse, no doubt Scylla could force him to reconsider.

He would hold to his Oath, even though healing

this monster would be such a rape of his skills that it would probably have the same destructive effect as breaking the Healer's Oath. It would despoil the one thing of value and meaning left in his life.

There was no escaping the crucible unscathed.

All he could do was hope that maybe afterward he could find some opportunity to make amends for what he had done. Maybe he would get a chance to treat some of Fist's subjects and begin redeeming himself. Maybe if he let himself be used and broken, he would be cast away and get a chance to escape on his ship and find help.

He took a deep breath. "Let's take a look at you," he said heavily. The heartsick resignation in his voice was no ploy. He climbed reluctantly to his feet and started toward his new patient.

Willing himself to walk deeper into the crucible.

Brother Fist produced a gun from a hidden pouch in the arm of his chair, pointed it at Marchey's chest.

Marchey froze midstep, eyes on the weapon. He knew just enough about arms to recognize the big, blued-steel handweapon as an old-style Fukura "Spring Flower" pistol. The folded alloy projectile it fired would make a fingerprint-sized hole going into a human body. It would exit the other side like a whirling dinner plate heaped with gore.

Brother Fist hacked gleefully. "Think of this as Malpractice Insurance." He gestured curtly with the gun. "Come on, get to it."

Marchey obeyed, tearing his gaze away from the weapon. "You don't have much faith in your fellowman for a priest," he said, trying for sarcasm but his voice coming out flat-line.

"Please, Doctor. I'm no priest, and you know it." He cocked his head. "But you're an intelligent man. Surely you must wonder what I am, and how I got here. I wasn't always Brother Fist, you know."

"No?" Marchey said tonelessly. "Give me your arm."

The old man offered his free hand, a bundle of twigs covered with wrinkled yellow parchment. Marchey took it, the cool dry skin like paper under his fingers. A silent command started the devices inside his prosthetics recording pulse, blood pressure, NFD, GSR, and a dozen other tests. Data whispered through his mind, the first bare threads in the warp of diagnosis.

Brother Fist settled back as if totally at ease, but kept his weapon centered on Marchey's solar plexus. "I came here not quite a decade ago. Back then about a fifth of the people on Ananke were wildcatters. The rest were members of a religious commune calling themselves the Immanuel Kindred. It looked like a perfect place to drop out of sight, further my studies, and entertain myself by practicing my specialty."

Marchey pressed a yellowed nail, let up. No color change. "What specialty is that? Slavery?"

A sardonic chuckle. "Nothing so crude. It is an art most often referred to as phagewar."

"Never heard of it." He began scanning Fist's extremities, the wasted limbs under the black cassock thin sticks vined with blue-black veins.

"What a pity. It is a lovely combination of the most effective elements of psychological and guerilla warfare, covert action, intelligence-guided subversion, terrorism, sabotage, propaganda, disinformation, and brainwashing. It is war fought without an army and prosecuted from within. Many of its stratagems are modeled on that splendidly successful, highly adaptable, and wholly admirable creature, the virus. I was—and remain—one of the top theorists and practitioners of this art. Remember the Martian Rebellion against UNSRA? I was the architect of its defeat. After that I went freelance. Undergound, really. You would find my real name turning up quite often in certain *sub rosa* literatures."

"A real Renaissance man," Marchey mumbled.

"Renaissance is rebirth, my dear doctor. You are more right than you know." He chuckled at some private joke.

"Anyway," Fist continued, "that life grew tiresome after a while. The governments and MuNats I worked for were reaping what I sowed, and even what you would call the worst of them had these archaic compunctions that prevented me from implementing my sharpest-cut plans. Then there was the growing temptation to bite the fat soft hands that fed me only scraps. So I decided to seek an out-of-the-way place to contemplate my arts and exercise them as I saw fit. A laboratory, if you will, complete with human rats."

Marchey had gone on to scanning and palpating Fist's sunken chest. The combination of the old man's sick pride in his work and what he was finding put a grim frown on his face. "Here," he said heavily, "on Ananke."

Fist nodded. "Just so. The Immanuel Kindred showed me the light, so to speak. They believed that man was made in God's image, and so remaking space in man's image served God. Isn't that a lovely sentiment? They were friendly, open-minded, tolerant, trusting, pacifistic, and, most importantly, industrious. They worked twice as hard as the wilders, believing they served a higher goal."

He sighed, tipping his free hand. "So many systems fail for lack of initiative. Their childish religion offered me possibilities far beyond what I could get from simply co-opting the politics of this place."

"So you took over the Immanuel Kindred," Marchey said to prove that he was still listening. This was nothing that he wanted to hear, but the more he knew, the better his chances. Moreover, the vague outline of an idea had occurred to him while he was examining Fist. A possible way out.

Fist showed him a sharkish smile. "I ate them *alive,* hallelujah and amen! Then I began turning them into something useful while bringing the wilders into the fold. On their knees, of course."

"You did this all by yourself?"

"I was a wolf among sheep. Oh, I had a mercy to

do the cruder bits of wet work. A Shock-trooper who'd killed an officer, deserted, and gone renegade."

Marchey looked up, confused. "Scylla?" There were female Shock-troopers, but she seemed too young.

The old despot's bubbling laughter made Marchey shiver as if ice water had been dribbled down his back. "My angel? Isn't she a lovely thing? But no, she came later. The mercy was an expendable who finally met his defining fate. Although you could say that the best part of him lives on to this day."

"Scylla's exo." Marchey stepped back. The woman inside that dead man's battle armor didn't even know it was machinery. As he had guessed before, she was just one more of this creature's countless victims.

"Exactly. Why have you stopped examining me?"

Time to bite the bullet. "I've learned all I can externally. Now I have to go inside." He already had a pretty good idea of what he would find. If he was right, he might just have a chance after all. Besides, before he could work as a Bergmann Surgeon Fist had to be—

—unconscious.

Those rheumy eyes brightened with interest. "Ah, now you perform the uncanny procedure which has made your kind outcasts among your small-minded fraternity. I can hardly wait to see you in action."

Marchey sighed. "Then we have a problem. You have to be unconscious for me to work." He'd wondered what was going to happen at this hurdle; it was hard to imagine Fist giving up control for even a moment. But he must have known he'd have to.

"Oh yes, the sacred rituals of Bergmann Surgery." That skeletal face took on a crafty look. "Tell me, does the name Dr. Keri Izzak ring a bell?"

"Yes." Reluctantly.

"Who is she?" Fist prompted sweetly.

"She—she's a Bergmann Surgeon, like me," Marchey answered unhappily, feeling new tentacles of cold trepidation curl through him. Fist's knowing Keri's name couldn't mean anything good.

"Not anymore. The lovely Dr. Izzak no longer practices your branch of medicine." He chuckled. "Or breathing, for that matter. About a year ago I had her kidnapped and taken to a quiet place on Earth. There she was subjected to some tests of my own devising. It was a tawdry business, and cost me a considerable sum. But I think it was money well spent. And she allowed me to prove a theory of mine."

The cold was all through him now. *Keri dead?*

He found his voice. "Theory?" he croaked. *Keri dead to prove a theory?*

Brother Fist wagged a bony finger at him in admonition. "You mustn't forget that I am a scholar. A scientist. I started getting sick about three years ago. So I began learning everything I could about you people and your specialty—as you well know, it's the most advanced form of medical technique presently available. Would you care to guess what I found?"

Marchey shook his head, both unwilling and unable to guess.

"A blind spot in the data. Something so simple that it has been overlooked all these years. It looked promising enough to be worth spending some of the credit my flock has so generously provided me on having a Bergmann Surgeon kidnapped and taken someplace quiet so I could put my conclusions to the test."

Fist paused a moment to make sure Marchey was getting all this. The shocked, sick look on his face said that he was.

"Dr. Izzak had the honor of being the subject of the tests. Unfortunately, she soon understood what I was trying to prove. Such a bright woman. I had to dispose of her—and the hirelings who tested her, of course—to protect what I had learned."

"You disposed of her," Marchey repeated tonelessly, unable to accept the offhanded way Fist had said it. Like her life had no more value than the wrapper around a stick of gum.

Fist shrugged. "I suppose it was wasteful, but I dared not try to bring here all the way out here. Too risky." He gazed at Marchey, a malicious sparkle in his eyes. "Don't look so crestfallen, Doctor. Rest assured that Dr. Izzak is still doing her part to hold up the traditions of medicine. As I understand it, she's part of the concrete footers under a new hospital complex in Djakarta."

Marchey absorbed this final hideous detail in silence, feeling utterly lost, weak, and doomed, as if buried up to his nose in concrete himself.

Fist cocked his head and adopted a pedantic tone. "Tell me, Doctor, what happens after one of your patients wakes up?"

"They remember," Marchey answered, his voice drained of all emotion. "They have nightmares. Any patient who sees me afterward becomes acutely hysterical. In the beginning we had several patients nearly die of fright. One actually did, though we managed to revive him."

Brother Fist clucked his tongue. "Not the basis for a very good doctor-patient relationship, is it? Such a shame that you're not equipped to properly savor terror. Think how different your life would have been if you were! But I digress. Your patients must be unconscious while you work. Why?"

"In many cases they are that way to begin with, and most surgery is easier to perform on a nonresponsive patient. For the others we soon learned that what we do, and how we look and act in our working trance is so frightening that it's easier that way."

"So I've seen. One of my assistants had to be kept from shooting the late Dr. Izzak. A devout Catholic, he thought she was possessed by Satan. This extreme deep trance state you work in. Is it absolutely necessary?"

Marchey frowned. "Absolutely? I'm not sure."

"Hazard a guess."

"Well, the trance guarantees total concentration. When you first start out you need it to maintain your limb image." A shrug. "I guess that technically I might be able to get by in a lighter trance now, but going

deep helps shut out the reactions of the other medical
people, and keeps me from getting too attached to the
patient. But I don't see—"

"Of course you don't," Fist replied archly. "No one
did until *I* came along." He looked enormously
pleased with himself. "It's really quite a wonderful
thing, the way your life has been made so needlessly
miserable. The irony is even more delicious because
you'll never get to use what I've learned on anyone
but me."

There was no way for Marchey to miss the implied
message that he would never leave Ananke alive. But
at that moment that didn't matter. Fist was telling him
that there was a way around the Nightmare Effect.
All he could think was: *What did we miss? What did
we overlook?*

"That's it, *think*," Fist whispered. "It's in the air
before you. Seize it."

Marchey didn't need him to push. His mind was
working furiously, going over the hints he'd just been
given, trying to put them together into the answer that
had eluded them for so long.

"You—you're saying that if the patient is
conscious . . ."

An encouraging nod. "And?"

"And . . ." He racked his brain, his thoughts going
in circles until they tripped over the obvious. The
blood drained from his face. It was *too* obvious—
wasn't it?

He said it out loud, trying it on for size. "And I do
my work in the lightest possible trance . . ."

Brother Fist nodded approvingly, as if he were a
student who had given the correct answer to a difficult
question. "Bravo, Doctor! You knew all along that
your tightly focused concentration creates psychic
scarring on a mind made especially impressionable by
unconsciousness. What you failed to deduce was that
the problem could be remedied by two simple changes
in *modus operandi*."

Marchey sagged inside. It couldn't be that simple.

It just *couldn't*! That was as simple and obvious as antiseptic procedure, as manual CPR, as the Heimlich maneuver—

—the oldest of which had been in use for just over two hundred years. The others were even newer than that; relatively recent innovations in the long history of medicine. It made perfect sense, and its very simplicity was what had made it so elusive.

He felt his pulse quicken. If this was true—

Everything would change.

No, not everything. The fear and mistrust and despite of other medical professionals would probably remain. He would still be regarded as a lunatic who had willingly mutilated himself to become some sort of bizarre faith healer. That opinion was too deeply entrenched to be changed quickly, if at all.

But he would no longer be forced to work on a blurry succession of faceless, senseless, unplugged meat machines who would remember him after only in their nightmares. He would be able to look patients in the eye before and after his work was done. He would be able to see them smile, see tangible proof that the price he'd paid had been worth it after all.

And that would make all the difference in the world.

"You must be eager to begin, Doctor." Brother Fist purred, wrenching Marchey back to the here and now. "You want to know if this will work or not, don't you?" It was not a question.

Marchey's silver hands closed into fists. He nodded. *Yes, I have to know.*

A moment later he understood just how steep and high the walls of the crucible were built. The creature that called itself Brother Fist had known all along that he would treat him, if not for sake of his Oath or for fear of Scylla, then to see if his deepest desire was truly within his grasp.

Now that it was, and the moment of wonder had passed, he realized that Fist had turned the gift into garbage—if you could call something purchased with the life of a friend a gift—even as he gave it. There was no way for Marchey to use this to heal him and ever feel clean again.

Fist would methodically strip him of everything he loved and believed. He would probably keep him alive to be his personal physician, and to torment by forbidding him to treat those of his subjects who needed and deserved his services. That would be entirely in character.

He found himself pitying the people of Ananke more than ever. In less than an hour Fist had turned him into a helpless puppet, so entangling him in his webs that there seemed to be no way he could ever get free again. They had endured nearly a decade of his merciless machinations.

The old monster was more than a mere madman, more than another tinpot tyrant. He was like some awful destroyer from myth. A Shiva, destroyer of worlds. A gorgon, whose gaze was death. A brilliant, malignant Midas whose very touch spread corruption and ruin. A Circe who warped innocent beauty into monstrosity, just as she had when she turned Scylla—

Scylla. The fair maiden turned into a monster.

Marchey's mood had been plummeting like a sparrow sideswiped by a supersonic fighter, the ground rushing up at it while tumbling helplessly end over end. But the thought of Scylla put air of possibility under its wings.

What and who had she been before Brother Fist laid his foul hands on her? Could some fragment of that lost soul still remain behind her horrific mask? Was there any way to reach her?

It was only the flimsiest straw of possibility, but there was nothing else within his grasp.

He remembered what she told him. *Even if you are alone with him, I will know what you say and do.* Was she listening? Hearing all this?

"Yes, I'm ready," he said slowly. "But old habits die hard. I want you to talk to me while I work."

"And what shall we talk about?" A death's-head grin. "Would you like to hear how Dr. Izzak died?"

"Not that," he answered curtly. The mention of Keri's death brought back the feelings of hopelessness and defeat he was struggling to rise above. He tried to make his voice flat, uninterested. "Tell me about Scylla."

Brother Fist settled back in his throne, hands in his lap still wrapped around the gun. He nodded, looking pleased. "Now there's a wonderful, heartwarming story. A veritable fairy tale! In some ways she's my most interesting creation."

Scylla's attention narrowed at the mention of her name, her blood pounding in her ears.

The talk about trances and the rest meant little to her. She had only half listened, her mind still reeling from the new version of her Master's advent on Ananke. One day-for-night different than the one she knew.

Could it . . . possibly be true?

If her Master, the font of all truth could lie about who and what he was, then how could she know truth when she heard it? Furthermore, if his being God's Chosen One was a lie—

—was *she* a lie?

Living a lie?

A living lie?

She shook her head. "No," she whispered, trying to push it all away with that one single word.

She *knew* that Brother Fist had been sent by God to lead them into the grace of perfect faith and righteousness. Knew it like she knew her own name and face.

She was His angel. God had made her to serve Him.

She sought her reflection in one of the screens. There was proof of this truth. Her very form was gilded with Heaven's power to make her a living instrument of obedience. Her might was an angel's might. She had been brought down for the express purpose of protecting God's Chosen One, and to chastise the faithless and punish the sinful. She knew this the way she knew she needed air to breathe; it was obvious and undeniable.

But—

Why did the story her Master told Marchey have this deeply resonating ring of truth? Why had it set loose what seemed to be remembrances of things she had never seen, of faces, of feelings, of frozen moments from a life she had never lived?

Why did her mind keep coming back to the hazy haunting sense image of a voice that might have been her own screaming, of a woman's face filled with despair as she was dragged away by something so bright that it hurt the eyes. A blank spot, then that face again, crying, pleading, begging her not to—

—not to . . .

The fragmented memory ended there, like a high, crumbling cliff edge poised over an abyss of deepest darkest horror.

Brother Fist began to tell a story. Her story. The story of her genesis. And the angel Scylla hung on his every word, seeking and dreading revelation.

"I had this place fairly well in the palm of my hand, but knew I would continue to need an enforcer. Unfortunately my pet mercy already had too much power for his own good or mine. Worse yet, he was beginning to get ideas. So I—"

The old man paused to give watching Marchey his full attention. He had waited a long time for this moment. Hopefully not too long.

Marchey ignored him. He stood before a high table, sleeves pushed back to his biceps, his gleaming prosthetics crossed before his chest. He began to breathe deeply, eyes closed, effortlessly sliding into that old familiar *pranayama*. His hands fluttered like silver doves in rhythm with his breathing. The grim expression darkening his face faded as he centered himself.

But instead of letting himself sink into that subterranean state in which he usually worked, he kept himself at what felt like a usable higher level. The rim of the deep cold well.

His eyes opened. There was a nagging urge to sink deeper, down to where habit told him he should go. He ignored it. Bending at the waist, he rested his arms on the table, palms up, hands still and sleeping. Reclosing his eyes, he took a deep breath and *let go.*

Breathing a sigh of what might have been pleasure, he straightened up and stepped back. His prosthetics remained on the table, inert and lifeless. The silver plates capping his stumps just below the elbows gleamed like mirrors.

He felt relaxed, oddly detached. In deep trance he'd always felt like the beam of a surgical laser, a straight hot true line of will so potent and tightly focused that neither emotion nor personality could fit into its narrow bandwidth.

This was like being in that state between sleep and wakefulness. For the moment, he was at peace. He turned toward his patient-to-be, a bemused expression on his face.

"Talk, old man." Speaking in trance was a new thing. His voice came out as a raspy whisper. He held his invisible hands up as if after scrubbing for surgery, feeling faint air currents slide through his fingers like silk. That indescribable sensation of being *able* glittered clear and bright as a diamond inside him.

Brother Fist blinked up at him uncertainly, then recovered his composure by tightening his grip on his weapon. He kept it trained on Marchey's belly as he drew near, a single slight tremor the only betrayal of his apprehension.

"Where was I?" he muttered. "Oh yes, I needed someone I could trust implicitly. One of the last holdouts was a Kindred named Anya. She had a daughter named Angel. I took Angel hostage. The girl had a birthmark on her back. When I sent it to Anya all rolled up and wrapped with a pretty pink ribbon she caved in." He snickered. "Of course my telling her that she would next receive the girl's fingers and toes strung together like pearls may have had some influence on her decision.

"Anyway, Angel's name made me think. I had set myself up as the Chosen of God, sent to rule and save them. I needed an enforcer I could trust. What would make a more fitting flunky than a Guardian Angel?"

Marchey leaned over Brother Fist and *reached,* the silver plates of his truncated arms stopping a handspan from the old man's sunken chest.

Fist licked his lips, his yellow eyes focused on Marchey's face. He knew that Marchey was reaching *inside* him, immaterial hands slipping through the heavy fabric of his cassock, through skin and muscle and bone as if they were not there. He knew all about Bergmann Surgery, about how those abandoned silver arms were nothing, even though they had come to symbolize his misunderstood specialty; it was their being put aside that had meaning. They were but a symbol of the flesh and bone each Bergmann Surgeon had sacrificed. He knew how a surgeon's hands are everything, and how Marchey and his compatriots' voluntarily having their own amputated had been the first deep cut of their severance from the rest of the medical community. He knew other things as well, things unknown and unsuspected by even the head of the Bergmann Institute.

Brother Fist smiled to himself. He was well aware of how vulnerable he was at that moment. Marchey could be holding his beating heart in his hands, with only the Oath he had mocked keeping him from turning to dead meat in his chest. The risk was small, but delicious, and the irony pure delight.

He felt no pain. The only sensation was a faint soothing warmth drifting gently through his insides. He returned to the telling of Scylla's genesis, to add another pleasure to this moment.

"So I turned Anya's daughter Angel into my angel. I tore her mind down and rebuilt it to my specifications. There was a doctor here. I made him imp the eye that lets me see what she sees, file and bond her teeth so she could bite a steel bar—to say nothing of an arm or leg—in half, then install her in my mercy's exo. He didn't need it anymore." He chuckled darkly. "Someone gassed him like a cockroach while he was sleeping."

Marchey changed position, his hypersensitive urfingers tracing the convoluted skeinings of his patient's nervous and circulatory systems upward. Toward the head. Toward the brain. A tight-lipped, disapproving frown shadowed his face.

Form V or mimetic cancer had turned the old man's thoracic area into a metastatic jungle of black-flowering malignancies. Lungs. Liver. Spleen. Stomach. Kidneys. The list went on and on.

"I turned her into the perfect enforcer and body-guard. She doesn't *believe* she is an angel, she *knows* it. Her certainty is absolute and unshakable. Every glance in the mirror confirms that certainty. I was the one who tattooed her face, by the way. A most enjoyable art form, in that it is the canvas and not the artist that suffers. Her loyalty is absolute. She will disbelieve her own senses before she doubts me or my orders."

He had to pause for breath. For the last few months he had not been able to get quite enough air.

"As for the name Scylla, that was a private joke only I was properly equipped to appreciate. When she was ready, I tested her. The first two tasks I gave her were simple. First I had her kill the doctor who made her what she was. Slowly, and with a certain bloody flair. Then I had her kill her own mother."

Marchey shook his head, displeased. One of Form V's mimetic variations was vascular. It insinuated itself into the structure of the patient's veins and capillaries, replacing healthy cells and mimicking their function. To destroy or excise it would cause vascular collapse.

That was what it had done inside Brother Fist's cranium. The old monster's brain was as rotten and tumorous as the abominations it housed. Remove the cancer and he would begin hemorrhaging in literally hundreds of thousands of places.

As Marchey explored the damage, some mental subsystem heard the story of how an innocent girl had been warped into a monster and felt sorrow. Another felt relief that there was almost no chance he would be able to perform a self-damning healing. But for the most part he was in the position of a fireman who has arrived on the scene only to find the house he is supposed to save already completely engulfed in flame.

Brother Fist could not resist fondling the grim bones of his works. "You should have seen it. The expression of shock and horror on her mother's face was one of the most exquisite things I have ever seen. She recognized her child. She wept. She pled. She cried Angel's name, but it meant nothing to my creation. Scylla flayed—"

The rest of that grisly description was blotted out by a wall-shuddering reverberating boom, deafening as the thunderclap riding a lightning strike, deep and foreboding as the first trump of the Apocalypse. Books and art objects jittered from their shelves, crashing to the floor.

It came again, this time bringing a stony rain and the tormented shriek of rending steel.

Brother Fist stared past Marchey, his face turning an ashy gray when he saw Scylla standing in the ragged hole where once there had been an armored door.

She was an apparition to strike fear. Dust swirled around her like smoke. Her demonic face was twisted into a terrifying mask of hatred. Her angel eye was aimed at her Master with the deadly intent of a gunsight while her other eye burned with an angel's wrath and glistened with an angel's unshed tears.

"—no—" Fist protested, his voice coming out as no more than a cracked whistle. He tried to aim the Fukura at her, but Marchey was in the way. He pawed at the larger man desperately, but Marchey remained oblivious, all his attention was focused on the impossible task at hand.

"Fist." Scylla's voice was cold, empty. The sound of a soul scoured by vacuum. She stepped across the bent steel and stone rubble that had once been a heavily reinforced door, pieces crunching under her metal feet. "You. *Devil.*"

Scylla stalked toward her maker, her steps measured and balletic, the gleaming silver metal of her exo flowing liquidly with her every motion. She seemed to glow with gathered power and purpose; a radiant, sword-sharp instrument of vengeance cast in argent and set into unstoppable motion. She was beautiful, the way a panther closing in for the kill is beautiful—form, function, and a terrible grace welded into one deadly purpose.

Brother Fist was in no position to appreciate the breathtaking perfection of his creation as she came toward him. His panic-stricken squirming finally let him get the gun pointed at her. He wasted no breath in warning, instead grimly taking aim at her face and pulling the trigger. The weapon roared and bucked in his hand, wrenching itself out of his feeble grasp.

Scylla's amped reflexes let her swat the folded steel missile screaming toward her forehead aside like a lazy fly. One glassy eye in the wall of screens shattered explosively and went blind. She bared her sharkish teeth in something too bloodcurdling to be a smile.

"I don't know if I am really an angel anymore," she said as she came up behind the oblivious Marchey, her voice flat and hopeless. She shoved him aside, bowling him off his feet. Then she reached for her creator.

"—but I am going to send you to Hell anyway." Her curved talons hissed from their sheaths and locked into place with a menacing snick. Each one ten centimeters of diamond-hard, microtome-sharp neoceramic, the ones on her left hand still crusted with her own blood.

"One piece at a time."

She reached toward him to begin.

Brother Fist cringed back in his chair. But it wasn't

deep enough to let him escape his angel's deadly caress.

Marchey found himself facedown on the floor with only a hazy idea how he had gotten there. He got himself onto his knees and turned around in time to see Scylla wrap her taloned silver fingers around Brother Fist's throat.

"No! Don't!" he shouted, lurching to his feet. He launched himself at her and wrapped his arms around her to restrain her.

They sank through her body as if they weren't there. He stared down at his stumps in dumb surprise.

Brother Fist writhed and kicked his feet, the liverish slash of his mouth stretched wide in a soundless howl. His bony fingers clawed in futile desperation at the vise clamped around his throat. Wet, livid red spattered his black cassock as the talons sank like hooks into his wattled neck.

With her head cocked to one side, Scylla stared down at his face as if seeing him clearly for the first time and trying to figure out what he might be. The anger was gone from her face. All that remained was a lifeless, moon-cold landscape.

"Don't do it Scyl—*Angel*," Marchey crooned soothingly as he centered himself and brought to bear the invisible hands which made him what he was. He sank them into her back and moved them gently inside her, playing her nervous system like a harp as he cautiously, delicately, probed first this bundle of nerves, then that one.

"I have to." Her voice was perfectly flat, emotionless as the metal that sheathed her tightening hands. Her shoulders sagged, but her grip did not loosen. Fist's face was turning bluish gray, his eyes bulging in terminal disbelief. His hands scrabbled like dying crabs, fingers slashed and bloody from clawing at Scylla's talons.

"You don't," Marchey said softly, insistently. "He's beaten now. Let him go. Look at him. He's old. Sick.

He's *dying*. Form V cancer, that's what he has, and its so advanced that even I can't do anything to save him. Let that kill him. Don't let him make a killer out of you."

Scylla's one eyelid was growing heavy as Marchey gently stole her consciousness. It sagged at half-mast, like a pale flag of reluctant surrender.

"But I already *am* a killer," she whispered, as if confiding a shameful secret. Her voice had become like a child's, high and breathy, each word coming out more slurred than the last. "I killed my muh—muh—*mother*! I did! An' others . . ."

Tears finally spilled from her one green eye. Human tears, salted with the stinging realization of guilt and loss.

"Scylla did that, Angel," Marchey whispered soothingly. "You are Angel. You loved your mother. You would never hurt her."

"Not . . . me?"

"Not you, Angel. Sleep now, Angel. Let Scylla go. Let this sick old man go. I'll take care of him for you."

"I—"

"Please, Angel."

"I—"

"Please, honey. Please. Do it for me."

"For . . . you . . ." she whispered, slowly relaxing her grip. Brother Fist fell back, gasping and wheezing as he tried to suck air through his bruised and bleeding throat.

Scylla's arms dropped to her side. She sighed heavily. "I . . . so . . . tired. . . ."

"I know, Angel, I know. You can let it all go now. Sleep. I'll watch over you. Sleep."

For Marchey the human body was an open book, and he knew every page, every line. He thought he could safely try to manipulate her voluntary muscles now that all the fight had gone out of her. But it was a slow, subtle business. If he'd tried before, she would have resisted, and probably killed him for trying.

He changed the position of his spectral hands, making that bundle of muscles contract, those slacken, gently guiding her down to the floor. Her eye was shut now, her face smoothing as sleep overtook her. He followed her down, still crooning her name, still telling her to sleep, still promising he'd watch over her.

At last Angel was stretched out on the floor, all but asleep, the vengeful angel Scylla quiescent.

Marchey knelt there beside her, gazing down and trying to see the Angel face hidden behind the face of the angel. He bit his lip. *Maybe if I just . . .*

He reached out hesitantly, then slowly swept an invisible hand across her face.

The demonic mask vanished under his touch line by line, revealing the pale, smooth face of a rather pretty woman in her mid-twenties. Her expression softened, as if she somehow knew what he had done. Like a light kindled after a long night, a shy half smile appeared, curving her lips.

Marchey sat back on his haunches, sudden tears in his eyes, utterly undone. She was so beautiful that it was almost frightening.

He reached toward her again, drawn to touch that sweet face one more time.

He never got the chance. He heard a rustling sound and a muffled grunt behind him.

Fist! He'd forgotten about F—

Realization came too late. Brother Fist crashed onto him from above, landing on his back and nearly knocking him down.

Marchey threw his head back and screamed as Fist drove the knife clutched in one bony hand deep into his back. He twisted desperately, white-hot pain ripping outward along every nerve as the knife was wrenched out of his flesh.

Operating on blind instinct alone he reared back, bucking his attacker off before he could strike again.

He spun around, slamming his knee down on the knife arm, hearing a satisfying crunch as Fist's brittle bones broke under it. The old man hissed in pain, the knife tumbling from his fingers.

A guttural curse at his lips, Marchey thrust one immaterial hand into Fist's scrawny neck and squeezed. Those hate-filled yellow eyes bulged as if about to explode from their sockets. His seamed mouth stretched wide in soundless, breathless agony.

Marchey felt his lips peeling back from his teeth in a feral grin. His pulse hammered in his ears. Adrenaline surged through him in a fierce red tide, washing away his reason and leaving only the urge to expunge the life from the vile creature writhing under him. To avenge Keri Izzak and Angel and her mother and every one of the countless faceless innocents who had suffered at his hands, to—

His spectral fingers closed around the old man's spinal cord and he braced himself to rip it right out of his body.

He took a deep breath, gathering himself to—

—*to become a killer, now that he could be a healer again.*

He let out a furious, frustrated growl. Changing his grip, he expertly and ungently snuffed out Brother Fist's consciousness.

But not his life.

Marchey sagged back, panting for breath and shuddering from the effort it took to get his emotions back under control, sickened by how close he had come to committing murder.

After a minute he heaved himself to his feet, gasping as the pain from the gash in his back came rushing back almost hard enough to knock him down again. Biting back a moan, he closed his eyes and recentered himself, then reached awkwardly behind him and closed the wound. He didn't wipe all the pain away; the residual ache would be a reminder to be more careful.

Now what? he asked himself, looking around dully.

He found himself drawn back to gaze down at the sleeping form of Scylla.

No, he reminded himself, *Angel.*

She looked so peaceful. Almost, well, angelic.

But sooner or later she would waken. What then?

She would need help, probably more help than anyone else in this terrible place if she was going to overcome the things which had been done to her. The fairly straightforward task of releasing her from the prison of that exo would only be the beginning of a long, slow, painful process. She had been a thing for years, and it might take just as many years to make her whole again. He would have to make Brother Fist tell him exactly what had been done to her to improve his chances of reversing the damage.

Which brought him to the fallen tyrant. The old monster was neutralized for the moment but would have to be watched closely for his own safety and everyone else's. There had to be some way to keep him from being killed by those who had ample reason to want him dead, providing a chance to pry his secrets from him before he died.

Thinking about it now, Marchey realized that he might owe Fist something for proving his Oath's precept that even the meanest human life had value. Abomination that Fist was, he had found a way for the lives of the surviving Bergmanns to have meaning once more.

Maybe so, but he hoped that this unwitting good work tormented the miserable son of a bitch to his dying day.

He had to get word back to Sal Bophanza, let him know that at least part of the dream could be salvaged. Let the others know that the Nightmare Effect was no more.

There were so many things to do. All Ananke was in need of his services. First to mind were a handless man, a scarred and trembling woman, and a one-eyed boy under the shadow of death. After that, who knew how many others.

As daunting as that task appeared, he knew that the wounds of the flesh would be simply and quickly repaired compared to the wounds of the spirit. Those would take him the longest to heal.

Him.

It finally dawned on him that he was assuming that these tasks were his to perform.

His blood went cold, chilled by an icy wave of doubt.

Had it been too long since he'd been anything other than a meat mechanic? Had he lost his touch? Had the years of drinking and apathy and disconnection damned him to be what the last years had made of him, now and forever?

He reached up, invisible fingers tracing the shape of the silver pin hanging from his slashed tunic. First it had been his pride and his hope, then his curse and his shame, and in the end the marker for a dead dream.

And now?

Could it be that this was his chance to begin putting his life back together in a new way? Had he met his own personal knight in shining armor in the form of a silver angel named Scylla, her entering his life as irrevocably changing it as his entering Merry's had done?

Such thoughts made him uneasy. He knew where he was and what he had to do. That was enough for now.

A world of suffering waited to be eased now that the old order had come apart.

He went and put on his arms, the better to begin picking up the pieces.

3

Diagnosis

Today is the day.

Marchey didn't look particularly ready for, or happy about it, however. Slouched on the bench seat of his ship's galley nook, he had an elbow propped on the tabletop and his chin cupped in one silver hand. His second cup of morning coffee sat in front of him, missing no more than a single disinterested sip.

A pad rested on the plastic tabletop in front of him, its screen displaying the continuing-care files for the people he had been treating on Ananke.

The device might as well have been turned off for all the attention he was paying to it. His eyes were hooded, his gaze turned inward. His thoughts kept skittering away from the task at hand, skipping through the day ahead to circle—but never quite settle on—its end, like moths drawn to a light they dared not approach.

He found it hard to believe that three weeks had passed since he'd found an angel in his temporary room at Litman. More had happened to him in the short time since then than in the three years preceding.

So much had changed since that shanghai visitation. And yet so much remained fundamentally the same, locked imperturbably in old orbits and rolling inexorably onward as if nothing had happened.

There were times it seemed to Marchey that human existence—or at least his—was nothing more than a groove cut into a circular disc of time, just like on an antique phonograph record. 'Round and 'round you whirled, creeping incrementally closer to the music's end. While the groove did give your life direction, the walls of the track abraded, grinding you down so that you fit it perfectly, and nowhere else. Even if you could jump the track, it would be pointless; you would only set yourself back, or skip ahead to a place you were bound to reach sooner or later anyway.

He shook his head, feeling his mood grow even darker. Picked up his coffee, took a sip, grimaced. It had gone cold.

A glance at the time told him why. Almost half an hour had been spent just sitting there, not quite thinking about all the things trying to creep into his awareness, and yet not completely shutting them out. Contemplating his navel and finding only lint.

He turned the pad off and pushed himself to his feet. There were a hundred loose ends he wanted to tie up before the day was over. He couldn't afford to waste any more time sitting around playing hide-and-seek with the contents of his head.

Besides, you never knew when something might come up behind you, tap you on the shoulder, and say *You're it*.

A drink—even a small one—would have been of immense help, but he had given that up. So far, anyway. Work was the only escape he had left, even though that was at least half of the problem.

Today was the day. No way to avoid it any longer.

So he headed toward the small inship clinic aft of the main compartment, hoping that work would be enough to make him forget, at least for a little while.

*   *   *

"Open your hand again."

Jon Halen did as Marchey asked, still fascinated by seeing it work. He was stretched out comfortably on the soft padding of the shipboard clinic's unibed, its sides folded down to turn it into an examination table.

Jon loved it here in the clinic. It was so warm and clean and brightly lit. And the air! Sweet and rich as wine—not that some wine wouldn't be nice, too. Beer, even. After almost a decade of abstinence he wasn't inclined to be fussy.

The hand in question was a three-fingered claw, the dark brown skin mottled with the startling pink of new tissue. It opened like a mechanical grapple; the stubby, rigid thumb opposed by two short unjointed fingers.

"Close it."

The thumb and single-phalanged fingers came together like pincers, closing smoothly. Jon had gotten to the point where he no longer had to concentrate to make them work. He shifted his attention to Marchey's broad, craggy face, pursing his lips thoughtfully at the grim expression there.

He'd watched the man who had rescued them become progressively withdrawn over the past two weeks, starting just a few days after his arrival. Turning dour and aloof. Putting all the distance he could between himself and everyone else. It was like he'd started leaving them even before the orders came down telling him to move on.

Marchey didn't notice Jon's scrutiny. All his attention was focused on the results of his handiwork. He knew he should be pleased by what he had accomplished, but couldn't help thinking about what he could have done with proper supplies and more time.

"Hey, Doc, you know what I did last night?" Jon asked, a mischievous gleam in his brown eyes.

"What?" Marchey asked distractedly. It looked like he was going to have to admit that this was the best he could do under the circumstances. Jon's hand had been crushed several years before and healed into a lumpy knot with the unmovable stumps of two fingers remaining. Over the space of four sessions he had freed up the fingers, reshaped fused bone and useless cartilage into a movable strut, molded atrophied muscle and tendon around it. Then he had coaxed nerves back into the rebuilt fingers and new-made thumb, turning a gnarled and useless lump into something at least marginally functional.

Still it looked like something a five-year-old might squeeze from a lump of clay. He shook his head. To think he'd once thought himself something of a sculptor. The problem was that he could only work with what was there. He could redistribute bone and tissue, but not make it out of thin air.

"Pinched Salli Baber."

That got Marchey's full attention. "You what?" he asked, staring at Jon blankly, unsure he'd heard him right. His patient grinned up at him, tickled by the reaction he'd provoked.

"Pinched Salli Baber. Right on the ass."

Marchey couldn't keep a grin from creeping onto his own face. "You pinched her."

Jon chuckled and nodded, then demonstrated his technique. "My fingers. Her fanny. *Yow!* You shoulda seen her jump!"

"I'm sure she did."

Marchey continued to be amazed by how quickly the people of Ananke had begun the monumental task of putting all they had suffered during Brother Fist's rule behind them, struggling to rebuild something like normal lives.

Not that everything was sunshine and roses now that Fist's hold over them had been broken. A considerable number of them had been so deeply traumatized that they might never fully recover. A few extreme cases still hid in their cubbies like wounded animals, cringing back in terror when anyone came near. A handful of others drifted continually through the cold, dim tunnels like blank-eyed ghosts, lost now that an iron hand no longer shaped every aspect of their existence.

Yet somehow the majority of them had begun trying to reassemble the fragments of their shattered lives. That they could do so after all they had been through was a testament to the resilience of the human spirit.

Some were more resilient than others, taking it on themselves to help the rest. People like Mardi Grandberg and Elias Acterelli, a former nurse and an ex-army medic, together helping him set up a make-shift hospital and institute a rudimentary health-care system. Raymo LaPaz, working day and night to coax more than the bare minimum out of Ananke's neglected life-support system. Jimmy and 'Lita Chee and their crew, trying to revive the long-disused hydroponics setup.

Hands moving again, helping and healing. And behind all of those projects and a dozen others like the mainspring of a multifaced clock was Jon Halen.

He had to be the strongest and bravest person Marchey had ever met. His wife and two daughters were dead. Forced labor in the mines had cost him both hands and a leg. He had been one of the discards working in the landing bay when Marchey had arrived, toiling away until the too-thin air and hypothermia killed him.

Yet within hours of Fist's fall he had begun hobbling tirelessly through the tunnels on his homemade crutch. Spreading the word that they were free at last. Reassuring them that this was the beginning, not the end. Cracking jokes. Chivvying others into motion, into action. Reaching into some deep inner reservoir and pulling out optimism, enthusiasm, and humor, then spreading them like a balm.

Jon had made sure that everyone had something to do, just mentioning that this or that needed to be done and making it sound like no one else could do the task. He'd assigned care of those worst off to those who had fallen into listless apathy, giving them a purpose to cling to, keeping them too busy worrying over another's welfare to dwell on their own misfortunes.

Before the end of the first day he had come to Marchey with a priority-indexed list of those who needed medical attention. When asked where he had learned triage, Jon had smiled and said that he had used the big fancy setup in Fist's quarters to do it for him, punching the data in one key at a time with a stylus he'd had someone tape to his useless hand because the machine refused to accept voice commands without a passphrase.

His own name had been on the list. Dead last.

Marchey had moved him up, and begun trying to shape a hand out of the ruin at the end of his right wrist. Now he was using those new fingers to cop a feel. Halen was some piece of work, no two ways about it.

Nor was he content with being just a patient. Marchey had managed to keep everyone on Ananke pretty much at arm's length. Everyone but Jon, that is. He kept waltzing past Marchey's guard like it was a fence with a ten-meter hole in it, slyly slipping bonds of friendship around him every chance he got.

"You know what that means, don't you?" Jon asked.

Marchey scratched his chin. "You're getting, um, horny?"

Jon's grin spread even wider. "Well, that too—and the look Salli give me makes me think I mightna be the only one." He grabbed the side of the table with his pinching equipment and levered himself around so he was sitting up, his good left leg dangling over the edge, the stump of his right braced off at an angle. His left arm, which ended just short of where his wrist should have been, rested in his lap.

Now he was eye to eye with Marchey. He held up his new hand between them. "Pretty damned ugly, in't it?"

Marchey had to agree. "Yes, and I'm sorry, but—"

"But *nothin',*" he stated flatly, looking Marchey

straight in the eye. "It mightna get me a job modellin' jewelry, but as far's I'm concerned it's *beautiful*! Have you got any idea how great it is to be able to hold a cup? To use a comp again?" Mischief crept back into that gaunt face. "Hell, Doc, do you know how wonderful it is to be able to pick your pluggin' nose when you needs to?"

"Well, I've heard . . ." Marchey answered, trying to keep a straight face, but failing miserably.

"It's a top-shelf experience," Jon assured him. His expression turned serious, showing something of the sharp-witted intensity he kept hidden behind his amiable grin and Belter's slur most of the time.

"When you come here, all I had was this big lump at the enda my arm. It hurt so bad all the time I used to think about stickin' it in one of the smelters to be rid of it. If that killed me, well, I could live with that. But I didn't, and now I'm glad. I've got me fingers again. The pain is gone. I can touch and hold and feel things. I can even grab Salli's ass and feel somethin' like a man again."

He tapped Marchey's chest with a stubby finger. "When you took Fist off'n our backs I kind of woke up, looked around me, and figured maybe I could do a little somethin' about our situation. Start fixin' some of the damage. So that's what I did. But I never once thought anythin' could be done with the mess at the enda my arm. I planned to just go on doin' my best with what couldn't be changed."

His voice dropped lower. "But you looked at it and saw somethin' I didn't. Saw that somethin' better might be made from it. I might've seen it myself, but I'd gotten resigned to it bein' the way it was, and it never occurred to me that I oughta think about it any differenter way."

He let his hand drop. "There's somethin' to be learned from that," he concluded, watching Marchey's face expectantly.

"It proves you don't know diddly about reconstructive surgery, Jon," he said, intentionally missing the point.

A flash of disappointment crossed Halen's face, then he shrugged and smiled. "I guess I surely don't." He slid off the table and onto his good leg. Marchey handed his crutch to him, then walked him to the clinic's door.

"By the way," Jon said with contrived disinterest, "You're sayin' good-bye to Angel before you leave, an't you?"

Marchey had expected him to bring this up sooner or later. Halen had been inordinately interested in his relationship to Angel from the very first. Not that there was one.

"Yes," he replied shortly. "Now you keep exercising that hand. Continue taking the Calcinstrate to build up bone mass."

"Butt out, in other words." Halen grinned disarmingly. "Hey, I can take me a hint, even if you can't." He limped on across the main compartment toward the airlock. "Wouldn't want to rub you the wrong way."

"More to the point," Marchey called after him, "don't you go rubbing *Salli* the wrong way."

Jon leaned on his crutch, looking back and leering. "Hell no, Doc! I plan to rub her the *right* way—providin' I haven't forgot how!" He waved his handless arm in farewell and continued across the main compartment and out the airlock.

Marchey went back to the console built in along one wall of the small clinic, shaking his head with amusement. He sat down, his smile fading. "Record update. Jon Halen."

"Ready," the comp replied.

"Halen's gains in finger strength and mobility have exceeded my expectations." Pinching Salli proved it. *Yow!*

"As noted before, all residents of Ananke are suffering from severe calcium leaching caused by inadequate diet and low gravity. In Halen's case, I had to redistribute bone for reconstructive purposes. The Calcinstrate is increasing bone density. At the present rate of accretion I should be able to begin building a second set of phalanges within another week—"

He paused, realizing what he had said. He would not be here in another week. It wasn't that he'd forgotten that fact; some traitorous part of his mind was still taking it for granted that he would finish the work he had started.

But it was not to be. MedArm was putting him back on the circuit. They said he had been here long enough.

He supposed they were right. Another week might allow him to give Jon those finger joints, but it would not let him do all that needed doing here. A year wouldn't be enough. It was the work of a lifetime.

It wasn't like he was abandoning them. MedArm had assured him that the medical help and supplies they needed would be sent soon. There wasn't much more that he could do until then anyway. His small inship clinic had never been designed to handle anything more than small-scale emergency work or the occasional single-patient transport.

He was out of most pharmaceuticals. The small bank of tissue cultures had been used up, and he lacked the equipment to grow more. He had no transplantable organs—not even such common ones as eyes, livers, hearts, and kidneys—and no temporary prosthetics. Requests through MedArm to the other hospitals and clinics in Jovian space had netted nothing yet. Not even regrets.

The emergency was over. He had stabilized the situation. None of the remaining tasks couldn't be done by others.

"Delete last sentence," he said gruffly. "Continue: It is my considered opinion that only plastic and orthopedic procedures be used on Halen's partially reconstructed hand, even though it might appear that more cosmetically correct results could be gained by full amputation and replacement. I believe he would refuse the latter course, anyway. This is not an irrational or neurotic response; he simply has a, ah, sentimental attachment to his hand.

"End update." *Let them figure* that *out.* "Close file."

There, he'd done all he could to look out for his patient. What Jon and the others needed now was a well-equipped team of specialists. Once MedArm got them on-site the people of Ananke would be in the best possible hands.

Just as whatever patient he was being sent to see would be getting the best help available to him or her. Ananke didn't really need a Bergmann Surgeon any longer, and this person, whoever he or she was, did.

He sat back, pinching the bridge of his nose and feeling a dull ache in his temples.

So why did he keep feeling so guilty about leaving? And in direct opposition to that, so relieved? And guilty about feeling relieved, and—

"Fuck," he muttered, leaning forward to open a storage compartment a bit above eye level. He stared at what was inside for almost a full minute before taking it out.

Just one. That's all.

He placed the bottle of vodka on the counter in front of him, a glass beside it. Creating a still life portrait of his existence before Ananke.

What's wrong with this picture? he asked himself.

That was an easy one. The bottle was still full.

The whole day had been a killer. Every one of the people he'd treated had asked him to stay. Some had asked him straight out, practically begging. Others, like Jon, had brought the subject up more obliquely. It felt like fingers and hooks being sunk into his skin in a thousand different places, trying to hold him here, to pull him toward the impossible.

Worst of all was how each and every one of them had been so damned grateful, their gratitude a sort of insidious reproach. After about the fifth one he'd had to bite back the urge to shout at them, to slap them back so things could remain on the safe clinical level where they belonged.

But he had gotten through it somehow. Now he just needed a little something to wash the taste out of his mouth. That was all.

He stared at the bottle, remembering how those first heady hours after Fist's fall had made him drunk on possibility. He'd let himself think. . . .

Marchey snatched up the bottle, face twisting into a bitter facsimile of a smile at his own naïveté. Giving up drinking had been a grand gesture. *I am whole again. I don't need this any longer.*

"I am full of shit," he muttered, pouring the clear truth into the glass.

He picked it up. The vodka sparkled with promise.

Finally being able to have contact with his patients had seemed like a wish finally granted by a suddenly benevolent universe.

For a few glorious hours, anyway.

But he had quickly found himself in the position of someone who, after years of wandering thirsty on a parched, endless desert, suddenly finds himself snatched up and hurled into the middle of a vast lake. It was no wonder he had begun to drown. There were too many of them, their need was so great, and each and every one wanted a piece of him.

It had been a sobering experience, making him step back and take a long hard look at his situation. The work still had to be done, but he had waded in only as deep as he absolutely had to, keeping his feet on the solid ground of detachment.

For a little while there he'd lost sight of who and what he was, but he'd come to his senses. He was still a Bergmann Surgeon. That meant sooner or later he would have to move on. Which was all the more reason to keep from getting too cozy.

The time to depart had come around again. It always had and always would. He reminded himself that he had left hundreds of places without a backward glance.

He brought the glass to his lips. Closed his eyes.

He'd be leaving this place, too. In just a few hours he would put the people who lived here behind him. Nothing to it. Like falling off a cliff.

Or a wagon.

The vodka went down easy. It brought tears to his eyes.

Angel strode along the gloomy tunnel. She was in a hurry, but made herself move slowly and deliberately. Some of the people she passed smiled at her. She smiled back, carefully keeping her mouth closed each time.

She had put in long hours of practice in front of a mirror to get it right. The face she saw reflected back was still a revelation. Her metal-and-glass angel eye still remained, but for the most part she saw the smooth white face of a young woman. This stranger in the mirror was *her*.

Slowly she had come to understand that it was a rather nice face. More than one person had even told her that she was pretty—though not the one she most wanted to hear say it.

Still, she had to be careful when she smiled. If she let her lips open, that exposed her teeth. They were *not* pretty. She now understood that they were not supposed to be. They had been filed to sharp points and capped with white and red ceramyl for the same reason her face had been tattooed; to help make her an object of terror and dread.

The trick still worked. Her teeth could turn her sweetest smile into something that harrowed up chilling recollections of Scylla, like skeletons buried under a thin layer of earth. She did her best to keep them hidden.

He had erased the Scylla face overlying her own with just a pass of his invisible hands. She had been as much asleep as awake, but she had felt it happen, felt it more acutely than anything else in her whole life. That touch had reached a place far below the surface of her metal carapace, deeper than her hidden skin, a secret place she had not even known she possessed.

All the terror and pain she had caused as Scylla could not be expunged so easily, or by another. She knew that. There were few certainties in this new life of hers, but that was one of them.

Not only did Scylla lurk behind her smile, waiting to show if she forgot herself, but her every thought and action had to be considered, guarding against lapses into Scylla-thought and reaction. The line between what she had been and what she wanted to be was fine, and oh so fragile.

There were times the task of rebuilding her life as Angel, and not the other, seemed impossible. Still wearing her angel skin—her *exo,* he called it—only made the task harder. As long as it was a part of her she could not help but remind both the Kindred and herself of what she had been and done to them.

She had awakened from the long dark dream that was life as Scylla to find herself not found, but lost. All she had known and believed had been cast into doubt. Bereft of purpose, and her identity in fragments, she felt like a creature trained to perform a task that no longer existed.

Now she knew that was exactly what Scylla had been—a monster created by a monster to unquestioningly carry out his monstrous acts. Not more than human, but less.

There was no way for her to know if the urge to serve, to be of use, that she found inside herself was something innate, or more of Fist's programming. In the end she decided that it did not matter. That was what she saw those she most admired doing, and to become a good person she must emulate good people.

Service gave her some renewed sense of purpose and a way in which to atone for her sins. The silver skin and sinew of what she had been made her better able to help repair some of the endless damage her former Master had wrought. It gave her a way to repay the Kindred for their forgiveness. A forgiveness she sometimes doubted she would ever deserve.

The payments were made by long hours spent doing the work of machines that had fallen into disrepair because Fist had decreed that all tools were to be locked away, being potential weapons and temptations to sabotage. Her exo allowed her to perform tasks which would have taken cranes or winches or twenty strong people. She became the engine powering the truckles that hauled the ores and ices to the processors. She became a human grabmaw, tearing away at Ananke's stony breast with her ceramyl-taloned hands, working as if it were her own sins she was rooting out of herself chip by chip.

She turned a corner, entering the wider main tunnel. Elias Acterelli trotted toward her, his short legs carrying him along at his usual breakneck pace. He had a bundle of blankets under one arm, a carry sack over the opposite shoulder, and three children hot on his heels. No doubt he was on his way to the crude hospital ward that had been set up in a former dining hall.

He slowed down and grinned at her. "Hi, Angel," he called cheerfully, brave or foolish enough to even pat her on the shoulder in passing. She smiled back, keeping her mouth closed.

Few others would do such a thing, perhaps fearing that touching her exo would somehow summon up Scylla like some terrible genie from inside her. The reaction of the children was more typical. They gave the silver-skinned ex-angel cautious smiles and as wide a berth as the tunnel allowed.

It was not that she did not want to be free of the armor in which she had been an unwitting prisoner. She hated it now. The gleaming biometal had gone from a source of pride to a mark of shame, tarnished by the blood of innocents and creaking with the memory of mindless cruelty.

At last she reached her destination, passing through the massive steel door that had once barred the way to the chapel and the chambers off it, including what had once been Fist's inner sanctum. Now it remained open wide, welcoming any and all back into the place which had been the center of the Kindreds' faith.

The chapel was one of the few rooms they had managed to complete before Fist's advent, the work of their finest artisans. Angel entered, sparing not a single glance at the radiant solar clockwork overhead or the intricately-set mosaic floor.

It was the altar table at the far end that had her whole attention. The webbed restraints that had once been bolted to it were gone now. She had torn them off herself. But bloodstains still darkened the scarred top of the white-stone slab, left there as a testament to those who had bled upon it.

A shudder passed through her. As always, the sight of the altar brought back memories of the "penances" she had meted out, and confessions she had extracted on it as Fist's punishing angel.

Although still in a hurry, she took the time to stop and kneel, her heart tightening in her chest.

In days since Fist's fall the altar had been quietly turned into a shrine to those who had been lost, lovingly created and tended by those who survived and remembered. A single precious real beeswax taper burned in a tall holder, its soft, lambent glow giving the objects spread across the bloodstained white stone the golden aura of cherished memories.

Indeed, that was what they were.

Dozens of flat and solido pictures of those who had died during Fist's reign of terror had been placed there. The faces were of every age and sex and color, each of them frozen in a moment from an innocent past. Scattered among them were other momentos. Locks of hair tied in bits of wire or ribbon. Wedding rings and inscribed bracelets. Lockets opened to show a face or faces that had been carried near the heart. Medals. A briar pipe with a well-chewed stem. A china bird with a broken wing. A pair of wire-framed eyeglasses, one lens cracked down the middle. An antique leather-bound Bible and a broken compad diary.

Dried flowers, their faded petals as fragile as the life that had once been in them.

The list went on, but of all the things that had been so loving placed there, she was always the most deeply touched by the saddest testimonials of all. These were toys that had outlived the children they had belonged to. There was an air of hopeless abandonment about them. The dolls and stuffed animals looked mournful, bereft, their staring eyes searching forlornly for the lost one who had loved them.

Angel blinked back a tear in her one green human eye. The blank-glass lens that replaced the other looked on with dry indifference.

There was little of her own childhood she could remember, no more than uncertain whispers. It had been torn from her mind and discarded as useless. Gone with her childhood were all but the most fleeting memories of her mother. The moment she remembered most clearly was the one she most wanted to forget, that moment when as Scylla she had killed her mother. She could recall only shards of that act, but they were vivid and sharp enough to cut her to the quick each time they surfaced.

Once she understood the purpose of the shrine, she had tried to find something of her mother's to put up there. After two days of fruitless searching she had given up, forced to admit that not a trace of Anya remained.

So she had made a vow that one day she would lay the silver skin of her exo down among the other offerings to the past. Until that time she would remember her mother and all the other dead by serving the living as best she could.

Angel raised her arms, holding her hands toward the altar, candlelight glinting off the polished metal. A mental flick of the wrist sent the ceramyl talons sliding from their sheaths. Try as she might, she could not entirely suppress the traitorous Scylla-thrill it set off.

"This is what I was," she said in a husky whisper,

addressing the dead gathered about her in the quiet chapel. "I still bear the mark of what I was, and it grows heavy on me. . . ."

She bowed her head, leaving the rest unspoken. There were some things she could not say aloud, and the deepest, most secret reason for wanting to shed the angel skin was one of them. Her mother and all the other dead knew what was in her heart, she was somehow sure of that. All she could do was hope they could forgive her for her selfish secret desires.

"I will never hurt one of yours again," she promised, retracting her claws. She gazed up at the altar, and speaking as if laying down Law to herself and whatever of Scylla remained inside, added, "I will never hurt anyone ever again."

She stood up, comforted by the renewal of her promises to them and to herself. Even so, she knew that in the end promises weighed no more than the breath on which they were spoken. That was one of the few truths she had learned from her old Master. Only actions had real weight; only the keeping of a promise had value or meaning.

Promises. They were holding her together and tearing her apart.

She had made a promise to prove that she was no longer a monster before she allowed herself to shed the skin of the one she had been. That promise had turned into an iron collar around her neck. Yet she could not bring herself to break it, not even now, when it looked like it might cost her release and acceptance and everything else she dared want for herself.

This seemed to be one of the many prices of becoming human.

Marchey did as much of his work as possible on his ship.

His main excuse was that his small inship clinic was better equipped than anything Ananke had to offer. While that was true, it wasn't the whole truth.

He felt safer there. More in control. It was his place,

it was where he belonged. At odd moments he thought about Ella locked away in a fortress of her own making, and found himself all too easily able to understand her fanatic reclusiveness.

Staying onboard also served to remind his patients that his stay was only temporary.

Still, he had to make rounds at the half-assed hospital he'd helped put together, and there were certain chores that had to be done in the office where the medicomp that had belonged to Ananke's former doctor had been set up.

There were no more patients to be seen that day. The end was in sight. All that remained was a bit of work in the office, his Final Appointment, and a last swing through the hospital. Then he could finally get the hell out of here.

"Dr. Marchey!"

It was a high, childish voice that called his name from somewhere behind him. He heard running footsteps, turned to see who it was.

Danny Hong skidded to a halt before him. Looking at him now, it was hard to believe that this was the same sick and frightened boy he'd seen when he first arrived on Ananke. His golden skin glowed with returning health. His straight black hair stuck up in every direction, as if set on end by all the energy inside. A white bandage covered the empty socket that had once contained the dangerously infected remains of one eye. A lopsided, long-lashed eye had been crudely drawn on the bandage with a black marker.

"Nice peeper, Danny," he said, pointing. "Did you draw it?"

"Yes sir. Well, Jimmy and 'Lita helped."

He nodded approvingly. "Good job. Pretty soon you'll get a real one."

Eyes had been on the list of needed tissues he'd sent to MedArm. There had been no way to save Danny's eye; gangrene had been too advanced. Even using conventional technique implanting a new one would have taken an hour at the most, but there had been none in his ship's small tissue bank. Nor had he been able to return sight to a woman who had been blinded by exposure to vacuum, or replace the steel-and-glass lens filling one of Angel's eye sockets.

The boy gave a squirming shrug, shoving his hands in his pockets. "I guess." He bit his lip, then squinted up at Marchey with his good eye. "I wish you didn't have to leave."

"I have to, Danny," he said gently. "There are other sick people who need me."

A glum nod. "I guess. I—well, I wanted to tell you a secret before you left. 'Lita said you can tell a doctor *anything* and it stays a secret."

"She's right. Secrets are part of our business. What's yours?"

Danny looked around to make sure they were alone, then lowering his voice to a whisper, said, "I know how to read and write, sir."

Marchey blinked in surprise. "Is that so?" He'd been expecting something more along the lines of an adolescent confession of confusing physical urges. Danny was about the right age for such things.

"Yes, sir. Brother Fist said we kids weren't s'posed to learn such stuff, that he and God would teach us everything we needed to know. But my mom, she taught me anyway. She made me promise never to tell anybody. She said it was our little secret. But now I guess it's okay to tell you, isn't it?"

Another of Fist's nasty little policies coming to light. Not that the old tyrant was the first god-pounder who preferred his flock to remain as ignorant as possible.

He bent down so that he and the boy were eye to eye. "It's okay to tell *everybody* now." He riffled the boy's hair. "God gave you brains so you could use them. Knowing how to read and write is a *wonderful* thing. It's something to be proud of, something you might even want to help teach the other kids."

Danny absorbed this solemnly. "Then it's not bad, not a 'bomination?"

He shook his head. "No, it's not. Let me tell you

something, Danny. Your mom was very wise and brave. Even though she knew it was dangerous, she passed on to you the most precious thing she possessed because she knew it was important. Saying that it was bad was the abomination."

Danny's mother had been dead for over a year, the boy all on his own at the age of thirteen and put to work in the mines like an adult. Jimmy and 'Lita Chee, their own daughter four years dead, had taken him in since Fist's fall. Families like this were springing up all over Ananke, like determined flowers sprouting from scorched earth.

"You should be proud of her and proud of yourself. Every time you read something you should remember her."

"I do. I read every minute I can." The boy hesitated, scuffing the ground with his toe, then peered at him slantwise. "I write stuff, too," he said quietly.

Before Marchey could ask what kind of stuff, the boy spoke in a rush, as if letting out something he'd kept bottled up far too long. Or getting it said before he lost his nerve.

"That's what I want to do when I grow up. I want to write about my mom. About what happened to her. About what happened to Jimmy and 'Lita and everybody else here. About how Brother Fist did such bad things to us. I want to write about you changing Scylla from an angel into our friend, and how that saved us all from Brother Fist. I want to make sure everybody knows about it, and if I can get it all written down just right, then nobody'll ever forget about my mom and everybody else, will they?"

Marchey stared at that small earnest face in dismay. He could see that the boy was frightened: of having said his dream out loud, of chancing exposing it to ridicule, of its sheer size and difficulty. But the boy's face was set with determination to achieve what he had set for himself in spite of his fear, in spite of everything. Like a mirror into the past, it reminded him of the burning sense of purpose he'd once had himself. To be a doctor. To be the best doctor ever. To do what other doctors could not . . .

What could he say? That the curse of humanity was forgetfulness, and history was nothing but generation after generation repeating the same mistakes? That idealism was the surest road to disappointment, and the higher you set your sights the more certain you were to fall short?

"I—" he said around the lump in his throat, "I think you're right. I also think your mother would be very proud of you. I know I am." He offered the boy one silver hand. "Good luck."

Danny shook it solemnly. His hand was small, but his grip was firm and sure.

Even though it was a constant reminder of a past she desperately wanted to put behind her, Angel had not been able to make herself give up her old cubby in a side room off the chapel. It was one of the few things in her life that had not been changed beyond all recognition by Marchey's arrival and Fist's fall.

She had another reason for keeping it. One darker and more complex, one that made her feel guilty and weak and unworthy.

Ashamed of what she was doing but helpless to stop herself, she crossed to the big multifunction communit at the end of the room. Trying to ignore the sense of sin she felt, she took it off standby and sat down on the end of her pallet, remote in hand and eyes on the meter-square main screen.

Then she began scanning through the hidden surveillance cameras, searching for Marchey the way she had once used them to sniff out indolence and blasphemy. Viewpoints bloomed and vanished in quick succession on the main screen, the tick of her thumb against the button the loudest sound in the room.

Finally, she found him approaching the door to the cubby he had been given, just down the tunnel from the makeshift hospital.

The pickup zoomed in until his head and shoulders

filled the screen. She glanced down at her hand, surprised to see one silver finger on the stud which had
called for the closeup.

She knew it was wrong to spy on him like this, but
could not seem to help herself. From the moment
when he had first touched her, first called her Angel,
she had been drawn to him. The pull was constant
and terrifyingly strong. It was like nothing she had
ever experienced, and far too powerful to be denied
by fear or shame.

Scarcely aware of what she was doing, she got off
her pallet and drifted closer to the screen.

Sadness whispered through her. He looked so tired.
There were bags under his eyes. His broad shoulders
were slumped as if his silver arms weighed a hundred
kilos each, and some vast unseen weight had been
piled on his back.

Angel automatically switched to the pickup inside
the cubby as he pushed through the door. She tabbed
the sound on. Now he was coming toward her, sitting
down, taking up a pad.

She watched him work, broad forehead wrinkled in
concentration and his voice a soft murmur. It wasn't
until her metal-clad fingers clicked up against the
smooth unyielding surface of the screen that she realized she had reached up to touch him. Trying to regain
that momentary contact, that scary and splendid connection, which had since eluded her.

"Angel?"

She jumped, the sudden, unexpected sound from behind her catching her so completely off guard that her
old angel-self responded reflexively. In the blink of an
eye she snatched her hand back and whirled around
to face the intruder, crouching down and preparing to
pounce. She bared her teeth, legs coiling themselves
to fling her across the room in a single bound, her
hooked fingers ready to sprout gleaming blades.

Her exo-accelerated senses gave her ample time to
recognize Salli Baber. To realize that there was no

threat. To understand that once again she had allowed
her old reflexes to betray her.

Salli's reactions only worked at normal human
speed. Even as Angel was untensing and beginning to
damn herself for her lapse, Salli was paling at the sight
she presented. Her mouth stretched into a frightened
O and the stack of folded clothing she carried went
flying from her hands like startled birds.

Angel compounded her first mistake with a second.
She saw Salli's legs start to fold under her and acted
instinctively. Her amped systems empowered her to
cross the room and catch the woman before she was
even halfway to the floor.

Her intentions might have been good, but fear of
the silver-skinned angel of vengeance had been so
deeply hammered into Anankeans' psyches that most
of them were still haunted by the stalking spectre of
Scylla in their dreams. Salli let out a strangled squeak
of terror and fainted dead away, her brown eyes rolling back into her head.

Angel stared down at the unconscious woman in
her arms for several long seconds, faced with further
proof of her own inadequacy. Shoulders slumped in
defeat, she carried Salli to her pallet and gently laid
her down on it.

Face tight with fury and shame, she shut off the
monitor, then rifled through her drawers in search of
a stim. Finally she found one, and trying to keep herself from thinking about how she had last used one
on a man who had passed out during an atonement,
pasted it on Salli's neck.

Then she stepped back out of Salli's line of sight,
hugging herself as she pensively watched over her and
waited for the stim to take effect.

Salli was a wiry, dark-haired woman in her early
forties. Like so many others, Fist had made her a
widow. Although of average height and fairly muscu-
lar, the baggy black coverall she wore made her look
smaller. Like everyone else, the years of Fist's rule

had left her painfully thin. No one got fat on two bowls of processed algae a day.

Her face was of the sort you would call handsome, good bones and too much character to be merely pretty. Her olive skin was almost completely smooth and unblemished now. Before Marchey had arrived and worked on her, the left side of her face had been twisted and ridged with rough brown scar tissue, a puckered hole large enough to let her broken teeth show through punched in one cheek. That whole side of her body had been similarly scarred, and her left arm had been weak and stiff.

Angel could not keep herself from remembering when Salli's accident had happened. An overage, undermaintained BoresAll head had exploded. One worker had been killed outright, decapitated by flying steel and stone. Salli had been standing a bit behind him, and so partially shielded from the blast by his body.

Fist had sent Scylla to check on Salli after her co-workers had carried her limp, bleeding body back into the living cubic. She had given them permission to remove the steel and stone splinters which had turned one side of her body to bloody meat, and at Fist's behest, given them a coagulant and antibiotic spray to use on her. This departure from the ban on secular medicine came about because Salli was their best surviving drill operator and Fist didn't want to lose her.

Nobody had mentioned the contradiction.

Nobody had suggested giving her any sort of painkiller. Not Fist, not herself, and least of all her comrades from the mines. They knew she was getting better care than most, and asking for such a forbidden thing would have earned them punishment.

Salli's head moved from side to side, as if denying wakefulness. Angel called her name.

The woman on the pallet moaned as the stim reeled her back to consciousness. Her head rolled in Angel's direction, and her brown eyes snapped open, bulging in terror as the fearsome silver afterimage burned into her retinas was replaced by the real thing.

"Forgive me—!" she cried, cringing back and flinging up her hands to ward Scylla off. As if that ever could have stopped her.

Angel hugged herself tighter, blinking her one green eye against the dampness she felt welling in it. "It's all right, Salli," she said soothingly, forcing the words past the constriction in her throat. "It's just me. Angel. Not Scylla. I will not hurt you."

"You won't hurt me?" Salli repeated in a small voice, sounding unconvinced. She peered past her upraised hands.

"I will never hurt anyone ever again," she answered with a quiet certainty. "I—I am sorry I scared you. You scared me, and I overreacted."

Salli's hands fell and she stared back in wide-eyed disbelief. "I scared *you*?" she said, surprise replacing her fear.

Angel forced a smile onto her face, carefully keeping her teeth hidden. "Startled me, anyway. I forgot you were coming." That last was half a lie; it was more a matter of someone else filling up every corner of her thoughts.

The other woman returned a tentative smile that let the knot in Angel's chest begin loosening. "I think maybe I better knock louder next time," she said with an uneasy laugh, sitting up and looking around. "I brought you some things . . ."

"I will get them." They were scattered all over the threshold where they had fallen. Angel went after them, careful to move slowly.

Salli was on her feet by the time Angel had gathered up the articles of clothing and carried them back.

"Thanks," she said. She selected one item, dropped the rest on the bed. "Let's see what we have here. I've had most of this stuff hidden away for years." She shook out the pair of pants she'd picked out, then held them up against Angel's waist.

"Too small." Salli tossed them aside, rummaged

around and found another pair. "Maybe. The color suits you." She put them aside for the final cut. Next she pulled out something small and sheer, looked at it, then at Angel's sexless, silver-sheathed body.

"I guess you don't really need panties, do you?" she said, chuckling as she tossed the silky undergarment atop the discarded pants. "Or a bra, for that matter. You could probably park an ore truck on them babies and they wouldn't sag."

Angel didn't know how to answer that. She watched Salli start pulling one item after another from the pile and measuring them against her. Before long she was chatting away as if nothing had happened, telling Angel about her first bra and her first pair of something called "crotchless panties" while she picked out things for her to wear.

Angel only stood there in wide-eyed dismay, stiff as a pot-metal mannikin. This was a lot more than she had bargained for when she asked Salli to help her dress like a regular woman for her final chance to see Marchey. All the different cuts and colors bewildered her. The rules for matching the various items seemed incomprehensible.

Getting the right things picked out would not be the end of it, either. Then she was going to have to ask Salli to help her put them on.

Rack her brain as she might, she could not remember ever getting dressed like a normal person. The girl she'd been before being turned into Scylla must have worn such things, but she couldn't remember it.

Marchey put the pad aside, his throat dry from almost an hour of straight dictation.

But he was done. The pad now contained the proper procedures for dealing with anything likely to come up with any of the patients he was leaving behind. The tap of a button copied it into the old Medicomp. He'd put new MedMems in both the pad and the Medicomp for Mardi and Elias to fall back on, but this would be faster and easier. All either of them would have to do was name the patient and his or her symptoms. The pad would search out the proper response and walk them through the correct course of action. It wasn't quite the same as being there, but it would have to do.

He settled back, taking a last look around the room. The Kindred had given him this cubby to use as a combination office and guest room just a couple days after his arrival. The rough-walled room contained the old Medicomp and chair along one side, and a bed at the far end. Along the other side they had placed a couch, table and chair set taken from Fist's chamber to give it a homey feel. It was supposed to be a place of his own here. They'd even put his name on the door, as if hanging out his shingle for him.

By then he had come to his senses enough to realize that he didn't belong here, and his stay would be temporary. There had been no polite way to turn it down, but he had used it as little as possible. The bed had never been slept in.

He poured a cup of water from the carafe at his elbow and took a sip. It was flat and tasteless. It eased the scratch in his throat, but did none of the things another sort of drink would do for him. A glance at the clock told him that the time for what he thought of as the Final Appointment had finally come around. Angel was due to show up any minute now.

Thinking about facing her only made him want a real drink all the more.

Just one more. That old familiar refrain.

Less than ten seconds' indecision passed before he reached toward his pouch for the small flask he'd brought with him in case he needed another shot of nerve tonic. No sense in letting such careful preparations go to waste.

Just as his hand closed around it he heard something thump against his door.

Angel stood before the door to Marchey's cubby, the present she had brought him clutched in one hand, the other poised to knock. She stood there like that for over a minute before she let her hand fall, admitting to herself that she had made a mistake.

She looked down at herself. The problem was with the clothes. She had worn a pair of coveralls once, using them to disguise her silver body when she had ventured into the steel corridors of the hospital wheel to kidnap Marchey. Fist had occasionally bidden her to wear a white ceremonial robe.

But all that had happened in another life. Those things had not been worn so that she might look like a normal woman. So she might look, well, *pretty*.

For all the life she could remember her silver armor had been enough. Never once had she felt a whisper of shame or self-consciousness. She hadn't even known that all the things which made her a woman were hidden under there.

Now she did know, and covering the places other women covered made her acutely aware of them, secret places that felt suddenly exposed by being doubly hidden.

All she had wanted to do was try to breach the wall *he* had thrown up between them, a wall that might as well have been built from meter-square blocks of nitrogen ice, it was so palpably cold and solid.

Scylla would have torn the wall down and forced him to acknowledge her. To Angel, it looked insurmountable.

In the beginning he had been so kind and warm. He smiled when he saw her, that smile making her feel like her insides were filled with warm syrup. He took time to talk to her, tried to make her laugh. He called her Angel, and when he said that name it made her want to be Angel more than ever.

Then suddenly one day the warmth and kindness were gone. It was almost as if he'd gone to bed one night as one man and woken up the next as a stranger.

From that moment on he had begun treating her with a brusque impatience that left her hurt and bewildered. He would grimace when he saw her, as if the

sight of her pained him, and speak only in monosylla-
bles, if at all.

Sometimes she thought that maybe he still saw her
as Scylla, as the monster who had threatened his life
and hurt him. Or maybe he was angry at her for refusing to let him release her from her exo. Maybe she
simply didn't deserve his attention. Hadn't earned it.
Maybe it was all that and more, each reason another
block in the wall.

When she had found that he was going to leave,
she had thought she was going to die. She had gone
to him, and though she had wanted to beg him to stay,
she had only asked that he give her an hour of his
time before he left. He had grudgingly agreed, and
she had kept herself away from him since then so that
he would not have an excuse to change his mind.

Now that fateful hour had come around, and with
it her last chance to break through. She had thought
that maybe if she looked different he might see her
differently. But this was not going to work. The blouse
and slacks were only making her so nervous that she
was sure to make a fool of herself.

So she put his present on the floor and began trying
to figure out how to remove the blouse. She remembered that it had fastened up the back—for reasons
Salli had not been able to make entirely clear. She
reached behind her and began fumbling at the buttons.

Either the exo limited her range of motion just
enough to make the operation impossible, or dealing
with things such as pearl buttons was an arcane, ac-
quired skill. No matter how she contorted herself, she
could not get even one button loose. Finally she abandoned that approach and tried to pull the blouse off
over her head.

Only to get hopelessly stuck when she had it half
on and half off. She wriggled and writhed in rising
desperation, face trapped in a fold of silky cloth, unable to see, afraid she would tear the fragile thing,
and wishing she had learned to curse.

Now in full-blown panic, she shuffled and shucked

and spun, only succeeding in kicking over the present she had brought.

She heard it skid across the stone floor. Her heart froze when it clunked up against the foamstone door panel. Moments later she heard the door open, followed by the surprised sound of a sharply indrawn breath.

Her first impulse was to shred the source of her humiliation into a thousand pieces as she ran away to hide. But this was her last chance to see him, and she couldn't bring herself to throw it away.

Angel made herself stand there, her hidden face red with shame as she waited for whatever happened next.

The sight that greeted Marchey when he opened the door stopped him cold. His eyes went wide as he saw Angel there in the tunnel, apparently being eaten by a shirt.

He almost laughed, but caught himself in time. After a moment he figured out what had probably happened. Like a child unskilled in dressing herself, she had gotten tangled up in the blouse that she was trying to either take off or put on.

Doing his best to keep a straight face, he went to her aid. "On or off?" he asked gently.

"Off!" came the muttered, muffled reply.

"Off it is." He didn't have any trouble getting it unbuttoned and peeled off her, even though it had been several years since he had helped a woman undress. There was something subtly erotic about it.

Or maybe not so subtle. When he stepped back it seemed like a good idea to hang on to the shirt and hold it in front of him.

Angel looked miserable, her pale face pinked with embarassment. She stood there with her head bowed, staring at her feet as if trying to figure out how to kick herself.

Marchey's heart went out to her. He was all too aware that she was caught somewhere between childhood and womanhood, with a stiff dose of delayed adolescence thrown in to make things even more difficult. Added to all that was her hardly knowing how to be a person.

The only way out of it was to pretend that nothing had happened, a coping mechanism that was hard to beat for all-around usefulness. So he bent down to retrieve the object on his doorstep. It was obviously a bottle, carefully wrapped in a piece of cast-off insulating foil. "For me?"

Angel nodded, refusing to look at him.

"Are you going to come in so I can unwrap it?"

She peeked shyly up at him. "Are you sure unwrapping me was not enough for you?"

Once he'd thought she didn't have a sense of humor. But she did, which as much as any other indicator told him that she had a chance to be a whole person again. This proved she also had timing.

At last it was safe to laugh. It felt good. It felt even better when he saw a sheepish smile creep out onto her face.

Angel followed him inside, hovering near the door, her hands nervously plucking at the material of the slacks she was still wearing as if trying to get rid of them one thread at a time.

"Why don't you sit on the couch?"

"All right," she said, edging over and sitting down on one end, her back ramrod straight. She looked up at him, her pale face solemn.

He smiled at her. "Let's see what we have here." The foil peeled away, and what a surprise, it was a bottle. His eyebrows climbed his forehead when he saw the label, and he had to take a second look to be sure he was reading it right.

"This is real single-malt scotch. Bottled in Scotland," he said softly, staring at Angel in amazement. "It's over seventy years old!"

Angel ducked her head. "I remembered you liking to drink that on the trip here. I—I hope it is still good, being so old and all."

Marchey chuckled. "Oh, I'm sure it is." He hefted the bottle in his hand, trying to guess its value. A couple hundred credits would probably just buy a shot—if an open bottle could even be found. "Where did you get it? Has this place got an AlkaHall nobody's told me about?"

"No," she answered seriously. "Broth—uh, my old Master had boxes and boxes of different kinds of bottles stored away." A frown appeared as she tried to remember the different kinds. "He had brandy, other kinds of whiskey, gin, vodka, bore—borebon? And wine. All kinds." She jumped up. "I can go get you some more. Just tell me what you want. Or I can take you there."

It was a tempting offer. If this was any example of what the old monster had stashed away, it had to be an alcoholic treasure trove, a tippler's Shangri-La.

But this bottle was the one she had picked out for him. One diamond alone is a treasure. When you have a whole sackful no one gem can have the same value and meaning.

"That's all right." He patted the bottle fondly. "You brought me the best one of the whole bunch."

"You are sure?"

"Positive." A thought occurred to him. "You might take Jon Halen and Elias Acterelli there, though. Let them, ah, inventory the stock." They would dole it out fairly, and if anyone deserved a stiff drink, it was the people of Ananke. He also knew that Mardi and Elias had quietly begun assembling a beer-brewing setup in a storage room just off the infirmary. It would be algae beer, since that was the only raw material they had on hand. Fist's stock would tide them over until they got into production.

"All right." She sat back down, perching on the edge of her seat as if ready to bolt and run. Her nervousness was painfully obvious. No doubt she was working herself up to something, and it wasn't too hard to guess what.

Fortunately he knew how to deal with both matters

at once. He had planned to keep their meeting short and formal. Somehow that hadn't worked out, but this might work out even better.

"Well, Angel," he said, "I think we ought to sample a little of this wonderful stuff. How does that sound to you?"

"I do not—" She made a helpless gesture, a jittery lift of her hands and shoulders. "I mean I do not know how. I have never consumed alcohol before."

"Then it's high time you learned." He found two cups and put them on the table, then cracked open the bottle. "Don't worry, you're in the hands of a very experienced teacher."

Half an hour later Marchey was slouched in the chair, his cup in one hand and his feet up on the table between it and the couch. He was feeling pretty good. The scotch was even better than he had thought it would be; taste and bouquet incomparably smooth, yet with a kick like a caber applied to the cerebrum.

Angel had been unsure if she really liked the taste or not, and the modest amount she had consumed had hit her hard. No surprise there; hundred-proof whiskey is not exactly an ideal drink for beginners.

Her earlier nervousness had been replaced by an almost feline abandon. She was sprawled across the couch, staring dreamily into space with a vague smile on her face.

Marchey took another sip, savoring the taste on his tongue as he contemplated his drinking partner.

Although it was not something he was particularly comfortable thinking about, he had to admit that she was attractive. Hell, she was beautiful. Who could have guessed that there had been a face so sweet under the tattooed horror?

Her filed teeth and the blank glass lens that replaced one eye did little to detract from her beauty. They were nothing more than repairable conditions his eyes automatically subtracted. In fact, he'd gotten to kind of like her teeth. As for her exo, it revealed enough of her form to make him wonder what was hidden. She'd come up with a pearl necklace from somewhere. The strand was looped around one tidy silver breast in a way that kept pulling his eye back again and again.

Her physical appearance accounted for only a small part of her allure. There was a freshness about her, a beguiling innocence. An inviting vulnerability completely at odds with the indestructable shell surrounding her body.

Then there was her eagerness to please him. The awe and yearning and yes, even the love that shone in her eyes when she looked at him. Any man would find that hard to resist. Especially one with far too many years of celibacy under his belt, so to speak. He found her so frighteningly enticing he dared not let himself be around her.

The bewildered hurt he'd seen in her face and eyes when he'd begun keeping her at arm's length had made him feel like as big a monster as her old Master. But it had to be done. He knew she couldn't understand why he had shut her out, and he doubted he could explain it to her. She was young and inexperienced enough to think anything was possible.

He was too old not to know better.

Still the impossible and yet so damn tempting notion of asking her to come with him kept recurring. He usually suppressed it the moment it glimmered in his mind, but seeing her there before him in all her glory made that difficult. Nor did the scotch he'd consumed help matters. It helped float his imagination easily over the low, leaky levee of his inhibitions.

He had to admit that he was tired of being alone. The close press of people here might be more than he could handle just yet, but the best face he could put on returning to the hermetic solitude of the circuit was a nerveless resignation which already needed help from his old friend alcohol to be maintained. For all that things had changed, his life would be pretty much the same.

Marchey sipped his drink, staring into his glass and feeling his mood curdle.

There was no point in tormenting himself with daydreams. He was going back to shuttling from hospital to hospital and patient to patient, with an emphasis on waiting out the periods of suffocating nothingness in between.

It would be like the glass in his hand. Mostly empty, with just a taste of what he needed to get him through puddled on the bottom. It was bad enough that he had to live like that. But to bring someone else into it?

She had a chance to lead something like a normal life now. Taking it away would be selfish and cruel. Maybe even criminal. She had to stay. He had to leave. End of story.

"Can't you stay here on Ananke?"

Marchey blinked in confusion. The question had risen up out of his own turgid thoughts, but he didn't think he'd said it aloud. He looked up from his glass toward Angel. She huddled on the couch, hugging herself as if against a chill, her one green eye squeezed shut.

It wasn't too hard to guess that it had slipped out of her mind and onto her tongue, greased by whiskey. He could answer, or pretend he hadn't heard. If he asked her what she said, she might say *Nothing,* and let the matter slide. But he doubted it. He'd been dreading this moment, fairly certain that the subject was going to come up sooner or later.

He decided to answer, as much to remind himself as to explain it to her.

"I wish I could." Saying it out loud made him realize just how much it was true. But once again it was a matter of knowing what was possible and what was not. This was not.

She hunched her shoulders as if gathering his answer in to keep. "Why can't you?" she asked, voice little more than a whisper. "Doctors cannot stay in one place?"

Marchey stared down at his silver hands, the polished metal reflecting his distorted face back at him, reminding him that he had no choice but to be what they made of him.

"My kind can't. At least not yet. There aren't very many of us, and we have a duty to go where we're most needed."

"It could not be done some other way?"

He shrugged. "Maybe it could. I don't really know. For now we're sent from place to place because it's the best, most efficient way for us to be used."

"I see." She sat up, finally looking directly at him. "Brother Fist's system used everyone very efficiently, too."

He shook his head. "It's not the same."

Her green eye narrowed, fixing on him as unblinkingly as the glass lens that replaced the other. "Isn't it?"

"No!" He snorted. "Not even close."

"Then tell me *how* it is different. You go where you are told to go, and do what you are told to do without question or complaint. You have let yourself be used for so long you have forgotten what it is to have a mind of your own."

Marchey glared at her. "You don't know what the hell you're talking about." He knocked back the rest of his drink.

"Don't I?" She shot back, her voice rising. "Have you forgotten who you are talking to? I am the one who kidnapped you and brought you here. You were so used to having your life controlled that you did not even put up a fight!"

"You threatened to rip me to frigging shreds if I didn't come with you!" Marchey snapped, on the verge of shouting. He couldn't believe that they were arguing about this, but he'd be damned if he'd let her get away with saying that she had just snapped her fingers and he'd followed after like a whipped dog.

"Yes, but you were easily coerced. You did not care where I took you. You did not even care if you lived or died! It has taken me some time to be sure I understood this, but what I have concluded is that you were almost completely dead inside when I found you. You had smothered your sense of self inside a bottle and corked it with apathy. Since you have been here you have been faced with the prospect of coming out and living again, and it so frightens you that you are running away!"

"I'm not running away," he spat. "I'm just doing my duty. You don't know what the fuck you're talking about."

"You keep saying that. Even I can see what you have been doing." She put her cup down with exaggerated care. "You have hidden on your ship almost the whole time you have been here. You have hidden from everyone, treating them like devices to be repaired, not like people. You have hidden from *me*. Every time I have tried to see you, you have always had somewhere to go or something else to do. You have run and hidden from me like you never did from Scylla."

"I haven't been hiding, dammit! I just want you to start leading a life of your own." He said it with all the force he could muster, as if that might help get it through her thick silver-plated skull.

Angel stared at him in disbelief. "That is what I have been trying to do!" She shook her head. "But not you. You want to seal yourself back in that ship like it was your coffin and go back to being dead inside."

"Me?" Marchey growled, her accusations making fury bubble through him. He levelled an accusing finger at her. "I'm not the one who's still hiding inside that fucking tin can, afraid to come out and be like the rest of us!"

She flinched as if he had slapped her, shocked hurt flitting across her face. "Afraid to come out?" she cried, lurching to her feet, lips peeling back from her jagged teeth. "This is *Scylla's* skin! She is in here with me! As long as I wear this I have to be on my guard against her every moment of every day!"

Hooked silver fingers clawed at her smooth, sexless silver breast. "Don't you know how much I want to be free of this prison? Of her? To be like everyone else? To have a chance to be a *woman*? To be a woman for a *man*? To—"

She couldn't say it. Not to him, of all people. She had said too much already. Her hand cut the air in a slashing motion, as if severing that line of thought and argument. Her voice dropped to an imploring whisper as she tried to make him understand. It was that or scream.

"I cannot let myself do that—have that—until I have finished paying for at least some of the evil I did. I have a duty to *earn* my way out. I have to give, to serve, to put what I want last or it will mean nothing."

Marchey had listened in glowering, tight-lipped silence, dismissing all she said as rationalization. A caustic mixture of frustration and resentment churned in his gut.

"Bullshit. You're afraid. Call it duty if you want, but you're just looking for something to replace Fist in your life." He spoke coldly, his voice sounding like that of a stranger. His face hardened. "Do you really want to know why I've been trying to stay away from you? Do you? Well, I'll tell you, little girl. Because I wasn't about to let you substitute *me* for *him*!"

The moment those brutal words left his mouth he regretted them. But there was no way to take them back. And it was true, dammit!

Angel stared at him, the color draining from her face. Anger and hurt beat at her insides with steel fists, seeking release. The ghost of Scylla stirred in the urge to return the hurt a hundred times over.

She turned away and stumbled toward the door, knowing she had to get away before she lost control. But she stopped short of it, wanting to repay him for what he had said, wanting to hurt herself for driving him to it, staggering under the weight of what she had said and wanted to say but had not been given the chance to tell him.

She took a shuddering breath. "I am afraid," she admitted in a low hopeless voice. "I am afraid I will have to live in this thing for the rest of my life. Because I am afraid you are the only one who can free me from it. Not just my body, but *me*. And you . . ."

She hunched her shoulders and ducked her head as if to protect herself from the results of what she dared not say, but which had to be said anyway. "You do not even care. About the people here. About me. About anything. Even about yourself. Or that someone might l-l-*love* you!"

That was it, that was the end. All the emotions surging inside her were too new, too raw and wild to be contained. She lifted her foot, her exo multiplying the power of her coiling leg muscles thirty times over, then lashed out with all of her strength.

The force of her kick ripped the door from its pins, flinging it against the unyielding stone of the tunnel's opposite wall and shattering it as completely as her hopes. Had anyone been in front of it, they would have been killed.

Angel was past such considerations. Shame and loss consumed her, sending her fleeing into the tunnel and away from all the things she had ruined, the door least among them.

Marchey stared at the empty doorway, feeling old and stupid. Worse yet, he felt ashamed.

I shouldn't let it end like this. He knew he should go after her, try to repair some of the damage. At least apologize.

He didn't move a muscle.

But it did have to end. Who said endings had to be happy?

"Are you all right?" Mardi puffed from the doorway. Her lined face was pale and frightened, and she'd come from the hospital ward just down the tunnel at a dead run, a bedpan clutched to her chest like a shield.

He gave her a meaningless smile and waved her away. "Just fine. Everything's all right. You go back. I'll be along shortly."

As soon as she was gone he picked up the bottle Angel had brought him. It was still nearly half-full. That might be enough nerve tonic to get him the hell out of there.

She has to live her own life. So do I. A clean break was probably for the best.

He uncorked the bottle and filled his cup. His silver hand dispensed the medication without a tremor.

"Life goes on," he informed the silence, raising his cup.

He drank half of it off in one desperate gulp. As he waited for that to hit bottom so he could inhale the rest he wondered why the gift she had given him suddenly tasted so bitter.

After committing the travesty of swilling the fine old scotch down like rotgut, Marchey made his last stop at the infirmary to leave the pad with Mardi and Elias. For some reason it seemed important to hang on to the all-but-empty bottle all the way to the lockbay.

The cavernous, stone-walled chamber was jammed with people there to see him off. Passing through the doors and into the bay he ran into a living wall. Dismayed by this one last barrier to making his escape, he'd stalled, knowing he should have expected something like this. But his mind had been on other things.

There was only one way to get to the other side. After a few moments to gather his nerve, he lowered his head, took a deep breath and waded in, the scotch bottle clutched protectively to his chest.

Every one of the people gathered there seemed to have put on their best clothes for the event, items hidden away for many long years, inappropriate to Fist's drab dictatorship. Most of this faded finery could best be described as glad-rags, and it was worn by people badly out of practice at having fun. Still, there reigned a festive air such as the place hadn't known for far too many years.

Jon Halen was waiting for him at the top of the ramp, right in front of the locktube doors. Instead of his usual coverall, he was decked out in a ratty wine-colored velveteen tux that hung on his emaciated frame as if on wire hangers, a tattered red-silk carnation on one lapel. To Marchey he looked like the master of ceremonies at a death-camp talent show.

Marchey stumbled up the ramp to Jon's side. He felt as if he had been kissed, thanked, hugged, and patted on the back by everyone at least twice. If he'd been sober, he couldn't have endured it. As it was, he felt like someone who had been thrust out naked and unprotected on Jupiter's surface, squeezed beyond endurance by an inescapable gravity and pressure. He hadn't seen any sign of Angel. One small favor.

Jon gave him a welcoming grin. "Well, Doc, this is it."

Marchey nodded distractedly, wanting only to get the hell out of there as soon as humanly possible. "What about Fist?"

"All aboard. Still sleepin' like the most uglysome baby you ever did see."

"Great. Thanks for taking care of that."

Jon snorted. "Hell, we're the ones should be thankin' you! We'd pay you good credit to haul his miserable ass outta here if he hadn't stole it all."

"It's no big deal. Any luck finding out what he did with everything he took from you?"

Halen shook his head. "Nah. I've started hackin' at his comp in my spare time, but I'm a few years outta practice, and that paranoid old bastard set up so many layers of protection it might take me years to chop through 'em all." He shrugged and grinned. "But let me tell you, it sure do feel good to be back in the saddle again." He rubbed the back of his neck. "I get my tap fixed, and my chances to break the bank'll be better."

Marchey had carried only two spare taps in his

ship's stores, and had been forced to use both on patients who needed the extended life-support and monitoring capabilities a direct linkage to their nervous systems offered. Those who'd had taps when Fist took over had been forced to submit to the injection of a black-market nanovirus that attacked their taps' nanostrand linkages, rendering them useless and unrepairable. A tap was a potent tool, which made it a threat to Fist's rule.

"Well, MedArm will fix you up soon. Good luck on your treasure hunt." He turned toward the locktube. "If Fist lets anything slip, I'll pass it along." He would have headed up the tube, but Jon put a restraining hand on his arm. He turned back reluctantly.

"Listen, Doc. That's a generous offer, but I want you to promise me you won't go messin' with him any more than you absolute have to. Okay?"

"All right," Marchey mumbled, casting a longing look up the tube. "Sure."

"One more thing."

"What?" He managed to bite back the *now*. Halen was staring at him, his face solemn. His gaze was so direct it made Marchey uneasy.

"You've done more for us than we can ever repay," he said with quiet force.

"That's all right," Marchey muttered, embarrassed.

"No it in't. We don't have much. But the honor of offerin' you what we do have has been given to me. It an't somethin' you have to take right now, and its value is somethin' only you can tote up."

Jon drew himself up, his lean humorous face suddenly turning stern and proud. Marchey had opened his mouth to say he didn't want anything, but was silenced by the man's magisterial air. The bay went silent as all talk, as though even breath itself, was withheld.

Jon began to speak, raising his voice so all could hear, his Belter's slur gone and his words ringing out clear and strong as the notes of a trumpet.

"Dr. Georgory Marchey, you were brought here

among us against your will, and as a stranger. You are a stranger no more. You have been a true friend to us all. Now you say that it is time for you to leave us. Although we wish you would stay, you depart with our blessings. But there are some things we want to give you before you go.

"Our friend, we give you our lives, for it is you who has redeemed them for us. We give you our trust, for that is the least of what you have earned. We give you our eternal friendship, for you have been a true friend to us when we needed a friend the most. We give you our love, for love is the font from which friendship and trust and even life itself flows."

Jon put his hand on Marchey's shoulder, his face grave as a judge's and yet suffused with pleasure. "Last of all, we give you our home. It is your home now, because home is the place where love and trust and friendship and life wait for you. Come in fear or come in joy, come in triumph or come in direst extremity; know that you can return here to your home and you will find us waiting to embrace you in full welcome."

Jon embraced Marchey then, kissing both of his cheeks. When he stepped back, his brown eyes sparkled with tears of joy. The Kindred had few rituals, and this was their oldest and most precious. It meant all the more to him and all the rest because it had so nearly died with them.

"Come home again, Brother Marchey," he intoned, completing the rite, "Come home to where your kindred wait for you."

No one broke the throbbing silence that followed. Every eye was upon Marchey, many of them gleaming with tears.

Marchey realized that they were waiting for him to respond. Their simple, sincere offering had moved him deeply, leaving him at a loss for words.

"Thank you," he said, the tightness in his chest and throat turning it into a strangled croak. He gazed out over their upturned faces, so many of them familiar to him now. His whole body felt rocked by the massive wave of love and gratitude washing over him, threatening to carry him away. Deep enough to drown him.

Vast enough to bury him there.

"Thank you!" This time it was a desperate shout, and a thunderous cheer echoed back from it, shivering him from end to end. It grew louder and more jubilant.

He clumsily turned toward the locktube, breathless and shaking. Jon offered his misshapen hand. He took it, silver fingers gripping the gnarled pink-and-black knot. There was no thought of its being an imperfect work. It was the hand of a friend.

"Fare you well, my friend," Jon yelled over the uproar. He winked. "It's still not too late to change your mind!"

Marchey ducked his head, an inarticulate yes and no all at once. Jon released his hand, and he hauled himself up the sagging guide-line into his ship with one arm, the bottle clutched to his chest in the other.

Once inside he banged on the lock's close bar with desperate haste. The doors hissed shut, silencing the cheers and farewells. He crossed the main compartment at a stumbling half run. When he reached the control board he 'ucked the bottle under his arm and slapped the pad that brought up the message

DEPARTURE SEQUENCE INITIATED

The ship rumbled into life around him like a steel beast preparing to digest what had fallen into its belly. He stood there, silver hands locked on to the edge of the board like vises, eyes blindly fixed on the orange ABORT pad.

The battered panels covering the docking area ground back to reveal the starry void. There was a slight jolt as the clamps were released, then the ship started to fall slowly toward the waiting emptiness.

A minute later it emerged from the uncovered blister on Ananke's stony, pockmarked surface into pale warmthless sunlight. The craft sideslipped, angling away, electronic senses casting for the next destination.

The ABORT pad still glowed as the time to change his mind ticked away. He closed his eyes, putting temptation out of sight.

The acceleration warning sounded. Ten seconds later the ship's primary drive flared. Weight settled over Marchey, pressing him down as the ship flung him away from Ananke, gathering speed with every passing second.

At last he opened his eyes, and stood there watching the barren gray moon dwindle to a smeary dot on the screen.

Such a small, pitiful place. Ugly inside and out. Barely 20 km in diameter, scarcely enough gravity to attract dust.

Yet he could feel it pulling at him, raising a tide in his blood. The stupendous gravity of Jupiter was a weak force beside it. That could only captivate the body.

"Doctor," he muttered tonelessly, "I diagnose a serious need for medication to help you recover from your time in near free fall." He turned his back on the screen and lurched toward the galley nook.

A pad combination he knew by heart got him a cup of synthetic vodka from the dispenser. As always, the ship was ready to provide him with what he needed. All forms of escape at his fingertips.

He tossed it back, shuddering as it went down. When his eyes quit watering enough to see the pad clearly he called for another.

This one he raised in mock salute. "Well, I made it. I'm safe now."

He laughed, but it had a hollow, mocking sound, and the expression on his face was not that of a man who has slipped free of a trap and regained his freedom.

Angel watched the shining blue mote centered in the star-flecked darkness of her bedroom screen dwindle and dim. When she could no longer differentiate it from the other glowing points, she turned the unit off.

The screen blanked, the light fading with it.

Her angel eye automatically shifted to a combination of light amplification and infrared, allowing her to see in the gloom. But there was nothing it could do to help her find her way through the blackness that had descended inside her. Only one light could do that, and now it was gone.

She hung her head, admitting defeat.

There were so many things she had wanted to tell him.

But she hadn't even said good-bye.

Angel heaved herself to her feet with a sigh. There was work to be done. Work at least was something she was good at. Good for.

Maybe if she filled all her hours with it, she could keep her mind off the endless, comfortless night that was the future.

Marchey managed to pry his eyelids open, even though they seemed to weigh several kilos each. Bright light crashed into his bloodshot eyes like broken glass fired from a shotgun. He squeezed them shut again to keep from getting holes in his brain.

He lay there for several seconds, steeling himself for another attempt. Groaning at the effort it took to lift his head, he squinted blearily around to get his bearings. Little by little his brain ground into action like a gearbox full of sand, rocks, and tar.

He licked his lips. *"Yurk."* His mouth felt like a dog with mange had slept in it.

He found out that he'd passed out at the galley table, which explained why one side of his face felt flat and numb. Clear memories of his first and second helpings of vodka remained. He recalled using the table's touchpad to check on his passenger, and remembered the drink he'd gotten himself as a reward for remembering to do so. After that things got kind of fuzzy.

A glance at the clock told him that twelve hours had passed since his last grip on reality. Wincing at the thunderous clang of his fingers against the auto-kitchen's touchpads, he punched in an order for coffee spiked with brandy. He gulped it down greedily, scalding the fur from his tongue.

That fortified him enough to get his feet under him and totter off to take a shower. The ship's real-water shower was more than a luxury; it was a lifesaver at times like this. In his delicate condition a sonic shower would probably have killed him.

Fifteen minutes later he returned to the galley, looking and feeling like he might be able to pass for human. He had changed into soft, baggy black trousers and embroidered slippers. Ignoring the water dripping from the hair at the back of his head, he pulled on a loose red-and-black tyon shirt.

He punched up a second coffee, straight this time, and forced himself to eat some sort of tasteless, nutritionally balanced breakfast cake that was gone before he quite figured out what it was supposed to be besides good for him.

When his cup was empty he considered a third, spiked again, but decided he'd better not. At least not yet.

There was something he had to do before he could talk himself out of it. Something best done when he had all his wits about him. Another drink or two of liquid courage might make him feel braver, but would only make the task more dangerous.

He had left the compartment housing the inship clinic brightly lit, as if its occupant were some sort of nocturnal monster the harsh glare could keep contained. Had such things been available, he might have even hung up a shitload of garlic and a gross of crucifixes just for safety's sake.

He hesitated in the doorway, reconsidering his decision to eschew another drink. Surely just one more would be more help than hurt.

Right. Then one more after that. He stuck to his plan and made himself go on inside.

A deepening chill that had nothing to do with the temperature made him shiver as he approached the unibed. The unit's sleek black sides had been folded up into patient transport mode, giving it a coffinlike appearance.

He went to the control side of the 'bed and gazed down at the skeletal figure of the man who called himself Brother Fist.

The old man lay there still as death, looking more like something recently exhumed than anything alive. Naked but for a blanket covering him up to his chest, the wrinkled parchment skin slackly draped over the bones of his emaciated body looked too gray and bloodless to be the skin of anything other than a cadaver. His eyes were closed and deeply sunken into their sockets. The liverish slash of his mouth hung slightly open. Only the faint rise and fall of his thin chest betrayed his tenacious hold on life.

Marchey knew that by all rights he should have been dead. Little better than death warmed over because of Form V cancer when he'd had Marchey kidnapped to cure him, his overthrow had been the beginning of the end. The Form V had immediately gone into its wildfire terminal stage.

The average interval between the beginning of terminal stage and death was a week. Anyone else would have been dead from it by now. But not Fist. Somehow he kept his decaying body and putrescent soul together by force of will alone.

Marchey laid one silver hand on the flat touchpad on the unibed's side, the circuits in his prosthetic directly interfacing with its complex systems. Data whispered into his mind, soft as music from another room: *Respiration slow and shallow [7/31], but consistent with patient's condition. Pulse slow and thready [14], blood pressure low and steady [40s/28d], but CWPC. Blood gasses—*

The data whispered on, Marchey interrupting every

so often to tweak an adjustment in the life-support parameters. The 'bed's neural fields were in Pain Suppression, Patient Immobilization, and Deep Sleep modes.

The old monster was fine just the way he was. Still alive, but dead to the world. A sleeping dragon, its fires banked and its hunger held in check. Although weighing barely over forty kilos and only days away from death, he was still almost as dangerous as he had ever been. As long as his mind functioned he would remain so.

Back on Ananke, Marchey had kept him locked in a storage room and buried under a sleepfield. The locks weren't to keep Fist in, the sleepfield would see to that, but to keep his former subjects out. There was no way he could guarantee Fist's safety, but he felt that he had a duty to do what he could to insure it.

The lock had seemed like a logical precaution. After all, his former subjects had ample reason to want at him. Most people would have been rabidly trying to get their hands on him, first to torture his secrets out of him, then lynch what was left after the interrogation.

But not the Kindred. They had learned their lesson and learned it well. To have *any* dealings with Fist was to flirt with destruction. He had enslaved them, tormented and murdered the ones they loved, perverted their faith, and stolen everything of value they had: the fruits of their labor, their freedom, their dignity, and their future. Fist would have seen to it that vengeance cost them all they had regained, and they knew it. They avoided him like the plague he was. After a few days Marchey quit locking the door.

Shortly after he had been given orders to go back on the circuit again he'd offered to take Fist with him and turn him over to whatever authorities would have him. It stood to reason that the people of Ananke would have a better chance of recovering from what had happened if the source of the infection were removed.

The offer had been made to the community as a

whole through Jon Halen, who had already emerged as something of a leader. Or at least a spokesman for the consensus. The Kindred had never been much for leaders before Fist, and it was doubtful they would want any others after him. Unsurprisingly enough, Jon returned saying they would gladly be rid of him.

Since then Marchey had toyed with the idea of trying to get Fist to reveal what he had done with the spoils from Ananke. Standing in the shower with the water beating down on his aching head, feeling a tidal pull from behind and faced with the empty hours and days ahead, the idea had taken on a new attraction.

It would help divert his thoughts from . . . other matters.

"Sleepfield off," he said, the unibed chiming in response to his command. "Bring the patient around. Keep immobile and anesthetized."

Wake the dragon. Up to now he had only let Fist rise up to a semiconscious state, first when repairing his broken arm and lacerated throat, then afterward during his daily check on him.

Marchey was perfectly willing to admit that Fist scared the living hell out of him. Anyone with half a brain would feel the same way. His heart beating faster in trepidation, he gripped the side of the bed as if to keep himself from running away. Playing with Fist was a dangerous diversion. Shaving his face with a hundred gigawatt mining laser would be far safer.

Fist's crepey eyelids fluttered as he began to come around.

Marchey could not shut out the memories of Fist's endless unapologetic cruelties. His utter delight in the suffering of others. The way he had nearly ruined his life. That brought him the tempting notion of shutting off the painfield as well.

The idea had its own dark magnetism, but he let it slide. Not only because it would be contrary to his Oath and all his principles, but also because he knew Fist would only sieze on it and use it against him. He had no doubt that the old man could surmount his own pain, then use it to cause someone else to suffer.

The frail draped birdcage of Fist's chest rose higher with each indrawn breath. His bony hands twitched weakly.

Marchey resisted the temptation to step back. Not only was the old man's breath unspeakably foul, reeking with death and disease, but he knew that the doors to a human chamber of horrors were about to open.

Fist's rheumy, pus-colored eyes opened slowly, blinked. If he was confused, it didn't show. The warped animus lurking behind those eyes stared out at what was around it with a cold, inhuman calculation empty of surprise or expectation or ungoverned emotion.

When Marchey was still in college he had visited Earth for the first and only time, and in a stone temple in a country named India seen a real live crocodile the monks kept there. It was said to be almost a hundred years old, one of the last natural-born specimens alive. The huge, cold-blooded creature had lain there half-submerged in its pool, regarding the world around it with that same fearless, carnivorous dispassion. Its soulless gaze assayed you as either meat or threat, and if you were lucky, it dismissed you as neither.

Fist turned his head to look up at Marchey, exposing the jagged scars Scylla's talons had carved into his thin neck. He stared up at him for several long, unpleasant seconds before speaking.

"You've taken me . . . off Ananke." Fist's voice was a papery whisper, sibilant and reptilian. The disease in his lungs had gone into full-blown terminal stage. There wasn't much more than a handful of functioning tissue left. All else was dark carcinomic growth, nightshade blooms spreading in the warm darkness.

"That's right," Marchey answered, reminding himself to choose his every word carefully. "You had pretty much worn out your welcome."

Haaaaaaaaaaaaaaa. Fist's laughter was a bubbling

ophidian hiss that raised the hackles at the back of Marchey's neck.

"I suppose . . . I did at that." The ghost of a shrug. "You took me away . . . so they could not kill . . . the poor old man . . . who has done . . . so much for them?"

Marchey shook his head, almost smiling because he had a chance to score a hit on the old man's ego. "Not one of them raised so much as a hand against you. I guess you didn't corrupt them as much as you thought." Of course keeping him buried under a sleepfield the whole time hadn't hurt. Fist could drive a saint to homicide.

"Or I taught them . . . better than they know." His hand twitched dismissively. "No matter. What of . . . my Scylla?"

"Her name is Angel," Marchey returned coldly, the pleasure he'd felt a moment before clabbering at the mention of her name and the memories it conjured. "Scylla was the name of the thing you tried to turn her into. But that didn't work out so well after all, did it? Remember how she very nearly took your goddamn head off? She's not Scylla anymore, and she's not yours."

Those cruel yellow eyes bored into Marchey's face, commanding his full attention. "If she is . . . my toy no longer . . . she must have . . . become yours. You subverted her . . . supplanted me. That makes her . . . yours."

Fist's smile was a horrific thing. Again it reminded Marchey of laughing, scythe-wielding Plague in medieval art. "Isn't she . . . a delightful possession?" He licked his thin black lips with a long gray tongue. "Young. Beautiful. Innocent. So eager . . . to please."

"She's nobody's possession," Marchey responded heavily. "She's not a pet or a puppet. She's her own person now. Nobody owns her—least of all me. Now that you're no longer pulling her strings she has a chance at a life of her own."

Fist's baleful, unblinking stare held all the warmth

of a breath of space. Under it confidence withered like an orchid blasted by frost. "You . . . abandoned her?" he asked, an ominous note of accusation sharpening his tone.

Marchey kept himself from looking away, feeling like he was pinned to a board under a microscope, being examined to see if he was fit for dissection. Besides, he wasn't sure he could if he wanted to.

"Yes." He hadn't really *abandoned* her, but he knew better than to try to argue the point. In a war of words he'd be the first and only casuality.

"Then you have . . . *doomed* her," Fist pronounced, looking pleased by the prospect.

"I set her free." He couldn't keep the defensive note out of his voice. "I gave her a chance to make something of herself."

"You have . . . doomed her," Fist repeated with a steely certainty that made Marchey's blood turn to neocaine. He told himself that Fist was just trying to bait him. Angel's life or death had meaning to Fist only as something he could use to his advantage.

Try as he might, Marchey still couldn't resist the bait. He had to ask Fist what he meant, even though he was almost certainly playing into the old man's hands.

"Explain what you mean by that." It came out more of an appeal than the demand he had intended.

Fist ignored his question. He examined what small part of his surroundings were visible from inside the unibed, then turned his attention back to Marchey. "Where are you . . . taking me?"

Marchey shook his head, unable to let the other matter drop. "First tell me what you meant by saying I've doomed Angel."

The bundle of paper-covered sticks that was Fist's hand twitched in a gesture that said the matter was of no real consequence. "Nothing." That *rictus sardonicus* of a smile again. "If she is . . . as you said . . . her own person . . . then her fate . . . is of her own making . . . and no concern . . . of yours." He peered at Marchey expectantly. "Is that . . . not so?"

Marchey opened his mouth to answer, closed it. His crash course in dealing with Fist had taught him that anything he said would only sink him deeper in the morass. So he reluctantly left the matter unresolved and answered Fist's question.

"We're headed for a place called Botha Station."

He saw something flicker across Fist's masklike face. It was there and gone too quickly to be identified for certain. He didn't think it had been fear, but it might have been . . . dismay?

Fist closed his eyes, his face unreadable. But the 'bed's monitoring equipment reported a transient spike in his pulse rate. His reaction had not been artifice.

"I would rest a while," Fist said imperiously, turning his head away. "Leave me."

Marchey stared down at the old man, trying to understand what had just happened. Fist ignored him, his face inscrutable.

After a couple minutes he rechecked the 'bed's settings, then reset the sleepfield on delay, allowing the old man to remain awake for another twenty minutes before it came back on.

He paused in the clinic's doorway, gazing thoughtfully back at his passenger. The mention of Botha Station had hit a nerve, that was fairly certain. Giving Fist time to dwell on the matter might prove useful. And in case his suspicion was correct—

"We reach Botha Station in four and a half days, old man." He left without waiting for a reaction, closing the door behind him.

"Then we have . . ." Fist whispered, something like a smile creeping out onto his shriveled face, "a deadline. . . ."

Marchey had killed a couple hours at a compad, finding out what he could about Botha Station. It had been fairly educational, but put him no closer to understanding Fist's reaction.

Botha Station was a regional control, secondary processing, and staging area owned by OmniMat, the second largest space-based mining and materials megacorp. Only AllMine was larger. Those two, plus United Resources, made up the Big Three—or the Unholy Trinity, as they were more often called. The next largest mining and materials combine after United Resources was not very large at all; anything even remotely capable of competing with the Trinity had been either gobbled up or driven out of business decades ago.

Botha was heliostationary, maintaining a position on the sunny side of Jupiter between the orbits of Himalia and Callisto, some 9 million kilometers out from Jupiter's surface. Ugly little Ananke was over a third of the way around Jupiter's vast bulk from Botha. While that was one hell of a distance to travel—some 18 million kilometers—it wasn't really all that long a trip. Some of his house calls took over three weeks to complete.

The volume of space encompassed by Jupiter's moons was huge, but it was a cozy neighborhood when compared with the Belt, which has a circumference roughly four times the distance between Earth and Jupiter. Although he couldn't say so for certain, Marchey was pretty sure he had made at least one, maybe two trips completely around the Belt.

His review of the facts and figures about Jovian space were more than a little disconcerting, and he had come to the conclusion that he ought to get some sort of medal for utter and unalloyed obliviousness. He'd traveled hundreds of millions of kilometers and been to almost every part of inhabited space, and yet didn't really have the faintest idea of where he'd been or how far he'd gone.

Studying the data on his pad, he'd been amazed by how heavily settled the Jovian system had become. Not so many years ago it had been the frontier. Only scientists and a few brave and crazy wilders had been willing to venture even farther than this, to Ixion Station—and beyond—in hopes of making their names and fortunes from Saturn's lunar real estate.

Now, every moon was either settled or being exploited. There were habs everywhere. In near Leda a shipping tycoon named King—everyone called him Crazy Eddie—had set up an odd combination hab/hotel/pleasure dome that he'd built and brought all the way out from the Belt. In fact, a woman who'd accidentally fallen into Fist's web while searching for an aunt a few years back had suggested asking King for aid. Jon Halen had contacted him just two days ago, and King had promised supplies on the next available transport.

AllMine and OmniMat were the big sticks in Jovian space. They had moved in and glommed onto what others had found or begun, just as they had done in the Belt, and before that on Mars. It was nearing the point where anyone who wanted to remain independent would have to move outward, toward Saturn. Already Ixion had become more of a way station than the end of the line it had been when he'd visited Ella there.

Somehow all of these changes had slipped past him, even though he had been sent to several stations and settlements over the last few years. One operating room looks pretty much like another—especially if you don't give a flying fuck where you are. His ship was fully automated, following instructions from elsewhere. All he had to do was get aboard and it did the rest. More often than not he hadn't even bothered to find out where he was bound next.

Looking back, he had to admit that he had been pretty well automated himself. *Dr. Georgory Marchey, Robot Surgeon*. Keep him well lubricated and he'll give you years of trouble-free service.

Angel's accusations kept coming back to haunt him. At each recurrence he would tell himself that caring where he went wouldn't have made any difference. It would be like caring that every year you got a little older. It happened. Dwelling on it changed nothing.

So here he was, in the middle of the evening of his first day back on the circuit. He'd done his homework on Botha Station. He'd played cat and mouse with Fist, and still had his whiskers and tail intact.

Unsurprisingly enough, there was a drink in his hand.

That was another of the day's great accomplishments. Admitting to himself that he couldn't face the silence and the solitude without it. Knowing full well how easy it would be to let himself resubmerge into the sodden life he'd led before, he'd devised a strictly controlled regimen of alcohol intake. Prescribing enough to pacify, but not enough to pickle. He hoped the little rules and schedules would give him something else to occupy his mind.

At least it had blunted the feeling of being caged by the steel box of the ship, and stopped his restless pacing. Although he had his doubts that the dosage was high enough, he'd kept himself from upping it. At least so far.

He sat at the galley table, rolling his glass between his silver hands and trying to concentrate on the medical journal he'd called up on the pad propped before him. But instead of staying on a new mutagenic strain of parasite fond of vacationing in the islets of Langerhans, his mind kept drifting back to the cold, dimly lit tunnels of Ananke.

"Screw this," he mumbled after reading the same sentence for the tenth time. He snapped off the pad in disgust and sat back, trying to put a name on the way he felt in hopes that would help him get a grip on it.

He felt . . . almost, well . . .

. . . *homesick.*

He scowled and gulped at his drink. What an utterly ridiculous notion!

It was just that he was having a hard time readjusting to life on the circuit. To the solitude. To semisobriety.

Still, he kept wondering how Jon was doing. And what about Salli and Ivor and Indira and Ray and Danny and Mardi and Elias and Laura and all the other people he'd met and treated? How were they getting along?

Then there was the sharp point on this pyramid of curiousity, the ten-million-credit question.

Was Angel all right?

He told himself that he kept wondering—all right, dammit, admit it, *worrying*—about her only because what Fist had said was stuck in his brain like a splinter, causing a festering doubt that infected all his thoughts.

You have doomed her.

Each time that sinister echo sounded again he reminded himself that this was the old psychopath's genius. Fist wielded abnegation with the skill and precision of a surgeon. Just as he himself could put his prosthetics aside and reach inside a patient's skull to smooth away an aneurysm or erase a tumor, Fist could just as easily reach inside a person's head and twist their brain's contents, warping pleasure into pain, hope into despair, and all certainty into a sucking quicksand of doubt.

He's lying. Making it up. That was easy enough to say, but not to really believe. Marchey knew it wasn't that simple.

The old monster was a consummate liar, but he could be just as easily telling the truth if he thought that would best serve his ends. He could be stitching the true and the false so seamlessly together that there was no way to tell where one ended and the other began, turning what he created into a straitjacket, a prison uniform, a jester's motley, a shroud.

Only one thing was certain. Fist had wanted him to worry.

The old bastard had succeeded. In spades.

Marchey stared into his glass. Was there any reason he *shouldn't* call Ananke to see how his former patients were doing? If something was wrong with Angel, they'd tell him. Even if it was something Fist wanted him to do, what harm could there be in it?

The only way to find out was the hard way.

He put his glass down and headed for the commboard. Less than a minute later he was apprehensively waiting to hear the sound of a familiar voice.

Angel trudged back to her cubby. The normally graceful swing and flow of her movements had been reduced to the ponderous plodding of some clumsy machine by nearly thirty straight hours of physical labor. Her last and only break had been her disastrous farewell to Marchey.

Her green eye was glazed with exhaustion. It kept drooping shut on her. Not that she could see straight when it was open.

Her angel eye had no lid to sag. It faithfully reported her slow, lurching progress through the tunnels. Messages scrolled along the top of the lens's view, firing back along her nano-encrusted optic nerve and into her fatigue-muddied mind.

WARNING!!! XO PHYSICAL SYSTEMS REDLINE!!! her second silver self warned in pulsating red letters.

REST AND NOURISHMENT PARAMETERS EXCEEDED. >>PARTIAL SYSTEMS OVERRIDE INVOKED<< HOST MUST EAT AND REST BEFORE IRREPARABLE DAMAGE OCCURS!

Angel had no idea what any of that meant. Nor did she care, now that she knew it was not instruction from God. Whatever tatters of concentration she could muster were wrapped around the strange way she felt. She knew she wasn't moving her legs. She was only *thinking* about moving them, and her exo was doing the rest, carrying her slack, numb body along inside it. It felt odd, but not unpleasant.

Suddenly she felt something being pushed against her lips. She peered woozily down past her nose, saw her hand forcing a cake of manna into her mouth. She chewed the bland biscuit out of reflex, swallowed the dry crumbs. Her pouch. There had been manna in her pouch. Was that distant gnawing sensation hunger?

Before long her pallet hove into view, doubling and blurring as her organic eye lost focus and track. She couldn't even remember having passed through the outer door to the chapel.

The next thing she knew she was stretched out on her bed, flat on her back and unable to move.

HOST FATIGUE LEVEL CRITICAL wrote itself inside her angel eye. ***EXTERNAL DANGER LEVEL NULL. FULL OVERRIDE IN-VOKED: VOLUNTARY SYSTEMS GOING TO ENFORCED REST STATUS***

For the first time in memory her angel eye went dark of its own accord, shutting down so that sensory input from it did not keep her awake. Everything vanished in the darkness that followed. Her pale, haggard face grew lax as she began to sink into an exhausted, dreamless sleep.

Moments later she was dragged back toward wakefulness by a loud, insistent buzzing sound. Her angel eye remained stubbornly dark, but she managed to pry the other one back open.

She was still blearily trying to make sense of the sound when it stopped. An instant later the meter-square main screen of her comm lit.

Angel's breath caught in her throat as Marchey stared out of it at her like a face from a dream. Her heart raced faster and her head swam at the rush of emotions that surged through her. The comm had been left on standby against the one-in-a-million chance that he might try to call her, and against all odds he had!

She tried to get up, desperately wanting to get closer, to touch him if he was real, to answer if he was calling her, but her silver-armored body lay stiff, as if cast from solid metal.

Panic set in. She strained and twisted, trying to flog

her body into motion but only able to lift her head slightly off the pillow. Commands to her traitorous limbs were swallowed up by a silent nothingness that furled tighter with every exertion.

WARNING!!! wrote itself in fiery red print inside her still-dark angel eye. ***REST IMPERATIVE/ THREAT LEVEL NULL >> XO-MEDSYSTEMS IN-VOKING INVOLUNTARY SEDATION<<***

Angel's head fell back, her breath sawing in and out in ragged sobs. Her head spun. Dizziness made everything unreal. She couldn't think straight, couldn't tell if she was really awake or trapped in a nightmare, wanting to reach him so badly the need was more than she could contain; but her exo and her weakness defeating her.

The last thing she saw through the tears welling up in her eye was a smile appearing on his face.

She tried to smile back—

4

Consultation

Jon Halen's lean, dark visage filled Marchey's screen, lighting up in a toothy grin when he saw him. "Hey there, Doc," he drawled, "If you're callin' bout your bill, the check's in the mail."

Marchey had to smile, and not just at that very old, very bad joke. Just seeing Halen again did more to lighten his mood than anything he'd drank lately.

"Glad to hear it. How are things back at the old homestead?"

"Tolerable. I did just get one bit of good news."

Marchey smirked. "Salli wants to have your children?"

That made Jon snicker. "No, that's not it. 'Sides, I've been too busy humpin' a keyboard for any of *that*."

"Any luck cracking Fist's accounts?"

Halen's grin slipped. "Naw, I'm 'fraid not. I've been spendin' ev'ry minute I can spare tryin' to get a handle on his records, but I'm still just sortin' the locked files from the open stuff. The old bastard had enough data squirreled away to keep me diggin' for years."

He scrubbed his stubbly chin with his misshapen hand, peering at Marchey with one eye. "You been, um, talkin' to him?"

"A little. Sorry, but he hasn't told me anything." *Nothing I wanted to hear, anyway. Or believe.*

Jon shook his head. "Don't be. I shouldn'ta even asked. Like I said before, don't go messin' with him any more'n you absolute have to."

"You said you have good news," Marchey prompted.

Halen's irrepressible grin reappeared. "I surely do! There's medical people and all those supplies you wrote up on the way. Just got the word that they're s'posed to arrive sometime late Friday."

That was about the same time he'd reach Botha Station. Marchey let out a sigh of relief. Now maybe he could stop feeling so guilty about leaving them. "That's great. I knew MedArm would come through."

Jon shook his head. "It an't them personally, it's some outfit called the Helping Hands Foundation."

Marchey sat there after saying good-bye to Jon, mulling things over.

By all rights he should have been feeling pretty good. Jon had accessed the medical files for him, and he had been pleased to see that not only were Mardi and Elias doing an excellent job of keeping them up-to-date, the people in their care were doing at least as well as could be expected. Jon had offered to get Mardi to report directly—Elias was sleeping—but he didn't want her to think he was checking up on them.

Medical help was on the way. That should have been a load off his mind. It was, mostly. But he had never heard of this Helping Hands Foundation, and couldn't help wondering why they were doing what was supposed to be MedArm's job. Bureaucracy at work, no doubt, some penny-pinching MedArm comptroller using a private group of do-gooders to pare his or her precious budget. Once this outfit arrived he'd have to check with Mardi and Elias to make sure they were doing a good job—and raise holy hell if they weren't

Jon hadn't seen Angel since bumping into her in a corridor the morning Marchey left. He'd looked disappointed when Marchey turned down his offer to track her down for him. It appeared that not even his departure had dampened Jon's desire to put the two of them together.

He got up from the commboard and drifted back to the galley. He'd refilled his glass with straight scotch and knocked half of it back before he remembered that he was rationing the booze.

"Just celebrating," he mumbled, scowling into his glass. Everything was turning out the way it was supposed to. Everything was coming up roses.

No news was good news. Angel was probably just fine.

He drained the glass. She was undoubtedly going on with her life, already forgetting about him.

Just like he was forgetting about her.

Marchey jerked in surprise and spilled his coffee when his arm chimed that next morning, having forgotten that the day before he'd set it to remind him when Fist's sleepfield was about to shut down. The unibed had been programmed to give the old man half an hour of wakefuless per day.

He started to get up, then changed his mind and settled back into the galley seat. Let the miserable old bastard stew a few minutes. After swabbing up the mess he'd made he refilled his cup from the dispenser. Took a sip, grimaced.

Brandy flavoring in coffee was not at all the same thing as the real thing. Not even close. He dumped it out.

It was still early in his second day back on the circuit. The two hours he'd been up felt like two days.

The long stretches of monotonous solitude had never grated on his nerves like this before, never made him feel this trapped and jittery.

Of course this was the first time he'd tried to do it this close to sober. He couldn't recall the countless other times he'd spent days—sometimes even weeks—like a machine on standby clearly enough to say he truly remembered them. They were like the hours spent in sleep. He knew they had passed, but darkly and disconnected from the normal flow of time.

Just three days before there hadn't been enough hours in the day. Now there were too many days in each hour. The minutes pass slowly when you're all alone and mostly sober. Any distraction was welcome.

Marchey stood up, bitterly amused by the realization that looking in on Fist was going to be the high point of his day.

"So glad to see you . . . my dear doctor," Fist wheezed, gazing up at Marchey with what passed for a friendly smile. The Grim Reaper had that sort of smile.

"Of course . . . I should be glad . . . to be able . . . to see anyone." He chuckled, a wet, tubercular, hacking sound.

Marchey's guard went up. He rested his hand on the touchpad, but withheld accessing the 'bed's systems. "How are you feeling?" he asked, telling himself to watch his step. Fist was up to something.

The old man's thin, blue-gray lips peeled back from his sharp white teeth. "Probably about . . . the way I look."

Marchey let the opening pass. "Any pain?" The neural field created by the Schmidt crystals should be keeping the worst of the pain suppressed, but with Form V you couldn't count on it. Not that Fist hadn't earned some suffering by forbidding medical care for his former subjects because it pleased him to hear them praying to be healed. Surely such cruelty ought to be repaid.

"Does my pain . . . truly disturb you? Or does . . . it seem just?" Fist asked sweetly, as if he had read Marchey's mind. "What would you do . . . if I said . . . I was in agony?"

The safest course was to ignore the first two questions and take the last at face value. "I'd increase the anesthetic field to emergency strength. If that didn't take care of it, I'd keep you under the sleepfield full-time since I'm out of superaspirin, syndorphins, and paraopiates."

A slight nod. "As I thought." That awful grin widened. "No pain . . . I cannot endure. Your agenda . . . will not be spoiled . . . by my infirmity."

Marchey almost asked him what he meant, but caught himself at the last moment. Fist was finessing him for some reason, trying to lure him into something like a fly into a pitcher-plant. So he said nothing.

"What agenda is that . . . you ask?" Fist wheezed. His voice dropped to a conspirational whisper. "What do I have . . . hidden away? What passphrases and . . . code keys unlock it? I may . . . tell you." The ghost of a shrug. "I may not. It depends . . . on you." He stared up, smugly expectant.

Well, here we go, Marchey thought glumly, not surprised that Fist knew what he wanted and intended to use it to his advantage. But this was an uncharacteristically straightforward approach. Of course, when dealing with Fist the most dangerous trap was the one you didn't see. There was sure to be one, probably already under his feet. One wrong word would make it snap shut.

He stared back at Fist, doing his best to maintain an impassive, indifferent expression. After a moment the old man nodded, and smiled.

"You are . . . an apt pupil, Doctor. Caution is . . . an admirable virtue. But a one-sided conversation . . . is no conversation at all." Fist released him by looking away. Marchey swallowed a sigh of relief. Yet this small victory felt hollow. Fist was handling him with kid gloves, he was sure of it. But why?

"We have . . . been friends," Fist said quietly, stressing the word *friends* with smirking sarcasm, "For only . . . a short time. Still, you are . . . not a stupid man. You have been trained . . . to observe . . . to make deductions . . . on the basis . . . of those observations." He turned his head back to look up at Marchey, who could only uneasily wait for him to get to the point.

"Have you deduced," Fist whispered, "what motivates me?"

Marchey stared at the old man, knowing that his surprise showed on his face. So he made himself smile.

"You're a psychopath," he answered blandly, knowing Fist would take exception to it. If they were going to play games, let him be the one on the defensive.

Sure enough, he frowned and shook his head. "That is a glib . . . meaningless description . . . and rather . . . unflattering at that." He held up his hand, waggling a bony finger. "Stop playing stupid. It ill . . . befits you."

"Self-interest?" Marchey had to admit that he was curious as to what motivated Fist. He was criminally insane, but that didn't mean he didn't have some sort of logical framework—no matter how twisted—for all his actions.

"Closer . . . but a vague category . . . not a specific motivation."

"Love?" He had to keep himself from being drawn in, from giving the responses Fist wanted to elicit.

Those pus-colored eyes narrowed. Fist stared at him for several long seconds, then grinned. "Excellent. As I said . . . you are . . . an apt pupil. You learn. Use what you . . . have learned. You believe . . . that I am leading you . . . into some sort of trap . . . don't you?" It was not a question.

"Aren't you?" Marchey parried.

"You would know for certain . . . if only you understood . . . my motivations." *Haaaaaaaaaaa.* Fist's laugh made his skin crawl, but he knew he'd managed a draw.

Now if he only knew what the hell the game was.

Fist cocked his head to one side. "No doubt you have . . . called Ananke by now. How are . . . our dear friends there?"

"Nobody said they missed you."

A look of mock disappointment. "After all I . . .

did for them. Such ingratitude. How will . . . they ever get along . . . without us?"

Marchey snorted. "They'll get along just fine. They needed you like they needed a plague. The medical help they need is on the way, so they'll be fine without me."

He glanced up at the clock, deciding that it was time to end his visit. He hadn't gotten anything concrete out of the old psychopath, but neither had he found himself up to his neck in concrete and sinking into the mud under forty feet of water. Besides, it was time for a well-earned drink.

Fist's bubbling chuckle snatched his attention back like a slap in the face. "Not from . . . MedArm," Fist said quietly.

Marchey frowned. "How did you know that?"

"The Helping Hands Foundation." A skeletal grin. "The game grows . . . more intriguing," he wheezed with ominous satisfaction. "I am pleased."

Marchey stared down at the old man, hands clamped tight on the unibed's sides to keep him from shaking some answers out of the smirking bastard. "What are you talking about?" he demanded.

Watch yourself, he warned himself. *He's sucking you in.* But he had to ask. Anything that pleased Fist could only spell disaster for everyone else.

Fist's hooded eyes glinted with perverse pleasure. "Motivation," he rasped. "Pleasure. Reward. Allegiance. Fulfillment. Accomplishment." A pregnant pause. *"Challenge."*

He let out a long sigh, unmistakably savoring the moment and the situation. "Yes, even love. I do love life when . . . it puts the sweet raw stuff . . . of possibility . . . in my hands." He closed his hands as if feeling what he spoke about in them and closed his eyes, an expression of something like serenity on his fleshless face.

"It has put . . . that same sweet stuff . . . in your hands, too," he added in a conspiratorial whisper, as if imparting some secret wisdom.

Marchey leaned closer. "What do you mean?" he demanded again, knowing that he was taking the bait even as he did so.

The only answer he received was an inscrutable half smile.

Marchey would have worried about himself if he *hadn't* wanted a drink after his little dance in the dragon's jaws.

But he sipped rather than gulped, brows knit and his face pensive as he tried to get a fix on the situation.

Fist was toying with him.

But why? Was he being led into the inital passages of an elaborate labyrinth constructed for the simple reason that Fist was unable to resist turning people into rats in a maze, and he was the only rat within reach? Or could it be the beginning of a payback for spoiling his fun on Ananke?

Although he couldn't say why, he had a feeling that Fist's agenda was more complex than mere revenge, that his objectives were clear and simple even if his methods of reaching them were not. But was it possible to see them through all the smoke and mirrors?

What motivates me?

The old bastard had known that this Helping Hands Foundation was bringing relief to Ananke, and thought it was funny—or wanted him to think he did. But which? And why?

There was no way to tell. Fist's every word was calculated, his every expression the manipulation of a mask. Any resemblance to humanity was artifice. The one time he had let his true self show had exposed something Marchey hoped to never see again. The conscienceless egopathy and remorseless brilliance and sheer malignant force of personality that burned inside him put him so far outside the human norm that he might as well be alien.

Fist wasn't giving anything away, that was for sure. Anything he offered was bound to be tainted—a free lunch where the sandwiches were buttered with arse-

nic. The smartest, safest course of action was to lock
the clinic door, remotely reset the unibed to keep the
old man under until they reached Botha Station, and
do his best to put the matter out of his mind.

Another sip. A reminder that forgetfulness came in
a tasty and convenient liquid form.

He just couldn't shake the nagging feeling that Fist
was holding himself in check. Manipulating him to be
sure, but gently compared to the cruel and ruthless
way he'd crushed Marchey's resistance on Ananke. He
wanted to start a game. There was something he
wanted at stake. He'd as much as offered up everything he'd stolen from the Kindred as incentive to
play.

Another sip of his drink. Here was one sure answer.
A few more of these and everything else would stop
mattering.

He made himself put the glass down, still half-full.
Maybe this would be a good time to call Sal Bophanza
back at the Bergmann Institute. He dealt with Med-
Arm on a day-to-day basis, and might just know something about this Helping Hands Foundation.

He had last spoken to the Institute's director over
two weeks before, only hours after he'd saved Fist
from Scylla. Seeing the look on Sal's face when he
told him of the simple solution to the Nightmare Effect had been one of the high points of his life.

Who would have guessed that a man raised in the
Lunar African enclave Mandela would know a Rebel
yell or an Irish jig? Sal had let out the first and given
an energetic performance of the second.

It had taken Sal a while to calm down. Once he
had, Marchey had gone on to explain the situation on
Ananke and request immediate relief. Then he had
told Sal that he needed to stay on for a while. Sal had
promised to do what he could.

When orders to leave Ananke and proceed to Botha
Station had come in a few days later, he had hated
himself for the sense of relief he felt. Yet at the same

time he'd been angered by not at least being allowed to stay on until help arrived. Anger and a sense of duty had won out. He'd called Sal to ask for permission to at least stay until then—although by then it was more out of a sense of duty than desire to stay.

Much to his surprise, his call had been routed straight to MedArm. The unsmiling woman with the Chinese face and Phoban accent he found himself talking to had asked him to state his business. He'd begun to hem and haw out his request. She had interrupted him sharply, stating that the case had been reviewed, and the six days he was being given were more than generous.

When he had tried to argue, she coldly informed him that those six days could be cut to four, or two, or even none, and broken the connection, not even giving him a chance to ask why he was talking to her instead of Sal.

This time his call at least went to Sal's office. He recognized the big real-wood desk and the meter-long crossed silver arms emblem on the wall behind it.

But the man sitting at Sal's desk and staring back at him was not his old friend. This man was white, and had the hard-mouthed, expressionless face and ramrod-straight posture of someone whose life was devoted to giving—and unquestioningly taking—orders. If the severe, tightly fitting black onepiece he wore wasn't a uniform, it might as well have been.

"Schnaubel here." He glanced at Marchey's silver arms, his posture subtly shifting from rigid attention to the impatience of someone forced to deal with a annoying underling. "State your business."

"I'd like to speak to Sal Bophanza if I could, please."

The answer was immediate and unequivocal. "You cannot. Dr. Bophanza is not presently available—" The pale blue eyes of the man on the screen flicked to one side. His hands were out of sight, but a slight movement of his shoulders told Marchey he was accessing. "—Dr. Marchey." *I know who and what you are,* his face said with thinly veiled contempt.

"Can you, um, tell me how I can reach him?" Sal was *always* available. The Bergmann Program was his life. His devotion to keeping the Institute going and to those who had become the first and only Bergmann Surgeons was total. He had never married, and lived in a suite just off his office. Those rare times he left the Institute he carried a full commlink with him so he could be instantly available to those who might be no more than a friendly voice away from suicide.

This didn't look good. Not good at all.

"I am sorry," the man behind the desk said, his tone belying his words. "I am in charge here. Please state your business, Dr. Marchey."

Marchey made himself smile, even though he felt a sinking feeling in his gut. "No business, really. I just called to, ah, shoot the shit with Sal. Can you at least tell me when he'll be available?"

"Oh, I'm certain we'll have Dr. Bophanza back soon," Schnaubel replied, the superior, completely humorless smile that appeared on his face making Marchey suddenly very afraid for his old friend. "Is there anything else?" *Are you done wasting my valuable time?*

"No," Marchey said in the most offhand tone he could muster, "I don't believe there is. Thanks." He reached out and broke the connection.

"Well," he told the blank screen, sitting back and rubbing his chin thoughtfully. "That certainly put my mind at ease."

But it hadn't. Nor did the rest of his drink.

Late that very same night he was dragged from a restless sleep by an insistent, earsplitting beeping.

After a few sleep-fuddled moments to get his bearings, he realized that the sound was coming from the commboard. He crawled out of bed and shuffled over to it, yawning and rubbing his eyes.

Squinting at the array of multicolored pads, he finally figured out that a comm mode he'd never used before had become active. He scratched his bald pate, unsure what he was supposed to do, then hit the **?** pad because it seemed to sum up the situation perfectly.

The beeping stopped. The main screen above the board lit and displayed the message:

RECEIVING REQUEST FOR SECURE TIGHTBEAM MESSAGE LINK. ACCEPT?

He peered at it a moment, then shrugged. Why not?

So he hit the ACCEPT pad, muddily trying to puzzle out who would be calling, and why they weren't using the usual comm channels. The secure beamlock commsystem was a leftover from the ship's earlier life as a UNSRA courier packet. He hadn't even known the damn thing worked.

PLEASE STAND BY FOR FULL RECIPROCAL ALIGNMENT, he was advised. A few seconds passed. BEAMS LOCKED, LOW-LEVEL ENCRYPTION MODE. BE ADVISED THAT THERE WILL BE A .5 SECOND ENCRYPTION/DECRYPTION LAG.

The message scrolled up to the top of the screen, vanished.

"Yeah, so?" he asked the blank screen, which blipped as if in response.

Now a woman stared out of the screen at him. Her face was thin and pale, with high cheekbones and deeply etched lines at the corners of her clear hazel eyes. Her hair was moonlight gray and spilled over her shoulders. Her wide, generous mouth was quirked in an expectant half smile, and her arms were crossed before her ample bosom.

"Gory," she said. Her voice was low and whiskey-hoarse, with the slightest trace of a Russian accent. Marchey stared at her, remembering that face when it had been smooth and unlined, that voice when it had been a soaring alto which could wring tears from your eyes when she sang a love song.

" 'Milla," he replied, voice husky with the rememberance of the thirty-two-year-old Ludmilla Prodaresk. Raven-haired heartbreaker. Songbird. Brilliant diagnostician and surgeon.

Fellow Bergmann Surgeon. Her bare arms were silver, just like his own. How many years had it been since he'd seen her last? Ten? Twelve?

They looked each other over in silence. Marchey gazed at her careworn face, tracing the lines with his eyes and saddened that the years had used her so harshly. She was still beautiful, but it was the beauty of an Acropolis or a faded rose, of something that endures as a diminished shadow of its former glory.

Did the years show as clearly on his own face? Not that he'd ever been beautiful. He reached up and ran his hand over the top of his head as if pushing his hair back into place so he'd look his best.

When he realized what he was doing a rueful smile crept onto his face. There wasn't any hair left to push back, was there? The little bit clinging for dear life to the back of his head hardly counted. He could have easily had it replaced, but why bother? Just as she could have had a rejuve, but had not.

The mischievous grin Ludmilla gave him was so familiar that it resurrected the young woman he had known in her face and eyes. "You are looking like shit, Gory," she said, then burst out laughing. Her laugh was still young, still as warm and fresh as a spring breeze. It melted away the snows of regret in an instant.

"So are you," he assured her, laughing himself, looking her in the eye and an unspoken message passing between them: *We're still here. We may be battered and bruised and old before our time. We might have screwed up our lives in ways we never could have imagined when we were young by giving ourselves over to a dream that turned sour, but you're here and I'm here and* dammit! *but it's good to see you again!*

"It has been some long time," Ludmilla said.

"That it has." Marchey agreed. A lifetime.

The smile faded from her face, letting the years

creep back over it. "Must keep reunion short. There is covered pad marked 'M-S-E-M' on right side of your board. Please push it."

"Okay," he said uncertainly, looking down to find it. He flipped the hinged cover up and tapped the pad underneath.

It chirped and glowed blue. Ludmilla vanished in a squall of sleeting static. A message appeared in red:

MAXIMUM SECURITY ENCODING MODE ENGAGED. PLEASE STAND BY.

After a few moments the picture built back up line by line, but in a low-resolution monochrome.

Ludmilla was no longer alone.

"Hey there, Gory," drawled the man now standing beside her with his arm around her waist, his voice sounding hollow and synthetic. The loose open-throated shirt he wore showed the ritual scarifications on his chest, put there when he had achieved manhood on Mandela.

Marchey dropped into the chair before the console, gawping back in surprise. The man smiled at him, looking tired, but enormously pleased by the reaction he'd provoked.

"Surprised?" he asked.

Marchey nodded. "I sure as hell am, Sal."

It took Marchey a few moments to figure out what to say next. "No wonder I couldn't reach you back at the Institute," he managed at last.

Sal gave him a crooked grin. "I ran away from home."

Marchey remembered the ominous comment made by the man who had taken over Sal's desk. "I think they want you back. Quite badly, in fact."

"I'm sure they do. I, ah, appropriated a few items from the Institute when I left."

"You always did have your eyes on that Kamir holosculpture in the lobby."

Sal looked pained. "Actually, I had to leave that behind." He shook his head ruefully. "Hated to, but I had all I could carry."

Marchey knew what he was supposed to ask, and obliged his old friend. "What did you take, then?"

Sal shrugged his thin shoulders. "Oh, just everything MedArm needed to start turning out more Bergmann Surgeons."

It took Marchey several seconds to get his mind around that. "You're joking, right?"

"I wish I were." Sal's face was utterly serious now.

"I don't get it. You're saying *MedArm* wanted to take over the program and start making more of us. Aside from the fact that they allowed the Institute to be largely autonomous, I thought they had decided we were—how was it they put it?"

"Unworkable," Ludmilla put in. " 'An intriguing but unworkable dead end.' " A sardonic chuckle escaped her. "How could we argue? If there is one thing flat-butt bureaucrats should know, is dead end."

"So why the sudden change?" He shook his head. "It doesn't make any sense."

Sal shrugged. "I can't say for sure, Gory. There've been a lot of changes in MedArm over the last few years, not many of them for the better as far as I can see. A lot of new faces in key positions, and damn few of them with any sort of medical background. Real sweethearts, some of them."

"I think I met one of them when I tried to call you earlier today. A man named Schnaubel. He was sitting at your desk like he owned it. Pleasant fellow. All the warmth and charm of an ice-covered proctoscope. He seems to be looking forward to your return."

Sal nodded. "I imagine he does, and I sure hope he has to get used to disappointment." He hesitated, biting his lip. Ludmilla gave him a reassuring squeeze, whispering something in his ear. He nodded, then stood up straight, like a man facing a firing squad.

"I took them by surprise, Gory. Not because I was clever or anything like that. They just didn't expect me to do anything." He spread his hand in a helpless gesture, looking Marchey in the eye, appealing to him to understand.

"I haven't been much more than a figurehead in charge of an empty shell for a long time now. It's been years since I've had anything to do with scheduling or itinerary. MedArm took that over, and I couldn't do one damn thing to stop them. About four years ago I went to them, trying to arrange a convocation for all of you. I figured it would do you good to get together again. It has always killed me to see all of you so isolated, so alone."

His face hardened. "My request was summarily refused. The reason I was given was that it would be a, quote, *'inefficient disposition of resources'* unquote."

"We're being used very efficiently," Marchey said heavily, remembering Angel's accusation. He also remembered his angry denial. Had she come too close to a truth he hadn't wanted to face?

"We are still people, but they do not treat us so," Ludmilla said quietly, "We are little better than *robota* now."

"Yeah," Marchey agreed. She had used the Czech word Karel Capek had given the world in his play *RUR*: **Robota.** *Slaves.* Robots.

"We *robota* have no rights. No say in how we are being used." Her tone sharpened. "After a while we *robota* become so worn-out we are needing replacement. We become too troublesome to maintain."

"Or it looks like a better robots can be made," Sal added. "I got a call from an old friend inside MedArm, someone who had been culdesacked—'promoted'—into a trivial job with no real power. Some information she wasn't supposed to see happened to cross her desk. She warned me that MedArm planned to 'retire' me, take over the Institute, and start cranking out a new batch of Bergmann Surgeons. Crash Priority."

Marchey shook his head in confusion. It was late, and this was too much to absorb and understand all at once. "I still don't see what brought on this sudden reversal of policy."

"I can't say for sure," Sal said, "but I don't think it's coincidence that all of this seemed to start right after you found a way around the Nightmare Effect."

Marchey's first impulse was to dismiss the idea. But on second thought, it did make a certain amount of sense. He himself had wondered if it might be possible to restart the program, now that at long last a cure had been found for one of its most destructive elements. The next generation of Bergmann Surgeons might be able to lead something like normal lives.

But why the big fucking hurry to restart something the powers that be had been insisting was a failure? Why the power play? He said as much to Sal and 'Milla.

"The obvious conclusion is that they want the program strictly under their control," Sal answered glumly. "But what would that give them that they don't already have? They already have total control over you and 'Milla and the others."

He sighed, looking down at his hands. "You were right, Gory."

"About what?"

"About things turning out like this. I remember when MedArm first instituted the circuit. You said that all of you had been reduced to nothing more than specialized medical machinery—to tools. I told you you were wrong."

His tone turned apologetic, edged with self-recrimination. "*I* was wrong. It only made a bad situation worse. In the beginning I had a say in your disposition, but when I complained that they were running you too hard, they started cutting me out of the loop. The harder I tried, the worse things got." He raised one hand, let it fall in a helpless gesture. "I had to give up before I made matters worse."

"You've stood by us all the way, Sal," Marchey said quietly. Ludmilla nodded in agreement.

"Have I? The most useful thing I've been able to

do for years now was to just be there when one of
you needed a friend."

"That is thing to be proud of, love," Ludmilla told
him, one silver arm hugging him tight. He stared at
her a few moments, then back at Marchey, still looking like someone who believed he had done more
wrong in his life than right. Marchey knew how he felt.

"When I heard what MedArm was planning, I knew
I had to do *something*. So I asked for a couple weeks'
vacation. They were glad to grant it because it would
put me conveniently out of the way when they took
over the Institute."

Something of the old Sal appeared in his grin.
"Well, I fooled the fuckers! I grabbed all the critical
stuff—the hypnoregimens, tests, and the rest—wiped
everything else, leaving dummy files in their place.
'Milla happened to be there for some repair work on
one of her arms. So I showed up at her airlock, told
her what was going on, and here we are."

"Where's here? And what are you going to do
next?"

Sal made a face. "Here is nowhere, and I wish to
hell we knew. We really didn't have time to plan
ahead. 'Milla disabled her ship's transponder, scrambled the circuits that let them control the autopilot,
and we hightailed to the outer edge of the Belt because it's a good place to lose yourself. We were kind
of hoping you might know of a good place for us to
hide until we get this mess straightened out."

Marchey scrubbed his face with his hands, totally at
a loss. The only thing that came to mind was the question he'd wanted to ask Sal in the first place. So he
asked it.

"By the way, have either of you ever heard of the
Helping Hands Foundation?"

Sal and 'Milla exchanged a puzzled glance. Sal
shook his head. "No, why?"

"I'll tell you some other time."

The unlikely fugitives watched him expectantly as
he sat there, his thoughts stumbling through all he had

just heard like it was some sort of mental obstacle course. He was beginning to get a sneaking suspicion that somehow all this crazy stuff was connected. Nothing he could put his finger on, just a feeling.

He rubbed his eyes, forcing himself to put all that aside. Right now the important thing was figuring out some safe place for them to hide. Some out-of-the-way place where the people around them could be trusted not to reveal their presence.

At last a question with an easy answer. Maybe even a great answer if this Helping Hands Foundation was some half-ass bunch of incompetant do-gooders.

"I know just the place for two renegade doctors to go," he told them with a chuckle, pleased that he could be of some help to his old friends after all. "It's not much to look at, but I'd trust the people who live there with my life."

Coffee.

No brandy in it.

Slouched in the galley seat. Chin propped in his hand like a cut-rate copy of Rodin's *Thinker*. Its head was generally made of hollow bronze. People forget that.

He'd already been up for over three hours, having given up on sleep as a lost cause and dragged himself out of the sack quite a bit earlier than normal. All he had been doing was tossing and turning anyway. He had gone back to bed after saying good-bye to Sal and 'Milla, but the occasional fits of uneasy slumber had been filled with disturbing dreams that had him grinding his teeth and curling into a protective fetal ball.

He had dreamed of the people of Ananke, all slat-ribbed and hollow-eyed, chains on their legs, and silver arms like his own held out in entreaty. Walking among them, he had tried to pretend they weren't there. One by one they they had crumpled behind him, whispering gratitude as they fell. Another had a colossal Brother Fist prodding him through a dark maze, laughing at him when he stumbled into dead end after dead end while desperately trying to reach the small silver figure sinking deeper and deeper into the quicksand at the maze's center. He had a rope to throw her. It was around his own neck. *Not* a restful night.

The morning, however, had been highly productive. He had spent most of it pacing. Back and forth. Around in circles. Getting nowhere just as fast as his feet could carry him.

It was as if his world had fractured into an antique jigsaw puzzle. But no two pieces would fit together, and what the finished picture would be was a mystery. Or if the pieces did fit together, he couldn't see the congruence.

Pieces like: What was MedArm up to? Why were they trying to cut Sal out and take over the Institute—which was independently funded from Bergmann's estate, and supposedly autonomous as long as it met certain basic requirements MedArm itself had set?

And what, if anything, did that have to do with them letting some foundation do their relief work for them on Ananke?

He scowled and slouched lower, eyes half-focused on the steam curling up from his cup. Just like those nebulous vapors, there didn't seem to anything he could get a solid grip on.

Maybe Sherlock Holmes could figure this mess out, but he sure couldn't. He took a sip of his coffee, put the cup down. Drinking nothing but coffee and staying sober was supposed to have let him think more clearly. So far all it had done was send him to the head twice and make him more jittery than ever. Much more and he'd end up spending the rest of the morning alphabetizing his socks.

A glance at the clock reminded him that in just under half an hour Fist would be waking up. Which in turn reminded him that he had a whole other puzzle to deal with. One probably twice as insoluble and considerably more dangerous, a cryptogram that could put him in a crypt.

He toyed with his cup. In a way he almost had to admire the diabolical old bastard. There he was, on his way to be turned over to the authorities, so close to death that he could probably read the population number from the WELCOME TO HELL sign. So what does he do? He laughs and jokes and tries to play with my head. He drops hints that there's something going on I should know about, and tries to draw me into playing guessing games about what he wants in trade for telling me about it. As if he—

Marchey froze, coffee cup halfway to his mouth, eyes going wide with realization.

There *was* something going on. MedArm was trying to force Sal out and take over the Institute. So they could restart the Bergmann program. Their own way, whatever that was.

Fist had done considerable research into the Bergmann Program. Enough to find a way around the Nightmare Effect. Which meant he had an information pipeline into it. But—

—But Sal had just told him that the Institute had been cut completely out of the process of choosing where the Bergmanns went and who they treated. Yet Fist had known precisely when and where to send Scylla to grab him. That could only mean—

—*he also had a pipeline into MedArm!*

Marchey sat up straighter, brow furrowing as he followed that line of reasoning.

Everything Fist did was based on information. He learned all there was to learn about something, pinpointing its strengths and weaknesses.

He proved that he knew enough about Bergmann Surgeons to subjugate me, using my own ethics against me. He hinted that he knows all about this business with the Helping Hands Foundation—which leads back to MedArm again. Which means—

The old bastard probably knows exactly *what Med-Arm is up to. All* of it. *He'd as much as come right*

*out and said so. Some of the information was sure to
be locked away in those files Jon has so far been unable
to crack, but the whole picture is stored away inside
that tumorous reptile cage Fist has for a brain.*

Some of what he'd said could be construed as an
offer to hand over part of that information. To help.

But why would he want to change sides?

Allegiance. Fist had said that, hadn't he?

But his only allegiance was to himself. He had no
more loyalty than a gun or knife or bomb. Marchey
remembered the old man saying that he had once
worked for countries and corporations as a—what was
it he called himself?

A phagewar specialist. He had been, in effect, a
mercy. A freelance soldier of misfortune who would
work for you if properly motivated.

What motivates me?

"Damn," he muttered, his line of reasoning turning
circular. It was like the old fairy tale about Rumple-
stiltskin. *Guess my name.* Only in this case it was
Name my price.

Marchey sat back, pondering Fist's motivations.

*He has some sort of stake in all this. Botha Station
figures into it. There's something he wants. But he
won't come right out and say what it is. He has to
make a game of it . . .*

Marchey sat very still, sensing but not quite clearly
seeing the shape of the puzzle piece in his hand. He
thought back over all Fist had said to him, searching
for a clue.

Challenge. Reward. Accomplishment. Fulfillment.

*He can't keep himself from playing deadly chess with
people's lives. Until I came along he had won the game
on Ananke. He could have lived like a king, but instead
had lived an almost monkish existence. Why?*

Because the winnings didn't matter to him?

Because only the game itself mattered?

Because . . . only the game was real?

That seemed close, but not quite right. Then it

turned itself around in his mind, taking on a whole new shape and meaning.

Because he was only real—only truly alive—when he was playing?

It sounded too bizarre to be possible, but then again so was the man himself. Rather than rejecting the idea out of hand, he tried using it as a lens for examining the situation.

Several things suddenly sprang into clear focus. For instance, he'd put the old man under a sleepfield right after his fall. That should have slowed the progress of his disease to some degree. But it hadn't. Instead, his condition had soon after turned terminal. Yet he seemed to have hit some sort of plateau since first being awakened here on the ship.

Since he started playing with me. Almost as if that fed him, gave him a reason to keep living.

Marchey's eyes narrowed thoughtfully. What was it he said?

Even love. I love life when it puts the sweet raw stuff of possibility in my hands.

But that wasn't all. Right after he'd said—

It's put that same sweet stuff in your hands as well.

What cards am I holding? Maybe jokers and deuces, but no aces.

After a moment Marchey sat back and began to chuckle to himself. The game was still a mystery, but he was beginning to get an idea as to what his next move ought to be.

If jokers are all you hold, then that's just what you have to play.

Marchey beamed down at his gruesome patient and passenger. One sweet warm shot of scotch was nestled in his belly and on his breath. Another had been carefully splashed onto his clothes. He could smell its tantalizing scent with every breath. The slight flare of Fist's nostrils told him he smelled it, too.

In one hand he carried a glass, in the other a bottle. Grinning like he had a head full of laughing gas and saying not a word, he put the glass aside and went to work.

First he racked in a second bottle next to the bottle of sterilized in the unibed's liquids dispenser, this one filled with amber fluid. The tap of a pad filled the siptube with liquid gold. Then he clipped the tube next to the one for water, where Fist could reach it just by turning his head.

"There you go," he said jovially as he straightened back up. "Have a snort, old man." He retrieved his glass, held it up. "Be sociable. It's Happy Hour, and the drinks are on me."

Fist had watched him stone-faced and silent through the whole process. "What is it?" he rasped.

"Phoban scotch." He shrugged. "It isn't as good as the stuff you had stashed away on Ananke, but it beats the hell out of the recycled piss you get from the dispenser."

Fist's pus-colored eyes narrowed in calculation. "Why?"

"Well, you see they use real malt for one thing, and age it in genuine wood barrels shipped all the way up from Earth. That gives it a—"

"*Silence,*" the old man hissed. "I ask why . . . you have . . . brought it to me."

"Sorry." Marchey took a sip of his drink, smacked his lips. "I wanted you to help me celebrate going all the way off the wagon."

A slow blink as that information was absorbed and processed. "Why have you decided . . . to become . . . a worthless drunk again?"

"A talent like mine is a terrible thing to waste," he answered with a chuckle.

Fist stared up at him. "You amuse . . . only yourself. Or are you afraid . . . to tell me?"

Marchey shrugged, his grin turning into a grimace. "Maybe. I don't know." He jerked his chin in Fist's direction. "You're so goddamned smart, why don't you tell me?"

"Everything," Fist whispered, "is falling apart."

Marchey hung his head. "Yeah, you're right. Jon Halen can't crack any of your files, and I can't crack you. Sal Bophanza called last night. He's on the run. MedArm is trying to take over the Institute and start making more of us. They're up to other stuff I can't even begin to figure out. Angel has started acting strange, it's probably my fault, and there's not one damn thing I can do about it."

He blinked, took a long slug of his drink. "I can't stand being back on the circuit, at least not sober. I'm sick of not knowing what the hell's going on, and I'm tired of beating my head against a brick wall worrying about it."

An expansive shrug. "So fuck it! I give up! I've been a drunk before. It's not a bad life. It makes everything so much simpler and easier to take. I figure if you can't cure the disease, you might as well medicate the symptoms."

He pointed at the siptube. "You could use a dose yourself, old man. You've already got one foot in a body bag and the other on a banana peel. So why don't you join me? Misery loves company."

Fist ignored the offer. "You are only besieged . . . not defeated. Surrender is . . . premature. There might be . . . a way out . . . of your strait."

Marchey chuckled and held up his glass. "Sure is. This is it." He took another sip. "And it tastes good, too."

"No," the old man grated with an impatient shake of his head. "Every dark cloud . . . has a silver lining."

Marchey guffawed. "Right. Let's see. 'It's always darkest just before the dawn.' "

Fist's eyes blazed with anger. "Don't be . . . a simpleton! Pay attention . . . to me! *Every dark cloud has . . . a silver lining!*" He gasped for breath, winded. "That's im . . . portant!"

"And all you need is love," Marchey returned agreeably, reaching down to pat one bony cheek. "Maybe you'd rather drink alone. I know I do. Less distraction that way." He saluted Fist with his glass, then turned to leave.

"I'll be back to check on you in a little while," he called over his shoulder. "You better enjoy yourself while you can, you miserable old sack of pus. Time's running out."

"Remember . . . what I said!" Fist wheezed, coming as close to a shout as his ruined lungs would allow. "Dark . . . cloud! Silver . . . lining! It's im . . . *portant!*"

Marchey was on his way to the commboard even as the clinic door slid shut behind him. He dropped into the chair before it, letting out a pent-up sigh of relief.

Jon Halen was already on-line waiting for him, looking apprehensive. He let out his own sigh of relief when he saw that Marchey had survived his visit to Fist's lair.

"Well, Doc," he said, "how'd it go?"

Good question. Fist would have smelled a lie even faster than he'd picked up on the scent of whiskey, so he'd had to walk the thin outer edge of the truth, and it had taken total concentration. He felt like he'd just walked a molecule-thin tightrope over a pit full of poisonous snakes, but was pretty sure he'd pulled it off. The trip left his whole body feeling clammy with sweat.

"We'll know soon enough. Try this phrase on Fist's files: *Every dark cloud has a silver lining.*"

"Fist said that?" Jon asked doubtfully.

"More than once." He held up his silver hands. "It might just open the locked files on the Bergmann program."

"Well, let's give her a whirl." Jon looked offcam and began trying it as a passphrase. Marchey waited, listening to the painfully slow *clack . . . clack* of keys from Jon's end. The residual tension from trying to run a bluff on Fist made him feel edgy and impatient. Jon seemed to be taking forever. He reminded himself that the man had not only to work a keyboard, he was doing it with only half of one hand.

"Holeeeee shit," Jon breathed, looking off-screen in wide-eyed amazement. "We just cracked us open a hundred and sixtysome megs of hard data." He peered more closely at what was before him, nodding to himself. "You were right, Doc. It seems to be all about the Bergmann Program."

Marchey slumped back in his chair. His guess that Fist would give him something useful—something to keep him playing—if he thought that his playmate was giving up had been right on the money. The gamble had paid off. The problem was, that didn't necessarily mean the file contained good news. More likely it was bad. It had only been given up because Fist was sure its contents would make him want to stay involved. There was even a chance that Fist had seen through his bluff and had planned to give him this all along.

There was only one way to find out. "Transmit it to me, would you?"

Jon nodded absently. "Already workin' on it." He turned his attention back to Marchey. "There. I'll wade through it, too, just in case there's any passphrases to other locked files in it."

"We can hope, but the old monster doesn't give away anything for free."

" 'Cept trouble. How'd you get this out of him? Torture?"

Marchey shook his head. "I just told him what the situation looks like from where I stand, and convinced him that I was about to give up." That part hadn't taken much acting ability. If anything, it was too close to the truth for comfort.

"But you aren't going to give up, are you?"

"Not yet, anyway." Not that he felt anything like optimism. If your past predicts your future then he was doomed to failure.

Doomed.

That word had tolled in his mind for two days now. No hour went by that it didn't knell. He glanced up at the empty scotch bottle he'd brought from Ananke.

Every time he looked at it he thought of her, but he hadn't made himself put it out of sight.

"By the way," he said, trying for nonchalance and sounding unconvincing even to himself, "how is Angel doing?"

His insides tightened at the pained look that appeared on Jon's face. For a fleeting moment he wished he hadn't asked.

"Not so hot," Jon said slowly. "She's been workin' herself like some sorta machine. Goin at it twenty—thirty hours at a knock. She's eatin' just enough of that manna stuff to keep body 'n' soul together. She holes up in her room ever so often, to sleep I guess, and works straight out the resta the time. And—"

He hesitated, obviously trying to decide how much more to say.

Jon's reluctance to lay more troubles on Marchey's doorstep was appreciated, but it only made him dread hearing what was yet unsaid all the more.

"Tell me all of it," he said quietly. "I have to know."

"All right. Do you 'member Danny Hong?"

Marchey was unlikely ever to forget.

That last time he'd seen the boy had touched him deeply. Beyond that, he might well be where he was now because of Danny. Seeing him in the lockbay back when he first arrived on Ananke had been the moment when he had truly begun at least trying to look at what was around him, and trying to do something about it. It had nearly gotten him killed back then.

Now it was just driving him crazy. That was progress of a sort, he supposed.

"I remember," he said shortly.

"Well, Danny told me he saw Angel in one of the tunnels just last night. He said she was walkin' funny, like some sort of robot from an old vid, and that her good eye was closed. He swore up and down that she was asleep, or near enough to it to make no difference. So I went to check on her earlier today. She was diggin' in the mines, usin' only her hands and claws, and goin' at it like the devil hisself was whippin' her on. I had a helluva time getting her to stop and talk to me. She's lost weight, I think—that exo makes it hard to tell—and looks worn to a ragass frazzle. I asked her if she was okay. She told me she was just fine. Maybe a little tired sometimes, but not to worry 'cause her exo was makin her rest when she needed to."

"Shit," Marchey growled, sagging lower in his chair. He knew enough exotech to recognize what Jon had just described. To make a prognosis.

A combat exo like Angel's was designed for short bursts of furious activity, not protracted periods of heavy labor. It allowed its human host to drive his or her body far beyond the limits where an unaugmented person would simply collapse. That was something combat exo'd soldiers were constantly warned against, because if they pushed too hard for too long, the exo would be forced to take compensating measures. Partial and total overrides. Controlling limbs that were supposed to control it, and invoked rest periods where it would, if all warnings were ignored, actually partially disconnect her from her own body for her own protection.

Angel had never received proper training. Not that long ago she'd thought the silver biometal covering her was her own skin. She didn't know that she was forcing the quasi-aware nanostrand linkages spun into her nervous system to weave themselves deeper and wider inside her. To change the nature of their interfacings to meet the excessive demands she was putting on her body.

Serious changes.

Irrevocable changes.

She didn't know that she was slowly frying her own nervous system and forcing the nanostrands to take an active rather than passive role.

That she was all too probably condemning herself to having to wear that exo for the rest of her life.

—*Doomed her,* Fist intoned in his mind, looking pleased at the prospect of seeing his lost toy broken.

"Are you all right, Doc?" Jon's voice seemed to come from a thousand kilometers away. But it was millions, not thousands, wasn't it? She needed help. And where was he?

He sighed, scrubbing his face as if to wipe away the sense of guilt and hopelessness that had fallen over him. "Yeah." He had to do something about her, but what? He couldn't think of anything he could say if he got a chance to talk to her. Judging by his performance so far, he would only make things worse.

Jon was eyeing him with obvious concern, waiting for him to say something. Anything.

"Tell everyone—" he began, forcing himself to sit up straight. Tell them *what*? Come on you numbnuts excuse for a doctor, prescribe something! You knew she was working. You should have seen this coming.

"Tell them that if they see her, they should try to talk to her, to slow her down and keep her from working. See if you can find something for her to do that isn't so physically demanding. You've *got* to make her take it easier, make her rest more often."

"All right," Jon said carefully. "You're tellin me she's messin' herself up by workin' so hard?"

Marchey nodded, not wanting to elaborate. "Just be subtle about making her ease off. If she figures out what you're up to, it just might make matters worse." Because of all that Fist had done to her, she could not help but react badly to someone trying to control her actions. She finally had a will of her own, and would die before she gave even a little of it up.

"Consider it done," Jon said soberly. "Anythin' else?"

There probably was, but he couldn't seem to pull his thoughts together enough to figure it out. "No, not now. I better start going over the stuff you sent me. Stay close to that board, though."

"I'm livin' here, practically," Jon assured him, then cut the connection.

One green pad remained lit on Marchey's board. It indicated that the new information Jon had sent was waiting for him, ready to be accessed. He sat there staring at it for several minutes, his thoughts more than a million kilometers away.

At last he roused himself from his reverie. The time had come to find out what the file contained. He had a sinking feeling that he wasn't going to learn anything he really wanted to know.

Only one way to find out.

He reached out and tapped the pad. If nothing else, studying the file would at least give him a temporary escape from the self-recrimination squatting on his chest like a dour and patient vulture, its cry the strangled sound *doom*.

Marchey's metal fingers clattered over the keypad in a quicksilver blur. Before giving up his arms he had been a terrible keyboarder. Immediately afterward he'd found that his prosthetics allowed him to type considerably faster than he could voice input or chase menus. The biometal machines that had replaced his meat fingers were untiring and unerring.

He finished instructing the comp with a final burst of machine-gun-fast keystrokes.

READY TO ABSTRACT AND ANALYZE MATERIALS AS PER SPECIFIED PARAMETERS read the prompt. He hammered the BEGIN key home hard, almost vengefully. Like driving another nail into his own coffin.

WORKING the comp replied. PLEASE STAND BY.

As if that wasn't what he'd been doing all along.

Confirm the probable diagnosis with the appropriate tests. That was how any prudent doctor would proceed.

He slumped back and rubbed his bloodshot eyes, wanting a drink in the worst possible way. Craving it so badly his head pounded dully to its call, the vibrations throbbing through his nerves and making them buzz and itch. He could almost smell it. He licked his lips, his mouth watering for the taste.

But he knew he didn't dare. He'd end up crawling inside the bottle and closing the cap after himself. Once he got inside, it would be a very long time before he came back out again. If ever.

The comp seemed to be taking forever, and alcohol's siren call was growing stronger by the second. There was no spar to tie himself to, no way to clap his hands over his ears and shut out the strident babble inside his own head. The urge to find something he could hold on to sent his right hand drifting up to caress the silver Bergmann emblem pinned over his heart. His sculpted metal fingers traced the familiar shape delicately, as if probing a wound.

Two silver arms, crossed at the wrists, fingers spread wide. For over fifteen years he had worn that badge, and in turn been worn down by what it represented. It still looked new. He didn't.

His silver fingers closed around it. He squeezed his eyes shut and ground his teeth together as the urge to tear it off and hurl it across the compartment swept through him like a hot stinging wind, a sirocco of rage and resentment.

Better yet, he could crush it. Mash it all out of shape, just like his life had been warped all out of shape by what it had made of him.

The comp chimed. He opened his eyes and stared at the screen dully. READY TO DISPLAY ANALYSIS, read the display.

Wonderful. But was he ready?

Because of the way he had instructed it to extract and analyze certain data in the "silver lining" file, he knew there would be a graph. It would show a rising line that documented his fall from illusory grace. It would show him what he should have seen for himself long ago.

Smoldering anger and disgust with himself—with everything—made him clench his hand tighter. Inside his fist the silver emblem began to bend.

He came within a heartbeat of crushing it into an unrecognizable lump before he let his hand fall to his lap. He stared down at the pin. It was bent, but still recognizable. In spite of the way he and the others who wore it had been exploited, it still represented an ideal, and the ideal still lived. He couldn't let go of it. Not yet.

Marchey made himself sit up straight, stare reality right in the eye, and see his diagnosis confirmed. The touch of a pad put it before him.

He was still a doctor. He knew that you never pronounced something as terminal until you had explored every option.

And if you wanted to excise a malignancy, you had to first find out precisely what kind it was, and how far it had spread.

Fist's crepey eyelids fluttered as the sleepfield's effects wore off. His breathing quickened.

Marchey waited for him to come around, his hands gripping the unibed's high sides to keep him from grabbing the old man's frail shoulders and shaking him awake.

Those pus-yellow crocodile eyes opened slowly, fixed on him. Fist opened his mouth to speak, but Marchey didn't give him a chance to say a single word.

"Just keep your damned mouth shut and listen," he said tightly. "I'm not here to play games with you."

Fist closed his mouth, his eyes hooded and watchful. Something that might have been faint amusement crept out onto his fleshless face.

"I've read your 'silver lining' file. I know what the Bergmann Surgeons, myself included, have become." Saying what he had learned out loud was going to be hard, but now that he had faced the facts there was no going back.

"A certain faction inside MedArm has taken control of our disposition. They've made it so that our services are no longer available to the general public."

Dr. Khan back in the Litman commissary. She'd hinted at this. It had gone right over his head.

His mouth twisted, every word tasting bitter as gall. "We've only been used to treat a select coterie of the rich and powerful, or those useful to them. When you had me kidnapped at Litman, I had been brought in to treat the manager of a banking syndicate. One that just happened to hold the notes on mining equipment owned by a wilders' settlement. I figure those notes are now in the hands of whoever was behind all this."

His voice dropped lower, thick with fury and menace. "MedArm has been corrupted. They're sending this Helping Hands Foundation to Ananke. You thought that was pretty funny. You know what they're up to. Tell me."

Fist said nothing, still looking mildly amused.

Marchey stared down at him, wanting to wipe that smirk off clear down to the bone. He felt his lips peel back from his teeth, felt the steel top rail under his hands begin to flatten.

"We're not quite two days out from Botha Station. I don't think you're particularly happy about going there. I had a hard time figuring out why. Imprisoning you is no threat, you're totally bedridden as it is, and you know as well as I do that you'll be dead meat inside a week—that's if you last even that long."

Now he had to venture into a thicket of conjecture, but he made himself smile, as if his guesses were a straight true path through the thorny tangle.

"It seems to me that you have very few things left to lose. One is whatever spoils you took from Ananke. Another is all the nasty secrets you've hoarded over the years. Lastly, and I think most precious, is your pride. Which is considerable."

Fist gave a slight shrug, as if modestly accepting a compliment.

"Botha Station is owned by OmniMat," Marchey went on, the more he spoke the more certain he was that he'd pieced together at least this one small corner of the puzzle. "UNSRA might be the law in space and on Botha, but OmniMat's pockets are deep enough to let them buy just about anything they want. The minute they ID you red flags are going to go up all over the place. Odds are that not long after I turn you over to UNSRA, you simply disappear."

He nodded, watching Fist's face carefully. "You'd be quite a prize. Not only is every credit you ever stole up for grabs, you probably have all sorts of interesting information about their competitors, about the people they buy from and sell to, and even dirt on OmniMat itself locked away in that rotten old brain of yours. They'd take you off someplace private, shoot you full of drugs, and peel your every secret out of you. You would lose the final round of the game. You would die broken and helpless, humiliated and despoiled."

Fist hadn't flinched, hadn't shown the slightest sign of fear or even dismay. That maddening half smile remained, looking like it had been put there by an undertaker.

After a moment it widened, sharp white teeth gleaming between liverish lips. "Yes," he said in a low voice. "That is what . . . I *don't* want." His tone made it clear that there were still things he did want.

Marchey leaned over him. "You have two choices, old man. Either tell me about the Helping Hands Foundation, the full and absolute truth with the files to back it up, or I turn the sleepfield back on, and the next time you wake up you will be in the hands of people who want *everything* you know."

He waited for a reaction, his hands gripping the now flat guardrail, forcing himself to meet Fist's cold, unblinking stare. The taut silence made his ears ring, and the rising tension was a tightening steel band wrapped around his chest.

Fist gazed back at him, still looking as if he'd found all Marchey had said little more than mildly amusing.

Marchey felt the sweat trickling down his sides and threatening to pop out on his forehead. Fist was going to push it to the limit, to make him back down if he was bluffing.

He clenched his jaw to keep his resolve inside and reached for the sleepfield's controls, his gaze still locked with Fist's in a battle of wills where he was fighting as hard as he could and his opponent was scarcely exerting himself.

His hand settled on the touchpad. "Say good night."

The old man grinned, letting out a bubbling chuckle. "As I have . . . said before . . . you are an apt pupil." His thin hand twitched dismissively. "I concede. You are not bluffing . . . are you?"

Marchey shook his head, wanting to pant for air but making himself act as if nothing had happened. "No. I'll still do it if I think you're lying to me."

"Yes," Fist replied agreeably, "I believe . . . you would. There will be . . . no need. When I strike a bargain . . . I stick to it."

"Like the devil sticks to his deals?" Marchey asked with heavy sarcasm. "Should I change my name to Dr. Faustus?"

The old man let out a hacking chuckle. "Ah, now there . . . is a name . . . to conjure with! You flatter me. I am not so . . . very different . . . from you. Just a man . . . who excels . . . at his art. That is how . . . I see myself . . . you know. As an . . . artist."

Marchey stared at him. "Is that so?" he asked at last. Fist might just be stalling, but he doubted it. This was probably the overture to the next level of whatever infernal game he was playing.

Although he'd said he was done playing games with the old man, he knew he had only just begun. As the stakes grew higher the chances of walking away from the table diminished. He couldn't pass up the chance that he might learn something useful. Like it or not, Fist had drawn him into the game, and made sure he'd won just enough to keep on playing. Even this apparent victory was like as not part of the hustle.

"I do. Artistry . . . may be defined . . . by a total mastery . . . over materials . . . shaped toward a vision." A sly look crossed his goblin's face. "Take your old love . . . Ella Prime . . . for example."

The mention of Ella's name rekindled an ache in the old scar tissue stitched across his heart. He knew he shouldn't be surprised that Fist knew about her. The sly bastard had proved again and again that Marchey's life was an open book to him. Dredging up Ella's name was supposed to be the first blood in this new fencing match.

"All right, let's," he returned blandly. Much to his surprise, when he tried to visualize Ella's face he saw Angel's instead, and the ache it caused was fresher, sharper, deeper.

If Fist was disappointed at his gambit's failure, he didn't let it show. "She is a sculptor. Her chosen material . . . is clay. Clay is base stuff . . . unformed earth . . . unformed man . . . if you believe . . . in the fable of god. It is nothing . . . until her hand . . . transforms it. I too am a . . . sculptor of sorts. People and lives . . . situations . . . are my clay."

"People and clay are nothing alike."

Fist's wispy eyebrows arched. "You think not?" The ghost of a shrug. "Perhaps you . . . are right. People are . . . more common. More mallable. Clay must be . . . found and dug. It does not . . . seek the hand. The human herd begs . . . to be shaped. They let outside influences . . . be impressed like thumbprints . . . into the shape . . . of their lives. They willingly become . . . slaves of wages . . . and possessions . . . of fashion or ideology . . . of another's opinion . . . of religion. They seek . . . rather than evade . . . being pressed into . . . armies . . . movements . . . mobs . . . into any shape . . . the artist . . . chooses. They are . . . an irresistible . . . material."

Fist paused, panting for breath after this speech. He held up one skeletal hand to say that he wasn't done. There was a feverish brightness in his gaze, and his usual ironic tone had been replaced with something like passion.

"As for . . . the artist . . . he must create . . . or

else . . . the fire inside . . . consumes him. He must make . . . his works . . . by his own . . . vision of beauty. No standard . . . but his own . . . has meaning . . . no critic . . . may rightly . . . judge him."

He dropped his hand, inviting rebuttal.

Marchey couldn't argue with his assertion that people let their lives be shaped by all sorts of outside forces, few of them worthy; he had only to look at his own life to see the painful truth of that. But he had seen Fist's "artistry" firsthand.

"You're an egopathic monstrosity," he returned bluntly. "Your so-called artistry is nothing more than calculated, conscienceless brutality. Hitler was not an artist, and neither was Van Hyaams."

He shook his head. "You can't justify your crimes by calling them art. You are a lot of things, old man, none of them any damn good. But I never suspected you to have a weakness for rationalization or self-delusion."

Fist only smiled. "Perhaps the self . . . itself . . . is a delusion. But I digress. You have learned . . . much from me. I have made . . . my mark on you. Yet I am not surprised . . . you cannot grasp . . . my aesthetic. Few can. But here is something . . . within your grasp: One is either . . . sculptor or clay. Maker . . . or made thing. There is no . . . middle ground. One shapes and commands . . . or is dumb earth . . . in another's hand."

Fist's gaze narrowed, turning sharp as a poisoned blade, stabbing into Marchey's eyes and nailing him in place. "That is all . . . there is to life. Use or be used. Fight or surrender. If you want . . . to no longer be clay . . . then look about you. Seek the means. Seize the moment. If you have . . . a way to shape things . . . be it tool . . . or weapon at hand . . . then *use* it."

Marchey shivered, feeling as if a breath of absolute zero had passed over him. There it was: *If you have a weapon at hand, use it.* He couldn't make it any more explicit than that, could he?

The weapon Fist was referring to was, of course, his own self. Everything up to now had been a maze of passages leading to this juncture. The climb up the mountain before the high and wide vista of temptation was revealed.

Oh yes, he was tempted. He wanted to make Med-Arm pay for what they had done to him. That caustic urge churned in his guts; it had an even stronger hold on him than drink. The more he thought about the things they had done, the more his thoughts turned to retribution and revenge.

Now he had been offered the keys to an engine of vengeance. Fist *was* a weapon, like some unspeakable doomsday computer given human form; tell him what you wanted destroyed, and he would tell you how to reduce it to smoldering ruins. He didn't have the slightest doubt that even though the old abomination was more dead than alive, he was still more than equal to the task.

Should I change my name to Dr. Faustus? He remembered asking that, not knowing how close to the truth he had come.

There was the rub. No matter how carefully the deal was struck there were bound to be hidden costs. It would be like opening Pandora's box. There would be no knowing what evils would come of it, and no way to put them back once they had been loosed.

"This has been all very interesting," he told Fist with a feigned indifference that sounded all too false. "But right now I need information, not philosophy, and you owe me some."

Fist stared up at him, searching for evidence that he had been tempted, prying at the lines of his face with cold, clever fingers, seeking the slightest crack in his facade.

Marchey pursed his lips. "Is it time for a long nap?"

Fist let out a sigh that might have been either pleasure or exasperation, letting his head roll to the side. "Very well. What was it . . . you wanted to know?"

"The Helping Hands Foundation."

Fist squinted up at him with one yellow eye, withered lips twitching into a grim smile. "It's not going . . . to make you happy . . . or make things easier."

Probably not. "Tell me."

"It is . . . a Trojan horse."

Marchey's heart sank. "Explain," he said bracing himself to hear the worst.

Fist did explain, expressing some admiration for the scheme's diabolical design. It wasn't hard to tell that the old villain was holding nothing back. He obviously thought that finding out just how dire the situation was would only make Marchey all the more likely to take him up on his offer and pay his still-unstated price.

As soon as Fist was through, Marchey raced to the comm to call Jon Halen and give him the bad news.

Jon had heard Marchey out, his customary good cheer eroding away, leaving his gaunt brown face looking old and tired, drooping like a sail with the wind taken out of it. His bony shoulders slumped inside the threadbare flowered shirt he wore, skinny arms draped limply over the arms of his chair.

It occured to Marchey that they were all of them old: himself, Jon, Sal, and 'Milla; old and out of their depths, thrashing about in a shark-filled sea of changes, trying to fight the remorseless currents and stay ahead of the teeth at their feet, too long past the vigor of youth to have much chance of reaching the shore.

Jon squared his shoulders, running his misshapen hand though his gray-flecked black hair. "So what should we do?"

Marchey spread his hands. "Keep them from landing if you can."

"If we can," Jon echoed uncertainly. "What if we can't?"

"I guess you have to try to keep them bottled up in their ship."

Jon didn't look particularly excited about Plan B. He leaned closer to the pickup. "Are you absolute *sure* Fist an't lyin' to you about all this?" he asked plaintively. "He'd think trickin' us into refusin' doctors and medical supplies was funnier'n a rubber crutch."

"He's telling the truth," Marchey replied tiredly. "There won't be any real doctors or nurses on that ship, just mercys with enough field medicine training to pass as medicos. You take them up on whatever little help they'll be able to offer, and it will cost you everything you have left."

"How can you be so sure?"

"Fist has a file on it. The passphrase is *Indian Blanket Benevolence.*"

Jon frowned and shook his head. "I don't get the reference."

"Old Earth history. The settlement of the American West and the subjugation of its native peoples. One of the most efficient and effective strategies for killing off the indigenous peoples so their land could be taken was giving them blankets."

"Blankets?"

"Blankets infested with highly infectious disease vectors. What looked like a philanthropic act was actually cold-blooded, premeditated genocide. A dozen blankets could wipe out a whole tribe."

Jon shuddered, looking sick. "They really did that?"

"They did. In this case they don't want you dead, but in debt. Accept their help, and you'll be signing over mining rights, equipment, and yourselves as a ready-made work force all at once. I didn't get all the mechanics, Fist just gave me the high points. It's all in the file."

"Just like old times," Jon muttered darkly. "Here we were thinkin' we were home free now we was rid of Fist."

"I know. That's why it's imperative that you have nothing to do with the Helping Hands Foundation. If they get off that ship or land supplies, they've as good as won. All they have to do is bully somebody into signing the acceptance contract, and I doubt they'll hesitate at using force."

"Okay, I got all that, Doc," Jon said evenly. "But I don't see how we can keep them off our backs forever."

"I'm trying to figure something out. If I can't, I'll just have to use my fallback plan."

"Mind tellin' me what that might be?"

Marchey sighed, not really wanting to say it out loud. "Worse comes to worst I point Fist at the situation and pull the trigger. He knows a way to stop them."

Jon stared at him, his brown eyes wide with disbelief. "You're kiddin' me, right?" he demanded.

"I don't know if I am or not," Marchey admitted bleakly. No matter how much he tried to make it sound like there might be some other way out of this mess, he couldn't see any alternative. All he could do was put it off until the last possible moment.

Jon's face hardened, and he leaned closer to the pickup. "Listen, Doc, and listen good. That old man fucks over everthin' he touches. He'll fuck you over, too, you give him the chance."

"That's a definite possibility," Marchey acknowledged. Once before Fist had given him what he wanted and very nearly destroyed him in the process. It was hard to imagine him passing up another chance.

"There has to be some other way out of this," Jon insisted, sounding as if he really believed it. "You'll find it. You won't haveta go that far."

"I sure as hell hope you're right." Jon's optimism and faith in him was reassuring, and yet at the same time unnerving. How could they trust him? He'd deserted them, and left them open to this. "The longer you keep them at bay the better my chances."

"I know I'm right. Anythin' else?"

"Keep an eye on Angel for me. Keep her out of this. I don't want her to get hurt." *Any more than she was already hurting herself. Any more than I've hurt her myself.*

Halen nodded soberly. "We'll do everthin' we can. You can count on us."

He knew he could, too. That was the one gleam of light in the byzantine labyrinth he had somehow strayed into, knowing he wasn't facing it entirely alone.

But then again, he was the least of those who would suffer if he failed.

Angel watched Marchey's face fade from the big main screen as the connection was broken. Jon's face had been displayed on a smaller side screen that blanked at the same time, but she never noticed.

She sat quietly at the end of her pallet. The toll taken by the past few days showed in her face. Too many hours of work and too few of rest had pared it down, sharpening the curves and throwing her cheekbones into prominence. Her green flesh eye was sunken and kohled with fatigue.

It had only been by chance that she had taken a moment to stop by her cubby on her way from the minehead to grab a handful of manna before going on to put in a ten-hour shift at the smelter. Only chance that she had been there at just the right moment to listen in on Marchey's call.

When she had gone into her room her mouth had been set in a grim line that said she was running on will alone. That line had begun softening when she saw *his* face, and now it was very nearly curved into a smile.

She had come within a heartbeat of breaking in and revealing that she could tap in on their call. It had been seeing the ghostly reflection of her own haggard face on the glassy surface of the screen that had stopped her. As badly as she wanted to make some sort of contact with him, she couldn't let him see her like this. Now she was glad. The missed chance had become a promising opportunity.

Angel took a deep breath, let it out slowly.

He hasn't forgotten about me.

He cares.

It was strange how your life could turn on such a small thing as the admission that you needed to eat. She had heard people use the word *fate,* but never really understood what it meant before this. *Sometimes fate smiles,* people said.

Yes, sometimes it did. Fate had given her a better way of atoning for her life as Scylla. A way to repay the Kindred for their forgiveness. A way of proving that she was Angel and not the hated other.

A way of helping *him,* and perhaps even proving that she was worthy of his attention.

Fate had given her the chance of a lifetime, and she intended to take it.

She crawled back onto her pallet and set her exo's internal alarm to waken her in six hours. She would go on as before so that no one would know she had eavesdropped, but would rest more often and eat better.

Now she had a reason to harbor her strength.

Angel closed one eye and switched the other off to better see Marchey's face inside her mind. Her face was placid. A tender smile of anticipation sweetened her lips.

Even before she fell asleep she was dreaming.

Marchey sprawled across his bed, his mind as restless as his body was still. *You've got to sleep,* he told himself for the hundredth time, only setting off a new chain of associations and memories.

To sleep, perchance to dream on if you think you've got to think maybe she'll be all right if only I'd . . .

Even if he did sleep, he would only dream of all the things that plagued his waking hours. There was no escape. He felt as if he had fallen into a version of *Alice in Wonderland* rewritten by Kafka and Dante. A quicksand rabbit hole to Hell.

He turned his head to stare longingly at the glass on his bedside table. Enough 140-proof grain alcohol to start him down the road to unconsciousness like he had wheels on his ass.

But would the road really end there? If he drank that magic potion, he could slip free from the bewildering web of conspiracy, deception, and intrigue he had somehow become trapped inside for a time. Once free, would he ever come back?

Sure he would.

He turned his head and went back to contemplating the smooth white overhead, mind turning but getting nowhere, like a lame gerbil on a squeaky treadwheel.

Somehow he'd found himself in the center of this whole mess, even though he was dead square in the middle of nowhere without the faintest idea where to go or what to do next.

"This is stupid," he muttered, sitting up and gazing blankly around him. He just couldn't shake the feeling that he was forgetting something, that there was some critical piece of the puzzle right in front of him. Something so obvious that he kept overlooking it.

When he was a boy there had been a program called *Smiling Stan the Answer Man.* Stump him and you won a prize. Where was old Smiling Stan now that he needed him?

In spite of himself, his gaze was drawn toward the door to the inship clinic.

"You could turn everything around, couldn't you?" It wasn't really a question.

A foreboding smile appeared on Fist's skull-like face. "Several ways. Some quite . . . delightful."

Marchey shivered, snugging his robe tighter about him. He had seen enough of Fist's works to find it easier to imagine what he might find delightful than was good for his peace of mind.

"Do you have a conscience?"

"No," Fist answered with absolute certainty and no small pride. "Why should I wear . . . a ring in my nose . . . so that others might . . . lead me around by it?"

Marchey was tempted to follow up on that, but the last thing he needed to hear was that he was agonizing over everything for nothing. That any sense of responsibility or even guilt was only a delusion.

He had to keep moving, keep hitting Fist with scattershot questions. The old man seemed to have only one weakness. His smug self-assurance made him so sure of himself and his own superiority that he could not resist making his infernal games more interesting by perversely putting possible victory in his opponent's hands without their knowing it. By dropping cryptic hints, or even whole answers spun in such a way as to seem like questions.

"Is there—is there really any chance you would give me the passphrases that would access everything you stole from Ananke?"

That maddening smile grew broader. "Yes. If . . . properly motivated."

That answer caught Marchey by surprise. He had expected coy evasion. "What would you want?"

"Something which would . . . please me even more."

Marchey knew he was supposed to ask what it was he wanted, so he sidestepped the question. "You aren't in any position to spend any of your gains," he pointed out instead, making himself smile. "You can't take it with you."

"Perhaps not." A dismissive twitch of one bony hand. "Many things . . . I have accrued . . . will remain behind . . . most to never be unearthed. Not much of a memorial . . . but I cannot think . . . of many who would raise . . . a monument in my honor."

"What else are you leaving behind?" Marchey could have pointed out that Fist's memorial was the trail of destruction and misery and death he had left in his wake. What outrages had he committed before coming to Ananke? How wide a swath had he cut?

Back on Ananke a woman named Elyse Pangborn had begun compiling a list of those who had died under Fist's reign. Almost three hundred names had been on it when he left, and still all the sorrows had

not been counted. He could remind Fist of that, but
the old architect of atrocity would probably thank him
and turn blackly nostalgic.

"Unused power," Fist husked, as if naming a remembered lover. "I am even now . . . a powerful man.
With a few words . . . I could cause . . . empires to
crumble. Could trample the mighty . . . under my
feet . . . even though . . . I can no longer . . . even
stand."

It was temptation time again. Marchey doubted Fist
was boasting. He had hired out to governments and
corporations alike before descending on Ananke like
a terrible predator. He would have as a matter of
course sniffed out their every weakness and shaken
hands with every skeleton in their closets, making certain that he could destroy them if the need—or even
just the whim—arose.

"Do you really like destroying things?"

Fist regarded him, one wispy eyebrow raised as if
surprised he could ask such a crass question. "I like
to . . . *change* things. It is so easy . . . it is irresistible.
As for the other . . . Rome was counted beautiful . . .
long after . . . its empire collapsed . . . and its . . .
great works crumbled. Destruction . . . like beauty
lies . . . in the eye . . . of the beholder."

None of that was anything he could, or should even
try to argue. He had to try another tack.

"Do you like being the way you are?"

Fist grinned slyly. "Do you?" A condescending note
entered his phlegmy voice. "At least I am . . . not
what others . . . have made of me . . . not blindly
playing . . . a fool's role . . . assigned to me."

Marchey felt a chill, knowing Fist had just told him
something important. He stared at the old man.
"What are you telling me?"

"The obvious." Cruel humor glinted in his yellow
eyes. "Isn't that obvious?" *Haaaaaaaaaaaa.*

Marchey licked his lips. "Go on."

Fist shook his head, feeble but unbendable. "This

game is played . . . one move at a time. Now it is your move . . . my dear doctor.''

Am I playing some sort of role? A fool's role at that?
He shook his head, frowning in concentration. That wasn't quite what Fist had said. *Am I still playing a fool's role assigned to me?* Assigned was a key word, he was sure of it.

He leaned back in the galley seat, drumming his metal fingers against the tabletop as thoughts rattled through his head.

What am I doing?
Going crazy. Wishing I was drunk. Wishing I'd never left Ananke. Wishing I had some way to help Angel. Feeling old and stupid. Playing mind games with a psychopath. Trying to figure out what the hell is going on inside MedArm while I'm stuck on this goddamn ship with the shit about to hit the fan back on Ananke—

He blinked, gray eyes widening as pieces fell into place with an almost audible click.

I'm stuck on this ship. Back on the circuit again. On my way to Botha Station.
But why?
Because it's my job, it's what I do. Because—
Because MedArm is sending me there!

He sat bolt upright, a chill running down his back. "Is that obvious enough for you, Doctor Dickhead?" he muttered to himself in sour amusement. His mind raced in a hundred directions as that one simple fact illuminated so many things that had been in darkness. He forced himself to calm down and go through it one step at a time.

They're sending me there to treat a single patient they rate as more important than all the people of Ananke.
Who was the patient? What was wrong with him or her?

They had never said. No name, no condition. Just the expectation that I would unquestioningly obey orders.

Why shouldn't they expect that? He always had.

He got up and began to pace the carpeted deck, the hem of his robe flapping around his bare legs. That led to a couple obvious conclusions. But there was something else . . . a further inference nagging at the edge of his thoughts. Two more unconnected pieces drifting closer together, very nearly locking into one.

Sal said that it appeared MedArm had suddenly decided to take over the Institute and restart the Program right after a way around the Nightmare Effect had been found.

Now he knew that MedArm—or at least some group inside it—had been using the Bergmann Surgeons to further some hidden agenda of their own by using them to treat only certain people. He and 'Milla and all the others had remained unaware of how their use had been corrupted because the Nightmare Effect made it pointless to try to get to know their patients— not that the speed with which they were shuffled around gave them much chance anyway. That dovetailed so neatly it had to be engineered.

He turned on his heel, pacing back the way he'd come. Even if he hadn't stumbled onto the "silver lining" file, the end to the Nightmare Effect meant that sooner or later he and the other Bergmanns would have realized that his patients were almost never your ordinary Joe or Jane. They weren't stupid. They'd figure it out. When that happened they would be appalled, just as he had been. They would be outraged.

As a group, they could best be described as battered idealists. Their idealism was what had led them to risk their hands and their careers in the Program in the first place, and its tattered remnants kept them clinging to its promise in spite of the ruin it had made of their lives. None of them had much to lose. Once they figured out how they were being used they would rebel.

Marchey stood stock-still, having reached the sharpened hook at the end of this chain of deduction.

When that happened, MedArm would need replace-

ments. They had too good a thing going to give it up now. 'Milla's comment about them becoming robots that had become too troublesome to maintain had been right on the mark, as had Sal's remark about better ones being made. Obviously the new group of Bergmann Surgeons would be operating under a very different set of inducements, expectations, and motivations than the originals.

Back to the obvious, now that at least a little of the murk surrounding the Institute takeover had cleared.

The patient waiting for him on Botha Station was important to MedArm. One of the select few allowed to receive what the Bergmanns had to offer. More important than all the people of Ananke.

How important?

Now there was a question worth pursuing.

He cinched the belt on his robe tighter and headed toward the commboard. It was about time he found out just who he was going to treat, and why. But he wasn't going to ask MedArm. No, he was going to give the doctor in charge of the case a friendly call. Colleague to colleague.

When that was done he was going to permit himself one single weak drink. Not to forget, but to celebrate.

After all, it wasn't every day that he went back into private practice.

5

Intervention

"Well, Doc, we've got us some visitors."

Jon Halen was wearing the same flowered shirt he'd worn the day before, only now it was wrinkled and rumpled, probably from being slept in. There was at least two days' worth of stubble on his cheeks and chin, and deep bags under his bloodshot brown eyes.

"I told 'em to piss off," he went on. "They didn't have no by-your-leave to land, but they ignored me. They overrode the outer landin' shaft doors somehow and they're comin' on in like they own the place." He made a face. "Rude bastids."

Marchey marvelled at how calm Jon sounded. He wanted to curse and pound on something at the unfairness of it all, but somehow kept his voice even. "Damn. All I needed was another half hour."

At this point he was running on fumes. Sleep had been out of the question as the deadline approached, and he'd spent hour after hour going over what information he had, searching for whatever leverage he could find. Now that the moment of truth was nearly upon him he felt unreadier than ever.

"We'll try to buy it for you." Jon grinned. "Hope our credit's still good. You really think this patient of yours—"

"Preston Valdemar." The name of the physician in charge at Botha's Medical Section was Dr. Raphael Moro. He had given Marchey Valdemar's name, but refused to disclose his condition or anything else about him. Was that out of simple pique because he'd called the man in the middle of the night and awakened him? Or was it on MedArm's orders?

"Right, I remember his name from the Helping Hands file. Let's hope he has the mojo to call 'em off. How're you gonna convince him?"

Now there was a part of his plan he hadn't let himself examine too closely. "Any way I can." He took a deep breath, let it out. "Just get me that half hour and keep them from getting a foothold."

I will.

Angel made herself tear her gaze away from Marchey's face on the screen and turned back toward her locker. Inside it was the most certain way of keeping that promise.

The most certain and the most dangerous.

She wanted to pray for guidance, but her new self had not yet decided if she believed in God or not—largely because her old self had been so sure of it.

It was strength she wanted to pray for, because in her weakness she found herself seriously contemplating a course of action which could all too easily end up welding the silver skin of Scylla forever around her. Because now that the moment she had been waiting for was nearly upon her she felt small and afraid, completely unequal to the task she had set for herself.

There seemed to be only one way to banish the fear. A way that would at the same time make her more than equal to the threat posed by the intruders. All she had to do was reach out and take it.

Scylla's silver bracers hung there before her on their charging hooks in the locker. They seemed to gleam with promises of power and completion. They could make everything all right.

She snatched one off its hook with a sudden, convulsive movement and clamped it against her arm.

It responded instantly, powering up the moment its receptors touched the scarred bare skin on the back of her left hand. The status display popped up in the left periphery of her angel eye as the biometal artifact wrapped itself around her forearm like a living thing. Words and numbers flickered, changing as the weapons systems built into the bracer locked themselves into the exo's circuits and her own nervous system.

A Scylla-thrill of coiled power radiated up her arm from the bracer, sweeping away her fear and doubt before it. With it surged the heady remembrance of *power*. With just a thought she could release a howling burst of energy capable of punching through the hardened steel of a ship's hull like so much foil. Even without her other bracer, nothing made of blood and bone could stand against her. The intruders were doomed if she went to them like this, with Scylla's armaments to back her up.

—If she went to them *as* Scylla.

The shadow self of Scylla was the returning memory of strength and certainty and purity of purpose. Of fearlessness.

Life as Angel had been nothing but a morass of doubt and confusion and longing. Angel was a creature of weakness and helplessness and futility, her lot fear and pain and failure.

Angel had vowed not to hurt anyone ever again, never suspecting the dire circumstances she would face.

Scylla would cut the invaders down like wheat before a scythe. Nothing could stand in her way.

Nothing.

Least of all that fragile construct named Angel. The person she was now. The one *he* wanted her to be.

"No," she whispered, giving the mental command while she was still able. The bracer went back to standby and reluctantly released itself to dangle from

her arm like some war god's notion of a charm brace-
let. She peeled it off and put it back on its hook.

There was a long, white, hooded robe in her locker,
one her old Master had made her wear sometimes.
She chose that over Scylla's most dangerous aspects,
shrugging into it and knotting the belt tightly. Then
she closed the door to her locker, leaving sure victory
behind as she turned on her heel and began her journey toward the landing bay.

More than the fatigue earned by the last few days
made her walk slowly. But Angel held her head high,
knowing that she had just won the first very important
skirmish of the battle to come.

Marchey's ship had approached Botha Station like
a steel bee homing in on the center of a gargantuan
chrome poppy, bathed in the light reflected from the
vast spreading petals of silvery superfilm reflectors ar-
rayed around the complex. Beyond it, Jupiter's cyclo-
pean bulk blotted out the stars with a seething chaos
of color endlessly swirled by a madman's brush; its
staggering size dwarfing the imagination. Earth herself
could disappear inside old Jove like a pea in a bucket,
and its untrammeled breadth never completely fit inside the human head. Jupiter was always far vaster
than you remembered, even if you had just seen it
less than an hour before.

Botha's artificially maintained heliostationary orbit
kept it always in sight of the bright nailhead of the
distant Sun. That took energy to burn. Its existence
made a loud, all-but-impossible-to-ignore statement
about the wealth and power the company had at its
command.

The station was OmniMat's center of Jupiter operations, a sprawling complex of docking trees, free-fall
manufactories and materials dumps, transfer site for
the refined raw materials extracted and excreted by
the huge autofactories gnawing at the moons in
toward the planet's surface. Reaching out from its center like ten-kilometer-long stamens were the magnetic

catapults used to launch ships and fling containers of
the more durable goods sunward.

Botha was a place of endless day and ceaseless activity. The autopilot in Marchey's ship had locked into
local traffic control and begun picking its way through
busy swarms of workpods and past ponderous container tugs a while earlier. Jon called back just as Marchey's ship was sliding into its assigned berth at one
end of the main residential cylinder of the sprawling
complex.

Marchey had already changed into soft gray trousers
and a pristine white tunic, and was just putting the
bent silver pin in its place over his heart when Jon
came back on-line.

"We got trouble, Doc," he said without preamble.

"Tell me." The pin in place, he picked up his coffee.
He wasn't thirsty, but he needed something to do with
his hands, and thanks to his prosthetics he would have
splintered his teeth trying to bite his nails.

"I think I'd best show you."

Jon's feed blipped into a small inset at the upper
left corner of the screen. The rest of it changed to a
view of Ananke's loading bay as seen from high
above. Marchey assumed that the feed came from one
of the spyeyes Fist had put in every corner of his
empire.

"They came into the same dock you used," Jon explained over the muted grumble of sound coming from
the bay. "No big surprise there 'cause we only got the
one workin'. But they overrode the locktube somehow, jammin' their lock right up against ours, bustin'
the outer doors."

Another inset appeared, the view from the pickup
outside the lock skewed off at an angle, but showing
a section of matte black hull up tight against the stone
wall. There was nothing to keep them from leaving
their ship and coming through the inner airlock doors.

Nothing but the small, white-clad figure standing in
the middle of the wide ramp before the inner doors
and barring the way.

"Angel," Marchey said, feeling his insides go cold as methane snow.

"Mebbe not."

"Then who?" he demanded, the moment he said it knowing what Jon's answer would be, and his foreboding warping into dread.

"Scylla." Jon made a helpless gesture. "Angel's not a fighter, but *she* sure as shootin' is. Hell, none of us are fighters, you know that. Since the greatest danger seemed to come from lettin' them split us up, we planned to all get in front of the lock, sit down and link arms—try to use passive resistance. Just as we were gettin' ready to put ourselves in place she showed up, pushin' right through, ignorin' everybody 'cept to tell 'em to get back. She planted herself there, and an't moved a muscle since."

The pickup zoomed in closer, but revealed little more. The robe she wore concealed her exo, its hem brushing the floor to hide even her feet. Her head was bowed as if in prayer, the robe's hood shrouding her head and face. Her arms were crossed before her chest, her hands hidden by the robe's sleeves.

"She may have slowed them down a mite," Halen continued. "Nothin's happened in the time it took me to get back here from the bay, but—"

"But sooner or later they're going to try to come out," Marchey finished with leaden certainty. He glanced at the stacks, seeing that he would be locked in and cleared to debark in about two minutes. His gaze was drawn back to the small white figure standing guard before the lock's double doors.

Somehow he knew he was seeing Angel, not Scylla. Scylla would never hide her exo, for instance. Nor would she have waited passively, she would have gone in after them. But it wasn't really a matter of Angel being there and Scylla being off somewhere safely out of the way, like Luna or Limbo or Los Angeles, was it?

She's in here with me. That's what Angel had told him. Like a violent genie in a fragile bottle. Rub it the wrong way and out she would burst in all her awful glory.

Angel was in way over her head. No matter how good her intentions, if the situation turned ugly, it could all too easily crack the fragile shell she had built around the creature Fist had made of her and cause her to revert to Scylla.

If that happened, the threat would probably be neutralized. He knew that the combination of Scylla's fierce persona and that combat exo probably made her a match for the half dozen or so mercys who would be on the ship. There would be no hesitation, no quarter given. She'd chew them up, spit them out, and grind their remains into the ground.

Chewing up and spitting out what was left of Angel in the process. There was no way she could escape what she had been twice.

"Damn," he muttered, cursing the situation, cursing himself for accusing her of being afraid to shed her exo and truly be Angel. He had a sinking feeling that she was trying to prove him wrong by a test of fire, willingly stepping into the sort of inferno where her darkling sister self could take control.

There was a drawer under the commboard. He pawed frantically through it, searching for a remote. When he found one he held it up for Jon to see. "I'll wear this so I can stay in touch. Scare one up and send it down to her . . ."

Hesitation overcame him as he tried to think of too many things at once. He took a deep shuddering breath and started again.

"Have one of the children take it down to her if you can. That will seem less threatening to the people on the ship, and she might be more likely to take it."

Jon nodded. "Hang on." He looked away, speaking in a hushed, urgent voice to someone offcam, listening for a few moments, then nodding curtly. He faced Marchey again.

"We're working on it. Marcy is here with me, and

she's talking to the ship. They're acting all innocent-like, saying they only want to come out and help."

"Stall as long as you can," Marchey implored him, slipping the remote into his ear, his body heat turning it on. He tapped it with one silver finger. "Keep me advised."

[You got it, Doc.] Jon's voice whispered over the remote as well as over the monitor. He cocked his head a moment, listening to Marcy. "Danny's on his way down with the remote. You think talking to her will help?"

"Probably not," Marchey snapped. Going on the evidence, he would only make matters worse.

The chime signalling that his ship's airlock had cycled through sounded. Time to go.

He grimaced. "Sorry about that, Jon," he added more gently, taking a last longing look at Angel and hoping he would get a chance to tell her he was sorry for the way he had treated her. She appeared so small, so helpless. In so many ways she was little more than a child. Innocent and vulnerable. Trusting. Could she possibly understand just how big a risk she was taking?

Yes, she probably did. Maybe because she had never learned how to lie to herself the way he had.

"Doc?"

Marchey tore his gaze away to look at Halen's face in the inset. "Yeah?" There seemed to be something stuck in his throat, thickening his voice to a rusty croak.

Jon held up his misshapen hand as if in benediction. "If anyone can make somethin' out of this mess, it's you. We trust you, brother. Don't let yourself forget that."

Marchey wondered where Halen's confidence came from. He could use a dose.

"I hope you're right." He sighed wearily. "But did you ever think that maybe none of this would've happened if I stayed there with you?" *If I hadn't been too willing to run back to my safe old life. If I hadn't* convinced myself that I had fulfilled all my responsibilities toward you. If, if, if—

"Could be," Jon replied imperturbably. Then he smiled, his face that of a man whose faith remained bouyant and unshakable. "God works in mysterious ways, my friend. Did you ever stop to think that maybe you had to leave here to find out what you needed to know, and get where you needed to be, so you could do what had to be done to stop it?"

Marchey could only hope he was right. And that if there truly was a god, he she or it was on their side.

The name of the physician in charge of the patient Marchey had come to see was Dr. Raphael Moro. Early forties. Born on Earth. Educated on Mars. Excellent credentials.

Marchey knocked at Moro's office door, hoping he didn't have to chase the man down, or wait for him to turn up before he could see the patient. Gilt lettering on the door said that Moro was director of the whole Medical Section on Botha. That wasn't encouraging. Too many administrators believed that the delay and inconvenience they caused others was the best measure of their own power and importance. Giving a Bergmann Surgeon an especially hard time was strictly mandatory.

The door swung open a few moments later. The sheer size of the man filling the opening made Marchey blink and take half a step backward.

Moro was huge, and built like a bear. Round-shouldered and slightly stooped, but still standing well over two meters tall. His skin had the coppery sheen of Polynesian bloodlines, set off by the rumpled white scrubs he wore. His stiff black hair stood straight up atop his head, and his wispy black beard had a stripe of pure white running through it.

He stared silently at Marchey, brown eyes magnified by archaic corrective lenses, the pinched look of distaste on his moon face saying that he disapproved of him on sight. Ignoring Marchey's greeting and profferred hand, Moro brusquely turned and walked away, leaving it up to Marchey to follow. A half-meter-long, tightly braided black queue draped down Moro's slab-like back, swinging with every step.

"Sit," he said, pointing at a chair facing his desk as he passed it.

Marchey didn't particularly care for being ordered around like an orderly called onto the carpet for some screwup, but did as he was told. He watched Moro lumber around the side of the desk and lower his bulk into his high-backed leatherite chair, then just sit there glowering at him.

Even though he could almost feel every precious second ticking by, raising the level of his impatience and anxiety like sand piling higher in the bottom of an hourglass, he dared not let it show. He had to proceed as if this were just another job.

He folded his silver hands on his lap to keep them still. His prosthetics had been left uncovered on purpose. The sight of them made most doctors—surgeons, especially—uncomfortable. Offering to shake hands usually guaranteed a minimum of delay in being taken to the patient.

"I can't say that I'm particularly pleased by having you brought in on this case, Dr. Marchey," Moro rumbled at last, his tone gruff and putting sarcastic emphasis on *Doctor*. That was nothing new. Sarcasm, truculence, and even outright contemptuous loathing—Marchey had heard it all before.

"You're not?" he replied neutrally.

[Danny's in the bay now.] Jon whispered in his ear over the remote a second later.

Moro put his hands flat on his desk. They were massive, with thick blunt fingers, more like the hands of a stonecutter than a surgeon. "No, I'm not. But I was overruled. MedArm insisted on bringing in one of your kind."

"My kind," Marchey echoed tonelessly. Hostility was nothing new. It looked like Moro intended to articulate his. He didn't care how vicious the attack was, as long as it was short. Time was running out.

"Your kind. The kind that provide special treatment for the high-and-mighty."

He watched Moro's mouth tighten, as if he were about to spit, turning that statement over in his mind. *Moro knew how they were being used.* Khan had as much as said the same thing. Was it general knowledge, or simply rumor and innuendo that had attached itself to them?

"I refused to give you the patient's condition when you called because I wanted to see your face. I wanted to see if you showed the slightest frigging sign of a conscience when I told you what you've come to do."

"Well," Marchey said mildly, "why don't you tell me what it is? That way we can both find out what we want to know."

"Your patient is Preston Valdemar."

"So you told me."

Moro's eyes widened behind the thick lenses. "The name means nothing to you?"

"No," he lied. "Should it?"

"Damn right it should," Moro growled. "Valdemar used to be Belt Operations Director for OmniMat. But he 'retired' to become MedArm's new Outer Zone Manager a few years back. As you know, the Outer Zone starts with Mars and her moons and comes on out here."

He hadn't. Though Moro didn't know it, he had just given Marchey the information he needed to understand how MedArm had managed to get away with some of the things it had done.

MedArm's control of off-Earth Health Care was total and nearly autonomous. Sometime in the past it had apparently split into what were in effect two *separate* MedArms. One to cover the cylties, the Venus stations, and the teeming tunnels of old Luna herself. The other, its evil twin, to cover the vast, more newly inhabited and less densely populated spaces of Mars and its moons, the Belt, and Jupiter's moons. Since the Bergmann Institute was on Deimos, it was under the Outer Zone's control.

It was a case of one hand not knowing what the other one was doing, and the body they belonged to—the UN Space Regulatory Agency—knowing even less. UNSRA's administrative base was, after all, on Luna. Inside the Inner Zone and far removed from the Outer. He had to wonder when this split had happened, and at whose behest.

Neither the "silver lining" or "Indian blanket" file had mentioned it. As for Valedemar, his name had been cited once, but not his position. *See file* it had said after his name. No doubt there was another locked file that held the missing pieces and would hyperlink the other two together. One Fist had held back, helpful son of a bitch that he was.

Why hadn't Sal told him about this split?

Ah, but maybe he had. *I just let it go in one ear and out the other. Having your head stuffed up your ass creates a fairly serious hearing impairment, to say nothing of how it affects cognitive function.*

The important thing was that if Valedemar ran the Outer Zone, then he was even more powerful than Marchey had first thought. This new information only made him all the more impatient to get to him. His feigned indifference even harder to maintain as he sat there waiting for Moro to finish venting his spleen.

"MedArm Outer Zone has been goddamn busy," Moro went on, making it sound like he held Marchey personally responsible. "You know how the system is supposed to run. Doctors are free to work where they want, even outside the system in private practice if they follow the regs. Inside the system we're subsidized, with incentives for working in depressed areas. Supposedly the only interference with our autonomy is that sometimes new system-educated doctors are assigned short residencies in places with inadequate medical care."

Some doctors are free to practice where they want, Marchey amended silently. He kept his mouth shut,

though. Moro's face was darkening, and he could almost smell the man's anger. Moro had an axe to grind,
and Marchey was about to see its edge.

"I'm AAA certified," Moro said with a scowl. "I
assume you know what that means."

"I do." AAA certification meant that he was quali-
fied to practice all forms of medicine—surgery,
obstetry, genetry, euthanasia, nanotony, and all the
rest—rating in the top 5 percent of the profession in
terms of skill and training. His own battered pride
made him add, "I'm AAAB certified myself."

Only triple A's had been admitted to the Bergmann
Program, which was the origin of that final—sometimes seemingly terminal—*B*.

"Good for you. What do you know about Carme,
then?"

Marchey shrugged. "Outer Jovian moon. Mostly in-
dependents and wilders."

Moro nodded. "That's where I used to practice. The
conditions were miserable. My whole infirmary wasn't
much bigger than this office. 'Pay what you can, if you
can,' is the motto for strict adherents to the Healer's
Oath, right? I had my own ore accounts 'cause that
was what I got paid with more often than not. Everything I made went toward keeping my practice afloat."

Moro's blocky hands tightened into knuckly fists
atop his desk. "I loved that cold, ugly damned place.
Those people meant a lot to me, and by Christ I meant
a lot to them! But MedArm ordered me to come here,
replacing me with some quack with a half dozen malps
hanging over his head. When I tried to refuse, they
threatened to punch my ticket to practice. So I came
here and tried to appeal, getting about as far as I
would trying to shovel vacuum. Valdemar laid it out
for me. I was here to stay as long as he did, like it or
not. Would you like to hear why?"

[Angel won't take the remote.] Jon whispered in his
ear while he waited. Moro was going to tell him
whether he wanted to hear or not. But he did, he
needed every handle on Valdemar he could get.

"Because I was, and I quote, *'Too good a doctor to be wasted on that grubber garbage!'*" Moro roared, thrusting himself to his feet, his big fists braced on the desk as if preparing to vault over it so he could beat the living hell out of Marchey.

He thrust out his jaw. "So here I sit on my ass in this fancy office like some high-class whore! This place is lousy with corporate high rollers. Sometimes I get to treat what he calls the 'little people,' ordinary workers and their families." His expression turned bitter, his voice dropping to a growl. "Otherwise, I do a lot of cosmetic surgery. Rejuves. Coddle 'xecs without the brains to eat right or exercise. Lots of heart and liver work, lots of substance abuse."

Marchey couldn't see why Moro was blaming him for all this, unless he simply had to blame somebody. He watched the big man bend over to yank open a desk drawer. "All that's just bones I'm thrown to keep me out of trouble. What I really am is Valdemar's personal physician. Here are his records." He flung a sheaf of hard-copy flimsies at Marchey as if challenging him to a duel.

They fluttered to the ground at Marchey's feet. His face a blank slate, he bent, picked them up. Straightened up and began skimming through the pages.

He was soon a lot closer to understanding Moro's fury. He looked up at the other doctor. "Valdemar is a Maxx addict."

"He calls it his *little vice*," Moro sneered. "One week's dosage costs the system more than all the pharmaceuticals and supplies I'd use for six whole months back on Carme. But it doesn't cost him a single frigging credit. It's his *medicine*."

Marchey sighed. Maxx was the street name for a synthesized combination of several naturally occurring neuronal proteins. Even doctors called it that. Its clinical uses included the treatment of spinal cord and other major nerve-bundle injuries, Third Form Autism, certain types of paralysis, Laskout's Anesthesia, persistent coma, and a handful of related conditions.

It stimulated and amplified neurotransmission and acted as a sense enhancer.

The drug's high cost came from the difficulty of its synthesis and terribly short shelf life. But it was potent stuff. In most cases one or two small doses did the trick. A protracted course of treatment almost never ran for more than a dozen doses administered over a twelve-week period.

Even in relatively high clinical dosages the user's body was able to deal with it, and its metabolized by-products. Taking it over a long period of time was another matter. Elimination was outpaced by intake. Wastes accumulated, eventually leading to liver and kidney damage. The brain's normal chemical balance went from subtly altered to completely and increasingly out of whack, resulting in paranoia, extreme mood swings, synesthesia, and a progressive deadening of the senses that the abuser would of course try to combat with increased dosages of the problem's cause.

Maxx was a prestige party drug for the rich, or rare champagne treat for the street-level abuser. Full-scale addicts were extremely rare; it took a combination of deep pockets and reliable black-market connections to maintain the habit.

That, or a direct legal pipeline into the supply.

"I'm sure you know that the best way to treat his condition," Moro growled, "is to take him off the damned stuff and help his system purge naturally." His tone turned caustic, and he glared at Marchey, eyes narrowing to slits behind his glasses. "Come to find out there is another way. A service one of your kind provided about eighteen months ago."

Marchey stared down at the flimsies, reading a notation that might as well have been an indictment. "Clean him out. Repair all the damage. Let him start all over again."

There it was before him, more proof of what they had become. His fellow Bergmann Surgeon Andre Fescu had done just that. But he couldn't blame Andre. He knew it could have just as easily been himself. He wouldn't have asked any questions, and not just because nobody would have answered them anyway. He would have done the job and been on his way. In the unlikely event that he'd stopped to wonder why he was treating a Maxx addict, he probably would have chalked it up to cleaning up after a botched treatment.

He looked up at Moro again, all too easily able to understand the man's anger and frustration. He felt it himself, and it frightened him. This was something else to eat away at the dispassion he so desperately needed.

"I've seen enough," he said, standing up and doing his best to keep his face a mask of indifference. "I think it's time to see my patient."

[The door to the ship is opening, Doc! Angel just took a step closer to our airlock doors!]

Moro stared at him as if he were some sort of human tumor. "You're still going to go through with it?"

Marchey shrugged. "We all do what we have to."

Moro dropped back into his chair. He jerked his bearded chin to one side. "Back out the way you came in, turn right. Follow the red line to Room P1." His mouth twisted. "I hope you understand that I don't care to assist in this travesty."

Marchey headed toward the door. "I work alone, anyway."

A scowling nod. "I don't doubt it. Good-bye, then. I don't believe we have anything else to talk about."

"No, I don't suppose we do." As unfair as Moro's attitude was, it suggested that if given all the facts he might be a potential ally. But there was no time to spare, and Marchey didn't dare risk compromising his chances to get to Valdemar.

The door slid open before him. He could feel Moro glowering at his back as he stepped through.

Just after it slid shut behind him and he started following the red line beneath his feet, Jon began cursing in his ear because all hell had broken loose.

*   *   *

Angel had taken one small step forward, but no more. Old reflexes told her to take the offense, but she caught herself, remembering that the task she had set for herself was one of defense. Standing her ground, not trying to gain it.

So she waited for the man who had just come through the inner-lock doors to come to her, keeping her head bowed and her eyes downcast. Her angel eye gave her above normal peripheral vision, allowing her to look him over surreptitiously.

He was tall and rawboned, his loose black jacket and trousers unable to completely disguise his muscle-bound body. As he strolled toward her she noted the arrogant self-assurance in his rolling stride, the tough-guy swagger. His big hands hung at his sides, loose and empty.

He had curly red hair close-shaved around his ears, and a dozen bangles hanging from his lobes. There was a friendly grin plastered on his ruddy face, but his eyes were hooded with lazy insolence.

"You the welcomin' committee, darlin'?" he drawled, offering one big square hand. His knobby knuckles were heavily scarred, suggesting that he had caused more injuries than he had ever dressed.

Angel ignored it. "No," she said quietly. "You are not welcome here."

His hand dropped, thick fingers working as if to stay limber. "Aw, don't be like that, sweetie! We's just good samarians, come to help get you poor folks fixed up."

"The term is *Samaritans,*" she corrected politely. "We are not deceived. We know why you are here, and how you intend to 'fix us up.' Go back to your ship and return to your masters. We will have nothing to do with you."

There were more teeth in his grin now, and he stared down at her with amused contempt. "Now that's not particular friendly, darlin'." His voice dropped an octave, turned wheedling. "I think mebbe you better give this a good rethink and start bein' nice to us." He chuckled. "Else we jus' might not be so nice ourselfs."

"Go away. *Now,*" she whispered hoarsely, hope that he would be reasonable deserting her completely. She clenched her hands tight inside her sleeves, trying to keep a grip herself. "*Please.* I am warning you."

"*Warnin'* me? Haw! What're you gonna do if I don't, sweetmeat? Stamp your little foot?" He guffawed, stepping closer. "We's here to stay, meatpie. I think you oughta be more friendly." The mercy's grin twisted into a leer. "Fact is, I like little grubber crackies like you to be especial friendly, if you know what I mean."

He put his rough scarred brawler's hand under her chin to tip her face up so he could see it. "Le's find out if you's a bagger or what."

Angel could have resisted, but she knew the time had come to risk her newfound self by showing him something of the hated face of Scylla. She prayed that would be enough.

Her face tilted up toward him, rising like a pale moon from behind the snowy hill of her hood.

The mercy's leer faltered when her steel-and-glass angel eye fixed on him like a gunsight. Deep inside her the unquiet angel stirred, drawn by the first faint scent of fear.

"What the fuck—" he began, beetling brow furrowing in surprise and confusion.

Angel smiled at him then. But not with the closed-mouth smile she had practiced so hard to perfect. Her cheeks tightened as her lips pulled back. She remembered how to do it, the Scylla-smile was a memory woven into her nerves with titanium wires, and as she showed it she felt the hated other trying to climb back into place behind it.

The red-haired mercy took one bulge-eyed, disbelieving look at the mouthful of sharklike teeth she showed him, each and every one tipped with livid red as if still bloody from a meal of raw meat before he yelped and snatched his hand back as if afraid she would bite it off.

Shocked eyes fixed on her smile, and cocky self-assurance gone, he fell back a step.

Angel pressed her advantage. "Don't you want to be friendly?" she asked sweetly, closing the distance between them and grinning up at him. Inside she exulted. *Scylla was still under control and the invader was on the run!*

The mercy retreated another step, then turned and headed back toward the airlock. Not running, but not dawdling either. A jubilant cry went up from the people filling the back part of the bay, and they started toward her.

Angel heard them. She turned to tell them to stay back.

She never got a chance.

The moment her back was turned the mercy spun back toward her, producing a matte black hand weapon with a fist-sized bore from inside his jacket, levelling it in her direction and firing.

No sound or light came from the weapon, but there was no mistaking that he had fired. The gun was a perennial favorite of mercys for close-up work, fondly called a meatblower or a roaster. It fired a tightly focused blast of mixed radiation that created such instantaneous and intense localized heat in its target that it explosively vaporized flesh, the very cells detonating like millions of little bombs as the water in them was turned into steam in a microsecond.

The burst caught Angel in the small of the back. The shot was intended to blow her in half.

Her robe went up like paper in a blast furnace, instantly swallowing her up in a ball of orange-red flame. The Kindred's forward rush collapsed like a wave against an invisible breakwater, those on the leading edge stumbling and falling. The jubilant roar changed to screams of terror and horror.

The smug grin was back on the mercy's face as he waited for Angel to fall. But it froze, then peeled off completely when instead she slowly turned back to face him, burning scraps of cloth creating a fiery, smoky halo around her.

The gleaming silver skin and strutwork the robe had hidden was exposed now, golden in the dying flames. The mercy's face went chalk white as he recognized the combat exo for what it was. He stumbled backwards, his shocked gaze welded to the fixed grin on the face of his intended victim, the weapon in his hand forgotten.

Angel stared back at him with a blank, unwavering expressionlessness that was far more frightening than any scowl or snarl could have been, a machine-cold indifference to everything but what was centered in her crosshairs.

Her still exterior gave no hint of her inner turmoil. The urge to strike back crackled through her a hundred times hotter and more consuming than the fire that had scorched her face. Stoking the rising inner flames was Scylla.

Images filled her head: She could—

—cross the space between them before he could so much as lift a single foot, take his head off with a single careless backhand, and have ample time to study the look of surprise on his face as it hit the ground.

—drive her bladed hand into his chest, rip his heart out, and show him its final bloody beat.

—pull him apart the way a child strips the petals from a daisy.

Scylla showed her all the wonders she could perform, promising that she would at last have an outlet for all the hurt and anger and frustration. That to take this man down would be right and feel so good . . .

Angel shuddered, blinking back the visions and somehow keeping the angel subsumed. Swallowing hard, she found her voice.

"Please leave! *Please!*" she wailed, unable to keep the naked entreaty from her voice. The mercy turned and ran.

She watched him disappear through the airlock
door, hoping with every fiber of her being that it was
truly the beginning of the invaders' retreat.

Marchey stood just outside sensor range of the door
to Valdemar's room, his head cocked to one side as
he listened to Jon telling him what had just happened
in the bay.

"Get everybody to hell out of there," was the only
advice he could offer.

[What about Angel?] Jon demanded.

"What about her?" he hissed through clenched
teeth, that question tolling over and over in his head.

He rubbed his forehead, trying to think. "Sorry.
You say she's got them stood off for the moment?"

*[Yeah, but I doubt it can last. Their sort won't give
up this easily.]*

He was afraid Jon was probably right on both
counts. This had been no more than a skirmish. A
testing of their defenses. Now that they knew they
were up against someone in a combat exo the gloves
would come off.

"She hasn't done anything overtly hostile?"

[Not yet.]

He couldn't even begin to guess which would be
worse for her: getting badly hurt or even killed as
Angel or reverting to Scylla. He hoped to hell he
could fix it so he didn't have to find out.

"Okay, I've got to go now," he began. The sooner
he got to Valdemar the better everyone's chances.

[Just a second, Doc—] Jon put in. Several seconds
passed.

*[Okay. The bay is almost completely evacuated, soon
as it is we'll seal it up. Danny just came back in. He
says Angel told him to tell you that she knows you're
trying to fix everything. She says she'll hold them back
until you can get them called off our backs. She
says . . . she says she'll try to make you proud of her
this time.]*

Marchey closed his eyes for a moment, daunted by

her courage. Her loyalty and trust. He found himself
remembering the first and last times he had seen her,
and all the mistakes he had made in between.

"Hang on, Angel," he muttered half under his
breath, opening his eyes to stare at the door to Valdemar's room, less than a dozen steps away. The final
barrier to his objective.

"This time I won't let you down," he whispered, an
apology and a promise all in one.

He started moving. Had there been anyone else in
the corridor to see him, the cold, tight-lipped expression on his face might have made them try to stop him.

Not that it would have done them any good.

Angel listened to her message being delivered as
she moved closer to the airlock doors. She had refused
the remote Danny brought her because her exo already allowed her to monitor the channels they were
using. She had not mentioned it because she did not
want them to know she was listening, to give them
the chance to try to talk her out of the task she had
set for herself.

The invaders were going to try to come out again.
Soon. Angel wanted to believe otherwise, but knew
better. Scylla knew it for certain, and was just waiting
for her chance to be reborn like a vengeful phoenix
in the heat and flames of battle.

All she could do now was wait.

The bay had been evacuated and sealed up tight.
That was good. It was one less thing to worry about.

Marchey would come through. She did not doubt it
for one single moment. He had helped deliver the
people of Ananke from oppression once before, and
he would do it again. Somehow the mantle of guardian
angel had been passed on to him.

For all her telling him that he was dead inside, she
knew that there was a strength in him, a steadfastness
that she had first seen clearly when he stared Scylla
straight in the eye—stared his own death straight in
the eye—and refused to back down. Not because he

did not care if he died, but because when pushed to stand by what he thought was right not even an angel's rage could move him. There was something deep inside him every bit as durable as his silver hands, just as bright and stainless. He was capable of so much more than he knew.

He would save them all. Only this time, she would be at his side. They would be . . . together.

[Hang on, Angel,] his voice whispered in her ear.

Her breath caught in her throat. He didn't know that she could hear him, but that didn't matter. It was enough that he had said it. And she knew—*knew*—that he was telling her to hold on to the identity he had given back to her, and not revert to the other.

[This time I won't let you down.]

Or I you, Angel vowed, placing herself directly in front of the airlock's double doors. Fatigue and apprehension and the effort it took to keep Scylla subsumed made her head swim.

But she stood tall and proud, a solitary silver sentinel with a gentle smile on her face. Knowing that he cared after all strengthened her, fortified her sense of purpose. She would protect those she had once terrorized. She would make her mother and all the other dead proud of her. She would prove once and for all that she was no longer what she had once been.

She would give Marchey the time he needed, no matter what it cost. This time her life was pledged to something worthy.

She would show her love for him the only way she could, and hope that when this was all over he would realize that she was more than just his ally, and it was more than just help she wanted to give him.

Preston Valdemar was sitting up in bed, dressed in pearly white silk pajamas, hunched over a sleek wood-trimmed pad and speaking into it when Marchey appeared in his doorway. He looked up, eyes narrowing and brow furrowing in suspicion.

"Who the hell are you?" he demanded, putting the

pad on standby and hugging it protectively to his chest.

Marchey didn't answer. He stood there, taking a good long look at his patient. Sizing him up.

Valdemar appeared to be in his late fifties, the skin of his face blotchy, loose pouches of flesh sagging under his eyes and chin. According to his records, he was in his late sixties. The full range of antigeria techniques had been used on him just over a year before, so he should have looked to be in his late thirties at most. Maxx addiction had undone most of that. His close-set eyes were muddied by it and medication, their whites bloodshot and jaundiced.

There was also an unhealthy saffron cast to his skin. It was unlikely that the bloodcleanser racked in beside his bed was there for show. His liver and kidneys were probably little better than spoiled meat.

"Answer me, dammit!"

He had the fat, greedy mouth of a libertine, and his thick lips were pressed together petulantly as he glared at Marchey, waiting for him to respond.

Marchey ignored him, checking the room over carefully. There was a full communit at his bedside, probably linked to the pad. Good. The door he had just come through was the only one in or out. He locked it so they wouldn't be disturbed.

Reconnaissance done, he faced Valdemar, his face stonily impassive. "I am Dr. Georgory Marchey." He held up his silver hands so there would be no mistaking what kind of doctor he was. "I'm here to treat you."

"It's about time you got here," Valdemar sniffed, slumping back onto the pillows. "I feel *terrible*! You should have been here weeks ago! I'm not some damn welf; I run the whole fucking medicine show around here! I deserve better treatment than this!"

Marchey stared down at the flabby little man on the big soft bed, and although he felt nothing kinder than loathing, he smiled.

"Well, I'm here." His smile subtly altered, an odd

glint kindling in his gray eyes. "It has taken me a long time to get to where I am now. Let's find out if it was worth the trip."

Angel could feel it.

Something was about to happen. The very air seemed charged with a gathering electricity. She had never experienced anything like terrestrial weather, but she had heard and finally understood what people meant by *the calm before the storm.*

Would they rush her? Would the airlock doors open on a dozen weapons all firing on her at once?

There were a dozen possibilities. She needed to be ready for each and every one of them, but really all she could do was wait, her silver-sheathed body so tense it was a wonder it didn't ring like a tuning fork with every apprehensive thump of her heart.

She watched the airlock's double doors, her attention so tightly focused on the vertical seam between them that when the explosion came, she kept staring at the still-intact steel panels, thinking that they had tried to blow the doors and failed.

That thought had scarcely been formed when it was blown away by the terrible, blood-freezing dragon's roar that was the sound of every spacers' deepest, darkest nightmare.

The deadly shrieking howl of pressure breach.

Adrenaline-fueled fear burst inside her like a bomb, kicking her exosystems into overdrive. Her head snapped around, homing in on the sound, and she saw the gaping, life-eating, meter-wide hole blown in the wall twenty meters away.

It's a diversion! The warning flashed in her mind like a starburst, but breach drill was one of the first things learned by every child born in the fragile steel-and-stone shells that kept the implacable enemy vacuum at bay. Her response was as deeply wired into her nerves as the monkey reflex of grabbing at anything within reach when falling.

Instinct had her already racing toward the rack of

emergency patches against the far wall, leaning into the gale and legs pumping under her like pistons.

Dust, gravel, and other debris filled the escaping air, stinging her face and pinging off her exo. A plastic packing crate came flying at her out of nowhere. She barely had time to fling up her arm to protect her face. The impact staggered her, whirling flinders snatched out of the air around her and sucked toward the hole. Her momentum and the magnetic soles of her exo were all that kept her from falling and being taken as well. She had to keep her vulnerable organic eye squeezed shut against the scouring whirlwind. Only the indifferent glass lens of her angel eye let her see to reach the rack.

Let her see that the rack was nearly empty. The few remaining ceramyl-backed foamstone patches were far too small to cover the rent.

But the thick meter-and-a-half-square foamstone panel forming one end of the rack was large enough to do the job. She grabbed hold of it, set her feet and heaved, wrenching it from its moorings. Then she got herself turned around and headed toward the hole.

The hurricane-force outrush of air tried to rip the panel from her grasp, and when it couldn't, snatched her off her feet and took them both.

Angel had only a fractured second in which to realize that if the unreinforced panel hit the wall at the speed they were travelling, it would shatter into a thousand useless pieces. Jaw clamped tight on the air the dropping pressure was trying to steal from her aching lungs, she twisted desperately, turning, trying to get her arms and legs braced before—

Less than a tenth of a second later the panel slammed into the wall, smashing Angel's body between it and the unyielding stone around the hole it was supposed to cover.

"I can't *move,*" Valdemar complained pettishly. A pale blue derm was plastered to his neck. Muscle relaxant.

"That's to make things easier," Marchey explained as he rolled a table over beside the bed. He didn't say easier for what. Valdemar would find out soon enough.

"They put me out last time. Aren't you going to?"

Marchey showed him his teeth. "I think we'll get better results if we do this while you're wide-awake."

"I suppose you know what you're doing." Valdemar sniffed.

Some dark bastard cousin of laughter welled up inside of him. "I've never been more on top of things in my whole life."

He laid his forearms on the table, palms up. He'd gotten a lot of practice slipping in and out of the light working trance he needed, and more quickly shucking off his prosthetics back on Ananke. He closed his eyes, took a deep breath, *let go.*

Their weight fell away. He opened his eyes, feeling like he had just taken off swaddling gloves. Now his hands felt impossibly supple and exquisitely sensitive, ready to operate.

Even though it had been done without fanfare, removing his prosthetics had made an impression on his patient. Out of the corner of his eye he watched Valdemar's eyes widen as he straightened up, watched him lick his thick lips nervously. It made him smile.

"This won't hurt, will it?" Valdemar whined in a small voice.

Marchey had also gotten a lot of practice at another skill since leaving Ananke. It was time to see if he was really the apt pupil Fist kept saying he was.

"Only if I don't want it to," he answered as he turned to face Valdemar, his smile widening. The flat silver biometal plates capping his stumps had the same cold gleam as his eyes.

"All right, you miserable little pile of shit," he rumbled, slowly reaching for his patient, the points where his hands should have been coming closer and closer. "Let's find out just what you're made of."

Valdemar tried to cringe away, but he might as well have tried to levitate. Thanks to the derm on his neck his body only trembled like a worm nailed to a board. Panic rising, he tried to reach for the call button, but his hands and arms never even twitched.

Totally helpless, all he could do was stare at the terrifying expression on Marchey's face, gurgling with terror and humiliation as his bladder let go.

Angel was in Hell.

Escaping air roared and squalled around her, cold, so cold, and the implacable void at her back tried to suck her through the hole and swallow her completely. She couldn't breathe. Jagged rock chips, scouring sand, and bullet-fast bits of debris exploded against her exo and lashed the exposed skin of her face.

She teetered over the immense pool of blackness that filled the back of her skull, welling up from where her head had bounced off unyielding stone. If not for the thin layer of biometal covering her where hair should have been, her skull would have split like a melon. She couldn't tell if the unending howl she heard was inside or outside her head. She could barely see; she had to keep her human eye closed tight or she would lose it, and the other one kept phasing in and out.

The foamstone panel was still in one piece, only because she had put her body between it and the wall to cushion its impact. The impact had been tremendous; people had felt it in the soles of their feet all over Ananke. If it hadn't been for her exo, every bone in her body would have been broken.

Now the relentless air pressure was turning the panel and the wall into the two jaws of a vise trying to squeeze the life out of her.

Blind, deafened, and dizzy, still one thought clanged endlessly through her reeling mind: *This is a diversion!* It felt like an eternity had turned since the explosion, but the passionless timesense built into her exo's circuits told her that less than twenty seconds had elapsed.

She still had a chance to stop them. If she could get

free before she was mashed flat or eaten by vacuum. Or simply passed out, letting the other dangers get her.

Angel tightened her grip on the panel and strained against it, the cords standing out in her neck. A cry broke through her clenched teeth when it looked like not even her exo gave her the strength to force it back.

Still she refused to give up. She kept pushing, throwing every iota of energy she could summon into her trembling arms, the strain making the suffocating blackness rise higher and higher. The panel groaned and thrummed, nearly stressed to the breaking point.

Just as her exhausted body was about to fail her, the panel moved, forced back to arm's length and tipping so that one side ground against the wall.

That gave her better leverage. Bracing it up with her trembling arms, she wriggled toward the widest part of the gap, moving like some small creature trying to crawl out from under a stony crushing foot. When she had gotten as far to one side as she could, she gave one final desperate heave, rolling and twisting as she did so.

The patch slammed home with an echoing boom, cracking down the middle but not breaking. The seal wasn't perfect; air still whistled around the edges, sucking airborne bits of debris in to wedge in the narrow cracks, but the cyclone was over.

The force of her push sent her crashing to the cold stone floor. She landed on her side, desperately gasping for breath in the too-thin, dust-filled air. Her lungs were on fire, every ragged breath stoking the flames higher.

She could have lain there forever. Her limbs felt like they weighed a ton apiece. Her head swam, and even thinking about moving seemed impossible.

Instead she heaved herself to her feet wearily, blood seeping from her ears and nose, trickling from her mouth. Operating on blind instinct alone she got herself oriented and staggered drunkenly toward the airlock.

The outer doors were just beginning to slide back when she got to within two meters of them, coming within blurry sight of five heavily armed mercys in goggles and breather masks, the red-haired man she had driven off earlier in the lead. It was obvious from the shocked expressions on their faces that they hadn't expected to find her waiting for them.

Angel was at the end of her strength and endurance. She didn't so much charge the invaders as start toppling in their direction and somehow manage to keep her feet under her.

The looks of slack-jawed, bug-eyed disbelief that appeared on their faces squeezed a hysterical laugh out of her. It was funny. Scylla was nowhere to be found inside her now, and she didn't have the strength left to fight them even if she wanted to. The worst she could do was collapse on top of them.

The mercys did not know that. Seeing a battered and bloody-faced silver-skinned wild woman laughing like a berserker as she lurched toward them drove them back to the big airlock's ruined outer doors.

Angel saw one last chance to slow them down. Her laughter turning to a racking coughing that put fresh blood on her lips, she staggered the last two steps to the airlock's inner doors. Then she flung her arms wide, extruded her talons, and grunting with effort, drove her barbed hands into the steel panels, sinking them in almost to her wrists. Gathering the tattered shreds of her failing strength, she heaved at the door panels to pull them shut.

Had she been fresh and rested, she could have easily overcome the mechanism that powered the lock doors. In her present condition she was barely able slowly to wrench them shut to the tormented shriek of stripping gears and steel grating against stone. The panels began to twist and buckle around her silver hands. Her grip was too close to their edges, but she dared not try for a fresh hold.

She heard the enemy shout, saw them start back toward her. That spurred her to one final all-out ef-

fort. Her whole existence narrowed down to herself
and the doors.

Just—

Their resistance was incredible. Her arms and insides were aflame. Red-and-black motes danced before her eye. She turned her face away as they began
firing at her, daring only to use rubber dumdums in
the enclosed space.

—close!

In the end her will was greater.

The closing mechanism gave way with a gunshot
crack and the doors slammed shut. The warped steel
panels would not close all the way, leaving a gap the
thickness of her hand between them, but it was the
best she could do.

Angel hung there by her wedged hands, panting for
breath in the rarefied air and grimly holding on to
consciousness. She tried to lock her exo, finding that
it refused to move anyway. The inside of her angel
eye flashed with warnings and damage reports, pulsing
in time with the hammering of her heart.

She heard muffled cursing. Gloved fingers appeared
in the gap, trying to pry the doors open again. Her
exo had turned into a silver vise, making that impossible. It took her three tries to find the breath to whisper, "Comm active," and she had to swallow a mixture
of blood and dust before she could speak again.

"Hurry," she gasped. Her throat tightened, and she
felt a gathering wetness in her eye; tears stained with
blood. "I can't . . . do any more."

As she was licking her bloody lips to speak again,
she heard one voice rise above the angry gabble at
the other side of the doors. "Go get another charge,"
it bellowed. "We'll blow the fuckin' door to hell and
the bitch with it!"

She rested her head on her arms, closed her eye.

So that would be how it ended. The silent darkness
was piled up so high inside her that she would probably never know when it happened. Consciousness had

turned to smoke in her hands. It kept trying to slip through her fingers and fade away.

Still she held on. This was her last chance to make things right.

There were so many things she had wanted to tell him. That she had never been truly alive until he had touched her and given a real life to her. That she was sorry for the things she had said, for driving him away. So many things . . .

Her head lolled to one side, and she found herself fighting a tidal wave of red-edged black. Had she blanked out? She couldn't be sure. She only knew that the next wave would take her all the way under, and there was no way to stop or evade it.

"Come back," she croaked breathlessly. "Pl—please give me . . . another chance . . ."

She wanted to explain what she meant, and hear if he answered, but the silent darkness took her before she had a chance to do either. It crashed over her.

It took her down.

Valdemar's compad lay on the bedside table, still on standby. Marchey had glanced at it while putting it aside, seeing that it was linked to the bedside comm, and willing to bet that his patient had been talking to the supposed mission of mercy on Ananke when he'd come in.

—so you could do what needed to be done to stop it, Jon had said. Soon now he would see if that was true.

Marchey stared down at Valdemar's pale, frightened face, trying to keep a handle on his emotions. The light working trance gave him some distance from them, but not much. Rage, hatred, and loathing hammered at his insides, demons shrieking to be let out.

"The Helping Hands Foundation," he growled softly.

Valdemar blinked in confusion, his eyes flicking to one side to glance guiltily at the compad before coming back to jitter nervously between Marchey's face and the invisible hands poised just over his chest.

He let Valdemar feel a slight weight and pressure,

watched fresh sweat blossom on his ashen forehead and upper lip.

"Wh—what about it?" he panted.

"At this very moment there is a so-called relief mission trying to steal Ananke from its rightful owners."

"They're not *stealing*," Valdemar protested.

"What would you call it, then?"

"They're uh, p-providing a service."

"For a price."

"Well, yeah, what's—"

Marchey cut him off. "With no chance to refuse this service. I'm hearing what is going on even as we speak." His mouth tightened. "Do you know what it makes me want to do?"

Valdemar shook his head meekly. Marchey's face filled his field of vision. It was the face of a man so filled with fury and contempt that he looked capable of anything. It came to him that he might just be staring his own death in the face.

Marchey's eyes narrowed. "It makes me want to give you the same deal. A service for a price." He sank his immaterial hands into Valdemar's body.

"Maybe a little heart surgery." A feather-light touch on a certain bundle of nerves set off a brief flare of pain deep in the man's chest. Valdemar let out a strangled squeak, eyes bulging and his face going the color of curdled milk.

"A heartless bastard like you could probably use a little work on the old ticker." Marchey did it again, hard enough to make Valdemar gag and his whole body convulse.

This was wrong, and Marchey knew it. Worse yet, it felt so *good*. The urge to make Valdemar squirm and beg wanted to pour out of his hands like a boiling poison bottled up past containment.

You're bluffing, he reminded himself desperately. *You can't* can't *can't do him any real harm!*

"Please!" Valdemar wailed, his voice shrill with terror. "You can't hurt me like this! You're a d-d-doctor!"

Marchey bent lower, putting his face inches from Valdemar's. "Yes I am. I talked to Dr. Moro. He told me how you said the people he served didn't deserve a doctor like him." A mirthless smile screwed itself onto his face. "Maybe *I'm* the sort of doctor *you* deserve."

Valdemar's mouth was moving, but nothing was coming out. Tears rolled down his cheeks, and he'd completed his own humiliation by losing control of his bowels as well as his bladder. He cowered there in stinking misery, utterly powerless to stop Marchey from doing whatever he wanted with him.

Marchey stared down at him in disgust, knowing it was time to finish this atrocity up and get the hell out of there before he lost it.

Suddenly a harsh crackle of static lanced into his ear from the remote, loud enough to make him jerk his head to one side. A moment afterward he heard an agonized whisper.

[Hurry . . . I can't do any more.]

His heart stopped mid-beat. *Angel!*

[They blew a hole in the friggin' wall!] Jon broke in, his normal unflappable calm reduced to wreckage. *[Angel patched it, it was unbelievable what she did, and now she's blockin' the airlock doors! I'm tryin' to get help to her and more air into the bay—]*

Then distant and muffled, made metallic by the remote's attempt to compensate, *[Go get another charge! We'll blow the fuckin' door to hell and the bitch with it!]* The slow rasping wheeze of Angel's breathing sawed his heart into quivering pieces. The doctor in him heard lung damage.

The man who had been cheated and frustrated and used tightened an invisible hand inside the user he had in his grasp. Valdemar made a strangled sound and went rigid, heels drumming against the mattress.

Marchey withdrew his other hand, reached for the pad. It floated through the air, coming to hang before Valdemar's pale and uncomprehending face.

"Call them off!" he hissed. *"Now!"*

Valdemar stared past the pad and up at his tormentor in bewildered terror. "I don't—"

"Call off your mercys," he roared, fighting the urge to grind the pad into the man's face. "Or I swear to God I'll take you apart one fucking piece at a time. From the *inside*." It was all he could do to keep from demonstrating.

"L-line reopen, n-no picture," Valdemar stammered.

The pad chimed, and after a moment's silence a woman's voice issued from it. "Sturges here, Mr. Valdemar."

"C-call back the troops! L-leave Ananke at once!"

"Are you all right, sir?" Sturges asked with obvious suspicion. "You sound funny."

Valdemar's eyes rolled up toward Marchey, and he saw the price of failure carved into his stony face.

Angel was still breathing. If that sound stopped—

"Never mind that," Valdemar puffed, trying to sound commanding but failing miserably. "Just do as I say!"

"But sir, we've almost—"

"*Do as I tell you to you stupid slot!*" Valdemar shrieked. "*Or I'll have the fucking lot of you brain-burned and sold for testmeat on Armageddon!*"

"Yes, sir," Sturges answered stiffly. "I'm recalling the team now." There were several endless seconds of anxious silence. Both Marchey and Valdemar held their breaths.

Sturges came back on-line. "They're coming back to the ship. Do you want us to return to Botha, sir?"

Valdemar looked to Marchey for instruction. He nodded and mouthed the word *hurry*. "Yes! And hurry!"

Marchey simply closed his spectral hand inside the pad, invisible fingers turning the circuits to useless junk. He let it fall. It bounced off Valdemar's chest and clattered to the floor.

The pitch of Angel's breathing suddenly changed. He froze, fear rising thick and acrid as vomit up against his teeth.

[Come back,] she whispered inside his head. A pause, panting for breath. *[Pl—please give me . . . another chance . . .]*

"Angel! I'm here!" he shouted, straining to hear an answer, trying to reach her across the gulf of time and distance and misunderstanding that lay between them. But there was no response, only a hopeless silence that seemed far vaster and emptier than the airless void that separated him from her.

[Hang on, Doc, we're getting back into the bay now,] Jon bawled in his ear, his voice like a lifeline to where his heart had gone. *[The bad guys are liftin' off! Mardi and Elias are runnin' over to Angel. We got two vac-crews, one to sealfoam the patch, the other to seal up the airlock door . . .]*

Marchey stood there, blind to the world, seeing it in his mind, seeing Angel's face, hoping and praying and promising—

[She's ALIVE!] Jon crowed. *[She's out cold and hurt pretty bad, and I don't know how the hell we're gonna cut her loose, but they've got a breather mask on her, and she's alive!]*

Marchey's legs threatened to go out from under him as relief swept through him. A sound that was half laugh and half sob escaped him. "I'm coming back," he told Jon. "Take good care of her until I get there!"

[Count on it! And thanks!]

Marchey closed his eyes for a moment, setting tears running down his cheeks. When he opened them again, his gaze turned back toward his patient. Valdemar paled and began to sob when Marchey's attention fell back on him like a lead weight.

"Someone who means a lot to me almost died because of you," he said quietly. The anger was still there inside him. The loathing. He had right here in his hands one of the ones who had turned his life into a living nightmare, and seen to it he had no way out. Who had nearly destroyed the things he loved, just when he had finally begun to understand that he did love them. Who had corrupted all he held holy for power and profit.

For so many years the saving of every life had left behind nightmares, and this pathetic creature had used that for his own advantage, for his own greedy purposes.

Nightmares . . .

It took him only a moment to reduce Valdemar to total unconsciousness, and a few moments more to pull the familiar icy cloak of full trance about himself. Anger faded. Hate dissolved. Everything but cold directed will leached away, leaving only himself, his patient, and the cure.

He wrapped his immaterial hands around Valdemar's head, fingertips sinking inside the man's skull. "Remember me," he rasped, his touch and deep trance guaranteeing that he was heard.

"Resign. Stop turning MedArm into garbage. Give up Maxx or *die*." He could feel brain activity sputtering and flickering under his fingers, knew that his every word was being incised inside that skull past any erasing.

"If you disobey me, I'll come back for you. Remember me and what I can do to you. *Remember . . .*"

He shifted his grip. A touch here, there, saw to it that Valdemar would not waken for several hours.

Letting go of Valdemar he stood back, shrugging off the trance state, then turning his back on his patient to reattach his silver arms.

He knew he should be ashamed of what he had just done. Maybe he would be. Yet he wouldn't take it back even if he could.

At that moment all he could think about was getting to his ship and getting his ass back to Ananke as fast as he could, because there was someone there who needed him.

Returning to his ship was no problem. It was upon reaching the berth where it was docked that he ran into an unforeseen complication.

His ship's airlock door gaped wide open.

He stood there staring, knowing damn well that he'd left the craft locked up tight when he left. It was doubtful that old Fist had tried to escape. Not only was he too weak to walk and buried under a sleepfield to boot, he had every reason to want to remain hidden while the ship was on Botha Station.

That left one logical conclusion. Somehow, someone must have suspected Fist's presence on the ship. There was no way to guess how. The important question was: Had they already spirited him away, or was the kidnapping still in progress?

There was only one way to find out. He continued on inside, moving quietly, cautiously, his home suddenly hostile territory.

The dimly lit main compartment was deserted. He crossed it, soft-soled shoes whispering across the carpeting, straining to hear any telltale sounds over the anxious thudding of his heart. The clinic's door was open, bright light flooding out. As he drew closer he heard voices. Moving with all the stealth he could muster, he crept to the doorway and peeked inside.

Two men were struggling to pull Fist over the high sides of the unibed. The burly one dressed in the red OmniMat Security uniform had his arms wrapped around Fist's thin chest. Marchey watched the old man turn his head and spit in the man's face.

"Old skig spit on me!" he cried, his mouth curled in disgust as he rubbed his cheek against his shoulder.

The other man, dressed in a dark blue 'xec's tailored onepiece, laughed. "I'll teach him some manners."

"Damn well better!"

Onepiece let go of Fist's feet, stepped around to the side of the bed, then backhanded him hard enough to snap his head back on his scrawny scarred neck. "You behave, grampa." He grabbed a thin wrist. "Act up again, and I'll break your goddamned fingers."

Fist's head came back up, and he glared at onepiece, those carious yellow eyes blazing with sneering malevolence. His bloodied mouth moved as he whispered something that made the 'xec's face redden. Fist laughed, a moment later whispering something else that made the 'xec let go and clench his fists. One drew back in threat. Fist laughed again, daring him.

Marchey almost had to laugh himself at the ornery old bastard's absolute, unbreakable cantankerousness. But he knew he had to do something before the old man goaded them into killing him, thereby taking all of his secrets to the grave.

He scrubbed his mouth, trying to figure out the best way to deal with the situation. No great plan came to mind. He was tired and impatient to be on his way, and he'd had a bellyful of deception, intrigue, and taking the subtle approach.

"Screw it," he muttered softly, squaring his shoulders and striding on into the clinic as if he owned the place.

"Who the plug are you?" onepiece demanded, dropping his clenched hands and stepping back.

"Don't worry, I'm a doctor," he told them with a reassuring smile as he sauntered toward the security man at the far end of the unibed. The guard let go of his burden and reached for the holster strapped to his hip.

He never got a chance to touch the weapon inside. Marchey, still beaming happily, stepped in close and put his broad shoulders behind a roundhouse punch that drove his biometal fist into the cleft in the man's chin like a silver sledgehammer. His blow knocked the guard clear off his feet and into the bulkhead behind him. He slammed up against the padded surface, hung there a second, then crumpled bonelessly to the deck.

Marchey gaped in amazement at the results of the first punch he had ever thrown in his whole life, then spun around to confront the other trespasser, brandishing his fists and ready for round two.

Onepiece took one look and fled.

Marchey flung himself after, crashing into the 'xec's lumbar region. They both went down, Marchey on top.

The 'xec's head bounced off the deck with a sickening thump that made Marchey wince.

"Bravo . . . Doctor!" Fist called from inside the unibed. "A remarkable . . . display . . . of fisticuffs!"

"Just shut up," Marchey grumbled, climbing off the 'xec's back, then rolling him over and peeling back an eyelid. The man was down for the count, but fundamentally undamaged. He crossed the compartment to check on the security guard.

In the process of checking pupil response he found out that he had knocked the man not only cold, but cross-eyed.

Forty minutes later he was already undocked and on his way back to Ananke. He had taped up the intruders' hands and feet, put a sedative derm on each to give him more time to make his escape, then stuffed them into an equipment cabinet in the lockbay.

Fist had suffered only a few minor cuts and bruises from his manhandling. Marchey treated them and put him back under the sleepfield. The old man had kept laughing and calling him by the name *Ali,* whatever the hell that meant.

Now that the battle of Botha Station was over, he was dead on his feet and more than ready to sleep. But there remained a couple loose ends he wanted to tie up before he let himself collapse. So he drew a cup of coffee with just a hint of brandy in it to offset the caffeine, seated himself at the commboard, and called Dr. Moro.

The bearish, bearded physician came on, his face knotting into a look of tight-lipped distaste. "You again."

"Valdemar is still an addict," Marchey informed him without preamble. "His condition remains fundamentally unchanged from when I arrived, though he will probably stay unconscious for at least another six hours."

Surprise replaced Moro's disapproval. "Why?"
Marchey told him.

Raphael Moro turned out to be a very good listener. The few questions he asked led Marchey to tell him everything: the Helping Hands visit to Ananke and Valdemar's place in the scheme; how he had gotten to Ananke and what had happened there; how the Bergmann Surgeons had been co-opted by a tainted MedArm, and how Sal Bophanza had fled the Institute. It took him almost an hour to lay out the whole story. By the time he was done Moro was looking at him in a very different manner.

Marchey slumped there in his chair, feeling drained. His cup was empty and his throat was dry, but he couldn't summon the energy to get up and go for a refill.

"Well, well, well," Moro said at last. "That's quite a story. Going back to one particular, did you know that MedArm sent a flash directive to all personnel? Anyone with information as to the whereabouts of Dr. Salvaz Bophanza is supposed to report it immediately. Both large rewards and severe penalties are mentioned."

Marchey rubbed his gritty eyes, trying to remember if he had told Moro where Sal and 'Milla were headed. "I should have expected that." He sighed. "What are you going to do about it?"

"Do about what?" Moro returned blandly, stroking the white streak in his beard. "So, what are you going to do next?"

"Damned if I know." Marchey let out a mordant chuckle. "I'm almost afraid to find out, considering how I've done so far."

Moro peered at him a long moment, his glasses making his eyes look huge, then smirked. "Yeah, you've frigged up royally."

He sat back, steepling his thick fingers. "Let's see. After years of doing the best work you could do under conditions so bad they turned you into a drunk—instead of suiciding, or just plain quitting—you let yourself be kidnapped by an exo'd maniac who thought she was an angel. She took you to Ananke. There you managed to keep your Oath, helped bring down the man who had brainwashed her and turned the moon into his private empire, started her back on the road to humanhood, and incidentally found the cure for one of the things that had been messing up the lives of all the Bergmanns while you were at it."

Marchey started to interrupt, but Moro held up his hand. "Please, no pleas until all the charges are read. After all that, you followed orders and went back on the circuit after doing three doctors' worth of work on Ananke. You kept yourself from becoming a drunk again, and figured out the danger they were in by playing head games with a dangerous psychopath who had nearly destroyed you once and was probably working up to another whack at it, saved the moon and the ex-angel *again*—you better watch it, it's always a bad sign when you start repeating yourself—*and* saved Ananke's stolen assets and who knows what else by punching out some trespassers. Now, to top all that off, you helped me out and treated me like an honorable colleague, even though I was a perfect asshole toward you because I was pissed at myself for knuckling under to pressure."

Moro leaned forward, one bushy eyebrow arching in inquiry. "You sure you can't walk on water, too? Or at least turn it to wine?"

Marchey had to smile. Talking to Moro like this made him realize how it sometimes took another person to help you put your own situation in perspective. That outside view was something he could have used for quite some time now.

"Thanks," he said simply. "I needed to hear that."

"No problem. It's the least I can do." Moro grinned and rubbed his big square hands together. "You've given me what will sooner or later turn into a ticket back to Carme. I'm going to call a few other disgruntled types like myself so that when this shit hits the newswebs we'll be ready to put in our two cents' wor—"

The stricken expression that had appeared on Marchey's face made Moro stop and stare. "Something wrong with that?"

Marchey hung his head, looking dazed. "Get this whole mess out on the newswebs." He let out a sickly laugh. "You know, I'd forgotten there even was such a thing."

"You'd forgotten—" Moro stared at him, trying to figure out if he was joking and finally seeing that he was not. "That's incredible. Where have you been the last few years, anyway?"

"Nowhere." Every time he turned around he came face-to-face with more proof of that fact. He wished there was some way to shake Moro's hand.

"Well, it sounds to me like you're coming back into it now," Moro assured him.

"You know, I think I am."

"Keep it up. You're doing just fine." Moro sat back, glanced off-screen. "I guess I better go check on my patient." A sly twinkle came into his eyes. "He's going to have a bitch of a time. I may just have to confine him for his own good. He might even try to fire me when I refuse to give him any more Maxx."

Moro's teeth were white and square, they gleamed as he bared them in a smile. "But he wanted me, he got me, and now he's going to be stuck with me for a little while longer . . ."

It appeared that this time Valdemar's detox was going to be of the no pain, no gain variety. Marchey couldn't work up any particular pity for the man. In fact—

"Keep a record of this communication," he told Moro. "If he gives you a hard time, just show him a picture of me."

That earned him a long speculative look. "You're not kidding, are you?"

Marchey shrugged, showing his fellow physician a cryptic half-smile.

Moro grinned and slapped his big hands onto his desk. "You're a pretty interesting fellow, Dr. Marchey. I hope you plan on staying in touch."

Being out of touch with the world around him had been at the root of so many of his problems, he knew that now. It had been a hard lesson, but one well worth learning, even this late in life.

"Count on it. I'm beginning to see that I need all the friends I can get."

Marchey cut the connection, then slumped back in his chair, rubbing his eyes and wondering where he was going to find the gumption to get up and go to bed. He couldn't remember ever being this bone weary, not even as an overworked intern living on coffee and catnaps.

Still, there remained one more thing he wanted to do, one last mile to go before he let himself sleep.

After first taking a deep breath and letting it out slowly in hopes that a little extra oxygen might blow away some of the cobwebs, he called Ananke.

Jon came on-line immediately. He looked pretty wiped out himself, but the sliver of a smile touched his lips and he nodded. "Thought maybe you'd be callin' back, Doc."

"How is she?" No need to say who *she* was.

"Hang on a sec, and we'll get us an update." The screen split, Jon on one side, Elias Acterelli peering owlishly out at him from the other.

"Hey there, Doc," the medic said. "Jon said you'd probably be calling."

Marchey searched Elias's face for some sign of what to expect. He couldn't read bad news written in its lines and folds, but neither could he read good. If Acterelli's expression reflected Angel's condition, then it was guarded.

"How is she?" he asked quietly.

"That's hard to say," Elias answered slowly, "I mean considering the beating she took, it's a wonder she's still alive. Here's how things stand. We got her cut loose, and took her back to her room since the air's still better in the area off the chapel than in a lot of the other tunnel sections."

"Good thinking. Has she regained consciousness?"

Elias shook his head. "No."

"Comatose?"

A reluctant nod. "I'm afraid so."

Marchey had already braced himself to hear this. The sheer amount of damage both her body and her exo had absorbed had almost guaranteed it.

"That's not necessarily a bad sign," he said, amazed by how calm he sounded. All he had to do was look at Jon and Elias to see that they could use some reassuring. "It could be simple physical collapse, in which case she'll come around in a day or so all on her own. It may be that her exo has gone into partial shutdown to protect her from further damage. Her vital signs are stable?"

"Yeah. Depressed but stable. Hang on and I'll show you." Elias looked down, squinting at the medicomp's keyboard and then tapping a button. "You got 'em?"

"Yes." Marchey studied the numbers scrolling along the bottom of his screen. Not great, but not bad, considering. Just as Elias said, depressed but stable.

"How about her exo?" he asked.

Elias shrugged. "It's locked solid, but far as we can tell its life-support functions are still working."

"There's a way to check that. Just below her right clavicle you'll see the faint outline of a diagnostic port. It's shaped like a long oval. If you look close you'll see a tiny raised bump at either end. Take a hammer and hit first one bump and then the other—hitting them just as hard as you can—continuing until each is struck ten times. The port will open then—"

He hesitated, becoming aware of the strange looks Jon and Elias were giving him. "What?"

"You want me to hit her with a *hammer*?" Elias asked, clearly aghast at the idea.

Marchey almost smiled. "I know it sounds crazy, but you have to remember that you could pound on that exo with a sledgehammer all day without hurting her. Usually a dipolar electric probe is used to open the port, but a hammer will do the job. Biometal is piezotic, the impact will be absorbed as an electric charge. The ten charges per side is to minimize the chance of accidental opening."

"If you say so, Doc." Elias still didn't look or sound particularly enthused at taking a hammer to his patient.

"Now when it opens you won't be able to plug into the port, that takes a special interface and cable, but there's also a row of tiny status lights. If the group of four on the left are all green, then the exo's critical life-support and internal medical systems are still functioning properly."

Fortunately those systems were triply redundant and nearly indestructible. He didn't tell them that there wasn't one damn thing they could do if any weren't working right. Nothing except—

"You've got her on glucose?"

Elias nodded. "That home-brewed stuff you showed Mardi how to make. We had to put the needle into the back of her hand. We've also got that ventilator you left us right by the bed. Other than that, there's not one hell of a lot we can do."

"You and Mardi have covered all the bases. You've done a fine job. I know she's in good hands." Marchey did his best to sound pleased. He thought he might have even pulled it off. "Just keep a close eye on her until I can get there. Call me if there's any change."

"Thanks, Doc," Elias said, sounding more sure of himself than when he had first come on. He grinned and scratched his chin. "I guess I better go try and scare up a hammer. Wait'll Mardi hears about this! Talk to you later."

"Tell me the truth," Jon said after Elias left the circuit. "Is she going to be all right?"

Marchey shook his head. "I don't know. I can't know until I see her."

"Can you fix her up?"

"If anyone can. Odds are she's sustained serious internal injuries, and because of her exo there's not one damn thing Elias or Mardi can do about them.

She may still come out of this in one piece if her condition doesn't deteriorate too quickly."

The next thing he said had to be said, and only numb exhaustion allowed him to say it calmly. "Mostly it depends on her lasting until I get there. We have to acknowledge the possibility that she might not."

Oddly enough, a smile broke onto Jon's face, as if this were good news rather than a worst case scenario that he should be braced for.

"Then she's gonna be all right," he breathed serenely.

Marchey stared at him. "What makes you say that?"

"Because no matter how bad she's hurt, she's gonna hang on until you come back."

"You can't be sure of that."

Jon stared him straight in the eye. "Yes I can. I think you know it, too."

Marchey went to bed shortly after. Maybe it was the sum of several sleepless nights, or maybe he had absorbed some of Jon's conviction. Whatever the reason, he immediately sank into a deep and dreamless sleep that lasted for ten straight hours. He might have slept even longer, but the signal for Fist's daily wake-up period saw to it that he was awake, too. He groaned and lay there, trying to make himself pretend he hadn't heard it.

It didn't work. Finally he gave up, rolling over and pulling himself upright on the side of the bed. Duty called.

"I'm getting too old for this crap," he muttered glumly, listening to his knees pop as he stood up. Pulling his robe on, he shuffled to the galley for a ration of strong coffee. After one scalding sip he headed for the clinic compartment, cup in hand, yawning and stretching as he went.

Fist was already conscious. All Marchey had to do was take one look to see that the old monster had failed badly in the last twelve hours. His skin was gray and bloodless, and his lips were a cyanotic blue, even though the unibed was oxygenating his air and blood for him.

His first words had nothing to do with his condition. He eyed Marchey's cup wistfully, nostrils twitching. "That coffee . . . smells . . . wonderful," he husked, his voice little more than a papery rattle.

Marchey glanced down at the cup in his hands, embarrassed by his lapse in bedside manners. "Sorry. I shouldn't have brought it in here." Fist's digestive system was completely shot to hell. Any liquids other than distilled water—or the nodine-tinted ethanol-and-water mix he had passed off as scotch the other day—or any sort of solid food would lead to all sorts of complications.

"Might I . . . have some?"

He thought about it a moment, then went and retrieved a sterile sponge from one of the storage cabinets. After soaking up a few drops of coffee with it, he put the sponge to Fist's withered lips. He told himself that it was unlikely any of the coffee would actually reach his stomach, and even if it did, he'd be dead long before it could cause any problems.

Fist sucked the few precious drops of coffee out of the sponge greedily, then let his head roll to one side when it was gone. "Thank you," he whispered.

Marchey stared at him in surprise. "This is the first time I've ever heard you use those two words."

A phlegmy chuckle. "I doubt . . . I'll live . . . long enough . . . for you to hear . . . me say them again. Though I suppose . . . I should also thank . . . you for intervening . . . in my . . . abduction. You could . . . have let . . . them take me."

This sentimental turn made Marchey uneasy. There was maybe one chance in a thousand that it was genuine. The old man had all the innate graciousness of a garrote around the neck.

"Don't think I wasn't tempted," he returned harshly. "But I was afraid the first thing they'd try to peel out of you was the whereabouts of everything you looted from Ananke. I figured I'd earned first crack at that by putting up with you these last few days."

Fist nodded weakly. The unibed's painfield was already at maximum strength. The way his jaw and hands were clenched told Marchey that he was still in considerable pain. Yet a mordant amusement quirked the old tyrant's thin lips.

"I suppose . . . you have. These have been . . . interesting times . . . but—" He was seized by a fit of coughing that racked his bony frame from end to end. Marchey reached down to help him, but the Fist waved him off.

He straightened back up and waited for the spasms to pass, already knowing what the *but* was: But the interesting times were nearly at an end. Not even Fist's indominitable will could hold his failing body together much longer. His chances of surviving the trip back to Ananke were nil.

At last Fist was able to speak again. "Tell me . . . what has happened. What . . . you have learned. What you . . . plan . . . to do."

Marchey stared down at the dying man, thinking it over. There was really no reason not to. Fist's attempts to use him had failed. Somehow he'd managed to evade most of the traps the old man had laid for him and come through safely to the other side.

Strangely enough, he wasn't even very afraid of him anymore. Instead he felt something closer to pity at the wasted potential of such flawed brilliance. So much useful energy so terribly misdirected, not unlike how the vast constructive power of fusion had in the last century been used for nothing but bombs.

"All right, I will," he began, going on to recount the story of his visit to Botha and the battle on Ananke. Telling about what he had done to Valdemar was hard, but telling about what had happened to Angel was even harder. He told himself that if Fist said even one cruel word about her, the sleepfield was going back on and they would be the last words he ever spoke.

When he was done he wasn't sure if Fist was still awake. His eyes were closed and his face completely lax. But after a moment he swallowed hard and opened his eyes.

"You . . . have triumphed. I . . . congratulate you."

"It's not over yet," Marchey pointed out. "I still have to get the media to listen to and believe me."

"They will. Checkmate . . . is certain. I concede. Yet I would offer . . . one final challenge . . . two things you . . . would find of value . . . for one modest price."

"What things?"

"First . . . the passphrase . . . to the file . . . detailing . . . all my . . . numbered accounts. Even including . . . what I had accrued . . . before Ananke. Their contents . . . are con . . . siderable."

Fist ran out of breath, his ruined lungs pumping and wheezing like leaky bellows, unable to continue. Marchey didn't need to 'face with the bed's systems to know what the effort of talking was costing him.

Yet as ever, Fist remained determined to have his say. "Second . . ." he went on in a bubbling whisper, "all hard data . . . you need to expose . . . MedArm's subverters. Not just . . . the head . . . but every tentacle. Who they are . . . what they . . . have done. All ready . . . to be fed . . . to the major . . . newswebs . . . on command."

Fist ran out of breath again, teeth clenched against the pain as he tried to draw air into his ruined lungs. But he stared unblinkingly up at Marchey, the mind behind those soulless yellow eyes still ticking over with the cold precision of the circuits in a smart weapon, untouched by his body's failings.

Well, there's the bait, Marchey thought sourly. *Now for the hook.* "What do you want in return?"

A diabolical gleam entered Fist's eyes. "I have . . . already told . . . you . . . word for . . . word."

Marchey stared down at the evil grin creeping onto

Fist's skull-like face. He shook his head in wonder. Once again, he almost had to admire the old monster. If consistency was a virtue, then at least one facet of his character was pure sterling.

Even now he has to try to run one last game. But this one sounded like more of a bargain than a trap. It occurred to Marchey that this might be his last chance to get this information. Fist couldn't hang on much longer.

Might as well play along.

"Let me see," he muttered, thinking back to when he had last asked Fist if he would give back what he'd looted from Ananke. He'd said he would, given the proper inducement. Something that would please him even more.

Another man in Fist's position might crave forgiveness, but Marchey had no illusions about the old fiend suddenly seeing the light. He thought the Kindred's forbearance was hilarious. Absolution was meaningless to him; he had no more sense of guilt or remorse than the tumors that were killing him.

What would any dying man want? Besides more time, more life.

What would I want if I were dying? he asked himself.

I wouldn't want to die alone. I know that now. Fist has that one covered. I'm here. I ended up being turned into his personal physician after all.

I'd want a chance to correct some of the mistakes I've made. To make amends. Fat chance of that for Fist. What else?

I would want to leave something behind. To be remembered.

At that thought the answer became obvious. The things which most pleased Fist were those that fed his voracious ego and tickled his twisted sense of humor. This would do both.

The thing he wanted would provide a sort of afterlife for his ego, and suit his perverse sense of humor perfectly.

It came to Marchey that although Fist might tell himself that it was really nothing more than a final ironic mark struck on those he had so misused, there might be even more to it than that, than an expression of the ego's drive to leave something behind.

It might just be a small sad human cry coming from some lost corner of the old monster's soul. A plea to be, if not loved, at least given some semblance of honor.

He remembered what Fist had said word for word, and as usual, what at the time seemed only a sarcasm was in fact the answer to the whole riddle. His price stated right down to the penny:

Not much of a memorial, but I cannot think of many who would raise a monument in my memory.

He stared at Fist, surprise that this had been the fundamental goal of all his machinations written all over his face.

Of course the cagey old devil read it clear as print. He didn't even bother to ask if it was a deal. He simply gave Marchey the passphrases, trusting him to live up to his part of the bargain.

"Pennies from heaven . . . An apple a day." Fist closed his eyes, fleshless cheeks hollowing in a satisfied smile.

"I always fancied . . . a bronze statue . . . of myself . . . with a book . . . in my hand. But I suppose . . . I will have . . . to take what . . . ever I . . . can get . . . considering . . . the . . . cir . . . cumstances."

The "an apple a day" file did everything Fist said it would and more. The information in it had been chillingly explicit, meticulously organized, exhaustively corroborated, and absolutely damning.

Jon, Moro, and Marchey first reviewed the file together to make sure Fist hadn't slipped any jokers into the deck, then released it late that afternoon. It made the same sort of splash as a meteor screaming down out of the sky into a placid sea, creating not ripples but tsunamis. Within hours there were several hundred arrests, resignations, indictments, sudden disappearances, and a handful of suicides.

Marchey spent a large part of the rest of his trip back to Ananke on the comm, wearily repeating testimony to hastily convened boards of inquiry, briefing high officials who were either deeply concerned about what had transpired and ready to do something productive, or just knew a good bandwagon when it passed by. He lost count of the interviews he gave to ecstatic newswebbers slavering over the spilled corporate, political, and bureaucratic blood. Like it or not—and he didn't—he was famous.

The corruption of MedArm ran even deeper than Marchey had suspected. He'd become entangled in one strand of a vast and tangled web of conspiracy begun over fifteen years before, for the unexceptional motive of lust for power and profit. The corporate prime mover behind it all was OmniMat—Number Two in the Unholy Trinity with its eyes firmly fixed on the goal of being Number One.

One of the more perceptive webbers had, as a sort of follow-up question, asked, "If you could cure just one disease, Dr. Marchey, what would it be?"

"Greed," he had answered solemnly.

Greed it had been. Essentially it was a matter of OmniMat seeing MedArm as a fat prize just waiting to be taken and exploited.

Their tactics had been classic: divide, subvert, and conquer. Once key bureaucratic positions had been taken over by handpicked operatives, the cabal's first objective had been splitting MedArm into two nearly autonomous zones or divisions. This process took time, and was executed with a diamond cutter's careful precision. Since UNSRA was headquartered on the Moon, and inside the newly created Inner Zone, the split gave them freer reign in the Outer Zone.

Their next moves solidified their control of the Outer Zone: placement of MedArm facilites in cubic owned by OmniMat either directly or by way of dummy corporations; buyouts of and similarly advantageous changes in providers of pharmaceuticals, medical equipment and supplies, and other nonmedical materials, along with slowly inflating prices. At the same time there began a cautious incremental skewing of the levies in OmniMat's favor. Like Jon had said: *A few million here, a few million there. Before long the bastids were raking in real money.*

Subversion of the Bergmann Program had begun just after its inception. The Institute was one of the spoils OmniMat wanted for its own. First had come subtle reinforcement of the distrust of and ill will toward the Bergmann Surgeons that already existed through a variety of means. Later on had come the establishment of the circuit, a successful testing of their growing clout. Once the Bergmanns were isolated from each other and the rest of the medical community, it became easier to keep them unaware that they were increasingly being used as a premium commodity—carefully leaked rumors causing only more resentment, which in turn increased their pariah status—and as a tool to further the rest of OmniMat's agenda.

Marchey had thought that all this was as deep as sleaze could get. He'd been wrong. It turned out that there had been another reason for the institution of the circuit, obvious only in retrospect.

The Bergmanns were also being used as mules. Their ships were ideally suited for use as an ultra-secure method of carrying data and communiqués too sensitive to be trusted to the normal channels, along with hard currency, drugs, art, gemstones, and other portable valuables for bonuses, bribes, and payoffs. Their craft received priority routing and docking and since MedArm was a branch of UNSRA, were never searched or inspected for contraband.

The corporate and political coconspirators had been able to take over the Outer Zone, almost completely and had commenced the process of subverting the rest of MedArm. They were well on their way to gaining what amounted to the power of life and death over every man, woman, and child living off Earth. Had they not been stopped, they would have eventually reduced all medical services to their primitive, chaotic, and grossly inequitable state in much of the world at the end of the twentieth century.

Medicine would have become a *commodity*. A commodity under their sole control, available only from them and at what the market would bear. To Marchey this return to the bloody Dark Ages was a horrific vision, a cruelty equal to banning analgesics and anesthetics.

Equally frightening was that even UNSRA itself had been infiltrated. Key people in several departments had been bought off or blackmailed into connivance. Certain documents Fist had provided hinted that, bloated with satisfaction at what it had achieved so far, UNSRA itself had become OmniMat's ultimate prize.

The whole ugly scheme was now coming apart at the seams like a Frankenstein's monster stitched together with dissolving sutures. Some parts were even funny. When the media talked about Preston Valdemar they generally stated that he was "under UNSRA guard on Botha Station, and in the care of his spokesman and personal physician, Dr. Raphael Moro." Valdemar was mentioned often because he promised to be a key witness. The media people generally went on to explain that Valdemar had recently undergone both a breakdown and something akin to a sudden and quite extreme religious conversion.

Sal Bophanza and Ludmilla were still on their way to Ananke. Much to Marchey's relief, they were no longer fugitives. Sal's name had already come up several times as a possible candidate to take over MedArm and spearhead a thorough housecleaning and reorganization of its operations.

Marchey hoped Sal got the job. He himself had been burned too badly ever to trust the agency again unless someone with his old friend's integrity was in charge.

All this activity served mainly to keep his mind from his too-slow progress to Ananke. Otherwise, it would have been unendurable not being where he wanted to be, where he needed to be.

Late in the morning of the fourth day, he had posted himself as unavailable so he'd have time to talk to Jon Halen, making the first of the at least two daily calls he made to check on Angel's condition.

There was nothing new to report. She had still not regained consciousness. Mardi and Elias lacked the equipment to monitor brain activity, and even if they'd had it, Angel's biometal skull covering would have prevented them from getting reliable readings. Though she was comatose, there were no overt signs that she had suffered brain damage from oxygen deprivation. Her vital signs remained depressed, but stable. All they could do was watch her around the clock and call if there was the slightest change.

No call had come, but he kept checking in anyway.

Their talk had drifted on to other subjects. Fist's assertion that his assets were considerable had proved to be something of an understatement. There were literally dozens of blind numbered accounts maintained under a variety of names. There was also real estate, shares in major corporations, and the contents of hundreds of safe-deposit boxes crammed full of cash, art, antiquities, and who knew what else. Now a good portion of all that belonged to Ananke.

Jon had been laughing over this strange new state of affairs, going from rags to riches in a single stroke, and—thanks to it—owing Fist a monument, when the call buzzer from the inship clinic sounded. Marchey bade Jon good-bye and headed back to check on his patient.

Halfway to the door he broke into a run when he realized that Fist was still under the sleepfield and shouldn't be awake.

But he was. Somehow he had fought off the field's effects, a feat Marchey would have said was damn near impossible even for a healthy man.

A quick glance at the reads told him that Fist had probably signed his own death warrant with that effort. Every indicator was deep in the red. He damped the field and, trying to keep the death sentence he'd seen in the reads off his face, leaned over the unibed's high sides.

He needn't have bothered to pretend.

"This . . . is it . . ." Fist wheezed, his voice no more than a faint rustle Marchey had to lean closer to hear. He grinned his death's-head grin. "Will you . . . miss me?"

Marchey made himself smile. "I'll be wearing black for months."

Haaaaaaa. Fist's laugh sounded like a death rattle now, but he hadn't given up his grip on life just yet.

"A final . . . puzzle . . . for you . . . my friend. Search . . . the names . . . Byron Forsythe . . . Bradley Freeling . . . and . . . Braun Fastyx."

"Why?" Marchey asked softly.

"I have led . . . many lives. Contain . . . multitudes," Fist gasped, that evil grin of his widening in malicious glee. "But just . . . who am I?" A thin finger twitched in his direction. "And what . . . marks . . . have I . . . made on you . . . my most apt . . . pupil? Who . . . and what . . . have . . . you . . . . become . . . under . . . my . . . splendid . . . tutelage?"

Haaaaaaaaaaaaaaaaaa . . .

Fist's laugh became a bubbling wheeze, the sound of something deflating as all the life escaped it, finally trailing off to breathless silence.

All the monitors had gone off at once, telling Marchey what he already knew. He reached over and shut them off. Silence descended, ringing with finality.

Fist lay still, staring sightlessly up at him with glazing yellow eyes, his malicious grin fixed on his face by death.

Well, old man, you had the last laugh, he thought, bemused to find himself sad to see Fist gone. *I hope you're happy.*

It was altogether in character that he had died

laughing. Laughing at life, and at death. Laughing at having left one last riddle to solve, and getting in a final dig at what was already a source of considerable self-doubt.

Fist had changed him. That was undeniable. Only time would tell just how much and in what way.

"I'd tell you that I hope you're in Hell, old man, but to you it would probably seem like a lifetime pass to Disneyland." He reached down, gently closing those sightless yellow eyes one last time. Then he instructed the unibed to cover itself and freeze Fist's lifeless clay.

When he left the clinic he closed the door and turned out the lights behind him.

After first jotting down the names Fist had given him before they could slip his mind, he made himself a single weak drink and raised his glass in the old man's name and memory, a small gesture to mark the passing of a nemesis and the end of an era.

At last the waiting was nearly over. Oddly enough, he wasn't all that impatient anymore. Mostly he had this strange feeling of returning to where he belonged. Of completion.

As his ship passed through the dented steel blister on Ananke's desolate surface Marchey couldn't help but think back to the first time he had come to Ananke. He'd been a prisoner then, and not just of Scylla. His own apathy and indifference had been the chains he'd not only worn, but embraced. Habit had forged the links, the manacles welded on by his own diminished expectations.

It seemed like all of that had happened a whole lifetime ago, or happened to him in a whole other life.

In the back of his mind a sly, crepitous voice whispered *I have led many lives.*

Marchey still didn't know quite what to make of what he'd learned from following up on the three names Fist had given him. Fist had told them to him for a reason, but what was it? Had it been a confession, a warning, a subtle lesson, or just something to trouble his sleep for years to come? Perhaps all of those, bound together by some convoluted impulse only the old man could have understood.

Whatever the case, he now knew volumes more about the man who had called himself Brother Fist, and understood him even less.

Byron Forsyth had graduated from UNSRA's Archimedes Base Military Academy at the top of his class, and been recruited into their Intelligence/Covert Operations branch at the time when the New Cold War with Mars was degenerating into the Rebellion. He had quickly risen to I/CO's highest ranks before leaving it just after the end of the Rebellion under circumstances still classified all these years later.

Braun Fastyx was the *nom de guerre* of the elusive mastermind who had written the definitive underground texts on phagewar. A shadowy figure rumored to be allied with and under the protection of the weapons cults on Armageddon, the list of crimes attributed to him ran for several pages. He had vanished without a trace over ten years ago, never to be heard from again.

Bradley Freeling was a faceless, reclusive author with two highly regarded novels to his name, both about an antihero named *Bryce Fullerton*.

The first book chronicled how Fullerton, a brilliant but strange young UNSRA officer had found himself drawn into the dark and shadowy world of Intelligence, Covert Operations, and the just-emerging black science of phagewar, only to find that he harbored inside himself a terrible aptitude for it. This diabolic art came to him so easily, and so took him over, that in the end he reinvented it and it consumed him, warping him into an uncanny, amoral avatar of calculated atrocity.

In the end, when Mars surrendered and peace was struck, the list of war crimes attributable to I/CO began coming to light. The branch was dismantled, and it was decided that it was in society's best interests that Fullerton be declared insane and confined. By the

end of the book, and in the course of escaping
UNSRA imprisonment, Fullerton learns that he was
recruited in the first place because his psychological
testing revealed evidence of a latent sociopathy the
I/CO branch felt they could channel and exploit. They
had subtly orchestrated its emergence, feeding his
growing egopathy and paranoia, purposely warping
him into the ruthless amoral monster he had become.
After all, there was a war on.

The second book was shorter, and even more trou-
bling. It detailed how Fullerton, decades older and
living under an assumed name while working as a mer-
cenary social assassin, and so far keeping the worst of
his sociopathic tendencies under control—or at least
channeled—begins feeling himself losing his tenuous
grip on reality.

Fullerton knows himself to be going irretrievably
mad, and with the remaining shreds of his sanity, real-
izes just how dangerous he would be if he went amok
in the heavily populated near-Earth areas. Since he is
incapable of even contemplating suicide, he banishes
himself to an isolated, poorly populated place on the
outer fringes of human inhabited space so the amount
of harm he could cause would be minimized. In this
manner he in effect saves the populated worlds from
himself.

The place sacrificed for the greater good was not
named, but there was no mistaking it.

Marchey remembered once calling Fist a Renaissance man. Fist had chuckled, pointing out that renaissance meant rebirth, and hinting that Marchey was
more right than he knew. Had Fist somehow inte-
grated those separate personas—separate selves—at
the very end? Had he remembered who he had been,
how he had gotten that way, and found something like
sanity in those memories? Had he even seen himself
as some sort of darkling hero?

Marchey would never know.

There was a distant vibration as the docking clamps
took hold of the ship. Below his feet the shutters

closed out the stars. His stomach grudgingly accommodated itself to *in* being *up*.

He knew he was a different man than the one who had come to Ananke last time. Some of the changes had been for the good. But others . . . were they indeed Fist's mark? Proof that he was the apt pupil the old monster kept saying he was, with perhaps a touch of Bryce Fullerton lurking inside?

There was no avoiding the fact that he'd been sly, manipulative, dissembling, and even ruthless. He'd tapped into unsuspected wells of rage and contempt and even cruelty. . . .

The old psychopath had changed him; there was no way to pretend that he hadn't.

Still, for all his twisted brilliance, there had been some things Fist had never really understood. In spite of everything he had done to Kindred, he had not been able truly to corrupt them. The fact that they had repudiated him rather than tried to revenge themselves on him proved that. He had subjugated them, but not subverted them.

Nor had he understood the full nature of his own crucible, that what the flame does not destroy it quite often refines.

Adversity could anneal, as well as annul; the iron hand trying to bend you to its will might ultimately only serve to make you stronger and purer in spirit.

But first adversity had to be acknowledged, and then met head on. At times he wondered if so much of the wreckage he'd made of his own life went back to Bergmann Surgery. Not the giving up his hands for a crazy dream, but—

The lockstack turned orange, aborting mid-cycle and flashing a warning about poor air quality. He overrode it, then folded his silver hands, waiting for it to finish its cycle.

—but Bergmann Surgery was supposed to be *perfect* surgery. No blood. No pain. A chance to heal the heretofore unhealable.

Yet when they had found out that it had a flaw,

they had let that flaw dictate how they used it. From that point on they had proceeded less on the basis of what they *could* do than on what they could not.

These were just some of the many things he wanted to get straightened out in his mind. He wanted all his past mistakes understood, and his future laid out for him as cleanly and precisely as sterilized surgical instruments on a tray. The high cost of living without a future was a lesson burned into him past all forgetting.

These thoughts, just like all others of late, led him back to one place. One person. No matter how much he might have learned, and no matter how many things he had managed to do right, if he couldn't repair the damage caused by this one particular failure, then all the rest would become meaningless.

The lockstack flashed green. The doors slid back. The stale, tired air of Ananke rolled in to greet him.

He started on the final leg of his journey, once more gingerly making his way down the sagging, roughly patched locktube. In some ways it was the culmination of a journey he had begun as an idealistic young man of thirty with a full head of hair and absolutely no concept of what he was facing. He was much older now. It remained to be seen if he was the least bit wiser.

Down the tube he went.

This time there was no angel behind him, forcing him out of the safe womb of his ship.

This time it was the woman who had been trapped inside that angel drawing him out.

He crossed the lock and emerged from the battered, crudely repaired inner doors to find Jon Halen leaning on his crutch and waiting for him. Jon gave him a clumsy, one-armed embrace, then stepped back, lumpish hand tight and warm on Marchey's upper arm.

"Welcome home," he said quietly.

Marchey nodded, covering Jon's hand with his own, silver on black. "Thanks." He did feel like he had come home.

Jon was not the only one who had been waiting for

his arrival. Marchey looked out over the cavernous bay, seeing that almost everyone who could squeeze inside had turned out to greet him. They stood shoulder to shoulder, their familiar and half-familiar faces all turned up toward him. Some faces were solemn, but most were smiling. Several nodded or winked when his gaze slid across them.

For all their numbers, they were uncannily quiet. Not even a whisper broke the silence, a silence that spoke far more eloquently than any cheering ever could.

Jon's hand still on his arm, they started down the ramp to the bay floor. The people of Ananke parted before them like the waters before Moses, opening an aisle to the doors on the far side. Each and every woman, man, and child whispered *Welcome home* as he came abreast of them, the greeting filling the air like the sound of the sea as they crossed the metal-laid stone floor. But not a one of them did anything that might impede their progress. Each and every one of them knew why he had returned and where he was bound.

The sea of faces became a river when they entered the tunnels; both sides were lined with well-wishers. Marchey let Jon bear him along through the tidings, so deeply moved by his welcome that he was caught by surprise when he found himself inside the chapel and before the door to Angel's cubby.

Jon ushered him inside, those who trailed after remaining in the chapel outside, joining the quiet vigil that had been maintained since they had borne Angel's stiff, unconscious body back to her room. People who had once been terrorized by her as Scylla now fervently prayed for her survival. Whatever she had done to them had been repaid a thousand times over by the way she had defended them.

Mardi left the bedside, meeting them halfway to the door. She gave Marchey a solemn nod, but said nothing. There was nothing to tell. Angel's condition had not changed in days. She delayed him only long enough to plant a soft kiss on his cheek, then went out to join the others in the chapel.

Jon led him to the end of Angel's pallet. The two men stood side by side, Jon leaning on his crutch and studying Marchey's face.

Angel lay there still as death, the bruises and burns starkly evident against the milky paleness of her face. Her features were so lax that it was obvious she was not merely sleeping; the animating spirit that made her who she was, was nowhere to be seen on that flat and damaged landscape. Only the evidence presented by the crude cardiac-monitoring equipment at her bedside and the slow rise and fall of her armored breast proved that she was even alive. Her barbed hands remained frozen in the position they had been in when the airlock doors had been cut from around them, as if trying to come together in prayer.

Marchey had watched a recording of her heroic efforts over and over again, had played and replayed it until he saw her struggle in his troubled dreams. Although it broke his heart to see her suffer so, the indomitable spirit she had shown gave him hope.

It gave him a whole new definition of what was possible.

"She's a very brave girl," he said quietly.

Jon was still watching him, his face unreadable. "She's a very brave *woman*," he corrected pointedly. "And I think she's waited long enough for you." He squeezed Marchey's shoulder, then hobbled back outside, leaving him alone with his patient.

Marchey edged slowly around to the side of the pallet, his gaze lingering on Angel's face. He remembered the first time he had seen that face without its horrific tattooed mask, and how she had smiled when he removed it. He recalled being deeply moved, and in some strange way frightened, as if confronted with something that threatened everything he was, and against which he had no defense.

He had run, and he had hidden, but she had reached him anyway. She had thrown rose petals against the stone wall he had erected, and brought it down just as surely as if she'd used a wrecking ball.

He held his breath as he reached out to touch her cheek, trembling at the feel of her soft skin against his silver fingers. They told him her temperature, accurate to a hundreth of a degree. Her pulse and galvanic skin response. He ignored the data, his mind on other things.

Flesh and silver.

So much of what had happened to and between them came down to flesh and silver. Each had for years lost some part of themselves to the harsh demands of the silver—she as a crippled creature named Scylla, and he clinging to the tarnished promise of Bergmann Surgery.

The metal had brought them together, and in doing so given each one the means to release the other.

Sometimes hindsight meant being able to see what an ass you've been. Looking back, it was all painfully clear. Angel had chosen to keep her exo not out of fear, but because she had understood that shedding that outward metal shell was of little consequence. Freeing herself inside was what really mattered.

She had been trying to be free, too, by heeding—and letting him know she felt—the surging tidal pull of the flesh.

He, the older, supposedly wiser one, had clung to his own silvery exo. He had hidden himself inside it from her, from the people of Ananke, from choice, from life itself. Too frightened to step outside his rusty armor and be a man.

For so many years he had resented the fact that all anyone saw when they looked at him were the silver prosthetics, the silver pin, and what they signified. Yet she had looked past them and seen something more, something of equal or greater value. She had reached out to him so that they might both step outside their silver cages, and he had refused even to look at what she was offering, or what his refusal might cost.

Now he had that rarest and most precious of things,

a second chance. All he had to do was reach out and take it in his hands.

He straightened back up, the feel of her cheek lingering on his fingertips like a kiss. He'd given up so many things when he'd given up his hands. But if the abilities he'd gained let him bring her back, then it would be worth the price. He'd go back and do it all over again if that made what he wanted to do possible.

It was time to shed his metal arms and see.

"I'm here, Angel," he said softly. "You're going to be just fine," he added, as much for his own benefit as for hers. He started to turn away, looking for a place to lay his prosthetics aside.

A faint movement just glimpsed out of the corner of his eye snapped his head back around. His breath stalled in his chest when he saw Angel's one human eye fluttering weakly under its lid like a butterfly trapped in its chrysalis.

"Angel?" he whispered uncertainly, bending closer and taking her silver-plated hands in his own. They tightened ever so slightly. He was sure of it.

Her eye still moved under its closed lid, but more slowly. Her grip slackened. He felt her slipping away.

Panic ignited in him, spitting hot searing sparks of terror into every corner of his soul. The bedside monitor shrilled a warning as her pulse rate spiraled downward and her blood pressure plummeted.

An inarticulate cry of denial ripped its way out of him. He fought to smother his panic, knowing that he had to reach inside her, take hold of whatever life flickered there and keep it from escaping. To do that he had to calm and center himself, had to shed these damned tin arms and cup that guttering flame the best way he could.

But somehow he could not let go of her hands. His silver fingers remained locked around hers like links of chain. It was as if the lifeless metal parts of both of them were uniting in conspiracy against the flesh.

Just as suddenly as panic had come, a calm descended over him. He went still as a sunrise inside, a

quiet wisdom whispering in his ear how he should proceed. Not as a Bergmann Surgeon, not as a physician,
not as anything he took the time to name.

He pulled himself close to her, putting his cheek
against hers, his lips next to her silver-shrouded ear,
and called her name.

"Angel."

And again, telling her he was there. Calling her out.

"Angel, I'm here."

Calling her back.

He crouched there, hands clamped tightly around
hers as if holding her to life, all his skills flung aside,
whispering her name over and over like a mantra to
invoke a miracle, begging her to come back. Trying
to reach her. Trying to touch her. Telling her he was
there. Telling her he wanted her to come back.

Telling her he needed her. Begging her to live.
For him.

He didn't see her one green eye slowly open.

But he did feel her hands close tight around his
own.

Angel sat up on her pallet, watching Marchey stand
with his broad back to her as he reattached his silver arms.

She couldn't stop smiling, and didn't give a damn if
her teeth showed or not, simply revelling in how good
it felt still to be alive. There remained some lingering
pain, but nothing like before. It paled in comparison
to the pleasure of seeing him again.

Already it was getting hard to remember the suffocating red darkness that had been piled over her,
pressing her down toward where nothingness awaited.
Above the smothering, senseless dark, there had been
only bright electric pain lighting a frozen emptiness
that made the coldest, darkest, dingiest tunnel of Ananke look like heaven. There was no reason to return
to that place. And yet she had resisted the pull of the
nothingness and the peace it promised, all curled
in on herself and blindly waiting for something that had

to come soon if she was to survive, hung on as long as she could. It had been getting harder, her grip slipping as she weakened. The peace below had loomed closer, the weight above relentlessly pushing her down.

Maybe the memory of that slow descent toward nothingness would fade and be forgotten. She hoped so. But she would never forget how an immaterial hand had reached down through it all, brushed against her, and brought her into momentary awareness, out into where the pain waited.

When it disappeared the pain had driven her back, driven her deeper, driven her down toward the place from which there was no escaping. The fall she had forestalled had begun in earnest, and there was no way for her to stop it.

Then the hand had come for her again, caught her as she fell, and she had clung to it with all her might. It had been a lifeline, pulling her back through the darkness and back into the pain. But the pain hadn't mattered then. Nothing had mattered but having the thing she had yearned for finally within reach. She would have followed it anywhere, through anything.

The hand he had offered, the hand that had saved her, was not metal, not flesh. It was the essence, the force he had used when he had first pulled her out of the monster she had been as Scylla, the part of himself he had withdrawn from her grasp shortly after, and taken completely away when he left Ananke.

She sat there watching him, knowing that she now understood something she hoped she could help him relearn. That the secret of his healing did not reside in what he could do as a Bergmann Surgeon, but inside himself. It sprang from his heart and soul and self. The first empowered the latter, which was only a conduit for something deeper and stranger and a thousand times more wonderful; something that could reach places the other could not ever touch; something he had let himself become convinced he could only express in one limited way. That was the part of him-

self that he gave to another. His skills might have
healed her, but only after his caring had saved her.

She understood all that because she at last fully understood a similar truth about herself. The secret in
being Angel had nothing to do with proving she was
not Scylla. It lay in simply touching people as Angel,
giving as Angel. That was the key to keep Scylla forever in chains.

When Marchey turned back toward her he wore a
solemn expression. "You messed yourself up pretty
good, young lady. It's taken me two hours to repair
the worst of your internal injuries, and it'll take at
least that long to finish the job. But the next step is
to get you the hell out of that exo while I still can."
He spoke quietly, looking right at her. Not through
her, or past her.

Both his face and voice softened. "You're not going
to argue with me about it this time, are you?"

"Hold on one damn minute!" The loud, unexpected
voice came from the doorwary, catching both of them
off-guard.

She and Marchey both turned to watch Jon Halen
limp into the cubby. "We've got us some things to
talk about first," he said heavily, heading toward the
bed. Angel stared at the tight-lipped frown on his face
in confusion.

Behind him were two strangers. One was a sad-eyed
man with dusky copper skin and short salt-and-pepper
hair. He was dressed in a white turtleneck and tailored
black pants. There was a silver crossed arms pin on
his chest. At his side was a woman with silver hands
just like Marchey's. She wore a pale blue caftan that
hung to the floor, her silver-gray hair cascading over
her shoulders. Her face was kind, and her bearing
regal. She, too, wore the silver pin.

The familiar faces of the Kindred filled the doorway
behind them, smiling shyly and waving, but remaining
outside. She saw Marchey nod uncertainly at the two
newcomers before returning his attention to Jon.

Halen parked himself on the side of the bed next

to her, that inexplicably stern expression still on his face. What had she done to make him angry?

"So," he said gruffly, "you figure you've earned the right to take that exo off, huh?"

"Yes," she replied meekly, unnerved by his close scrutiny.

"Are you *sure*?" he demanded, as if certain she was not.

Before she could answer Marchey spoke up in her defense. "What the hell's the matter with you, Jon?" he growled. "She damn near killed herself for you people!"

Jon peered up at him as if surprised by his ability to speak. "What's it to you, Doc?"

Marchey stared at him for what felt to Angel like an hour or more, his face caught between expressions and lost for a place to go. His mouth moved, but nothing came out.

"Answer him, Gory," the strange man put in quietly. The woman at his side nodded and echoed him. Angel couldn't read either of their faces, so she looked back at Marchey.

Gory. She liked the sound of it.

"I don't know," he said at last. His gaze sought hers, mute appeal in his gray eyes. She could feel his uncertainty; it was not so different from her own. It was one thing to know that there was something there between you and another person, but another thing entirely to define it. It was hard to know where you stood in relation to someone else when the how and what and who of *you* was still so uncertain.

But then again, maybe you had to let the existence of a connection with someone else be the beginning point, and let everything else flower outward from there. She reached out and took his hand, after a moment feeling it tighten around her own.

"She's important to me," he said at last, the rough planes of his face softening. He hadn't looked back at Jon to answer, he was still gazing at her, his eyes seeking hers. They met, locked. "You're important to me."

At those four words time seemed to stop. A shiver
went through her. Suddenly there beneath her feet
was the solid ground she had so desperately wanted
to build her new life upon. A place to stand, a place
truly to begin anew. And buried deep beneath this
ground, powerless and past any resurrection, were the
remains of a fallen angel named Scylla.

Time began to move again when Jon suddenly
reached out to cover their linked hands with his own.
Angel stared down at their three hands, two gleaming
silver and one mottled black and pink, then up at
Jon's face. A chill ran through her as she realized
what he was doing.

To her surprise Jon said nothing about it. He only
gripped their hands as best as he could for a moment,
giving her a secret smile, then let go and beckoned
the two strangers over.

She sat there in wordless openmouthed amazement.
Wasn't he going to tell Marchey what he had just
done?

Marchey stood there with Angel's hand in his, feeling very strange indeed. Saying what he had just said
had been like stepping through some long impassable
door to enter a new and uncertain world as someone
completely different from who he had been just moments before.

He knew that Jon's gesture had some special sig-
nificance, but Jon didn't give him a chance to ask
about it. Instead Halen invited Sal and 'Milla over.

"Angel," Jon said, his normal kindly tone back once
more, "this gentleman is Doc's boss, Dr. Sal Bophanza. The lovely lady with him is his colleague, Dr.
'Milla Prodaresk. The two of 'em landed just over an
hour ago and wanted very much to meet you before
they took off again."

Bophanza bowed toward Angel as if greeting a
queen, murmuring, "I'm honored." 'Milla nodded and
smiled approvingly, then gave her a conspiratorial
wink.

Marchey shook himself out of the dazed state that had fallen over him. "You two are leaving already? You just got here!"

Sal smirked at him for several seconds before answering. "This is just a pit stop. As soon as the folks here can scrape up a few odds and ends we're heading back insystem."

"What's the big hurry?"

Marchey remembered the smug, *I've got a secret,* look that appeared on Sal's face from the old days. "I've been on vacation long enough, Gory. It's time to get my butt back to work."

"At the Institute?"

"No, as head of MedArm's Outer Zone."

"Hey, that's great!" he told his old friend, seizing his hand and pumping it in congratulations. Then he frowned as he realized the implications of Sal's promotion. "What about the Institute and the Program?"

"What about them?" Sal asked blandly.

Marchey took a deep breath. "We can't go on doing things the way we have been."

Sal looked mildly interested. "Is that so? Why not?"

Marchey thought hard for a few seconds, trying to pull all the things he'd learned in the last month into some sort of order. Where to begin?

At the beginning. "We started off on the wrong foot from the very first, letting ourselves be cut off from the mainstream. Letting ourselves be forced to keep moving from place to place."

"Nobody wanted you to stay on," Sal pointed out. "It would have been cruel to make you stay where you weren't welcome."

"Maybe so, but giving in didn't do anything to help them come to terms with us and what we could do. When we made the changeover to the circuit that nailed our marginalization shut. It separated us from each other and from everything else, and convinced us that we were all we could ever become. We never made a stand, so we ended up on the run."

"Okay, maybe you're right," Sal returned patiently.

"Now we do know that the circuit was largely started to make you easier to co-opt. That still doesn't change the fact that it originally made it possible for you to do the most good in the greatest number of places."

"Yeah, and look how it turned out!" Marchey shot back. He rubbed his chin, making himself stay calm. "We got used badly because we let ourselves be used. As for the other—" He thought for a second, sure there had to be a way around Sal's objection.

"Okay, maybe there are still too few of us to go around. But Jesus, the circuit so dehumanized us that some of us could only fight back by committing suicide. Remember Ivan? Grace? Josiah?"

He shook his head, not allowing himself to dwell on all the terrible waste of time, of potential, of lives. "I used to think they were the weak ones. But suicide was more of a human response than what the rest of us showed. We accepted being dehumanized. We got so used to it—I got so used to it—I couldn't imagine things being any other way."

Sal stood there with his arms crossed before his chest, looking unconvinced. "So what other way is there to do it?"

Marchey shrugged. "There has to be some sort of middle ground. Most of us, myself included, couldn't handle jumping back into the mainstream with both feet. We're too messed up. Maybe what we need are places for us to work from. *Our* places. Centrally located clinics or hospitals to act as bases for us. We could do most of our work from there—and have other medical people come in to work with us and start getting used to us. Now that the Nightmare Effect is gone and we've gotten some good press, that should be easier. Even those times we had to go out on call, we would have a place and people to come back to."

"You're saying that's important?" Sal asked quietly.

Marchey looked to the faces of those around him before answering. At Jon, the first real friend he'd made in years. At the faces of the people filling the doorway, people whose lives had become inextricably entwined in his whether he'd wanted them to or not. At Angel, who smiled back in encouragement. At Sal and 'Milla, his oldest friends and fellow survivors. Then there was Raphael Moro, and back in the dim distant past a woman named Delores Esterbrook, who had rescued him from despair for a while. The answer to Sal's question was so obvious he had to wonder how it had escaped him for so many years.

"It is," he said, his voice filled with unshakable certainty. "We need people around us. We need friends." Memories of Fist came to him then, and he knew that he'd even gained something of value from that prickly relationship. It was Fist who showed him just how dangerous and destructive letting another take control of your life could be. The old villain had just been such an extreme case that even a brain-dead boozehound couldn't miss the lesson.

He laughed. "Hell, we even need enemies. We've been out in the cold too long, Sal. We need to come home."

Sal nodded solemnly, his dark eyes intent. "It sounds like you have this pretty well thought out, Gory."

Marchey was surprised. It did sound that way. But that was only because he was finally thinking ahead, instead of blindly plodding along on the treadmill his life had been. It didn't matter that he'd been dragged off it against his will. What did matter was that he had left it behind, and found some horizon beyond the bottom of his next bottle. Somewhere along the way he'd learned that answers never came to those who refused to face that fact that there were questions.

"To tell you the truth," Sal went on, "it sounds to me like you ought to be the one to run the program from now on."

Marchey stared at him. He should have seen this coming, but he'd been too caught up in trying to make

Sal understand all the things he was still trying to understand himself. He shook his head. "Not me."

Sal arched an eyebrow. "And why not?"

"I don't want it."

"I need a better reason than that," Sal said patiently.

Marchey took a deep breath, and said it out loud. "Because I'm staying right here on Ananke. This is my home now." It felt good to have it out, to be able to say it and really mean it. Funny how each new commitment only served to make him feel all the more free.

Oddly enough Sal didn't look very surprised. Ludmilla grinned and nudged him. Marchey frowned, beginning to smell conspiracy.

He turned to glare at Jon, who only spread his misshapen hand and tried to look innocent. Marchey wasn't fooled. He'd had an hour to talk to Sal and 'Milla, and his earlier performance proved he had his own agenda.

When he looked at Angel the smile she gave him made him glad he'd said it.

"So what?" Sal said behind him.

"So what?" he echoed, rounding on him. "What the hell do you mean, *so what*?"

Sal shrugged. "So run it from here. I agree that there should be one or two of you in each populated area. One is needed out here. You're here. This would make as good a base as anywhere."

"But there's no goddamn hospital here!" Marchey shot back in exasperation.

"Ah, well," Jon put in, drawing his attention. He scratched his head, puckering his face up as if in the process of puzzling something out. "We sure could use a hospital, sccin' how a lot of us are still pretty messed up." A sly look crossed his face as he squinted up at Marchey. " 'Sides, you must remember that damn fool promise you went and made Fist on our behalf, don't you?"

He could only stare down at Jon, baffled by his bringing that up now.

"A monument, you promised him," Jon prompted. "His last laugh at our expense?" That mischievous grin of Jon's reappeared full force.

"Yeah, what about it?"

"We figure helpin' build a Memorial Hospital in his name with some of his money oughta have him spinnin' in his grave so fast he just about *hums*!"

After that, Marchey had to admit that he was beaten. By the time the others left Angel's cubby he had agreed not only to start up a Bergmann Hospital on Ananke, but also resurrect the Institute in it. He would run both, some of the old Institute staff and perhaps another Bergmann Surgeon to come on board later.

Sal had even hinted at starting to recruit again. The events of the past few days had brought about a fundamental change in how the Bergmanns were perceived, and there was no longer the Nightmare Effect to contend with. Sal had everything needed to restart the program on the ship with him, and would leave it all there when he left.

Marchey supposed that maybe after things settled down it might be time to try again. If learning came from making mistakes, then maybe they'd made enough to have figured out how to do it right next time.

Ludmilla and Sal had unsurprisingly enough become lovers during their time as fugitives. She was going back with Sal to take charge of the task of locating homes/hospitals for the other Bergmanns, including one for herself and Sal. Seeing the way they looked at each other in unguarded moments, he knew his old friends had a very good chance of being very happy together. They had a lot in common, and each had spent far too much of their life alone.

Jon had shooed everyone but Marchey out of Angel's cubby at last, sending them out to join the celebration going on all over Ananke. He paused in the doorway, giving them both a long, thoughtful look before going on out and closing the door behind him.

An uncomfortable silence sprang up once he was gone. All they had been through had not prepared them for being alone together. Each was convinced that he or she was the one who had spoiled things before and fearful of doing it again.

"I better leave, too, so you can get some rest," Marchey mumbled at last, carefully not looking toward her on the bed. It seemed like the right thing to say.

Her voice came to him, soft and shy. "I will rest better if you stay."

He ducked his head. "All right."

She patted a spot beside her. "You can come and sit down if you want."

"Thanks. I'd like that." He edged onto the pallet beside her and sat there stiffly, staring at his hands. But after a minute or two the tension of the past few days and even the tension of the moment began slowly melting away, thawed by the simple comfort of being beside her. He still felt nervous and unsure of himself, of what she expected of him, but even that seemed less and less unimportant.

He watched Angel's hand creep over to cover his, wondering where she found the nerve that he hadn't been able to summon in himself. But then she'd always been braver than he, more willing to take chances. Not because she didn't understand the risks, but because she was willing to believe something might be gained from them.

He contemplated their two hands. Both were silver, but each had been created for a completely different purpose. They were yin and yang; the hurter's hand and the healer's hand, joined now for a reason that had nothing to do with the silver biometal's shaping purpose.

Holding her hand brought a peaceful feeling, sweeter and deeper than anything drinking had ever brought him. It felt right.

"The Kindred began as a kind of religious community," Angel said quietly, breaking the silence. "They do not have a lot of laws or anything, but they do have some of their own customs and rituals."

"I know. They're a very special people." Although it hadn't seemed so at the time, being brought here had been one of the most fortunate turns of his life. The people here had been poor, but they had given him riches. He had a home now because of them, his life had human connection and meaning once more.

He turned his head to gaze at Angel. She was staring down at their linked hands as if they were some sort of puzzle she was trying to solve. "They do not put many restrictions or expectations on each other," she went on. "Most of their rituals have little if anything at all to do with religion."

He watched her take a deep breath, as if about to dive into water that was way over her head. "Do you remember when Jon covered both our hands with his?" she asked softly.

"Sure." She looked so serious. He wanted to say something to make her smile, but let it slide. This was obviously something very important to her.

"That is called a hand-bonding. It is a way for the whole community to, uh, recognize that two people . . ." She shrugged, a slight helpless lift of her silver shoulders. "Well, that they mean something to each other. To recognize and approve of a . . ." Her voice trailed off to nothing.

"A what?"

Her head bent lower. "A commitment to each other," she whispered, her voice barely audible.

He blinked in surprise. *Well I'll be damned.*

"You mean like an engagement or something?" he asked, gazing at the curve of the side of her face and captivated by the color that had rushed there. Jon had sandbagged him but good, sealing the match he had tried so hard to make. He owed Jon something for this, but what?

Angel shrugged again. "It can mean that," she said,

then added with desperate haste, "—but it does not *have* to. We could be adoptive family to each other, or heart-friends, or—"

"Or two people who love each other?" he asked, amazed at how easily those once unutterable words came to him. "Two people who have a lot to learn about love, and want to get to know each other better and see where their love leads them?"

"Yes," she agreed in a small voice. "It could mean that."

He was a tired old man, twice her age, and with so many kilometers on him that if he was a ship, he'd be ready for the scrap heap. Even if his ability to love was repaired, it would never be what it once was. She was half his age, innocent and new, in some ways not even a month old. Young enough to believe that anything was possible.

He'd once thought himself too old not to know better. But she'd taught him a new definition of what was possible, hadn't she? Who knew what else she could teach him or help him do.

There was only one way to find out.

"Then that's probably what it should mean," he said, settling back and putting one silver arm around her. She sat stiffly for a few seconds, her body trembling, then turned toward him and hid her face against his chest.

He said her name, letting it roll slowly off his tongue and finding that it tasted like the answer to a prayer. After a moment's hesitation he tightened his hold on her and stroked her back with his free hand.

That hand was nothing more than a clever device, and under it her back was sheathed with impermeable metal. You would think such a caress would be cold, mechanical.

Yet now all the silver biometal between them could not keep the touch from connecting. It slipped past those barriers like they weren't even there, reaching surely and easily into the deep places where love lives.

Soon he felt a warm damp spot made by tears as

they soaked into his shirt over his heart, right next to the bent silver Bergmann pin. "There, there," he chided gently, "you'll make yourself all rusty."

A sound that was half laugh and half sob escaped her. "I am so glad you came back," she husked.

"So am I." Marchey cradled her in his arms, smiling to himself and kissing the smooth silver top of her head. She snuggled her cheek against his chest, locking her arms around him and holding on so tight he had the feeling she would never let him go.

That was all right with him.

He wasn't going anywhere.

Daniel Hong-Chee
written on Ananke, Botha Station and Carme

May we never forget.

Dennis L. McKiernan

Praise for the *HÈL'S CRUCIBLE* Duology:
"Page-turning adventure."—Michael A. Stackpole,
New York Times bestselling author of the
Star Wars: X-Wing series

"Storytelling at its best...evocative and compelling."
—Jennifer Roberson

"McKiernan brews magic with an insightful blend of
laughter, tears, and high courage."—Janny Wurts, author
of *Curse of the Mistwraith*

**Book One of the *Hèl's Crucible* Duology
INTO THE FORGE**
❏ 0-451-45700-5/$6.99

Coming in September

GIANT BONES
by Peter S. Beagle
Nominated for the World Fantasy Award
Trade Paperback

New York Times Bestselling Author
Simon R. Green
DEATHSTALKER DESTINY

The Legend of King Arthur Lives!
PERCIVAL'S ANGEL
by Anne Eliot Crompton

The Acclaimed Saga
JERICHO MOON
by Matthew Woodring Stover